W9-CHG-126

THE YESHIVA

Volume II

Also by Chaim Grade

The Agunah
The Seven Little Lanes
The Well
The Yeshiva (Volume I)

THE YESHIVA

Volume II

Masters and Disciples

by Chaim Grade

Translated from the Yiddish
by Curt Leviant

The Bobbs-Merrill Company, Inc.
INDIANAPOLIS NEW YORK

Published by The Bobbs-Merrill Company, Inc.
Indianapolis New York

Designed by Ingrid Beckman
Manufactured in the United States of America

First printing

Library of Congress Cataloging in Publication Data

Grade, Chaim, 1910–
The Yeshiva.

Translation of Tsemakh Atlas.
I. Title.
PZ4.G73Ye [PJ5129.G68] 839'.09'33 76-11608
ISBN 0-672-52344-2

To the memory of my father,
the dreamer and Hebrew teacher
Shlomo-Motte Grade

CONTENTS

CAST OF CHARACTERS

In Valkenik

TSEMAKH ATLAS—the founder of the Valkenik yeshiva; since he comes from Lomzhe, he's also known as Tsemakh Lomzher, or the Lomzher
REB AVRAHAM-SHAYE KOSOVER—a renowned scholar, rabbi, and sage; also known as the author of *The Vision of Avraham*, his most famous work
HADASSAH—Reb Avraham-Shaye's sister
BERELE—Hadassah's son
REB YISROEL—a tailor and yeshiva supporter
REB MENAKHEM-MENDL SEGAL—a teacher at the Valkenik yeshiva
REB MORDEKHAI-AARON SHAPIRO—the rabbi of Valkenik
HERSHL ZHVIRER—the Valkenik rabbi's son
SENDER SHISHLEVITZER—the Valkenik rabbi's son-in-law
CHAIKL—a yeshiva student; since he comes from Vilna, he's also known as Chaikl Vilner, or the Vilner
MELECHKE—a yeshiva student; also known as Melechke Vilner
VOVA BARBITOLER—a tobacco merchant
HERTZKE—Vova's son
CONFRADA—Vova's runaway wife
SROLEYZER—a bricklayer; a thief and a fence
REB LIPPA-YOSSE—the ritual slaughterer of Valkenik
HANNAH-LEAH—Reb Lippa-Yosse's daughter
RONYA—Reb Lippa-Yosse's daughter
YUDEL—Hannah-Leah's husband
AZRIEL WEINSTOCK—Ronya's husband
REB SHLOMO-MOTTE—Chaikl's father
FREYDA VOROBEY—Reb Shlomo-Motte's landlady in Valkenik
KREYNDL—Freyda's daughter

LEITSHE—a cook in the yeshiva kitchen
GITL—Leitshe's mother, also a cook
YOSEF VARSHEVER—a yeshiva student
GEDALYA ZONDAK—Yosef's father-in-law
SLAVA—Tsemakh's wife
MEYERKE PODVAL—a supporter of the library
REB HIRSHE GORDON—Valkenik's leading citizen; a strictly religious textile merchant; a leader of the ultraorthodox faction and a supporter of the Agudah
BAYNISH—Hirshe's son
MOSHE OKUN—a supporter of the library
ELTZIK BLOCH—Hirshe's brother-in-law; a leader of Valkenik's enlightened religious faction; a supporter of the Mizrachi
DAN DUNIETZ—a supporter of the library
SOYEH-ETL—the old caretaker of the Valkenik guest house and the Jewish cemetery
YOEL UZDER—a yeshiva scholar
SHEEYA LIPNISHKER—a yeshiva scholar

In Dekshne

GAVRIEL LEVIN—a farmer
ELKE KOGAN—a mental patient
WOLF KRISHKI—a mental patient

In Amdur

DVORELE NAMIOT—Tsemakh's first fiancée
FALK NAMIOT—Dvorele's father
REB YAAKOV-YITZHOK—an innkeeper
REB BARUKH RUBIN—the Amdur rabbi

In Lomzhe

TSERTELE—Tsemakh's aunt
REB ZIML ATLAS—Tsemakh's uncle; Tsertele's husband
VOLODYA STUPEL—owner of a flour shop; Tsemakh's brother-in-law
NAUM STUPEL—Volodya's elder brother

HERMAN YOFFE—an actor
FEIVL SOKOLOVSKY—a grain merchant
ZEVULUN HALPERIN—a Hebrew teacher

In Vilna

VELLA—Chaikl's mother; Reb Shlomo-Motte's wife; a fruit peddler
YUDIS—Reb Avraham-Shaye's wife
ZELDA—Melechke's mother; owner of a large fruit shop
ZELDA'S THREE DAUGHTERS—with their mother they are known as "the Sennacheribs," after the blasphemous King Sennacherib
MINDL—Vova Barbitoler's wife

In Nareva

MOSHE CHAYIT LOHOYSKER—a yeshiva student, ostracized for his heretical ways
REB SIMKHA FEINERMAN—the head of the Nareva yeshiva
YANKL POLTAVER—a student at the Nareva yeshiva
ZUNDL KONOTOPER—an associate of Reb Simkha
DUBER LIFSCHITZ—a yeshiva scholar and teacher
REB ZUSHE SULKES—trustee of the Free Loan Society
REUVEN RATNER—a yeshiva student
SHIMSHL KUPISHKER—a yeshiva student
DANIEL HOMLER—a yeshiva student
ASHER-LEML KRASNER—a yeshiva student
HENEKH MALARITER—a yeshiva student
BEYLA GUTGESHTALT—Chaikl's landlady in Nareva

PART I

1

THE VALKENIK ROSH YESHIVA, Reb Tsemakh Atlas, had ceased giving Musar talks. Sadness cast a shadow over him; he was like a lone pine on a hillside with a dark cloud over it.

Since Reb Avraham-Shaye Kosover, celebrated author of *The Vision of Avraham* and one of the shining lights of Jewry, had warned Reb Tsemakh that although his students weren't mature enough to understand the intent of his sermons, they might remember his remarks and discover his doubts, the yeshiva principal had found it easier to stop speaking than to watch his words. Now he spent an hour every day in the yeshiva and then went to his room in Reb Yisroel the tailor's house or to the attic chamber in the synagogue for private meditation. More often, however, he could be found in the deserted women's gallery of the Cold Shul, the old wooden synagogue on the hill. But no matter where Tsemakh was, he tormented himself with the same question: Should he return home? And he always answered, No! If he had found no rest in the world of Torah, he would certainly not find it in the merchants' world of his wife Slava's family in Lomzhe. Moreover, he dared not renounce his responsibility for the yeshiva he had founded, especially since no one was forcing him to take action against his will.

Not having to weigh his words before the students and spending day after day alone set Tsemakh's rebellious thoughts free. As a youth his beard and earlocks had covered his doubts, but now the questions grew with the beard and earlocks, as though his heresy had insinuated its way into their roots. Once he had burrowed into philosophical texts that proved the existence of the First Cause, but now he knew that a deity discovered through logic was not a God sensed in the heart. He was even less sure of the existence of a personal Divine Providence. If one were to judge by the tears of the oppressed, then perhaps it was correct to say that the world was run by eternal laws at the hand of a Divine Providence to whom it made no difference whether a man squashed a worm or a lion devoured a prophet. In response to the age-old anguished cry from the time of the prophets and Job—Why do the wicked thrive and the righteous suffer?—sages in every generation had replied: The righteous will be rewarded in the world to come. But what if there were no other world? Blessed are the innocent who believe in another world, just as they believe in the Divine Revelation of Torah. Their proof is that the world heard the thunder and saw the miracles at Mount Sinai. But someone not graced with such faith can question precepts that are not rationally comprehensible. Tsemakh did not know whether his intensified doubt was a consequence of his failures in life or whether he had failed because he wavered. The only thing he did not doubt was the Musar teaching that man was evil from birth but could become good through constant effort at self-improvement.

The yearly summer guests—the Lithuanian Torah scholars—began to appear in the village again. Tsemakh kept aloof from them too. He had never liked these distinguished young men who sought worthy and well-paid positions as religious functionaries. And besides, he knew that there was a more profound difference between him and the other Torah scholars. They either believed in or didn't think about fundamental principles, while his faith was tainted to its very depths. Therefore, when he encountered such young people he felt like a liar for having a beard and earlocks, wearing rabbinic garb, and being a rosh yeshiva. Tsemakh shivered with fear that someone might discover what was happening to him and call him a hypocrite—which to his mind was the worst possible stain. The other rosh yeshiva, his friend Reb Menakhem-Mendl Segal, couldn't understand him. The only man who understood his torments of doubt was Reb Avraham-Shaye Kosover. But he, apparently, would keep his silence.

Tsemakh was afraid of the new Valkenik rabbi, Reb Mordekhai-Aaron Shapiro, and his children. The rabbi's son and son-in-law knew him from Navaredok, from his early years of wandering in Russia and later on in Poland. Tsemakh was sure that new complaints had now been added to the old. Zundl Konotoper and Reb Duber Lifschitz had spread the word among their friends that when they went to Lomzhe to bring Tsemakh back to the true path, he had spoken heresy. The fact that he had later abandoned his wealthy Lomzhe in-laws and founded a yeshiva was no proof that he had changed. No Navaredker who passed through Valkenik spent the Sabbath with Tsemakh Atlas. He also noticed that the rabbi avoided him, surely on the advice of his children. Now the rabbi's son and son-in-law had come to visit their father, and Tsemakh murmured to himself the words of Job: That which I feared has come to pass.

As a youth the rabbi's son, Sender Shishlevitzer, had had a reputation as a good calligrapher. He had copied down the Musar talks of the Old Man, Reb Yosef-Yoizl, and had them printed in booklets. Reb Sender Shishlevitzer had a broad, round face and a round beard, as if hammered out of copper. Judging by his full lips, his pink and white face, and his large, astonished eyes, one might have thought him a naïve youth. But when he looked at a youngster, the boy felt that everything he wanted to conceal was being pulled out of him with a corkscrew. Only when Reb Sender saw a pupil shivering under his penetrating glance would he give an odd laugh, put his arms around him, and pace back and forth with him in the beth medresh until the boy felt honored and uplifted by his tenderness.

Reb Sender's brother-in-law, swarthy, thin, and bony Hershl Zhvirer, also had a considerable reputation. The brothers-in-law lived in the Beth Yosef, the Navaredker center in Mezeritch. The Mezeritch rosh yeshiva often sent Hershl out to a distant village to be a teacher for beginners. When Hershl Zhvirer first entered the yeshiva, he didn't impress the students. His Musar talks had no depth, his Talmud lessons no sparkle or acumen. Moreover, no one ever saw him studying. He scratched himself and wandered about in the beth medresh, the house of study, or sat in a corner dozing, his head resting against a prayer stand. This pattern would continue until the village principal asked him to lead the Evening Service. It was then that everyone would realize who this seemingly drowsy Musarist leader was. Hershl Zhvirer would put on his coat, approach the prayer stand, and shriek out the opening phrase of the prayer with such feeling that the students of the snow-covered village would fall into a pre–Rosh Hashana ecstasy on an ordinary winter's night. People also said great things about Hershl Zhvirer's marriage. His father-in-law, Reb Mordekhai-Aaron Shapiro, who was then the Shishlevitz rabbi, had wanted to tell him about the dowry and the years of free board. But the groom waved his hand and said, "It makes no difference!" Immediately after the wedding, he and his young wife had returned to the Mezeritch yeshiva to live on rye bread and meager meals so as to remain close to the Torah, according to the Navaredker way.

Reb Menakhem-Mendl had known the rabbi's son and son-in-law since they were youths. Seeing the two men entering the beth medresh, he ran joyfully up to them. But when Reb Menakhem-Mendl asked Reb Sender Shishlevitzer to give a talk in the yeshiva, the latter replied, "I've come to Valkenik for a vacation and not to give talks."

"Lately our principal, Reb Tsemakh, has stopped addressing the students. He rarely sets foot in the beth medresh, but sits by himself and studies Musar," Menakhem-Mendl confided to his old friends. But neither of them said a word; they merely exchanged glances and left the house of study.

"Reb Menakhem-Mendl is as naïve as he was in his youth. He doesn't understand that Tsemakh Lomzher, who now sits and, as he puts it, studies Musar in private, is also capable of studying Musar without a hat on," Reb Sender told his brother-in-law as they left the synagogue courtyard and walked down the hill to the rabbi's house.

The following morning the rabbi, accompanied by his son and son-in-law, visited the cottage in the green courtyard of the former pitch factory where Reb Avraham-Shaye spent his summers. As usual, Reb Mordekhai-Aaron Shapiro laced his conversation with Midrashic phrases and sermonic explications; Reb Avraham-Shaye listened silently, occasionally laughed out loud, then again fell silent. The two brothers-in-law let their father talk and never took their eyes off Reb Avraham-Shaye Kosover, whom they were meeting for the first time. Sitting with them in the courtyard was Chaikl Vilner, once a student at Reb Tsemakh's yeshiva, now studying with Reb Avraham-Shaye. He gazed with curiosity at the rabbi's son's round, rosy face and at the son-in-law's thin, bony one. It seemed to Chaikl that the two Navaredkers were looking at Reb Avraham-Shaye not only with awe because of his learning but with hidden contempt too. He was, after all, an old-fashioned Talmud scholar who presumably had no understanding of a subtle Musar sermon.

Reb Mordekhai-Aaron Shapiro cast several angry glances at the insolent yeshiva student who didn't have enough sense to leave when his elders were speaking. But Chaikl didn't budge; he wanted to see and hear everything.

"I've been in Valkenik only since Lag B'Omer, and the community already owes me a week's wages," the rabbi complained. "And even if they paid me on time it wouldn't be enough for my living expenses. I have asked them for a raise, which the community leaders are ready to give—but then they'd have to raise the meat tax, and the leaders are afraid this will enrage the ordinary people."

"The meat tax should by no means be raised," Reb Avraham-Shaye said.

"And I'm not asking that it should." Reb Mordekhai-Aaron put both hands to his ears and shook his long gray beard, as though to shake off unwarranted suspicion from himself. "The leaders want to raise the meat tax anyway. Expenses are large and the householders aren't paying their community taxes."

"You must warn the community leaders and the butchers that you will proclaim a ban on the meat." Red blotches appeared on Reb Avraham-Shaye's face. "It goes without saying that it's an injustice to fleece the poor, but nowadays you can't even overcharge the rich for kosher meat or they'll buy unkosher meat."

The two brothers-in-law were amazed at Reb Avraham-Shaye's sharp words. Nevertheless, they didn't interfere because they were afraid of their angry father.

"Wouldn't you be afraid of proclaiming a ban against the rich men and the butchers in a village where you had just assumed a post?"

"If I were a rabbi in a village I would surely do it." Reb Avraham-Shaye placed a heavy fist on the table.

Chaikl listened to this conversation, holding his breath and staring at the rabbi's hand. He had often wondered why the slightly built Reb Avraham-Shaye had such big hands and fleshy fingers.

Seeing that the student still wasn't budging and that his teacher didn't dream of sending him away, Reb Mordekhai-Aaron Shapiro stood up with a groan and went out into the courtyard, accompanied by his children and by Reb Avraham-Shaye. The rabbi was boiling with rage; he was holding his cane behind his back and nervously scraping the sand. Chaikl, at the window, saw that the argument was continuing there and was disappointed at not being present. He would never have thought that Reb Avraham-Shaye would stand up for the Valkenik Jews, whom he rarely met and with whom he hardly exchanged a word.

In the fresh air Reb Mordekhai-Aaron's anger began to simmer down. He once again posed a question on a biblical verse and responded with an analytical parable. Then he suddenly asked his sons to tell what they knew about the Valkenik principal, Reb Tsemakh Atlas. "I have recently told Reb Avraham-Shaye why I don't interfere in the affairs of the local yeshiva. The present rosh yeshiva, Reb Tsemakh Atlas, is—"

"—a great man!" Reb Avraham-Shaye cut in, as if giving strict warning that no one was to contradict him.

"Of course Reb Tsemakh Lomzher is a man of great strength. He always was," Reb Sender agreed, and his broad smile brought out the dimples in his full cheeks.

"And have you visited the yeshiva?" Reb Avraham-Shaye asked the rabbi's son-in-law, whom he liked because of his discreet silence.

"Yes, we've gone in," Hershl Zhvirer replied, unwilling to discuss the matter any further.

It was apparent that the principal's former friends did not wish to speak ill of him, but they also wanted nothing to do with Reb Tsemakh. Looking worried, Reb Avraham-Shaye addressed the rabbi angrily: "On your first visit here you said you were afraid that Reb Tsemakh Atlas might persecute you. Now you have to watch yourself lest your fear of being persecuted make *you* a persecutor."

"What?" Reb Mordekhai-Aaron flared again, looking at his children as if he could murder them for standing there like dunderheads. "How can you say that my fear of being persecuted will make me a persecutor?"

"There's only a hairline of difference between being persecuted and persecuting. With the blink of an eye the roles can be reversed." Reb Avraham-Shaye turned to the young men. Perhaps they—the Musar students—could understand what their father failed to understand.

"At the moment when the persecuted person gathers strength and becomes the persecutor, at that very minute he loses all his previous merit, and the Creator sides with the newly persecuted, even if he is a wicked man."

"We don't intend to cause the Lomzher any harm, God forbid. We don't want to hurt him." Hershl looked hesitantly at his father-in-law.

But Reb Avraham-Shaye answered heatedly, "If you, the principal's former friends, don't visit his yeshiva, you'll cause suspicion to fall on him from both the students and the townspeople. A snub of that sort is equal to endless persecution."

"We have no choice," Reb Sender answered, turning his head away, which made him seem even more secretive.

But the words began to pour quickly from Hershl Zhvirer. One followed on the heels of another, as though he had awakened from a nap in the middle of prayers and wanted to catch up with those he had drowsed through. "Reb Menakhem-Mendl Segal told us that Reb Tsemakh has stopped giving Musar talks. So Reb Menakhem-Mendl asked Reb Sender to give a talk. But Reb Tsemakh would surely have viewed this as a way of pushing him out of the yeshiva. So we're actually doing him a favor by not interfering with his school." Hershl suddenly fell silent, apparently not used to speaking so much.

"You *should* have given a talk if you were asked to," Reb Mordekhai-Aaron shouted at his son, and his eyes also burned with anger at his ineffective son-in-law. The rabbi seized his chin as if he wanted to drag himself out of the courtyard by the beard, and, accompanied by his children, went out the gate.

Reb Avraham-Shaye stood in the middle of the courtyard lost in thought: There's no doubt that the two Navaredkers want nothing to do with the principal because they don't trust his religious feelings. But they implied something more and at the same time tried not to enrage their father. A shadow of fear and astonishment briefly crossed Reb Avraham-Shaye's face, as though he had seen a wet gray snow falling in midsummer, and an embarrassed smile touched the corners of his mouth. He should have realized before that Reb Mordekhai-

Aaron Shapiro wanted either his son or his son-in-law to become the principal of the local yeshiva. That was why he had begun the conversation by groaning about his meager salary and then started talking about Reb Tsemakh. Reb Mordekhai-Aaron considered this goal quite just and proper. Since he was the rabbi here, the yeshiva by rights should belong to him and his children. The young men, however, had no wish to arrogate the livelihood of an old friend—so they were Musarists after all! Reb Avraham-Shaye gave an angry, mocking laugh. The two Navaredkers had come with their father to visit him so they could learn what he thought of the principal. Gradually they would let themselves be persuaded by their father and would even ascribe motives of self-sacrifice to themselves: Reb Tsemakh Atlas was not properly caring for the pupils; he was not giving any Musar talks; the yeshiva was likely to disintegrate—and a place of Torah study had to be saved.

Reb Avraham-Shaye sat down on the bench next to the table in the courtyard to calm himself. Why was he taking the principal's bad fortune so much to heart? That Reb Tsemakh Atlas was a terribly arrogant man. If he couldn't run the yeshiva according to his wishes he wouldn't speak to the students at all. He sat in the dark, and his conduct prompted others to say that he wasn't fit to be a principal. His pride showed that he was no believer. A person who believed in the Creator was not so arrogant. It was hard to understand why he didn't leave Valkenik altogether; after all, he had a wealthy family, Reb Avraham-Shaye said to himself, and felt his face burning with anguish. He was astonished and upset at being so drawn to the tall, gloomy principal.

Reb Avraham-Shaye went up to the porch of the cottage and stopped again, staring at his fingertips; he was ready to go to the village and tell the principal that his silence was the cause of his own ruin. But Reb Tsemakh was by nature contentious, uncompromising, terribly stubborn, full of stormy passions. In a discussion with him Reb Tsemakh might, out of bitterness, say something that ought not to be heard, and then he would indeed have to be persecuted. Reb Avraham-Shaye would by law be compelled to persecute him and remove him from the yeshiva. So for Reb Tsemakh's own sake it would be better not to call on him or say anything to him.

2

AFTER SHEVUOS, the Feast of the First Fruits, old and young Torah scholars began coming to spend their vacation in Valkenik. Each arriving guest enhanced the mood of cheer in the village. The householders painted their summer cottages, polished the furniture, aired the bedding. Scrubbed windowpanes faced the road with the curiosity of a bride awaiting the wagon that brings her in-laws to the wedding.

The first to appear were the scholars of Kletzk, yeshiva youths with their hats atilt, a confident stride, squared shoulders—sturdy in the war for Torah. Their method of Talmud learning was thorough study and not pious pilpul. To bring Kletzk into the path of Musar, the Slobodka yeshiva had at one time sent fourteen of its finest scholars there—like the fourteen volumes in Maimonides' *Code of Law*. At the same time the Old Man, Reb Yosef-Yoizl Hurwitz, had come down from Navaredok with his "Cossacks." The Kletzk yeshiva had then agreed to study Musar for a quarter of an hour a day and not a minute more.

The Kletzk rosh yeshiva had come on vacation with his students. He was a small man with a short beard and short earlocks. His great wide-brimmed rabbinic hat made him look like a mushroom. He walked quickly, spoke quickly, but still hadn't the strength to catch up with the new interpretations continually tumbling in his mind. Although his students nearly wrote their fingers off trying to jot down the outlines of his insights into Talmud, they couldn't keep up with him. It was said of the Kletzk rosh yeshiva that in his mind he could leaf through the entire Babylonian and Jerusalem Talmuds faster than the wind fluttering through the leaves in the woods. His students crowded around him proudly and proclaimed at every opportunity: "If you want brisk, lively studies, go to Kletzk!"

The students of the noted sage Chafetz-Chaim of Radun were for the most part tall and thin, with gaunt, pale faces. Even on vacation they spoke softly and went to walk in the woods with the intent of strengthening their bodies for the Torah. In like manner they went to their morning prayers and, in Radun, to the old rabbi for a talk. During the Sabbath the ninety-year-old Chafetz-Chaim sat on his couch, propped up by little pillows; on his desk lay a huge open Pentateuch with Rashi's Commentary. On low stools around him sat older Torah scholars who had come together for the Sabbath to visit the rabbi of all of Jewry. Behind the guests stood pious youths with closed mouths. The holy old man moaned: "Ay, ay, my children. Today or tomorrow the Messiah will come, and the Jews still aren't ready." The old gray-beards sighed along, and behind their bent backs the students swayed like thin nut trees during a storm that makes old oaks creak. The young students of Chafetz-Chaim had faith in their rabbi's prophecy that today or tomorrow the Messiah would come; hence they studied the Talmudic tractates dealing with the offering of sacrifices in the Holy Temple.

The saintly old man did not leave Radun; because of his advanced age his family was afraid for him to travel. His sons, sons-in-law, and grandsons, however, did go away for vacations. Among the heirs there was a quiet battle over who would be Chafetz-Chaim's successor. The older students didn't want to hear that someone would be their yeshiva leader through rights of dynastic succession, grabbing the limbs of the great tree just because the sage was his father, father-in-law, or grandfather. The younger students squabbled with the older ones and among themselves too. Some of the students argued that their rosh yeshiva should be an analytical scholar because they already possessed a thorough knowledge of the Talmud. Opponents responded that they needed a rosh yeshiva with thorough knowledge because they were already analytical scholars. A third group demanded a spiritual leader; a fourth sought a good administrator. Since Chafetz-Chaim was still alive and an open conflict would be a disgrace for the whole family, the heirs had decided that for appearance' sake they would lead the yeshiva together. But the competition still continued quietly, and each one of the leaders had his own group of students whom he brought to the resort community of Valkenik.

Outsiders would have found it difficult to pick out the rosh yeshiva, the guide, the spiritual leader, and the administrator among the heirs. All were broad-shouldered and thick-bearded, with hair growing up to their eyes. They had protruding paunches and heavy buttocks, and their brand-new split gaberdines burst at the seams, front and back. They promenaded through the village with measured stride, coughed with slow dignity. Their large, hairy nostrils inhaled the dried-pine aroma with gusto. They stopped every few feet, since running did not befit Talmud scholars, especially since they were on vacation with no need to rush. Each of the principals held a big black umbrella in his right hand, left hand behind his back as though out for a Sabbath stroll. When the sun began to blaze, Chafetz-Chaim's heirs held the open umbrellas over the heads of their pupils, each one protecting his own group of followers. Occasionally the spiritual leader bent his head toward a keen student who whispered something into his ear concerning the administrator. The elder listened to the younger and smiled under his mustache, which began to bite and cut him like the teeth of a steel comb. Nevertheless, he mastered the temptation and spoke no evil about his brother-in-law or cousin. He didn't say a word. But from the way the older man held the black silk umbrella over the head of the slanderer, he could guess how much his whispered words were appreciated.

At the resort there was also a rosh yeshiva without students, a man who gave an occasional lecture in Baranovitch or in Slonim. He was a talkative, jovial man with a bared chest and rumpled ritual fringes. He wandered about with a farmer's thick, plain walking stick and stopped to talk with the Jewish villagers who were carrying wood to the cardboard factory in their carts. He was seen standing by barns when women were milking the cows, and even in the midst of the market place patting a horse. He had inflamed eyelids and watery, good-natured eyes full of childish amazement. Judging by his beard, which was not at all threadbare or plucked out in spots, it was clear that he did not mull too long over Talmud studies. He said quite openly that he held no high opinion of the modern Talmudic analysts who burrowed to the very root of such topics as whether one must throw all bread out before Passover because one is forbidden to keep it in the house or merely because one is forbidden to look at it during that period. Such remarks made by a man who taught youngsters in Baranovitch or Slonim caused the Kletzk prodigies to turn away in contempt, as if from a kindergarten teacher. But this didn't bother the rosh yeshiva with his farmer's walking stick. He strolled in the forest alone; stared at the trees; bent down to examine a fern, a wild flower, a strawberry, a worm; muttering all the while in amazement, "The wonders of God; the wonders of God!"

The princes of the Lithuanian Torah scholars were the yeshiva students of Mir. Even in the sands of Valkenik they were decked out in pressed suits, wary lest a speck of dust fall on them. They wrote with gold-tipped American fountain pens, kept their glasses in flat leather cases, and wore wrist watches with decorated bands. Even a young yeshiva boy, since he was already a student at Mir, would look around three times to see who was talking to him before he replied. And when he finally did reply, he would frown and ask, "Do you understand?" as if a profound thought were concealed in everything he said. The Mir yeshiva was especially famous for its older students; indeed, many of them were over forty. It was hard to find suitable matches for them. Either the dowry wasn't big enough for the learning of the Mir student, or the bride was too old for his passion. Sitting so long on the yeshiva benches had made these bachelors lazy. They spent half their days in their rooms reading the Warsaw newspapers. They saved money from the funds doled out to them and collected books, suits, ties. In Valkenik the people from Mir sat on the verandas eating cheese, sour cream, and blintzes, ceaselessly tapping their necks and stroking their neatly trimmed cheeks to see if they had fattened up. In the forest the Mir people lay in deep hammocks perusing books of philosophy or the Kabbala which they had brought especially for their vacation reading. But when a younger student came by and wanted to look at the book, the older one would say, "It's not for you, lad; you're too young for mystical texts. Why don't you look into a commentary on the *Code of Law* in the meantime?"

Hence one can imagine how the older Mir students felt, now that a group of students had recently come from America. The Americans had money but not a crumb of decorum. In the beth medresh they hung their coats on other people's hangers and threw their galoshes about. There was a fine of at least ten groschen for breaking the rules, but the Americans laughed and paid twenty. They went around with open jackets and unbuttoned collars. Polka-dotted ties dangled from their necks. They weren't ashamed to hitch up their trousers in public and jingle the coins in their pockets. When it was hot they simply took off their jackets. They wore their caps pulled down low over their hard heads, their thick, disheveled shocks of hair hanging down to their eyes. They spoke with chewing gum in their mouths. The Americans found it right and proper to shout to one another, "Hey, Jack! Hey, Joe!" and they boxed in the middle of the street, jumping around like goats. It wasn't surprising that when an older Mir student saw this, he was so ashamed that he didn't know where to hide.

The exact opposite of these youths from across the sea was the yeshiva students from Germany. They dressed neatly, wore brown shoes with double soles and broad-lapelled jackets of thick wool. They were very pious and good-humored, but when one of them didn't find his Talmud on his prayer stand, he flared up immediately. All these youths from Frankfurt and Hamburg had studied in the *Gymnasium*, so they weren't drawn to reading forbidden secular books, but they lacked keenness and acumen. If a Lithuanian made a clever remark, the Germans gaped naïvely and didn't understand. If a German cracked a joke, he alone laughed. An American student might sway violently at prayers, as though to shake off the impudence he had brought from across the sea, but the German simpleton stood as straight as a taut string.

The housewives who had German boarders would say, "They're fine honest youngsters, but there's no spark to them."

But both the Americans and the Germans were useful in the yeshiva. For the most part they lagged behind in their studies and hired poor Lithuanian students to tutor them in the difficult Talmudic passages. After graduation they would return to their gentile surroundings and teach Torah there. But there was no benefit to be had from the Polish youths. In the rich Hasidic homes of Lodz and Warsaw it had become the fashion to send their sons to a Lithuanian yeshiva for a few years. And so young Hasidim sent to Mir strolled around in small hats and polished boots. They wore soft white collars in midweek and satin gaberdines with silk belts for the Sabbath. One could already see the thick beards that would cover their faces in the future, their fine homes, the big businesses they would run, and the places of honor they would have at Hasidic rebbes' tables. The Polish youths had an aggressive bearing; they paced back and forth during prayers with thumbs hooked into their belts. They stopped in the middle of the beth medresh, swaying passionately from side to side; when it came to the *Alenu* prayer they spat—right on the floor. For doing that in the yeshiva one was fined half a zloty, but when the cleanliness monitor demanded the fine from the Hasidim, they laughed in his face and addressed him as "thou." The monitor, a gentle, modest scholar from Zamet, who would not have called even a little boy "thou," froze in his tracks in confusion at such vulgar disrespect, and the Polish youths turned away from him as if he were a stray billygoat in the synagogue courtyard.

Once a week the spiritual leader of the Mir yeshiva gave a talk in his attic chamber. The Polish youths shoved their way in as if it were a rebbe's table, but they derived no pleasure from this pushing. At the rebbe's table, when the elder Hasidim shouted at them, "Watch it, you boor, or you'll get slapped," they snapped back impudently. But the older Mir students let themselves be shoved by the Polish youths. They merely shrugged and looked through their glasses with their cold Lithuanian eyes. While the leader was talking there was total silence in the chamber. His followers gathered around him, their faces brimming with Torah secrets. A dozen times the leader would interrupt his talk and whisper, "There's a terrible smell of charcoal here. The room is full of fumes." His followers would frown and whisper, "There's a terrible smell of charcoal here. The room is full of fumes." The Polish youths couldn't grasp the profundity of the leader's words—no matter how much they inhaled, they didn't feel the fumes. And when one of the Hasidim couldn't restrain himself he would punch one of the followers and ask in his thick Polish accent, "What's he talking about? I don't understand his Lithuanian jargon."

The older Mir students trembled with fear that one of the vacationing Americans or Poles might follow them back to their yeshiva and cause them untold embarrassment. The Mir scholars deigned to exchange a few words with the students of Radun, but they regarded the Kletzk students as mere brats. The Kletzkers in turn laughed at the arrogant Mirers with their gold-tipped fountain pens for not being methodical in their studies. The yeshiva of Mir existed only by virtue of notebooks that had been handed down from Reb Chaim Brisker—their rosh yeshiva had no time for Talmud lectures. Even during the summer he had to wander all over America to raise funds to support his unmarried scholars who were fattening themselves at Valkenik.

Nevertheless, peace and affection were maintained among the scholars of the various yeshivas, even if only for the sake of appearances. And they all shared the fear that a wagonload of Navaredker Musarniks might suddenly inundate the town. From their experience in other rabbinic resorts they knew that Reb Yosef-Yoizl's pupils could troop into a town and swarm over it like locusts. Lately some of the Navaredkers had begun to dress neatly and behave temperately, but the stricter Musarists among them still went about in rags and tatters. They wore rumpled trousers, frayed jackets with holes in the elbows, wrinkled, greasy hats, battered shoes, and long, faded ritual fringes. And even though they came to the resort for a rest, they knew no rest. They turned summer into Yom Kippur. The students of the other yeshivas would be reciting the Afternoon Service in the woods, swaying even more silently than the trees. Suddenly they would hear the shriek of a Navaredker pounding a tree trunk and banging his head against the bark. But the Navaredkers' greatest joy was to surround a Mirer ben Torah and rebuke him with pleasant mien, as it were. If the latter said a word of protest, they would attack him in earnest.

"At Mir you get all gussied up like peasant youths for a village feast. At Mir hair grows wild as horses' manes. At Mir you offer a hundred excuses to justify a wrong deed—you find proof in the Talmud that a scholar who finds a stain on his suit is worthy of death. But at Mir there is no fear for stains on the soul," the Navaredkers would scream. And the disparaged student couldn't slip away from them—it was as if he had touched a beehive or put his hand into an ant hill.

3

ONE SUMMER AFTERNOON Reb Avraham-Shaye Kosover and Chaikl went swimming for the first time. Carrying a blanket and two towels, Chaikl ambled along slowly, and Reb Avraham-Shaye leaned lightly on his shoulder. Eyes half closed in the sunlight, he thought of his Torah studies as usual. The student had noticed that when the rabbi spoke to people he floated up out of the Talmud for a while and then swam back again. His face looked like a forest covered with a warm mist, near and far at the same time. Sometimes his silence was as clear as a deep lake; sometimes as hard and dry as a rocky hill. Mount Sinai, Chaikl mused, probably looked like the rabbi's huge bare forehead. . . .

They followed the trodden grass trail near the green fields. Parallel to the trail ran the yellow sand path. In the noon light it sparkled as if covered with glass splinters. The lush, sun-drenched fields were bordered by a high wall of thin birches whose branches waved sleepily and blended in the distance with the silvery horizon. On the hill above the path dark green pines became denser and turned deep blue. In the drowsy afternoon a bee zoomed by Chaikl's nose and left a steely buzz in its wake. The voices of young peasant women gathering blackberries rang out in the forest. Two storks, beating their dry, hard wings, flew low overhead. In a flash they crossed the sown stretches and landed on a swampy marsh. Two whooping peasant lads were struggling with a brown cow with black spots on its knees. One of the lads pulled a rope attached to its horns; the other prodded it with a branch from behind. But the cow stretched its tail out like a stick and refused to budge. Chaikl felt like letting out a whoop just for the fun of it. He wanted to run across the bridge, strip quickly, and jump into the water. At his side the rabbi was conversing in his thoughts with the

Talmudic sages. His entire world was locked behind the wrinkles in his brow: the portion of the Talmud that gives the laws of agriculture, the commentary of Maimonides, and the medieval Talmudic commentators from France.

"I'm sorry you have to go so slowly because of me, Chaikl. You know, when I was a youngster I didn't play many pranks. Quite often I get the urge to bang on a strange window and hide," Reb Avraham-Shaye said, and his smile shone like the window of the cottage where one was born and which one sees years later.

The rabbi and his student passed the large courtyard of the cardboard factory. In front of the red brick building electric lights glowed as if it were night, casting a dusty, yellowish glow. The muted roar of the machine saws sounded like the panting of a slow, steam-puffing locomotive. Opposite the factory at the edge of the forest stood a long one-story log house with many windows, which housed the vacationing yeshiva students. They sat on the porch, talking loudly and laughing. Seeing Reb Avraham-Shaye passing, they fell silent and gazed at him. He hastened by taking larger strides to keep the students from detaining him. When he reached the wooden bridge, however, he slowed down again and, face beaming, listened to the Torah scholars on the porch resume their animated discussion. "Precious youths," he muttered, his eyes shining with joy. Chaikl knew that Reb Avraham-Shaye had great affection for the yeshiva students and spoke well of them. One would be a gaon. Another had a noble character. A third had spiritual gifts. But he didn't praise them to their face and was glad they didn't visit him.

Every evening the yeshiva students swam naked at a bend in the river hidden by thick bushes and overhanging willows. No one was there in the afternoon. Chaikl spread the blanket on the ground, and Reb Avraham-Shaye quickly threw off his cloak before he sat down. He fixed his gaze on the sky, as if even bathing were done for the sake of heaven, then drew his ritual fringes over his head.

Chaikl also sat down and untied his shoes, but stood up immediately and muttered, "I can't stand sitting on the ground. I like a tree trunk, but there are no stumps here—I see some farther off."

"Can it be, Chaikl, that you haven't come up with an idea?" Reb Avraham-Shaye wondered. "Pull out a tree trunk and sit on it. Can you swim?"

"Yes, a little," Chaikl answered.

"Why the sudden modesty? *You* admitting to only a little?" Reb Avraham-Shaye teased. He finished undressing. Chaikl moved away. Something strange was happening to him. He couldn't comprehend it while it was occurring, nor afterwards, when he was ashamed to discuss it with anyone: He didn't want to see the rabbi naked. He chided himself that it was a wild, foolish notion, for he went to the bathhouse with his father. Even the yeshiva students went swimming with their principals. Still, he absolutely could not persuade himself to raise his eyes and look at the naked Reb Avraham-Shaye.

Chaikl undressed as far away as possible, then quickly jumped into the water, where he dived and swam back and forth, using the breast stroke. But he took great pains not to swim near the place where the rabbi stood up to his neck in the river, splashing the water with his hands.

On the way back Reb Avraham-Shaye walked even more slowly, smiling at the sun as it dried his washed beard and earlocks. As they reached the old pitch factory, a couple emerged from the woods. The young man had a black mustache and thinning hair; he was wearing a checked suit with patch pockets. Holding his hat in one hand, he led a short, broad-shouldered, full-fleshed woman with the other. She wore a thin beige outfit adorned with birds, flowers, and leaves. Her full breasts swung under her loosely buttoned blouse. Her blond hair gleamed and her lips were painted red; her arms, bare to the shoulders, glowed with a fresh tan. She carried the man's walking stick and leaned her heavy, swollen body against him. When the couple passed Chaikl, he saw her green-shadowed eyes.

Suddenly the young woman called out to her friend, "These wild young people with their beards and earlocks are sprouting up all over the forest. There isn't a place where one can hide from them." Chaikl knew from her accent that she spoke Polish at home and with her friends; now she had purposely spoken Yiddish for the two bearded Jews to understand. The sweet-faced lover and his girl friend certainly weren't spinning fringes in the forest, Chaikl thought, and both envy and zealousness flared up in him.

"You don't like Jews with beards and earlocks?" Chaikl shouted. "Then shut your eyes. Your grandfather Haman and your great-grandfather Pharaoh also hated Jews."

"What's he saying?" the man asked the woman in Polish, his mustache bristling like worms. Chaikl stepped closer to the couple, prepared to argue and even fight. But then, seeing the rabbi running into the courtyard, he too ran to catch up, though he thought angrily that the young cavalier would surely consider him a coward.

"You're not a ben Torah," Reb Avraham-Shaye said, and proceeded to the cottage porch.

"And how *should* a ben Torah reply?" Chaikl clenched his fists as if intending to run back to the couple with a suitable reply.

"A ben Torah doesn't reply at all," Reb Avraham-Shaye shouted, and went into the house.

That evening the kerosene lamp cast a weak light on the cot where Reb Avraham-Shaye lay, his myopic eyes peering into his little Talmud. In his strenuous efforts to get the proper explanation from the Mishna, he pressed his fists to his temples and began chanting in a bitter, strident voice, as if demanding to know why God's Torah was so difficult. Then he lay motionless without making a sound. His eyes shone cold and deep. Chaikl swayed silently over the Talmud and thought that Reb Avraham-Shaye probably regretted his invitation; the rabbi obviously considered him a bigmouth.

"Come and eat," Reb Avraham-Shaye said, finally getting up from his cot.

"I don't want to," Chaikl grunted. He wanted the rabbi to know that he detested being shouted at. Reb Avraham-Shaye laughed and left the room.

After eating, the rabbi returned and sat next to the low window, motionless once more. Good heavens, he's thinking of Torah again, Chaikl shouted to himself. The rabbi had apparently forgotten that Chaikl too was in the room, hungry. Being a pupil of the author of *The Vision of Avraham* was difficult and boring. Chaikl looked around as if he were sitting behind a barred window. Just then the rabbi's sister Hadassah opened the door and said, "Come and eat; the meal is ready." Chaikl realized that the rabbi had asked his sister to invite him to the dining room; this time he accepted.

Hadassah's husband had gone to America on a fund-raising trip with the rosh yeshiva of Mir. The Mir scholars had a good time in Valkenik even without their leader, but without her husband Hadassah hardly knew what to do with her large family. Nevertheless, no one ever heard her shouting at her blond little boys and at her darkly charming gap-toothed little girls. She had only to say a word or pat someone on the head and that child would immediately quiet down. When Hadassah and her brother were talking, it looked as though they were whispering. They never raised their voices. At times she wouldn't leave her bedroom and her cough could be heard from behind closed doors. A doctor came and went; the maid ran to the village pharmacy for medicine; Berele brought his mother the hot-water bottle; and Reb Avraham-Shaye left his sister's room worried. But everything was done quietly, as if in absolute secrecy.

After resting in her room for a couple of hours, Hadassah would rejoin her family at the table. She sat with a shawl over her shoulders, shivering with cold in midsummer. Her face looked blue; her full lips were dry; her chin sagged. Only her clever, bright gray eyes smiled. Chaikl wasn't so much enchanted by Hadassah's appearance as by her regal behavior, and she felt that he watched her every movement. Her brother had told her about Chaikl's wildness and about his talents. Hadassah thought that her brother still didn't know his pupil well and that the seventeen-year-old youth didn't know himself, either. To keep him from noticing how much his inquisitive glances offended her, Hadassah constantly smiled graciously and maternally at him; but this made him even more restless, and he was ashamed to touch the food. Hadassah had to remind him, "Don't be absent-minded. The food is getting cold." She addressed him in the same calm way she spoke to her children.

Now Chaikl sat alone in the dining room, angry and dejected. He was a freeloader here, superfluous, a stranger. The rabbi and his sister had a distinguished lineage, while he wasn't even a rabbi's son—that was why they couldn't stand his behavior. The rabbi had probably told his sister how he had insulted the couple at the gate, and she too probably regretted having taken him in. He could tell by the way she had prepared his supper—as if he were a starving man—and then left the room. On the table she had set a plate with two boiled eggs, a basket of sliced bread, a pot of tea, and a bowl of cold sorrel soup with sour cream and pieces of hard cheese. Displeased with the food, Chaikl bolted it, washed it down with tea, said grace, and went out to the porch.

From the high grass and the marsh came heavy buzzing and quacking. A white fog slowly rose from the meadows over the treetops and floated up to the cold chimney of the pitch factory. From the patch of fog a phantom materialized—the white-skinned, full-fleshed young woman; her black-mustached boy friend remained swallowed in the mist. Chaikl turned to the door as if to flee his unclean thoughts and run to the rabbi—when through the dining-room window he saw the rabbi's sister with uncovered hair.

He had never seen Hadassah without a kerchief. Holding his breath, he gazed at her black hair tumbling to her shoulders. She picked up the teakettle with both hands, covered the bread basket with a small cloth, and carried the dirty dishes to the kitchen. She did all this quickly, as if afraid that the walls and ceiling might gaze too long at her uncovered hair. After washing the dishes, she went through the dining room toward her bedroom. As she walked she turned her head restlessly, and her undone hair made her face look like a frightened bird in a leafy thicket. I've never met such pious people as Reb Avraham-Shaye and his sister, Chaikl thought, and went into the rabbi's room in a state of excitement. He was ashamed both of his suppressed crass desire for the voluptuous young woman in the woods and of his pouncing at her and her escort.

Exhausted by studying, Reb Avraham-Shaye would fall asleep in his light summer clothes on week nights. Only on Friday nights would he crawl out of his cot and undress with great effort. This time too Chaikl found him lying in bed in his robe, trousers, and socks, his little Talmud at his side.

The next morning Chaikl found an extra pillow under his head. Seeing that he slept with his head low, the rabbi had given him his own pillow. Wrapped in his tallis, Reb Avraham-Shaye was facing the wall and praying with ecstatic devotion. At one prayer he raised his eyes and his clenched fists to the ceiling as if storming the gates of heaven. At another his voice rang out with the meekness and joy of a man who has nothing and wants nothing, for his happiness is in speaking face to face with his Creator. During the Silent Devotion he sank into a deep silence. It seemed to Chaikl that the rabbi had divested himself of his tallis-wrapped body and his soul had gone over hill and dale to a place where the sun rose large, round, and radiant. The needles of the pines on the hill opposite the window glinted with the gold of lighted candelabras. Reb Avraham-Shaye concluded the

Silent Devotion and immediately began to undo his tefillin. "Why don't you say the prayers that come after the Silent Devotion?" Chaikl had once asked him.

"I have no more strength," he replied.

At breakfast the rabbi reminded Chaikl to visit his father. Walking through the forest to Valkenik, Chaikl thought: Although the rabbi had reminded him about the mitzva of honoring one's father, Reb Avraham-Shaye really didn't like his father because he was a maskil, an intellectual who sought secular as well as Hebrew learning. Chaikl looked up at the trees, trying to guess their names. When he lived in Freyda Vorobey's house he had often strolled on the outskirts of town with his father. His father would push his dark blue glasses up to his forehead and with his cane point out oak, maple, elder, and nut trees. But the rabbi, even though he studied the Mishna's Order of Seeds day and night, paid no heed to trees, bushes, or plants. He studied the laws about the plants of the Land of Israel the same way he studied the laws pertaining to the sacrifices that would be offered when the Messiah came and the Holy Temple was rebuilt.

4

DURING THE SUMMER one section of the community guest house was crowded with poor beggars, but the other section still housed the yeshiva boys, since they had slept there all winter. Early one evening Melechke Vilner, Chaikl's fellow townsman and the baby of the yeshiva, saw Vova Barbitoler, the tobacco merchant from Vilna, who a year ago had given him a set of ritual fringes and a kiss on the head. Now Hertzke Barbitoler's father looked like a beggar—in tatters and with hair grown wild. Frightened, Melechke hid from him. The next day all Valkenik was talking about the Vilna householder who had come to Valkenik during the winter to prevent his wife from taking his son away from the yeshiva. Everyone knew that Vova had failed: Hertzke had left for Argentina with his mother, that harridan with the caracul coat and two silver fox furs. Vova, the father of the rebellious son, wasn't spoken well of in Valkenik either, but no one had expected him to deteriorate into such a sad state in so short a time.

When he arrived this time, Vova Barbitoler had gone from door to door begging from the shop owners in the market. He also went to the inn where he had stayed in the winter. The innkeeper and his wife had heard he was in town but hardly recognized him. He was dressed in rags and covered with dust. His beard was a cluster of cobwebs. Nevertheless, the innkeeper treated him with respect, asked him to be seated, and invited him to eat with them. "Do you hear from your son in Argentina? And how have you come to such a pass?" But the former tobacco merchant wouldn't sit down and declined to eat. "I can't spare the time," he said. "I haven't heard from my son and my poverty is my own fault. But I'm not ashamed to go begging from door to door."

The innkeeper handed the poor man a zloty and his wife gave him a challa, half a noodle pudding, and a slice of cold fish—everything she had left over from the Sabbath. Vova put all the food in his beggar's bag. Before leaving he asked the address of the bricklayer who had given his son Sabbath meals during the past winter. As soon as he had gone the innkeeper's wife wrung her hands and began to cry. "Oh, woe, that a man could come to this!" To keep himself from bursting into tears, the innkeeper shouted, "Stop bawling, woman! Anything can happen in life!" Nevertheless, the couple weren't sure it was want that had prompted the Vilna merchant to become a beggar. They felt that somehow all this might be a mad joke for him. Any moment now he would return with a laugh and fling their gifts into their faces. Everyone knew he was a strange, crude man—he had tormented his son and refused to send his wife in Argentina a bill of divorce for fifteen years—so who could tell what his present intentions were? Other Valkenik residents too looked at him with pity and suspicion: Had Vova gone mad? Didn't he want people to pity him now, just as he had once wanted to elicit slander and scorn? Everyone noticed that he paraded around with the beggar's bag under his arm with the dignity of a congregant carrying his tallis bag.

Sroleyzer the bricklayer, who had connived in Hertzke's running away, had managed to hide from Vova twice, but the third time the beggar caught up with him. Sroleyzer jumped up in fright, as if a corpse from the cemetery had come to choke him. "It's not my fault!" Sroleyzer yelled. "That Hertzke is a bastard, a snitcher, and his mother is a bloody whore. May they both drown before they get to Argentina!"

"Don't curse them. It's not your fault, and it isn't Hertzke's or his mother's fault. It's mine." Vova Barbitoler stood by the door and stretched out his hand. "Give me a donation."

Later, in the beth medresh, Sroleyzer swore before a group of congregants, "If Hertzke's father had punched my face with a pair of brass knuckles, I wouldn't have been as stunned as I was to see that outstretched hand asking for money. I begged the poor man, 'Vova, eat in my house, sleep here. I'll take care of you as if you were my own flesh-and-blood brother.' But he—he absolutely refused, he just wanted a donation. I gave him a fiver. So he gives back the fiver and says he doesn't deserve that much. So he ended up taking one zloty. Poor man!" the bricklayer whined. "My heart is torn to pieces with sympathy for him."

The congregants exchanged glances: Just look at that compassionate thief. First he helped the woman from Argentina take his son away and make the father miserable, and now he's weeping for him. That fence had expected the befuddled tobacco merchant to slit his throat. That extorter knew he deserved to be torn to pieces—that's why he redeemed himself with a zloty.

The old ritual slaughterer, Reb Lippa-Yosse, and his family recalled the Vilna merchant's visit to Reb Tsemakh Atlas, who at that time was living with them. But now Vova hadn't even asked about the rosh yeshiva. He didn't ask for a donation either; he just wanted to eat. Aware that Vova had refused meals at other houses, they viewed his request to eat as a good sign. But he was as impudent as the most seasoned mendicant. He slurped his soup and bolted his meat, then asked for another plate of soup and more meat. He seemed purposely to call disgust down upon himself and test the family's patience. The old slaughterer, his two daughters, Hannah-Leah and Ronya, and their boarder, Reb Menakhem-Mendl Segal, sat quietly. But Yudel, Hannah-Leah's husband, felt nauseated. His stomach was turning; he thought he wouldn't be able to sit at the table any longer. But he didn't get up because he was afraid that Vova would make a scene.

Obviously wanting to debase himself even more, Vova Barbitoler declared that he was no longer a tobacco merchant and had begun dealing in sacred objects. "I sold prayer shawls and ritual fringes until I realized I wouldn't be able to make a living from that. So I established a Free Bread Society to provide bread in midweek and challa on Sabbath for recently impoverished congregants. I'm the trustee of the society and its collector and distributor. But Vilna already has a society like this. It too makes such gifts without fanfare, and even has a similiar name—The Free Loaf Society. The trustees of that group raised a fuss. They said I was competing with them and they accused me of taking more for myself than I was distributing to others. Imagine! I was taking more than I was giving others." And the former merchant bared his teeth as his son Hertzke used to do.

The old slaughterer gave Vova a contribution. Reb Menakhem-Mendl Segal, on the other hand, couldn't bring himself to give money to a man who had recently been such a generous philanthropist and who in Vilna had paid him to teach Chaikl Vilner. But Vova Barbitoler stood there with his hand outstretched as if demanding a debt, and finally Reb Menakhem-Mendl gave him a coin. Vova didn't even glance at the sum and left the house without saying good-bye.

The people around the table then began to talk. It seemed that the Vilna merchant had obviously taken a penance upon himself. But a man who wanted to torment himself for past sins made no demands on anyone and didn't brag about himself. Hannah-Leah whispered with her younger sister, Ronya, who looked very dejected. She was very grieved because Tsemakh had not returned to the house, if only to visit her children. The men had said that Tsemakh Atlas was visiting the yeshiva less frequently. He sat alone in the attic or in the women's gallery of the Cold Shul. Ronya felt that the tobacco merchant's appearance in the village had some connection with their former lodger and that new sufferings would accrue to Tsemakh's previous ones.

After the visit to the slaughterer, Vova Barbitoler went to his old Vilna friend, Reb Shlomo-Motte, the Hebrew teacher. In the presence of Chaikl's father Vova didn't play the role of the beggar or assume the guise of a madman. Reb Shlomo-Motte talked to him with quiet distress, as if both were continuing the conversation they had begun long ago in Vilna, in the tavern at the corner of Butchers Street.

"It's no good, Reb Vova. You're not behaving decently. For fifteen years you've lived with the consolation that your runaway wife in Argentina was suffering because she wasn't getting the divorce from you and that her children from her second husband were bastards. But when Confrada came from Argentina this past winter, and you saw how little she cared that her children from her second husband weren't kosher according to Jewish law, you began to punish yourself. There was a period when you hated her and longed for her at the same time. And now you're tormenting yourself because you dreamed of her all the time. It's no good, Reb Vova; it's no good."

"But I feel good this way, very good." Hertzke's father laughed. "Is your Chaikl still studying in Reb Tsemakh Atlas' yeshiva?"

"No, my son is no longer studying with him."

"What? He couldn't keep your son either? What is Chaikl doing now?"

The old teacher hesitated at length before telling Vova the news. "Chaikl is now studying with a great scholar who's vacationing here in Valkenik."

"And my son isn't studying with anyone. Hertzke doesn't even put on his tefillin," Vova chanted sadly, pounding the table with two fingers in accompaniment. "Well, I must go now. I'll come to see you again, Reb Shlomo-Motte. I'll also visit Chaikl and the man who's teaching him."

"His current teacher is a famous sage and a very noble man, but he's weak and ailing. He must not become excited. Even rabbis and friends visit him rarely so as not to tire him," Reb Shlomo-Motte said with increasing uneasiness.

But his visitor only laughed. "I was the one who hired your son's previous teacher, Reb Menakhem-Mendl Segal; I can meet his present one too."

At the doorway he stopped beside the landlady. Tall, thin Freyda the American looked at him with her kind and foolish eyes. He looked like a beggar, but since Reb Shlomo-Motte was spending time with him, he must be a respectable man. At first Vova Barbitoler made a motion with his hand as though intending to ask the poor woman for a donation. But Reb Shlomo-Motte silently pleaded with Vova not to shame him in front of the landlady. Vova dropped his upraised hand and his eyes gleamed with the licentiousness of an old sinner who secretly wants to pinch the maid's behind.

5

THAT NIGHT the Hebrew teacher slept poorly. He had decided that in the morning he would send his landlady to Chaikl with a note warning him of Vova Barbitoler's impending arrival. But the landlady's daughter, Kreyndl, did not leave the house all morning long and Reb Shlomo-Motte was afraid to ask a favor of Freyda while Kreyndl was at home because he couldn't bear to hear the girl shriek at her mother, "You fool, why do you let yourself be taken advantage of?" The old man sat on the edge of his bed and thought gloomily: Once upon a time he had not been intimidated by the persecutions of rabbis who opposed the Haskalah. Nor had he kowtowed to rich householders to get their children as students. But now he had to shiver in fear before a young witch like Kreyndl lest she tell him to find lodging elsewhere.

To keep people from laughing at her as they had laughed at the poor cook Leitshe when her supposed fiancé Yosef Varshever had jilted her, Kreyndl began to befriend the maids in town and with them began to make fun of the bench warmer who had been her mother's boarder. "It's true," she said, "I once thought Chaikl was a modern young man despite his being in the yeshiva, but then I realized he was a fanatic. If he weren't a fanatic, he wouldn't have become an assistant to the vacationing rabbi. But I'm letting his father stay on with us out of pity for him," Kreyndl told her friends. In private, however, she squabbled with her mother. "You fishwife," she said, "don't think I don't see you're in love with Reb Shlomo-Motte! You never take your eyes off him!"

Freyda looked at her daughter as if she'd gone crazy. What nonsense! When a woman had a husband who was a boor—Bentsye the Golem was one of his nicknames—and who was living in a village with a peasant woman, it was a pleasure to have an intelligent, well-educated man with a beautiful white beard in one's house. The Divine Presence hovered over Reb Shlomo-Motte; his high forehead shone like the sun. Freyda liked Chaikl too. Although she regretted that he had moved out, she was glad he was living and studying with a great rabbi. When Chaikl came to visit his father, Freyda always stood in the kitchen, her long thin hands on her apron, gazing at him with awe, as if he too were already a great rabbi.

Reb Shlomo-Motte whispered to the landlady, "When your daughter leaves I'd like to send you to the forest with an important message for Chaikl." Freyda understood that it was in connection with the visit of the tattered man with the disheveled beard who had so upset Reb Shlomo-Motte. The mother waited impatiently for her daughter's departure, but Kreyndl fussed about in her little room humming to herself, as if she'd guessed something was up and was acting out of spite. The more calmly the girl hummed, the more gloomily Freyda looked out at the path which led to the village known as the Black Blacksmith, where her husband Bentsye the Apostate was living with a gentile woman and giving her his wages. Suddenly she saw someone coming and clapped her hands with joy.

"Reb Shlomo-Motte, your son is coming!"

While Chaikl listened to his father telling him all about the tobacco merchant, Kreyndl sang loudly in her little room: "Money is round, money is round, and it soon rolls away." Chaikl knew that she was directing this song at him, as if to say he was eager for a large dowry. But Chaikl now had bigger worries, and he pleaded with his father not to make him more apprehensive about the tobacco merchant's visit.

"Why should Vova come to the rabbi's cottage and start a scandal? In Reb Shaulke's beth medresh in Vilna he wept in our presence and admitted it was all his fault. Both Mother and his wife Mindl said he's humiliating himself because he has become a penitent."

"He's become a penitent," the father mimicked his son angrily. "Only your wild Musarniks and foolish housewives can persuade themselves that a man can change overnight. His weeping in Vilna and his beating his breast for his past sins still doesn't mean a thing. Either he had a moment of true penitence or he was putting on a show even then. In any case, he still considers himself in the right. At first he would get drunk in order to rage, and now he prefers being a beggar in order to rage."

Kreyndl now sang another song about how money goes from hand to hand; it warned against boasting because money is lost so easily. Although the girl was trying to annoy him, Chaikl was still thinking of the tobacco merchant, not of her.

"I don't understand why a man should go begging from door to door in order to rage," he said.

His father replied softly so that Kreyndl would not hear, "She's quite a girl. But if a lad like you learns a trade and can meet any girl he wants to without being afraid of a rosh yeshiva, he looks for a fine girl, not a witch like her. You say you don't understand why a man should go begging from door to door just to be able to rage? What about you? Weren't you enthralled by Reb Tsemakh Atlas because you felt you'd be able to rant and rave just like him? You've forgotten already, but the tobacco merchant still remembers that you helped Reb Tsemakh Atlas take his son Hertzke away from Vilna to the yeshiva here. It's not for nothing that he asked me who you were studying with. Your teacher is the sort of person who can't bear scandals, so you must tell him everything before Vova does, and when you see the tobacco merchant coming, both you and your teacher should go out the window and run to the woods."

Reb Shlomo-Motte's last remark was not without irony. Chaikl had told him that when Reb Avraham-Shaye saw rabbis or yeshiva students coming into the courtyard, he called, "Guests are coming!" and then went out by the low window and into the woods. The old maskil held that a person who avoids others cannot be a guide for a young man who has to be shown the correct path in life. But to avoid a meeting with Vova Barbitoler, such a ruse was certainly acceptable.

In the meantime Kreyndl had finished singing another song, this one about modern youths who were as trustworthy as street curs—obviously referring to the romance she had had with Chaikl, and his rejection of her. Then she suddenly came out between the curtains of her little alcove. She was all decked out in a pleated pink dress and a wide-brimmed straw hat. She wore white gloves, carried a white purse, and had on white shoes with such high heels that she almost reached the low ceiling. Reb Shlomo-Motte nearly smacked his lips in derision. Freyda too, peeling potatoes in the kitchen, stood open-mouthed: In the middle of the day, when all the boys and girls were working and the town was empty, why was she getting all dressed up for the Valkenik sands? But Kreyndl was hurrying off as if a troop of bridegrooms were waiting.

Kreyndl saw Chaikl and stopped in astonishment, as if surprised to see him in her house. "Well, look who's here! He turns up everywhere, like weeds. And wherever he goes he sows trouble. Sroleyzer says that he and the crazy rosh yeshiva fooled that boy into coming to Valkenik—the one who later went to Argentina with his mother and whose father later went mad from sorrow. And now this madman has come to town and is going from door to door begging for money."

"It's a sad business if you have to make friends with that thief Sroleyzer and his gang," Freyda yelled, holding the kitchen knife in one hand and an unpeeled potato in the other.

"Then who should I make friends with, a bench warmer?" Kreyndl pointed a white glove at Chaikl. "I swear, any working boy has more honesty in him than all the bench warmers put together." And before leaving she added with a haughty little laugh, "And just to spite everyone, I'm going out now with one of the cavaliers from Sroleyzer's group."

Hardly twenty-four hours had passed since Chaikl had tongue-lashed the couple by the gate of the rabbi's vacation cottage, and his ears were still ringing with the scolding the rabbi had given him: "A ben Torah doesn't answer at all!" Therefore he kept silent now.

His father looked at him out of the corner of his eye and said softly, "I'm going to write your mother to wish us *mazel tov.* I'll tell her that Chaikl's new teacher has had a great influence on him. Chaikl has learned to keep quiet."

On his way back Chaikl stopped at the synagogue courtyard. Every time he passed the Cold Shul on the hill, with its turreted roof and octagonal windows, he was reminded of Noah's Ark on Mount Ararat. But now he had no time for such fantasies. He hesitated for a moment and then went through the low door into the women's gallery to see if Reb Tsemakh was there. Indeed, he was sitting in a corner next to a prayer stand, holding a Musar booklet and looking as if he hadn't left the shul since Chaikl had met him there months ago. His cheeks had become more sunken; his large black eyes were like jewels that sparkle but see nothing. The Vilna youth groaned like an old man who has come to rid himself of an evil eye.

"You probably know that Hertzke's father is in Valkenik, begging from door to door. Valkenik is saying that it was the two of us, you and I, who brought him to such a state. What am I supposed to do if he comes up to the rabbi's house and makes a scandal?"

"What should you do?" Tsemakh repeated as if from sleep. "What can you do? Neither of us can deny that we brought Hertzke here."

"But I didn't want to interfere. You told me in Vilna that if I didn't help you I wouldn't be a true Navaredker Musarnik and would never forgive myself for having seen a friend in anguish and not helped him. I obeyed you, so why should I suffer now?" Chaikl muttered.

"You're right," the principal responded weakly. "What you're saying is absolutely true. But now it's too late."

"My father feels that Vova Barbitoler is just putting on a show. First he used to get drunk in order to rant and rave, and now he's become a beggar to do the same thing."

"Your father's right. He has common sense." A sharp smile flashed on the principal's face and immediately faded.

Chaikl didn't know the primary reason why Reb Tsemakh was so dejected, but he sensed that his leaving the yeshiva had added to the principal's gloom. Reb Tsemakh didn't ask how his studies with his new teacher were progressing and no longer even felt like rebuking him. Chaikl left the Cold Shul more depressed than before.

On Synagogue Street he saw Melechke Vilner approaching. Melechke, always indignant that Reb Avraham-Shaye had not taken him as a pupil, was nevertheless glad to meet his fellow townsman and immediately confided his secret to him.

"In the other part of the guest house, where the poor wayfarers lodge, there's an organ grinder who's going around Valkenik holding a cage with a green parrot in it. The parrot is chained to the cage and the man also has a big white mouse that pulls little fortune cards out of a box. True, it's a waste of time from Torah studies, but I can't help myself." Melechke groaned. "It's as if pincers are dragging me over there to see the green parrot that chatters like a man and the mouse with sharp little teeth that nibbles from your hand. And I'm dying of curiosity to see what's written on those little fortune cards. But the organ grinder is mean. If you don't give him ten groschen, he doesn't let the mouse pull out a single fortune card. I've given him all my ten-groschen coins. I think I've even spent the three zlotys that my mother sent me for expenses." Melechke sighed like an old recluse in a shul admitting that he has succumbed to temptation.

"Have you seen Hertzke's father in the guest house?" Chaikl asked. "I hear he's staying there. Have you spoken to him?"

"At first I hid from him," Melechke answered, "because he frightened me with his wild eyes and bedraggled looks. But yesterday while I was standing next to the organ grinder and the mouse was pulling out a fortune card for me, I felt someone patting me on the head. So I turned around, and it was Hertzke's father. The tobacco merchant asked me how I was and lectured me: it wasn't fitting for a yeshiva student to be drawing fortune cards. "A field mouse can't predict anyone's fortune," he said. "A man makes the fortune he himself deserves." Melechke groaned again. "I can't help it—I can't stay away from those little creatures, especially the parrot. It's green all over and has a yellow tuft of hair and a hooked beak. It's probably a hundred years old; that's what the organ grind—"

"Has Vova Barbitoler asked you about me?" Chaikl interrupted him.

"He told me he knows who you're studying with and he's going to see your teacher. He also told me that before he leaves he'll give me a nice present," Melechke said, looking modestly down at his babyish hands and fingers.

"Why the present? Because you're playing with a mouse?" Chaikl asked suspiciously. This little plaster saint loved to tattle and had probably blurted out to the tobacco merchant the whole story of his romance with Kreyndl. "Tell me the truth; what did you tell him about me that made him promise you a present?"

Melechke's eyes, which had been glowing with the dream of the green parrot, now flared with anger. "Common knowledge isn't considered slander, and I didn't ask Hertzke's father for a present. He volunteered to give it to me because he's sure I'm going to continue my

Torah studies. But he told me that you won't continue with yours." And Melechke backed away from the older townsman, eyes blazing.

This means that Hertzke's father will come to the rabbi's cottage, Chaikl thought. But since he didn't want to be frightened ahead of time, when he went into the rabbi's room he immediately opened the Talmud and began reciting. Reb Avraham-Shaye, standing with the little Talmud folio in his hand, realized the extent of Chaikl's agitation by the quaver in his voice.

"What's happened? How's your father?" the rabbi asked.

"Vova Barbitoler is in Valkenik!" the pupil burst out. He told the rabbi who Vova Barbitoler was and why he was a blood enemy of both Reb Tsemakh and Chaikl himself. Reb Avraham-Shaye, eyes wide and nose pale, listened in astonishment and trepidation.

"You're wild and so is the rosh yeshiva." The rabbi laughed and shrugged with some irritation. "Every youngster in town was already committed to Torah studies, isn't that right?" the rabbi said sarcastically. "And so the only one needed in the yeshiva—that's what you and the principal felt—was the tobacco merchant's son, a boy who, according to you, has been accused of being a pickpocket."

"I know for sure that Vova Barbitoler is preparing to visit you to make a scandal," Chaikl said loudly, waiting for the rabbi to shake with fear. Reb Avraham-Shaye didn't reply; he acted as if he hadn't heard. He thought for a long while, then said, "Reb Tsemakh Atlas is a hero, but a hero on the outside—while according to the Torah a hero is a man with internal heroic qualities, one who can subdue his bad inclinations. Even for a man who wants to sacrifice himself, the Jewish law has established boundaries between causes for which a man can give up his life and those for which he may not. Bringing a youngster into a yeshiva is a sanctification of God's name. But bringing that kind of boy—especially against his father's will—turns sanctification into desecration. And even the greatest hero is a wild ass if he doesn't know where to stop."

"What will happen when Vova Barbitoler shows up here? Are we going to run into the woods?" Chaikl asked.

"I don't know what will happen then," the rabbi answered. He straightened his mustache with his thumb. "Come, let's go back to our studies. You know what? You're a gaon at finding ways to waste time. Let me hear you recite that passage again. . . ."

6

Dear Tsemakh,

Aunt Tsertele is dead. One night she lay down to sleep and did not wake up again. . . .

Tsemakh's eyes filled with tears and he couldn't finish reading his Uncle Ziml's letter. Hands behind his head, he lay fully dressed in bed in his room and recalled his trip from the yeshiva back to Lomzhe. His short, squat aunt had stood by the table, offering him the bread basket and the salt shaker. Her kind, toilworn hands and emaciated head had trembled with old age. Behind her stood Uncle Ziml, looking like a long, cold chimney, staring up at the ceiling as if toward heaven. At first their three sons, his cousins, had treated him decently, but now they detested him; his brothers-in-law were his enemies too; and his wife, their sister Slava, bitterly resented him. Why shouldn't she? She had come to Valkenik to ask him to come home and he had let her return to Lomzhe in humiliation.

Only Ronya, Reb Lippa-Yosse's daughter, had remained devoted to him and was concerned about him, even though he had humiliated and insulted her too. Yesterday Ronya had come unexpectedly into Reb Yisroel's house with her two little boys and told the tailor's wife, "I just dropped by during our walk because since Reb Tsemakh has moved out of our house and into yours, the children are always asking about their uncle." Tsemakh's landlady knocked at his door and let Ronya and her children in. "Here's uncle," Ronya cried to her children, and quickly told Tsemakh in a low voice, "The father of the boy whose mother took him to Argentina has come to town. He's either half crazy or just pretending—who knows what he's planning to do?" Tsemakh noticed that Ronya had become thinner and seemed younger. She looked around the room, eager to see how he lived. "Why am I saying this? Of course you know he's in town," she said in haste. Then she grabbed her children by the hands and left the room.

A pale secretive smile illuminated Tsemakh's face. It was pleasant to lie in bed thinking about Ronya. Soon his smile sank into the corners of his mouth. He recalled how, during the past winter, he had struggled with himself not to fall into temptation with her. But what was the result? He had exhausted himself to overcome his *yetzer ha-ra* for a married woman, and the fire of Musar had cooled within him. He froze in the middle of the summer, both in his room and in the synagogue.

Tsemakh went on with his uncle's letter.

> My sons want me to move in with them, but I don't want to leave my home because I often think that Tsertele is still with me. And if I go to my children she'll be left all alone in the house. I don't always think that my dearest one is still with me, but at such times I feel the mourning in every corner and I understand what I never understood before. I never properly appreciated my good fortune in life. Oh, if I could only take her place in the store so she could go to the wholesaler for merchandise or go home and cook supper! That's the way people are. If things are going well, a man doesn't appreciate his good fortune; and when he finally realizes that he has to thank the Provider of all Good for his measure of good luck, it's too late to repair the damage.

For years his strange Uncle Ziml had dreamed of becoming a recluse. And he had also advised him, his nephew, to marry his first fiancée from Amdur and to become a recluse immediately after the wedding. Later his uncle had dreamed of picking up the wanderer's staff and advised Tsemakh to follow suit. Now the old man regretted not properly appreciating his life with his Tsertele, and was warning Tsemakh to return to his wife before it was too late.

In the afternoon Tsemakh went to the Cold Shul. Once more he sat in the women's gallery, knowing that on the other side, in the men's section, a placard hung on a pillar listing the Thirteen Articles of Faith. It stared right at him through the latticed window. Yes—he admitted it—he lacked faith in the Creator. So why was he sitting here? He had dreamed of students who could comprehend a profound sermon and had no fear of contemplating the most fundamental aspects of one's faith. Studying Talmud with beginners wasn't for him. Fate had caused him to get entangled here, unable to extricate himself until someone came and pushed him out.

Tsemakh sat with closed eyes, his face tense. His memory sank down into the depths of his soul and burrowed there like someone climbing down a ladder into a shul cellar to look for a fragment in the mounds of rotting pages of torn holy books. Suddenly he heard light footfalls. The wall of the women's gallery faced the high fence of a garden. Between the wall and the fence was a deep ditch overgrown with stinging nettles. Tsemakh looked out a dusty little window; in the ditch stood Vova Barbitoler, waist-high in nettles.

Tsemakh gave a start. He had anticipated the tobacco merchant's visit and was expecting him. But his enemy's crawling through the ditch made it seem as if he wanted to attack him from behind with an ax. But Tsemakh soon gathered that Vova had missed the low side door of the women's gallery and stumbled into the overgrown ditch. With a few long strides Tsemakh was outside.

"You're looking for me, no doubt. Come in."

His hands burned by the nettles, his enraged hairy face visible through the tall, prickly grass, Vova Barbitoler looked like a wild beast. But when the rosh yeshiva called him, he laughed gaily and began to crawl out.

Tsemakh returned to the women's gallery and sat behind a prayer stand. Vova Barbitoler followed him and sat in a chair facing him. A dirty set of ritual fringes hung out of his tattered gaberdine and fell over his knees. He wore a stiff black hat with a torn brim and large, crooked, dust-covered shoes. Filth wafted from him, the sweaty smell of a man who sleeps in his clothes for weeks at a time. He scratched his pricked hands with his dirty nails, his face contorted with the pleasure of scratching. His feverish eyes gleamed with joy and also with affection for his victim; Vova was glad that he could play with Tsemakh before devouring him.

"I heard that you rarely come to the yeshiva. Ever since I've known you, I've felt that you destroy everything you touch. I was afraid you'd destroy the yeshiva too, but now I hear and see that, thank God, the yeshiva has remained a yeshiva and *you're* destroyed. You look like a scarecrow, like a wax dummy. God is now repaying you for having reduced me to beggary. People still pity me and give me a donation, but you're a headache to them."

As hard as Tsemakh had tried of late to wrench himself out of his apathy, he had not succeeded. Now all his strength awakened. He felt a hidden joy, a dark harbinger of redemption. If the tobacco merchant tried to drive him out of the village, well and good.

Tsemakh replied calmly, smiling, as if he had wagered with his enemy which one would raise his voice first. "It is not I who have reduced you to beggary—it's your own corrupt nature that has brought you to this. And your son has your blood. You don't know anything about forgiveness, and Hertzke couldn't forget how savagely you beat him. He doesn't trust a Jew with beard and earlocks because you have a beard and earlocks. He didn't take his ritual fringes and tefillin to Argentina because you put on ritual fringes and tefillin. The only people Hertzke liked were his mother's brothers, members of the Vilna underworld, because you hated them. And that's why he purposely befriended people in Valkenik who were part-time or full-fledged thieves. Your son took revenge on you, just as you took revenge on his runaway mother by torturing him and by not giving his mother a divorce, and just as you have come now to take revenge on the Valkenik Jews."

"I've come here to take revenge on the Valkenik Jews?" Vova wondered, but his mocking eyes admitted that the principal had guessed right.

"Yes, to take revenge on the Valkenik Jews—and most of all, naturally, to have your revenge of me. After all, the local Jews looked on and remained silent when your wife from Argentina took Hertzke away. Some of the residents even felt that you deserved to have the boy taken away from you. That's why you want everyone to see how troubles have made you a pauper and then let them all feel guilty toward you! I'm confident that if you made the attempt you could still do business. But it's easier for you to go begging from door to door, so everyone can see the state to which evil people have brought you. And where you feel you can make a bigger impression at playing the role of a broken penitent—you say there that it's all your fault and you beat your breast, crying, 'I'm a sinner.' But no matter what you do, people won't trust you. People think you're a clown—just putting on a show."

"Yes, I've become a clown." Vova Barbitoler nodded like a drunkard who sobers up and complains about his addiction to the bitter drop. Then the clownish mien disappeared from his face and, in a voice of anguish, he loosed a torrent of words:

"Yes, perhaps I'm a clown now—I'm a clown for sure. When I was still running around Vilna after Hertzke left, telling everyone it was all my fault, I really meant it. I was waiting for good friends to console me and tell me that even though I had made mistakes during my life, others were also responsible for my troubles. But they listened to me and chimed in, 'Yes, yes, you alone are at fault.' Decent people remained silent. Some tried to soothe me and say I wasn't the worst. Even a blind man could have seen that they said it halfheartedly just for convention's sake. They didn't even have enough patience to hear me out. I noticed that when I made scandals they were afraid of me, and others even said I was right. But when I berated myself, they winked and made fun of me. They laughed at me as if I were some kind of shlimazel, and people turned away from me as from a moron. Even though the holy books say it's better to be considered a moron than a wicked man, they preferred making fun of the moron to hating the wicked man. What's more, when I used to fight with everyone, deep down I knew I was wrong and felt guilty before God and man. But I didn't want to admit it, because then I was still sure I'd prevail. But once I realized that I had lost it all and began to beat my breast in contrition, people began to turn away from me. The only thing they needed me for was to criticize me. 'He's finished. Done for. Let him drop dead,' they said. So I said to myself: They won't live to see the day. I won't beat my breast anymore."

7

VOVA BARBITOLER fell silent and sat with his arms dangling at his sides, legs thrust forward and spread apart. Tsemakh Atlas too was silent and morose. The gloom within each man increased the enmity and rancor between them. The cold and empty men's shul was visible through the latticed windows. The tall grasses swayed sadly and quietly on the outside wall of the women's gallery. Vova and Tsemakh looked like two corpses sitting in a tomb, fighting over grievances they had had while still alive. Tsemakh's passion for admonition was so aroused that he looked daggers at Vova.

"I see that you're an even bigger clown and buffoon than I thought. A true penitent's greatest pleasure is having people humiliate him. But you—not for one second did you have deeply felt regrets for your perverted deeds. You just said that in the presence of people you beat your breast in contrition. You expected people to fall on their knees and plead, 'Reb Vova, have pity on the world and don't weep! Reb Vova, don't say bad things about yourself! Reb Vova, you're as innocent as a newborn babe, even though for fifteen years you refused to give your wife a divorce! You're not guilty either, Reb Vova, of tearing the wig off your third wife's head and inhumanly humiliating her in the presence of the whole congregation.' This is what you wanted to hear from everyone who watched you beating your breast. And because people didn't console you by proclaiming your innocence, you took to playing the role of a beggar. What do your first wife's children say about your new role? They probably don't know where to hide for shame. Indeed, that's what you want. As sure as I'm standing here, I know that just as you want to take revenge on me and on the Valkenik Jews, you also want to take revenge on your first wife's children for running away from home because of the constant fights. You want your children to bury their heads in shame because they have a beggar for a father. You buffoon!"

"I can't churn out such a mad torrent of words—after all I'm not a Musarnik. What I'd like to know is, can a Musarnik only talk, or can he listen too?" Vova asked, wiping the perspiration from his brow.

"Of course a Musarnik can listen," Tsemakh called out with wild joy and curiosity. "A Musarnik can have even more faults than other people, but he has one attribute: he can listen to the truth and not lose his temper. What do you have to say?"

But the words did not come easily to the tobacco merchant. They stumbled laboriously from his mouth as though all his lifelong sufferings had become embedded in his throat:

"How could you grab me by the lapels and call me a wicked Haman because I humiliated my wife? You humiliated your wife even more! My excuse could be that I was very embittered when I humiliated my Mindl, and dead drunk to boot. But you, Musarnik, you married a young, beautiful woman from a fine family and then ran away from her after the wedding, just like Confrada ran away from me. From this I conclude—"

"Yes, what do you conclude from this?" Tsemakh yearned to be castigated for not being with his wife.

"—that you attacked me in Reb Shaulke's beth medresh not because I humiliated my Mindl but because you like to stick your nose in wherever there's confusion and trouble. You come alive when you're in a fight. Without a fight, you don't know what purpose you have in this world. You dragged Hertzke here because I was against it. You dragged Chaikl here because his father, Reb Shlomo-Motte the teacher, was against it. But because you attracted those two little bastards by turning them against their fathers, and not by gentleness and Torah, they both abandoned you: Hertske by going with his mother to Argentina and Reb Shlomo-Motte's punk by switching to another teacher. People say he's a great scholar and a holy man. Don't you worry; I'll be talking to him about his pupil. . . . But now it's you I'm concerned with. When you tore Hertzke away from me in Vilna, you knew that I'd locked him up in a little pantry for theft. I also told you then that his mother's brothers, those gangsters, were lying in wait for him. So you gave me your word that you'd watch him carefully—and may God protect you for the way you kept your word! How could you have watched my son when your mind was somewhere else?" Vova's half-closed eyes opened, full of smoky flames.

"Where was it?" Tsemakh asked, his heart stopping in fear that his temptation with Ronya had become known.

"Your mind was on fighting with your wife, so how could you have watched my son?"

Vova Barbitoler noticed the principal's confusion. His hairy face trembled with the lust for revenge: he imagined how he would stop the Torah reading on the Sabbath until the worshipers would let him have his say. He would make no demands except that they listen to his remarks about their rosh yeshiva. This Tsemakh Atlas, he would say, had once broken an engagement . . .

If he knew about Ronya, he would not have kept it quiet, Tsemakh thought, breathing more easily. "Is that so? You even know that I broke an engagement?" Tsemakh asked, strangely delighted.

"Yes, I know. One of the students told me. That's how much your pupils like you." Vova laughed in his face.

"On Sabbath morning the first minyan holds services here in the shul. Where will you stop the Torah reading—in the beth medresh or in the shul?" Tsemakh baited and teased him even more.

"First I'll stop the reading in the shul, and then I'll go to the beth medresh," Vova replied.

"Fine!" Tsemakh stood. His fear was gone. "On Sabbath morning I'll pray with the first minyan in the Cold Shul, and then I'll come to the Torah reading at the beth medresh so that you can see me as you tell the congregants who I am. Are you happy now?"

Vova stood too and looked through the window to the men's section. On the pillar next to the pulpit he saw the placard with the Thirteen Articles of Faith. For a minute sweet repose rested on his face, as though he had awakened from a bad dream in the morning sunshine. But as soon as he turned to Tsemakh, he became furious again.

"I want you to know that even though I thought you were insensitive and not too clever, at least you were honest and just. You took up the cause of a humiliated woman, and you were ready to sacrifice yourself for children who study Torah. That's why I gave in each time you attacked me. But when I found out how you—who demands things from others—treat your own wife, and that lately you don't even care about your students, then you're going to pay for everything. I've never forgiven my runaway wife the torments and shame she's caused me, so do you expect me to forgive you, a perfect stranger? I'm going to stay here in Valkenik and make your life miserable till you're forced to run away. I swear this as sure as there's a God in this world. I believe in God. I put on tefillin every day, and after saying my prayers I recite: I believe with perfect faith in the Creator, blessed be He, who created the world and is the Creator of all His creatures." Vova pointed to the placard on the other side of the latticed window. "I believe that there is a God in this world, and that he'll pay you back for everything you've done to me."

"Look, I knew you believed in God." Tsemakh gagged with hatred. "I knew that a wicked Haman like you needs God as a partner to his deeds. A sensualist like you also has to be promised the world to come. If you didn't act the buffoon and lie to yourself, you'd be ashamed to believe in an all-merciful God while you yourself are a cruel brute. Just as a man has two eyes, you have two manias in life: lust and revenge. You're an old man already. But even after you're dead and there's nothing left of you, your unsatisfied lust and unsatisfied revenge will live on with a life of their own. You believe in a God of Israel, yet you nearly beat Hertzke to death for not putting on ritual fringes. You saw to it that all the Vilna orphans had ritual fringes—but none of that is worth a cent. Even if you melt with tears under your tallis, even if you beat your breast till you damage your heart, even if you spend the rest of your life wandering about as a penitent beggar—it will be absolutely worthless. Fulfilling the mitzvas is not hard; studying Torah day and night is not hard; believing in the Master of the Universe the way you believe is not hard. It's even easy; it's a pleasure! What *is* hard is to deny yourself your beastly desires. You can go and tell this to the vacationing rabbi in my name. I know you aim to go there to take your revenge on Chaikl too—a boy who's totally blameless. It was I who forced him to help me bring your Hertzke to Valkenik. You're burning for revenge, and you want to drive him away from his teacher just as you want to drive me out of town. So when you visit the rabbi, I want you to tell him what I think of your belief in God and your putting on tefillin. And if you tell him this, I assure you that Reb Avraham-Shaye, the saintly gaon, will side with you and not with me."

"You also fought with Chaikl's teacher? Are you sure he'll side with me? All right then, I'll tell him what you said." A smile bloomed like nettles in the wrinkles of Vova Barbitoler's rough, hairy face.

"And when you prevent them from reading the Torah on Sabbath morning, tell the congregants what I think about your belief in God, too. And now get out of here. I don't want to see your face again until the Sabbath."

"I'm going; I'm going." Vova cheerfully strode forward on his crooked legs. "And remember my oath! I won't budge till I drive you out of the yeshiva and out of town."

As soon as Tsemakh was alone again, he pressed his forehead to the prayer stand and groaned. "I'm sick and tormented," he murmured. "I want to rest my bones in Aunt Tsertele's living room. She'll cover me with her shawl as she did when I returned, broken, from wandering away from home. I'm even lonelier than Vova Barbitoler in the Valkenik guest house. I wish it would all end. Let Hertzke's father make it difficult for me here and force me to run away."

In the synagogue courtyard Vova Barbitoler stood, daydreaming of Hertzke sitting in the beth medresh and studying Torah. The sun baked the old man's face, perspiration ran down his forehead, and his feet buckled from too much walking. But the chanting voices of the yeshiva students nailed him to the spot. He just managed to tear his feet away, as though the ground were hot cement. Swaying as he went, he headed for the guest house.

Following him for quite a distance was Yosef Varshever, Gedalya Zondak's son-in-law, fashionable in a light straw hat and leather sandals. He walked slowly, as if lost in thought. Only when the tattered Vova turned in between two rows of trees did Yosef catch up to him.

"Well, did you tell him about his first fiancée and his wife? Did the scandal you're planning for him during the Sabbath Torah reading scare him?"

"I told him everything, but he didn't get scared," Vova growled.

"He got scared all right. He's just pretending he's not frightened," Yosef triumphed with anger and pride.

Vova turned his troubled, careworn glance on him. "Why do you hate him? After all, you made a good match in his yeshiva."

Enraged, Yosef Varshever bit his thin lips and spoke quickly, afraid someone else might hear. "Aside from the fact that the principal nagged the life out of me for not marrying Leitshe the cook, lately he's insulted me even more. I can't stand listening to my father-in-law telling me that I'm a freeloader. So I decided to become a fund raiser for a great yeshiva and travel around like Azriel Weinstock, the slaughterer's son-in-law. To be entrusted with such a mission I'd have to have a recommendation to the Yeshiva Council. And right now the man who wrote *The Vision of Avraham* happens to be vacationing in Valkenik, and a letter from him to the Yeshiva Council would open all doors for me. So although it galled me, I still had to go to the principal and ask him to speak to Reb Avraham-Shaye Kosover. But Reb Tsemakh answered: 'Reb Avraham-Shaye won't give you a letter in response to my request, and indeed you *can't* be trusted. If you could fool a Jewish girl, you're also capable of pocketing the money that people donate for a yeshiva.' These were his very words; do you expect me to forgive and forget?" Yosef Varshever looked around to see if anyone had seen him talking to the beggar.

"But I'll get what I want. I'll travel around the world, and when I'm in Argentina, I'll bring you regards from your son."

"A rascal like you can even be a rabbi in Argentina for my wife Confrada and her husband," the tattered Vova barked into Varshever's face. "Thieves have rabbis too, and you surely would have made a rabbinic decision that Confrada's bastards from her second husband are one hundred percent kosher children."

"I'm helping you against your enemy, and now you're insulting me?" The milk-white skin of Yosef Varshever's thin face quivered with rage. "Don't you dare breathe a word I told you about the principal's conduct. That's all I need! If you so much as mention my name, I'll deny it absolutely."

"Don't worry; I won't call on you as a witness. Tsemakh Atlas and I are open enemies, but you're a sneaky worm!" the beggar raved, and Yosef Varshever departed trembling. Vova dragged his tired legs to the guest house, muttering to himself, "Blast the mad Musarnik for the kind of students he has trained."

8

TOWARD EVENING a guest came into the rabbi's courtyard and looked around. Chaikl spotted him from the porch and ran breathlessly to the rabbi. "He's coming! Vova Barbitoler is coming!" Chaikl was ready to help the rabbi crawl out of the low window and into the woods. "Sit still," Reb Avraham-Shaye said sternly, not moving from his bed.

"I have no intention of running away," Chaikl mumbled and sat down over his Talmud at the table.

Vova Barbitoler came in quickly, in a festive mood and humming a little tune. He glared at Chaikl, then turned humbly to the rabbi, who had begun to get out of bed.

"Don't be angry at me, rabbi, for disturbing you. I'm a poor man, begging from door to door," Vova said pathetically, but his eyes laughed slyly, like those of a Purim player who knows that everyone knows that his white Mordecai beard is pasted on. With a quick gesture he pulled a folded piece of paper from his shirt pocket and handed it to Reb Avraham-Shaye. "Here's a letter of introduction from a Vilna rabbi which bears witness that I once was a respectable, well-to-do householder who has now become impoverished, and that Jews who are known as compassionate should treat me with consideration. Read it, rabbi."

"I believe you without reading it." Nevertheless, Reb Avraham-Shaye looked at length into the folded paper as though he were counting the letters. "It's true; it says you need bread." And he returned the note to the impoverished man.

"You see, rabbi, I'm not lying to you. Still, there are Jews in Valkenik who don't believe that I need bread. Even my old Vilna friend, Reb Shlomo-Motte the teacher, doesn't believe me. Yes, your father." He pointed a finger at Chaikl. "Your pupil probably told you who I am and how I've come to such a pass."

"Yes, I have heard. What can I do for you?"

"What can you do for me?" the visitor shouted unexpectedly, as though to tear the house out of the nocturnal stillness that had settled over it. "You can't do a thing for me. I'm not asking anything of you. I just want to get to know you better. Before I became poor, I was concerned that your student shouldn't grow up to be a street ruffian. I hired a teacher for him, the very same Reb Menakhem-Mendl who is now a Talmud teacher at the yeshiva. So I also want to get to know his newer and greater teacher. Isn't it true, Chaikl, that I hired a teacher for you, and you raised a prayer stand against me because I asked you to show me your ritual fringes? You hear, rabbi? A youngster who threatens an older man with a prayer stand won't remain a Torah scholar. Never in his life! Now he's quiet. Now he's pretending to be a little saint. But I know how his anger is seething in him. It's his good luck that he's in your house, or I would settle accounts with him right now. . . ."

"Watch out! He's likely to raise a prayer stand again, and if there's no prayer stand, he might grab hold of the lighted lamp," Reb Avraham-Shaye joked. But his ringing voice sternly warned the visitor not to dare raise his hand. Vova Barbitoler stood there tongue-tied, and Chaikl was astonished too. He understood the rabbi's hint that he wouldn't let Vova touch him.

"Someday he'll raise a prayer stand against you too. I don't mean a prayer stand itself; I mean he'll do just the opposite of what you're teaching him." Vova attempted to make his voice higher pitched, but he became more and more confused. He had apparently not expected the rabbi to be so unimpressed by his threats. For a moment Reb Avraham-Shaye's chin twitched and trembled. Then he suddenly laughed gaily, as though both he and his visitor had been joking.

"Of course Chaikl is a stubborn rascal. No matter what I say, he says just the opposite. Have you eaten supper? It's a long walk here from the village, and you're probably hungry."

Vova was thrown off balance, subdued by the rabbi's simplicity and gentleness. When not ranting, however, he didn't know how to behave or speak.

"I'm not hungry," he mumbled.

"But you won't refuse a cup of tea," the rabbi said.

"I won't refuse a cup of tea." Vova smoothed down his disheveled beard with his fingers. Reb Avraham-Shaye's addressing him as if he were an honored guest had awakened in him the desire to be respectable.

At the dining-room table Vova Barbitoler sat a few minutes beneath the electric light, gazing at the tablecloth. The rabbi entered with a glass of tea and a plate of cookies. The visitor whispered a blessing, slowly sipped the tea, and dourly listened to the rabbi's remarks.

"The Talmud says about youngsters like Chaikl: 'Be careful with the sons of the poor, because from them Torah will emanate.' The Torah considers him privileged because he is a child of poor parents; hence I have to deal more gently and carefully with him than I would with a rich man's or a rabbi's son. Because of his poor origins, and for other reasons too, he's ashamed, even though he doesn't seem submissive. Therefore there's a chance that he may rebel against his benefactor. The prophet Jeremiah says: 'The heart is deceitful above all things, and exceedingly feeble: who can know it?' But the All-Knowing can see into the heart of man. So we must wait until Chaikl feels confident in Torah learning and then the impudence in him will disappear of its own accord. The Torah which teaches that man is mere dust also strengthens him and lifts him up."

"And do you think he will remain a Torah scholar?" Vova asked.

"I'm not sure, but since his conduct is improving daily, one shouldn't speculate about future developments. When I think about it, I'm confident that even if he doesn't remain with Torah studies, the Torah will remain in him and with him."

The tobacco merchant couldn't remove his intense, penetrating glance from the rabbi, who confided in him as though he were an equal. If he had such feeling for a brat from Butchers Street, he wouldn't be any less sympathetic for a broken old man. Vova Barbitoler quickly finished the tea and crunched the hard biscuits with appetite, as though after a long fast.

At that moment Reb Avraham-Shaye's thoughts were rummaging in the cupboard where the cold foods were stored. But since his guest had previously stated that he wasn't hungry, he would not insist lest Vova think he was being treated like a pauper.

"And don't neglect the fruit." Reb Avraham-Shaye pointed to the apples. "Please, say the blessing."

Reb Avraham-Shaye's head and shoulders were hunched toward the table; he appeared to melt into the shadows. Only his high, vaulted forehead gleamed golden yellow under the electric light. The visitor too was webbed into the evening darkness. Knife in hand, he peeled an apple, cut it into sections, and chewed a piece, carefully keeping his mouth closed. This manner of eating distorted his face, as if he were grimacing at himself in a mirror.

"What do you say about the local principal, Reb Tsemakh Atlas? You've probably heard what he did to me. Was it right for him to butt into my life and tear my son away from me?"

"Not only should he not have done that, but it was also a most foolish blunder on his part. I don't understand his behavior, unless he's simply a wild man and in his wildness does foolish things." Reb Avraham-Shaye said what was on his mind, but at the same time he calculated that he was also doing the principal a favor by talking ill of him. The more he sided with the embittered man, the more his hatred would subside.

"I thought that when he saw me all broken up, he'd apologize for having ruined my life. But instead he insulted me yesterday more than ever before." Vova Barbitoler tapped a finger on the empty tea glass and his eyes burned. "Well, if I'm the cruel brute he says I am, I'll pay him back for everything. I'll make it so miserable for him here that he'll be forced to run away from town."

Reb Avraham-Shaye listened with lowered eyes, his left hand on his forehead. He was longing for the joy of lying on his cot and thinking about a dispute between the sages of the Mishna. The principal and this man would surely destroy each other rather than submit. Reb Avraham-Shaye sensed that this time he couldn't say: I'm not intervening in a fight; I'm a weak man and don't want to take time away from Torah studies. This time he would have to intervene, because this dispute could result in a great desecration of God's name. And besides, now more than ever before, he felt compassion for the rosh yeshiva. He had to be saved.

"If you really want to drive Reb Tsemakh Atlas out of town, you'll succeed, but it will break you even more," Reb Avraham-Shaye said after a long silence.

"Why should it break me?" Vova stared with wide, bloodshot eyes.

"As long as your plans haven't been carried out, you assume that revenge will satisfy you. But revenge is not the Jewish way—and it will break you once and for all."

The silence of the night forest wafted darkly in the window. The bulb's yellowish light and the dining-room shadows added deeper mystery to Reb Avraham-Shaye's whispering. Vova looked at the frail rabbi with concealed fear. He's right, he thought. If I had sent Confrada a divorce years ago, she wouldn't have come from Argentina to take Hertzke. And even if she had come, Hertzke wouldn't have left hating me so.

"An argument with no heavenly intent has no real winner who can exult in victory." Reb Avraham-Shaye stood with hunched shoulders and placed one hand over the other. "From all I've heard about you and can now see for myself, there's no doubt that you have suffered. But Reb Tsemakh Atlas is also miserable; miserable because of his character."

"He's still as crazy as ever. I've told you that his insults yesterday were worse than when he tore my son away from me in Vilna," Vova said, slowly getting to his feet.

"He reviled you because he feels guilty," Reb Avraham-Shaye replied, exhausted by the talk.

"Rabbi, now I don't agree with you. He still thinks he's in the right, and no matter what I do he'll still consider me the same good-for-nothing brute." Vova waved his heavy hand despondently and stumbled to the doorway.

"What he thinks shouldn't bother you. You have to think about yourself and your peace of mind," Reb Avraham-Shaye said, delighted that his visitor was leaving.

On the porch they encountered the thick darkness which in one ink smear fused the courtyard and the nearby wooded hill. A man should not leave in such darkness, Reb Avraham-Shaye thought, and felt a prickly perspiration on his partly bare head. What did they want of him? He had defended Tsemakh Atlas against the Valkenik rabbi and his son and son-in-law. And now, for an entire evening, he had had to defend him against an obdurate man, hard as steel. Should he have this difficult man spend the night here? A minute later the host took his visitor by the hand and said, "In such absolute darkness you won't find your way to town. You must spend the night here in the cottage."

"What?" Vova asked in a muffled voice. "The principal calls me a wicked Haman and a cruel brute, and you want me to spend the night here?"

"A man can't testify against himself that he is wicked," Reb Avraham-Shaye laughed, and in the darkness his face burned with shame at his fleeting anxiety that the visitor might have to stay the night.

9

THE IMPOVERISHED FORMER MERCHANT stood in the middle of Reb Avraham-Shaye's room, head up, listening to his own thoughts as though they were hidden voices from nocturnal depths. From behind the table lamp Chaikl gazed at him, wondering where Hertzke's father would sleep. There were only two beds in the room, and anyway, why should he sleep here? How had he managed to find favor in the rabbi's eyes? But Vova Barbitoler neither spoke to Chaikl nor looked at him.

Reb Avraham-Shaye went to his sister for bedding and returned laden with sheets, pillows, and a quilt. He looked at Chaikl and asked sternly, "Why haven't you taken your sheets off your cot?" But to Vova he said gently, "I'm sorry you'll have to sleep so uncomfortably." Vova still stood in the middle of the room in mute amazement, looking through the open window into the darkness. Chaikl prepared his bed on the long bench by the table and then wanted to make Vova Barbitoler's bed. But Reb Avraham-Shaye thrust him aside and made the bed himself. Not used to such work, he was soon tired out. "I'm not a good hostess," he said, laughing. "You can undress now," he told Vova. "If you have to step outside, Chaikl will show you the way." Once more Vova didn't reply. He sat on the edge of the cot, incredulous that all this was actually happening to him.

Reb Avraham-Shaye, who usually studied in bed until after midnight and usually fell asleep in his clothes, this time undressed before he slipped under his blanket, as he usually did only on Friday and holiday nights. Chaikl understood that the rabbi didn't want to disturb Vova and that he must do the same. But a wild urge to study now came over him, and he continued swaying silently over his Talmud.

"Put out the light and go to sleep!" Reb Avraham-Shaye shouted.

In angry silence Chaikl blew out the kerosene lamp with all his might. He undressed in the dark and stretched out on the hard, narrow bench. Had he been told earlier that he would have to sleep without a straw mattress he would have gone back to the village. Distressed that Hertzke's father had heard the rabbi shouting at him, he was set to flee into the forest in the middle of the night. He lifted his head from the pillow and listened intently, confident that neither the visitor nor the rabbi was sleeping. Vova Barbitoler coughed, moistly smacking his lips as though there weren't a tooth in his mouth. Then he sighed deeply and lay still. Chaikl couldn't fall asleep for a long time. It seemed to him that Vova Barbitoler's silence made the air in the room suffocatingly thick.

All other mornings Reb Avraham-Shaye prayed aloud; this time he prayed silently so as not to awaken his guest. When Chaikl awoke, Reb Avraham-Shaye was not in the room. He had abridged his prayers so as to lend his tallis and tefillin to the visitor. Vova Barbitoler moved his lips slowly, apparently still ruminating over his hidden nocturnal thoughts. As soon as Vova had finished the Silent Devotion, Reb Avraham-Shaye returned and invited him to breakfast.

The guest and his host sat in the dining room opposite each other, eating boiled eggs and not saying a word. After tea and grace Vova Barbitoler muttered, "It's time to go." Reb Avraham-Shaye accompanied him to the path that led to the village. Then the beggar took a bundle of paper money from his chest pocket.

"I'll try to make something of myself again. I'm going to try to become a merchant once more, so I don't want to touch the money I've collected. Distribute it among the poor or the yeshiva students, rabbi. Give it to whomever you wish."

"Why should I become your assistant in distributing charity? Every Jew has to distribute his own charity." Reb Avraham-Shaye smiled.

The tops of the nearby trees glinted with a crown—the sun hung over the treetops, round and radiant. The pine trees sparkled with millions of golden-green needles, pearled with dew. But Vova Barbitoler was still gloomy, his brow furrowed as though he had forgotten where he was going. He replaced the money in his pocket and frowned even more deeply.

"I've taken an oath and vowed that I won't leave until I've driven Tsemakh Atlas out of town."

"I hereby release you from your vow and take upon myself the sin of breaking your oath." Reb Avraham-Shaye placed his hand on his heart. "But you ought to remember too that because of your dispute the yeshiva may be destroyed. No matter what complaints you have against the yeshiva principal, Jewish children who study Torah should not be made to suffer."

Vova turned away and looked down at the path for a long time. When he turned back his face was wet with tears.

"No, rabbi, I'm not going to take revenge on other Jewish children just because my Hertzke isn't putting on tefillin. I've made peace with almost everything, but there's one thing I can't make peace with nor forget. I can't forget how, at the Vilna station, I pleaded with my son to take the little book of Psalms with him." Vova took a little book with black covers from the pocket of his shabby overcoat and held it in the palms of his hands. "I begged him: Say a psalm every day for me, your father, and also for your mother, who has sinned against God and me. But he pushed the little book back at me—and his mother stood there laughing, beaming with joy. That's what I can't forget. I'll remember that to my dying day." Vova Barbitoler put the little book back into his pocket, wiped the tears from his face and beard, and spoke more softly. "I don't know why that Tsemakh Atlas is moping in the Cold Shul. He looks like an exorcised dybbuk and I hear he hardly ever sets foot in the yeshiva. But when he was reviling me, he felt better. 'Your belief,' he shouted, 'your belief in God and your putting on tefillin every day have no value as far as I'm concerned; and you can tell the rabbi that in my name. He'll side with you, too,' is what he shouted at me. I can see that he's at daggers drawn with everyone—and I only wish I were lying. He himself will bring the yeshiva to ruin, but I don't want to help him do it. I'll obey you, rabbi. I won't have any more dealings with him. No one has ever spoken so kindly to me or treated me so well . . . Rabbi, bless me."

Reb Avraham-Shaye felt dizzy: Tsemakh Atlas was going to start a conflagration. But he had no time to think of this now. He must ponder carefully whether to mention Vova's undivorced wife in Argentina. If he remained silent now, the Divine Presence might accuse him of closing his eyes to the sin of adultery just for the sake of his own peace.

"Rabbi, I see that you don't want to bless me. You don't think I deserve it." Vova shook his head. "I thought you would give me a blessing."

"I'm not a Hasidic rebbe, so I can't bless you. The All-Merciful Father in heaven will bless you if you obey Him." Reb Avraham-Shaye hunched into himself and spoke softly, his voice breaking. "Our sages say that one mitzva spurs another, one good deed draws another into its path. When you forgive the rosh yeshiva, you'll see that bearing other grudges is not worthwhile. As long as you don't send your wife a divorce, you are causing a Jewish woman to sin continually. But if you free her according to the laws of the Torah, she will no longer incite your son against you. He'll remember that you sent him to a yeshiva and perhaps he'll put on tefillin again. Now go in peace and good health, and may He who uplifts the fallen help you too."

Reb Avraham-Shaye pressed Vova's hand and quickly went back into the courtyard. Excessive pleading was as contrary to his nature as giving blessings.

Vova Barbitoler left Valkenik that very evening. The next morning the village was in a turmoil, as it had been when he arrived. People said that the impoverished merchant had left his beggar's pack of food in the guest house for the other beggars and had given all the money he had collected to the town rabbi for charity. Vova also kept his promise to give Melechke Vilner a present—the little book of Psalms that Hertzke had refused to take with him to Argentina. But Melechke felt mightily deceived: he wasn't an ignorant carter who could only recite a chapter of Psalms between the Afternoon and Evening Services; he was already an independent Talmud scholar with his own original interpretations.

Vova Barbitoler didn't stop to say good-bye to his old friend Reb Shlomo-Motte. When Chaikl told his father about the tobacco merchant's night at the cottage, Reb Shlomo-Motte sat in silent astonishment for a long while and then said thoughtfully, "I assumed that if your teacher runs from visiting rabbis he would surely run from someone who came to start a scandal. But I see now that I was mistaken about Reb Avraham-Shaye."

When Reb Tsemakh Atlas heard that Vova Barbitoler had distributed everything he had begged, he grimaced with disgust: What a buffoon! Vova had wanted to impress the town at his departure as he had at his arrival.

The villagers knew that Vova had slept in Reb Avraham-Shaye's cottage the night before he left. Tsemakh realized that it was Reb Avraham-Shaye who had persuaded Hertzke's father not to create a scandal. And Tsemakh remained alone in the women's gallery of the Cold Shul—his place of refuge, his voluntary prison.

PART II

1

NO SOONER had the season for blackberries, sunny currants, and wine-red cherries ended than the time for the purple plums began. They were so cheap that they were sold by the pailful. But since pious Jews do not eat meat or new fruits—and do not go swimming, either—between the Seventeenth of Tammuz and the Tisha B'Av fast days, landlords reserved their butter, cheese, and sour cream for the summer visitors while they and their families made do with black bread soaked in sorrel soup thickened with a bit of milk. The days were hot, and the dust from the roads settled in one's throat. The peasants were working hard in the fields and didn't come to the village. The market place was deserted. The older generation sat on the sun-baked porches of the cottages and the steps of the shops. In their hearts the exiled Divine Presence murmured like a dove the opening words of the Book of Lamentations: "How doth the city sit forlorn . . ."

The younger generation was even more sober and subdued. The cardboard factory beyond the woods had no place to sell its merchandise. The saws no longer gasped all night; work had stopped on two of the three shifts. Having grown accustomed to the factory whistle, the town youths still awoke to the minute, even without the signal, but they heard only eerie silence from the forest. The factory was still in operation during the day, but except for ten older Jews, the manager kept only the village peasants on, because they would work for less and were not troublemakers. The factory manager, a young, black-bearded, fiery-eyed Hasid from Poland, argued that it was no mitzva to provide a livelihood for such Jewish sinners. Praying among the cold, stiff non-Hasidic Litvaks, he alone swayed like a tree in a storm. He liked to have guests at his table seven days a week, but he couldn't stand these inciters of labor unrest. The Valkenik youths who had been fired gossiped that he ran after gentile girls, and, hating him, they began to hate the town's pious Jews as well as the vacationing yeshiva scholars.

The summer guests sat on the porches eating juicy red radishes and scallions in sour cream. They coated their potatoes with butter and gobbled stacks of omelets, big and round and clear as the sun. They drank rich thick cocoa and ate little cheese-filled pastries and puffy cakes sprinkled with cinnamon and sugar. Heeding the advice of their landladies, they ate dozens of raw eggs. The women also bought tender chickens for them, blowing into the rear feathers of hens to see if they were fat enough. This caused consternation among the town Jews.

"Are Torah scholars eating meat during the three weeks between the Seventeenth of Tammuz and Tisha B'Av?"

To which the landladies answered, "Our lodgers are merely following doctors' orders, and we all know that, according to the Talmud, even the Sabbath may be violated to save one's life." The villagers then turned directly to the yeshiva scholars. The latter replied to their ignorant questioners, "Not eating meat during the Three Weeks is only a custom, not a law. In fact some scholars hold that the custom is valid only for the first nine days of Av and not for the entire Three Weeks."

A couple of Valkenik lads swore that in their aunt's house they had seen a group of yeshiva boys secretly eating on the fast of the Seventeenth of Tammuz, but these backbiters were quickly silenced. "They probably got permission from their rosh yeshivas. They study Torah—and studying, the holy books say, makes one weak. How can you compare yourselves to them? It's all right for the students."

"Then it's all right for us too," the youths answered, and they began to put their arms around their girl friends' waists in public. The girls would swing their broad hips and, their wanton eyes shining, laugh pertly into the faces of the bewigged old women who looked back at them disdainfully from their porches.

The daughters of Valkenik grew tall and full-bodied like ripe cucumbers under moonlight. Nubile girls with full breasts like pumpkins and faces like risen dough peered out from the curtained windows of their small houses. Like tiny flower pots holding rosebushes, these poor little cottages were too small for the Valkenik girls with their large bodies and thick, beribboned braids. With nothing to do and nowhere to go, the local girls stayed indoors from the moment they awoke, heads heavy and eyelids leaden. In the evening they went to the bridge to meet boys. They chewed sunflower seeds and spat the shells into the water. They heard the carters' jokes for the hundredth time and slapped their hands when they got fresh. The young men had no intention of falling in love and getting married. They dreamed of Brazil, they wanted to go to Australia—anywhere, just so they could get out of town. The young people strolled around the back lanes, watching the setting sun finally sink like a stone into the cold blue lakes—far off where the sky touched the earth and the roads strayed to the Lithuanian border. The youths were so bored that they even lost interest in dancing, so the girls danced among themselves, singing and keeping rhythm with their high heels. The brides without grooms would gather in a friend's house around the big speaker of a rusty phonograph. Like stuffed birds with glass eyes they would sit and listen to the cracked record grating out its wornout waltz, turning incessantly—just as the three Valkenik rivers turned, and just as their thoughts turned around the lost hope of getting married and managing a household. Finally the girls became too lazy to meet and dance. They sat at home, took their trousseaus out of their dressers, and counted tablecloths, sheets, towels, linens, and lace-embroidered underwear until dark. They held their trousseaus in their slack hands and wondered: For whom is all this prepared? Where are our bridegrooms?

With the arrival of the vacationing yeshiva students a hope stole into the girls' hearts: the scholars were so fine and gentle; they never let a vulgar word cross their lips. What harm was there in having a religious Jew for a husband? Who cared if he grew a beard a couple of years after the wedding? But the girls soon realized that they couldn't count on the summer visitors either. Torah students wouldn't even talk to a poor girl. They didn't seem to mind looking—their eyes devoured the girls' hips, their bare knees and legs; they longed to put a hand on a plump shoulder. Some of the scholars literally drooled. But as for marriage—they thought only of rich matches. To spite the community leaders as well as their own parents, the girls stayed out with the local youths till after midnight, inciting them against the pious idlers, those gluttonous summer guests.

Completely bored and angry with the whole world, the youths were spoiling for a fight with both the pious local Jews and the visiting band of "God's thieves," as they called the students. Depressed by the heat wave and by their annual gloom at the destruction of ancient Jerusalem, the religious townsmen in turn became increasingly angry with the impudent, irreligious youths who lolled about in the woods by day and in the high grass at the river's edge by night. The smoldering argument finally blazed up unexpectedly, precipitated by those responsible for putting fires out—the Valkenik firemen.

The heat wave had caused forest fires in the region. One fire destroyed all the dry underbrush and left tree stumps burning for days, then spread to a swampy region. It was almost to the point of burning itself out; only a little smoke curled slowly up into the blue sky. Then suddenly a wind came and blew the blaze into another section of the woods. And just then the Valkenik fire brigade got the wild notion of having a fire-fighting exercise. They set fire to a pile of wood on the river bank and then ran down with pumps, ladders, and axes. They swung the axes and sprayed the water hoses, shouting, "Tear the roof down! Break down the walls!" At first the older Valkenik onlookers made fun of them, and their barbed remarks fell like sparks on the exhausted firemen. Then, as though the devil had had a hand in it, along came a gust of wind, and a red sheen spread over the river. Women holding babies screamed, "Help!" and the men shouted, "Our houses are going to burn up!" The frightened firemen just barely managed to smother the smoldering chunks of wood. Infuriated at their humiliation, their smoke-blackened faces red with rage, they accosted the bearded Jews with axes in hand. "Hunchbacks, why are you shoving?" But the latter snapped, "Go to hell and take your antics with you!" After this incident the brigade assembled in secret and made plans to repair their tarnished reputation and get even with the pious elders.

One afternoon the townsmen were sitting on the steps of their houses or shops as usual, swaying in a doze. Drops of perspiration ran down behind their ears and from their foreheads to their chins, but they didn't lift a hand to wipe their wet faces or shoo away the flies perched on their noses in a Silent Devotion of buzzing. The heat made the yeshiva students drowsy over their Talmuds. Not a sound was heard from the beth medresh. Suddenly the boom of a bass drum and a resounding trumpet call broke the stillness. The fire brigade band was marching up one of the back lanes near the river, approaching Synagogue Street. The bandmaster walked backward, facing the musicians and conducting with his hands. One bandsman slid the trombone back and forth, a second moved his fingers on the keys of the clarinet, a third blew into a tuba, a fourth clanged the cymbals, and finally a short-legged fellow last in line pounded away at the drum. Following the band was the fire brigade commander, decked out in shiny boots and a sky-blue uniform adorned with silver threads and fringes plus a whistle and medals. The strap of his cocked hat was stretched tight under his raised chin like a Polish cavalryman's. Next came the helmeted, square-shouldered brigade of youths with their round, strong faces; they marched in step, axes hanging from the belts at their sides. One of them was wearing a Red Cross armband and carrying a first-aid kit. The helmets and the brass instruments flashed in the sun. There seemed to be a lively competition between the metallic sounds of the brass instruments and the cymbals and the thumping of the big bass drum to see which could make the greater racket and deafen the village.

Valkenik was stunned. The townsmen awoke from their drowse and gaped at the sky, as if Elijah the Prophet were up there riding in his chariot and blowing the ram's horn to herald the Messiah's coming, and before Tisha B'Av no less. From his house near the road the old slaughterer Lippa-Yosse ran out in his long underwear, pillow feathers clinging to his skullcap and the fear of death in his eyes, as if expecting a pogrom. Seeing the firemen, Lippa-Yosse thundered with all the strength of a pensioned-off slaughterer and cantor.

"Heathens! How dare you parade around with music during the days Jerusalem was destroyed!" His upraised hands trembled as if a bound ox had broken away from under his slaughterer's knife.

But the commander shouted to his brigade, "Forward march! One, two, three, four," as a signal to ignore everything. And with brisk march step the group headed for the market place, where on both sides of the street the villagers stood shouting abuse at them. The musicians played on, and the youths marched smartly without saying a word in reply. They were accomplishing what they had set out to do. The local people were now seeing that the fire fighters could carry off a secretly planned parade even more successfully than a mock fire exercise. Suddenly the band stopped playing and the marchers halted.

Swaying toward them with black silk umbrellas held aloft were the pious summer residents, on their way to the forest to breathe the fresh piny air and rock in their hammocks. Each umbrella carried by a rosh yeshiva was flanked by the lowered heads of two younger yeshiva students who looked like mushrooms in the shade of a spreading tree. Seeing the firemen surrounded by the local Jews, the vacationers stopped: the two camps faced each other. On one side stood helmeted youths in uniforms and boots, carrying axes like bayonets; on the other side were the Torah scholars in their gaberdines and soft hats. Ashamed to have the students witness their humiliation, the villagers shook their heads in mute complaint: You see our misfortune? These are our heirs, woe unto us! The yeshiva students remained silent and, smiling faintly, tried to walk around the crowd. But their cold, arrogant silence and their desire to slip away incited the firemen even more. The youths broke out of line and lunged at the vacationers.

"Spongers! Poor people give money for them to sit and study Torah, but instead they fatten themselves up in the country. Just look at their fat potbellies. They look like a herd of cows coming home from pasture with their udders full."

Frightened, the summer residents stopped dead in their tracks, hands and feet paralyzed. But the villagers attacked the firemen with fists flying. "Apostates! May the earth swallow you up!" At that the vacationing students took advantage of the confusion and ran to the forest, their lowered umbrellas bent and twisted like shot-down birds with wings outspread.

The feud that began that summer day encompassed all of Valkenik and, like the forest fires, lasted for weeks. One day it would flare intensely, another day it would be nearly out, and on a third it would flicker to life again. Most incensed at the firemen were the owners of the summer cottages and the carters who transported passengers from the train station. They were afraid the vacationers would leave early and not come back next year. Sroleyzer the bricklayer and his gang also opposed the firemen. During a dispute Sroleyzer and his pack usually sided with the religious community.

On the other hand, the youths who supported the secular library sided with the fire fighters. The "library demons," as they were called, were sharp-tongued, impudent brats and open heretics. They took no part in the constant conflict between the people who sided with the Mizrachi party and those who supported the Agudah. In their view, both were narrow-minded fanatics. While the village seethed with the drawn-out squabble as to who would be the new rabbi in Valkenik—an old-fashioned scholar or a secularly educated one—the library group had said that no matter who the new rabbi might be, he would in any case side with the speculators and bloodsuckers. The villagers knew that the source of these words was the Bolshevik Meyerke Podval from Panashishok.

Panashishok was a Jewish village just across the Lithuanian border. Meyerke was an orphan from childhood who had been tossed from one Valkenik Talmud Torah to another until he grew up and could study on his own in the beth medresh. The Valkenik people said he had been a radical even as a youngster. Still, they had supported him because they saw signs of genius and had high hopes of his becoming a great scholar. But he had dropped his Torah studies and had gone to Vilna to work in a sawmill on the Viliye River. In Vilna he had befriended the leftists, was caught and imprisoned. After serving his sentence, he had returned to Valkenik and gone to work in the cardboard factory, where he immediately began to incite the workers. It was because of him that the manager, the Polish Hasid, had fired the Valkenik youths and kept the peasants on.

A short man, Meyerke Podval had a low, hairy forehead and an irascible glint in his half-closed eyes. When he debated with an opponent he would stand a hand's breadth away from him, one foot forward, head back, and both hands shoved into his trouser pockets. The Valkenik residents were more afraid of this gesture and the angry twinkle in his eyes than of his acerbic remarks. They sensed that Meyerke Podval could cold-bloodedly—and just for the fun of it—set the town ablaze.

On the Sabbath before Tisha B'Av the fire fighters and the library group stood behind the pulpit in the beth medresh laughing and talking. While the Reader was chanting verses from Isaiah in the traditional plaintive melody: "A seed of evil-doers, children who are corrupt," the congregation nodded in the direction of the heretics. That's exactly whom the prophet had in mind! But the youths laughed in their faces.

After services some of the town elders went to the firemen and said amiably, "You boors! The only things that used to interest you were having fire drills, spraying water from your hoses, and practicing your instruments. You never meddled in politics. Why did you suddenly give a concert during the Three Weeks before Tisha B'Av and furthermore attack the yeshiva students who provide a livelihood for our village? Tell us what you want."

The firemen scratched their necks, exchanged glances, and replied, "We want money for new water pumps, more brass instruments, and a big banquet. Why should only the Burial Society have a big feast every year? The Burial Society buries the dead; the Fire Fighters Society rescues the living."

Meanwhile Valkenik's leading citizen was approaching from his place along the eastern wall. Since the crowd had blocked Reb Hirshe Gordon's path, he stood listening with one ear cupped. The congregants gazed at him and waited for him to respond to the firemen.

"And what do *you* want?" Reb Hirshe turned to the library crowd.

Long, lanky Moshe Okun stepped forward. His height and his bulging eyes made him look like a skinny fish. No matter how loud he tried to speak, he couldn't make himself heard ten feet away. One merely saw him opening and closing his mouth. His gestures recalled the soft movements of water weeds and his rhetoric that of a public servant and chairman of conferences. After heated debates in all the Valkenik clubs, Moshe Okun would read interparty resolutions which he composed himself.

Now Moshe took the floor and declared, "On principle the library opposes a religious community, and especially the rule of the clergy. But until the community constitution is changed, the library presents three demands: First, one of our representatives must be included in a democratically elected commission that oversees the community finances. Second, the budget must include funds to support the Valkenik Dramatic Club. Third, the community must provide funds from its own resources for the purchase of new books."

"And what will you do if the community doesn't submit to these demands?" Reb Hirshe Gordon looked down over his glasses at the lanky youth.

"We'll keep on fighting till we win," Moshe Okun answered.

"Then fight," Reb Hirshe said and turned to the firemen. "You'll get money for a water pump and even for a banquet. And the community is prepared to give the library money—on condition that you buy wood and burn all the books."

Gordon left the beth medresh, followed by the congregants who sided with him. But his older brother-in-law, Eltzik Bloch, stayed in the beth medresh, fuming. "The Mizrachi *does* want to provide money to buy Hebrew books. Reb Hirshe Gordon has no right to speak for the entire community. He is not a councilman."

But Eltzik Bloch raged in vain. The congregants didn't hear what he had to say because they were so intent on looking at and listening to Meyerke Podval from Panashishok.

He spoke calmly, as usual, hands in his pockets and that glint in his half-closed eyes. "It's the Valkenik exploiters that the Prophet Isaiah had in mind when he used the phrase 'You rulers of Sodom.' And when that selfsame Isaiah said, 'When you make many prayers, I will not hear: your hands are full of blood,' he's once again referring to the Valkenik bloodsuckers. Your community leaders are a rebellious band of thieves. The pillars of the town are usurpers and crooks. Every one of you loves bribes and chases payoffs—every one of you loves to have his palm greased." Meyerke wanted to go on to cite Isaiah in connection with the way the Valkenikers treated orphans and widows. But the congregants slipped out of the beth medresh thinking: An orphan of his type had no business growing up. Nicer people were rotting in the earth.

2

ON THE MORNING of the Sabbath of Consolation, the week after Tisha B'Av, a group of twenty Jews made their way from their home in Dekshne to Valkenik. They wore peaked cloth caps, frayed gaberdines, and heavy, dust-covered boots. Their patched weekday prayer shawls were draped around their shoulders. No matter how these farmers tried to keep their belts snug, their sunken hips could hardly hold up their trousers. Their sparse gray beards looked like the skinny, sparse cornstalks in the stony Dekshne fields, and their emaciated faces were lined from hard work and worry. On this bright morning of the Sabbath of Consolation sadness darkened their eyes. The arid land that Czar Nicholas I had distributed among their grandfathers was still sucking the marrow from their bones. Despite their hard labor in the fields, the bread they reaped never lasted until the next harvest; nor were there enough potatoes and beets for the winter. The colonists felled trees in the forest and transported the big logs to the cardboard factory, and they also tried their hand at beekeeping and selling the honey. But each family's main source of income was caring for a mentally ill boarder.

The Dekshne patients were harmless, incurable melancholiacs; they came from well-to-do families who paid a monthly rent for their upkeep. Some of the lunatics had roved about in the village for more than thirty years. When a stranger came to Dekshne, the madmen would take the newcomer off to a corner. One would describe how his wife and children wanted to poison him; another would ask if the world was still insane. But visitors rarely strayed into the village, and the disturbed residents paid no attention to their landlords, so they usually smiled and gestured and talked to themselves. They would wander in a daze through the long village street, sit on heaps of refuse by the barns and on the steps of houses, making faces, until night came. From the time they had been normal one bright hour glimmered in the dimmed minds of these confused souls, like a stripe of light on the horizon when heaven and earth are all one darkness—but gradually even this single bright spot faded from the memories of these sick people. Sensing night covering their bodies like a wet, hairy beast, they would scream in terror. The second scream was wilder and more hair-raising. The third was accompanied by grating of teeth and raucous laughter that broke and crumbled as though their minds were falling apart. Having unburdened themselves of these shrieks, they would shudder, twitch, and shiver until paralysis beset them. Occasionally a landlord would find his lodger numb and stiff in the morning, like a beetle frozen during the night. The farmer would stand there looking numb too, and think how delighted the patient's relatives would be at the news that their payments could stop. And then, thinking of his wife and children, the farmer would realize that he and his family would have to suffer until he got another lodger.

Even though Dekshne had its own little shul, the colonists walked to the Valkenik beth medresh for festivals and important Sabbaths. For a couple of hours, at least, they liked to get away from their dismal settlement. Hence, in honor of the Sabbath of Consolation, they came to the Valkenik beth medresh and sat around the table at the western wall. But this time the Dekshners waited in vain to hear sweet melodies and cantorial trills. The beth medresh was in an uproar. The congregants were talking in every part of the room and the cantor Yudel rushed through the service. As the congregation grew, so did the tumult. When they reached the Shma Yisroel, the place buzzed like a market fair; during the Silent Devotion even the desk-pounding calls for silence were of no avail. The noise lessened only during the Torah reading, when the library group behind the pulpit went outside for a consultation.

The library club had a guest, Dan Dunietz. He was studying at a modern Jewish school in Vilna and had come to visit his parents in Valkenik for a two-week vacation. Dan's father was a quiet man who tended orchards. He sat in a corner of the beth medresh keeping his eyes on the Siddur, as if feeling guilty for having a son who was his exact opposite in character and behavior. Dan Dunietz was talking, bursting with heat like an overboiled pot. As he spoke, a shock of black hair fell out from under his blue-and-white school cap. He gesticulated with his long hands, and his eyes glowed with the fever of the undrained swamps of pioneering Palestine. He laughed sarcastically at the pious Valkenik Jews who were waiting for a miracle to transport them to the Land of Israel as if it were an esrog in a silver container. "You want a land flowing with milk and honey. A Messiah who will come riding on a white mule over the refuse heap of the Valkenik synagogue courtyard. That's what you petty shopkeepers of Valkenik are waiting for."

Dan Dunietz didn't approve of the local youths either. There had once been a pioneer organization in the village but there was not one now because the illegal immigration to Palestine had stopped. Where was endurance, perseverance? Dan Dunietz asked. Nevertheless, he befriended the leftists of the library club, and they chose him to be their representative before the "masses" in the beth medresh. Since he had been educated at a modern school and spoke Hebrew, the provincials would trust him more. Moreover, he was a guest in town, and the congregants had no complaints about his uncivilized behavior as they had about that of the local youths. They merely warned him, "Don't get excited or people won't be able to understand you."

Everyone knew that the Sabbath of Consolation was a "Zionist Sabbath" and that Eltzik Bloch, the head of the pro-Zionist Mizrachi, should have the honor of chanting the Haftora. Instead, the honor had gone to his brother-in-law, the leader of the anti-Zionist Agudah, under the pretext that he was commemorating the Yohrzeit of a deceased grandfather or great-grandfather. Reb Hirshe Gordon chanted the chapter of Isaiah hoarsely and without melody. When he came to the verse, "O thou that tells Zion good tidings, get thee up into the high mountain," he broke into bitter tears. Eltzik Bloch actually jumped from his place. How could a man be so brazenly hypocritical? Reb Hirshe Gordon hated the Zionists! Reb Hirshe was weeping tears of anguish because the Mizrachi people were dragging the prophet Isaiah into their heathenish faction.

At that moment the library supporters marched in and, standing shoulder to shoulder, approached the Holy Ark as if taking up battle positions. Reb Hirshe peered at them over his glasses, which were dripping with tears, and continued reciting from the parchment in his hands until he finished the Haftora and then the blessings. The congregation knew that the library club wanted one of their members to be allowed to speak. The worshipers turned to the pulpit, curious to see how Reb Hirshe would handle the situation. To their amazement Reb Hirshe winked to the cantor not to take the Torah back to the Ark just yet. If these apostates wanted to talk, let them talk.

Dan Dunietz went up to the steps of the Holy Ark and began, "The Midrash says . . ."

Reb Hirshe Gordon had previously arranged with his supporters that the heretics should be allowed to say what they had to say and then the congregation could continue with the Musaf prayers undisturbed. And when the time came to provide money for books, they'd be put in their places. But Reb Hirshe had not expected Dunietz to have the gall to begin with a verse from the Midrash. The blood rushed to his temples; his face turned red.

"You're quoting the sages? First show me your fringes! Let me see that you have on ritual fringes like me and everybody else in this beth medresh," Gordon shouted and with both hands pulled the fringes out from beneath his gaberdine.

Dan Dunietz was bewildered. Even his shock of hair seemed afraid to peek from under his blue-and-white cap.

Meyerke Podval from Panashishok answered for him. "And are ritual fringes obligatory if one is wearing a tallis?"

"Whether they are or not, you're a Bolshevik and a convicted jailbird. You shouldn't have lived to get out of prison!" Reb Hirshe screamed. He pointed at Dan Dunietz. "Get him out of here!"

Sroleyzer the bricklayer and his gang of helpers suddenly materialized by the Holy Ark. Eltzik Bloch lunged at them. "Let him speak! The Mizrachi wants him to speak. The Mizrachi wants community funds allocated for Hebrew books. We're not asking Reb Hirshe's opinion. He's not a member of the community council."

But Gordon was now ranting at the highest pitch: "Drag that rebel down from there!" And his side chimed in, "Get him down, down!"

Dan Dunietz had recovered by now. He was fuming and waving his hands. "The Valkenik Jews would rather wail over the destruction of the Holy Temple than build up the Land of Israel. The main thing for them is to pray daily, 'Let us witness your return to Zion in mercy.' Those liars! Do they really mean it? They prefer the Exile in Valkenik, their Valkenik Diaspora, over the return to Zion."

But Dan Dunietz got no further. Hands stretched out to grab him, and in a flash he was flying down the steps. One of the town crooks jabbed five hard fingers into the cheek of the intellectual Moshe Okun. "You half-dead corpse! Who are you shoving?"

"I protest," Moshe Okun answered softly and, clawing with all his fingers, he bloodied the crook's face.

The fight spread. The red-eyed, iron-fisted roughnecks fought with silent, methodical anger. Their forceful blows were well aimed: a knee in the belly, a fist in the chest, a head butt to the chin. The library crowd returned the blows with blind fury, almost foaming at the mouth. They attacked with prayer stands and smacked heads with heavy Talmuds; they swung their elbows and kicked left and right. They were out for blood: to gouge out eyes, to lacerate faces, to bite into jugular veins. They wanted to murder the underworld crowd by beating them to death.

There was another commotion at the seats of the well-to-do worshipers; it sounded like the wheels of a water mill turning. Reb Hirshe's faction was squabbling with Eltzik Bloch, while other congregants shouted: "A plague on both your houses! Every Sabbath there's another to-do in the shul," they complained. "We have to eat stone-cold cholent because of these delays in the services. Let those rabble-rousers eat stones!" Two congregants almost came to blows. One shouted, "Why are you standing up for these heathens?" and the second shouted back, "Your talking and a dog's barking is all one to me. You consider *my* son a heathen?"

During all this the old ritual slaughterer Reb Lippa-Yosse was banging on the prayer stand and screaming with all his might, "You bastards! You're desecrating the Sabbath." Reb Yisroel the tailor and yeshiva supporter shut his eyes and groaned, "Woe unto the eyes that have seen this." The rabbi, Reb Mordekhai-Aaron Shapiro, was all hunched over; his small, sharp eyes darted about like those of a little animal in a trap. He cursed the day he decided to leave Shishlevitz for Valkenik. The rabbi realized that all the factions would later complain and ask why he had been afraid to intervene and silence the conflict.

Only one person derived pleasure from the fight: Yosef Varshever, wrapped in his silk tallis. It made no difference to him who was beating whom, so long as they kept beating and hurting one another. That's how much he hated Valkenik and all its residents. Varshever just barely managed to keep himself from shouting, "Good! Excellent!" His only regret was that his father-in-law, Gedalya Zondak, was not in the midst of the fray.

To everyone's amazement Sroleyzer's gang gradually retreated from the library group. The toughs were frightened by the intellectuals' murderous fury and their threats while exchanging blows: "Informers! We'll shoot every one of you down like dogs. . . . Horse thieves! When the revolution comes, the proletariat will settle accounts with you." And some of the congregants were shouting at the roughnecks from their seats: "You touch my son and there'll be nothing left of you."

"Murderer! You'll rot in jail!"

"Cutthroat! Who are you waving your paws at? Youngsters!"

"People, help! Do something! They're making cripples out of our children!"

"We're defending the holy Torah and now you're attacking us?" the bloodied and tattered Sroleyzer spat at the congregants. "Damn you all!" he shouted, and he ordered his bloody forces to withdraw.

The victors were also black and blue, with ribs battered, gasping, and drenched with perspiration. They scarcely had time to draw a breath before the disheveled Dan Dunietz pointed at Reb Hirshe Gordon.

"He ordered me dragged away from the Holy Ark, so we'll drag him off the pulpit." At which the entire band pounced at the pulpit like a pack of wolves.

"Just try it!" Reb Hirshe removed his tallis, prepared to resist them singlehandedly, like Samson against the Philistines. The noise increased. Someone shouted, "You're not going to hit the rabbi's son-in-law?" Someone else put his hands to his head. "Help! They're going to desecrate the Holy Scrolls."

From the rear benches came the carters, who could lift a laden wagon with one shoulder; and butchers, who with their bare hands could twist an ox's horn until he fell to the ground. They fell upon the library supporters, shouting, "There'll be nothing left of you." The youths fled to the door as though a cyclone had blown them off a mountain. Fists fell upon their necks; blows rained down on their sides. Before they could turn around they were thrown out into the anteroom of the beth medresh. Dan Dunietz tore himself away from a pair of hefty hands for a moment and shouted, "Fanatics! The Prophet Isaiah who said 'comfort ye, comfort ye, my people,' was not the Prophet Isaiah the son of Amoz, but another Isaiah. There were two Isaiahs, three Isaiahs . . ."

"May you break your arms and legs!" The carter booted him out of the beth medresh and slammed the door.

Throughout all this the Dekshners had sat still at the rear table. When the congregation had quieted down and Reb Hirshe had given the order to proceed with the Musaf service, one farmer turned to his neighbor as if in a daze.

"Praying in our own little shul would have been more enjoyable."

The other man agreed. "Compared to these Valkenik loudmouths, our Dekshne madmen are a quiet sort." And the village Jews sank back into their gloomy silence.

3

SOYEH-ETL, the old caretaker of the guest house, had lived to see good times. Besides attending to her permanent lodgers, the yeshiva students, during the summer, she also took care of the wandering beggars who slept in the other section of the guest house. The remaining few hours of her day were spent at the cemetery. When the snow melted and the rosebuds bloomed, Soyeh-Etl went among the tombstones like a rich housewife among her cold parlors that had been closed off for the winter. For decades now she had been the cemetery caretaker; nevertheless, she still gazed in wonder at a stone adorned with the Ten Commandments, or at the bas-relief hands raised in blessing that indicated a Kohen's grave. She still marveled at the carved candelabra, the Stars of David, and the chiseled flowers and leaves that decorated the old tombstones. Soyeh-Etl could not read the inscriptions because they were in unvocalized Hebrew and many letters were rubbed away and faded. In fact, she didn't care what was written on the stones. Soyeh-Etl knew the names and lineage of the dead better than the living younger generation of Valkenik residents. Sometimes she stood on Synagogue Street staring at a youth and wondering: Whose grandson is he? The youth would look at the old woman's high, furrowed brow as if at an ancient tombstone inscribed with an undecipherable script.

Soyeh-Etl always had work to do at the cemetery. In one place she would straighten a board on the grave of a pauper whose heirs had no money for a tombstone. In another she would clean some greenish-yellow moss from a headstone. In a third she would perform the mitzva of putting another pebble on the tombstone of a holy man. When a woman forgot the location of an old uncle's grave, Soyeh-Etl, chuckling good-naturedly, would make her way through the high grass and the bushes overgrown with wild, prickly teasel. She couldn't understand how someone could forget the location of a kinsman's grave. But when the woman would burst into tears and shout at the mound of her uncle, asking him to intercede for a sick child, Soyeh-Etl too would weep. Strange screechy sounds came from her throat, as though she had nearly lost her voice among the mute tombstones. Returning from the cemetery, the woman, comforted, would think that Soyeh-Etl was a mother to the living no less than the dead. The only trouble was that, because of her old age and constant solitude, she had become a bit confused. But Soyeh-Etl didn't feel lonely at all, even though she had outlived her husband and all her children. On summer evenings she sat on a bench next to the cemetery gate, gazing out across the river to the village and asking the All-Merciful not to let the black box escorted by a group of Jews appear. Instead of graves in the cemetery, she prayed, let there be more young scholars to sleep in the guest house.

But lately old Soyeh-Etl had become very ill at ease. She had grown accustomed to having her young lodgers study their big books aloud in the evening or take a walk at the river bank. Now they had suddenly stopped strolling and chanting their sweet melody. Soyeh-Etl peered through the crevices in her little room into the students' section and saw that some of the boys were sitting around the table and others were in bed. All were deeply immersed in reading. They were so preoccupied with their books that they didn't look up except to exchange an occasional furtive glance and to eye the door as if afraid a stranger might enter.

The old caretaker noticed and remembered the shapes and sizes of the little books the students were reading so quietly. When she cleaned their quarters the next morning, the little books were not on the table along with the Talmuds, Pentateuchs, and prayer books. Soyeh-Etl realized that the youngsters were hiding the books—probably letter-writing primers, she surmised—in their trunks. The old woman felt a strange sadness, but when she began straightening the cover to Melechke Vilner's bed, her lined face brightened. Her long, thin, vein-webbed hands stroked his little pillow as if it were a grandchild's head. Soyeh-Etl loved the rosy-cheeked little boy because he was the most diligent of all the young students and was a sweet lad. When he came to her little room for a pot of tea, she had to place it on a chair because out of piety he took nothing directly from a woman's hand.

When the old woman lifted up Melechke's pillow to fluff the feathers and make it soft, she found a little book without covers or binding. As soon as Soyeh-Etl picked it up, she realized that it was neither one of the books the men read nor a woman's book of prayers in Yiddish. Somehow it looked too flimsy and too profane to be a Jewish book. As a girl, Soyeh-Etl had learned to read and to write with a slate pencil on a blackboard. But it had been many years since she had read or written anything—she knew her Hebrew and Yiddish prayers by heart—hence she had to strain now to make the individual letters cohere into words. The printed letters on the title page were big and black. She moved from one to another until she finally read, "Pi . . . Pitti . . . Pittigrilli."

The old woman raised her head like a rooster when he finds no seeds on the ground. Then she concentrated on the title page again until the strung-together letters hung in the air in three rows before her eyes like birds sitting on telegraph wires:

PITTIGRILLI

THE CHASTITY BELT

AND OTHER STORIES

Not having the faintest idea what these words meant, Soyeh-Etl put the letter-writing primer back under Melechke's little pillow.

That evening she looked through the crevices again and saw some lodgers sitting around the table just as they had the night before, while others lay in bed equally engrossed in reading. A youth came into the guest house with a well-filled linen bag. Since the old caretaker didn't know Meyerke Podval from Panashishok, she couldn't ask why the biggest heretic in the village was mingling with the pious young scholars, but she was amazed that the yeshiva boys didn't hide their little books from the stranger. Instead they gathered around him, smiling, and returned the borrowed books while he gave them others from his bag. Soyeh-Etl couldn't hear their whispers; she only saw that they had secrets. And she saw that as soon as the sack-carrying man left, the young scholars once again resumed their reading.

Carrying the bundle of books he had collected, Meyerke returned to the library, rubbing his jaw with pleasure. After he and his group were ejected from the beth medresh, he had outlined a plan to combat the reactionaries from without and sabotage them from within. He had struck up a friendship with the younger yeshiva boys and had begun to recite entire pages of the Talmud by heart, along with incisive interpretations remembered from long ago. Seeing that his erudition and expertise had won their trust, he began to persuade them to read the forbidden secular books. "True," he told his new friends, "there is a statement in the Talmud that he who reads forbidden books loses his share in the world to come. But the Talmud and various commentators teach us that what they really mean is that one is forbidden to read these books to a group, and one must not spend hours studying them as one does Holy Writ. But it is perfectly permissible to read them alone in private." And he told the library group, "The little students have been caught on the fishhook."

However, Meyerke soon noticed that the little students were cowards and complete hypocrites. He had assumed that the youngsters would flee the beth medresh after reading a couple of books. Instead, they read his books at night and during the day swayed over their Talmuds in the beth medresh. Waiting for a couple of youngsters to go astray and cast off Torah learning offered a doubtful victory, Meyerke thought. He wanted to do in the entire yeshiva with one stroke. Although he had given the boys his sacred word that not a soul in the village would know about their reading, Meyerke hinted to his friends that they could spread the word. The latter told their fathers,

"The community refused to support the library because secular books lead one astray from piety, but the local yeshiva boys can't tear themselves away from such books." The matter was discussed in the beth medresh and the congregants came to Reb Menakhem-Mendl: "What's going on? People here are depriving themselves to support the yeshiva boys, but instead of studying Torah they're reading forbidden trash."

Reb Menakhem-Mendl had already noticed that lately his students had not been prepared for their lessons and weren't keeping up with the yeshiva's order of studies. He felt that it was primarily Reb Tsemakh's fault because he hadn't been coming to the beth medresh. But during the summer the usual order of studies wasn't scrupulously followed even in the great yeshivas. The best scholars of Mir, Kletzk, and Radun, for instance, were vacationing in Valkenik. The Valkenik students, then, were following the precedent of their more famous elders and were idling too. But once Reb Menakhem-Mendl was informed that his little yeshiva had been infected with the plague of heretical books, he trembled with fear. As soon as the boys who lived in the guest house came to the beth medresh, he slipped out and with his small brisk steps went directly to the guest house.

In the Navaredker yeshivas it was an accepted practice that an older Musarnik could rummage in the trunk of a younger lad to see if he had any forbidden books. The older students even intercepted letters home to find out whether the student was complaining that he had fallen into a yeshiva where they studied too much Musar, or that his allowance was too small and his lodgings uncomfortable. When a youth discovered that his mail was being opened and protested that centuries ago Rabbenu Gershom had placed a ban on opening someone else's mail, the rosh yeshiva or the group leader would answer calmly, "It's permissible if it's done to spread Torah. We know better." When Menakhem-Mendl studied at Navaredok in his youth, he had not been able to tolerate such behavior. That was why the sharp Musarniks—Tsemakh Lomzher, for instance—had considered him a run-of-the-mill pious lad with limited intellectual abilities . . . And now Reb Menakhem-Mendl himself had to spy on his pupils.

Soyeh-Etl was in the middle of the bedroom sweeping the floor. Reb Menakhem-Mendl knew that the old caretaker was an honest woman, so he asked her what her lodgers were doing in the evening.

Her frightened look and her silence told him that everything he had heard about his students was true.

"What about Melechke Vilner?" he asked.

"He's reading Pittigrilli, *The Chastity Belt and Other Stories*," Soyeh-Etl replied in her hen's voice, pulling the little book from under Melechke's pillow. Reb Menakhem-Mendl stumbled over the strange name: What had she said? Pi . . . Pitti . . . Pittigrilli? After reading a couple of lines here and there, his hair bristled. This wasn't heresy but downright obscenity—pornography. "Is this what Melechke is reading?"

"Yes, yes, this is the letter-writing primer he's reading." The caretaker nodded, holding the broom in her hand.

Reb Menakhem-Mendl threw the trash on Melechke's cot and began searching under the other pillows. But the other readers, more careful, didn't keep their books there. He bent down and pulled trunks from under the cots. In the first he found a well-read book, as frayed as an oft-used Siddur. Its title was *Tsilke the Wild One.* Reb Menakhem-Mendl shrugged. What kind of foolish story was this? He had heard of wild ducks but he'd never heard of a wild "Tsilke" before. From under a second bed he pulled a locked wicker basket. The caretaker looked on uneasily as the rabbi twisted the lock with his thin, pale fingers and then, unable to open it, pushed the basket back under the bed. Under a third bed he found a small open suitcase; at the top lay a thick book with red binding called *The Descent of Man.* On the title page and in the book itself Reb Menakhem-Mendl saw pictures of all kinds of birds, snakes and monkeys. Finally it dawned on him that this must be the sort of book that asserts that man stems from the apes. He flung the book back into the suitcase, grimacing with distaste as if he'd held a slimy worm in his hand. Just then he noticed another book in the suitcase. The reader, bless him, was a hard-working scholar: he was reading two at a time, Reb Menakhem-Mendl thought, smiling crookedly. The title, *Political Economy*, stabbed him in the heart. As if heresy and obscenity did not suffice, they were also reading Communist books. Reb Menakhem-Mendl didn't want to see any more. He had had enough anguish and humiliation.

He stood by the table in the dormitory, shaking his head sadly and eulogizing the holy books that the yeshiva boys had abandoned and disgraced. He turned a page in a Vilna edition of the Talmud, fondled a little volume of *The Path of the Upright*, picked up a large Pentateuch with Rashi's commentary, and then spotted another secular book. On the cover, bound with faded green cloth, was a photograph of a man with spectacles and a trimmed beard. Reb Menakhem-Mendl had certainly heard of this writer. He was Mendele Mocher Seforim, the leading Yiddish writer, and the title of this abomination was *The Nag*. Although Reb Menakhem-Mendl had never seen the book before, he had heard that the writer abused and berated everyone—community leaders, rabbis, and fine respectable Jews. And a Navaredker ben Torah had placed this very Mendele—may the name of the wicked be blotted out—alongside *The Path of the Upright*, a Talmud folio, and the Five Books of Moses. Which one of his Torah scholars, Reb Menakhem-Mendl wondered, was reading this gem? Was it Araner or Podbrodzer? On the other hand, it made no difference who read the work of that scoundrel who compared the community of Israel to a dead nag; it made no difference who read a book that stated that man stems from the apes or one that was full of obscenities. The principal, who had hurried into the guest house, now left slowly, gloomy and lost in thought. The old caretaker stood leaning on the broom, looking out at the cemetery. When the trees and tall grasses rustled, Soyeh-Etl knew that the dead were telling one another about events in the village, even though no one had reported to them. Now the tall grasses swayed and whispered that the students had gone astray, much to the great distress of their teacher.

That evening Reb Menakhem-Mendl was scheduled to give a Talmud lecture. But instead of discussing the Talmudic passages, he rocked back and forth excitedly for a time, then asked the students: "What would you say about someone who eats unkosher food and then recites the Grace After Meals with utter devotion? What would you say about someone who fasts every Monday and Thursday but eats on Yom Kippur?"

Since raising his voice and pounding on a prayer stand was contrary to Reb Menakhem-Mendl's nature, he spoke with a tremulous voice, shaking with anger and pale with anguish. "Aren't you Torah students ashamed to read books full of heresy and obscenity and then return to study the Talmud and the Musar books?"

The pupils were momentarily confused, but they immediately recovered and had a ready answer. "The vacationing yeshiva students of

Mir, Kletzk, and Radun freely read the Warsaw newspapers and no one scolds them."

Reb Menakhem-Mendl had assumed that at first the students would deny the accusation completely, and that later they would beat their breasts in contrition and admit their guilt. But instead, here they were whitewashing their wrong, shouting that it was permitted.

"And what do you have to say, Melechke?" Reb Menakhem-Mendl turned to the youngster, the modest, thin-shouldered pupil who was sitting before him with a meek and pious demeanor, as if he had no connection whatever with the group that read secular books. "After all, you aspire to grow up to be a saint and a gaon—and yet you're busy reading a certain Pittigrilli's *The Chastity Belt and Other Stories!*"

Melechke said at once, "*The Ethics of the Fathers* tells us: 'Know how to respond to the heretics.' "

"Do you already know how to respond to a basic Talmudic problem?" Reb Menakhem-Mendl pinched his arm so hard that Melechke's face contorted with pain. "You read filthy books and then you coat the filth with purity by suggesting that you're reading them for the sole purpose of knowing how to respond to a heretic!" It no longer befitted Zelda's only son to burst into tears like a little boy. Instead, he stood up and proclaimed that he was going home. Fear swept over Reb Menakhem-Mendl—Melechke might indeed leave and others might follow suit. He put aside the dignity of a yeshiva principal and began to apologize. Reb Menakhem-Mendl saw that the students felt no fear or awe of him. Now he would have to turn to the great Navaredkers, the rabbi's son and son-in-law, and ask them to save the yeshiva.

4

"THESE BOOKS are even worse than the Moabite women who seduced the Israelites in the desert. But here there is no zealot, no Phinehas to stand up for the honor of the Torah and stop the plague," Reb Menakhem-Mendl told the Valkenik rabbi.

Reb Mordekhai-Aaron Shapiro couldn't bear for a stranger to look straight into his eyes while he was eating; what's more, he was eating cold fish and was afraid a bone might stick in his throat. Sitting at the table with him were his son and son-in-law and their wives—young rebbetsins whose pale faces seemed coated with chalk. They too were afraid their father might swallow a bone. The new Valkenik rabbi had heard that Reb Hirshe Gordon, the former rabbi's son-in-law, was stirring up the congregants because he wouldn't intervene in the fight the community was waging against the library club. Reb Mordekhai-Aaron pictured himself left without a livelihood. The community would no longer pay him wages; the housewives would stop buying Sabbath candles and yeast for challas from his rebbetsin; he would weep and rue the day he had exchanged Shishlevitz for Valkenik. And now, as if it weren't enough that he had Reb Hirshe Gordon on his neck, along came Reb Menakhem-Mendl with his complaints.

"It's none of my business. Reb Tsemakh Atlas has to tend to his yeshiva," said the rabbi, wiping his greasy fingers with a napkin.

Reb Menakhem-Mendl turned to two younger men. "Look here, you're Navaredker activists, after all, and you go from place to place to strengthen the yeshivas in the villages. Why haven't you come to the Valkenik yeshiva to give a talk and inspire the students?"

The rabbi's son-in-law jerked forward with the full force of his bony shoulders. "My father-in-law told you that this is the rosh yeshiva's concern, not ours." Reb Menakhem-Mendl waited to hear the response of the rabbi's son, the great Navaredker thinker and writer. Rosy-faced Reb Sender, his perpetual smile blooming on his youthful lips, realized that an answer was expected of him. His large, seemingly innocent eyes suddenly flashed sharply, and his voice turned sharp too. "I can't offer any help. Navaredok still hasn't forgotten what Reb Tsemakh Atlas once did."

"But he has long since repented," Reb Menakhem-Mendl replied, and quoted the Prophet Ezekiel's remark that even the most wicked man's sins were not held against him if he repented with all his heart. The two brothers-in-law exchanged smiles and said nothing. The rabbi gave the two young men who had suddenly lost their tongues a scathing look. They didn't care for the rosh yeshiva but were afraid to start trouble with him because Reb Avraham-Shaye was on his side.

And people said that Reb Avraham-Shaye was not always as quiet a man as he seemed to be.

"Reb Avraham-Shaye Kosover won't let a speck of dust fall on that Reb Tsemakh Atlas. He supports him wholeheartedly. Go to Reb Avraham-Shaye Kosover and tell him what's happening in the yeshiva," the rabbi shouted at Reb Menakhem-Mendl. "And tell Reb Tsemakh Atlas it's one thing or the other. If he wants to continue as rosh yeshiva, he must look after the students. If he wants to sit in silent meditation in the Cold Shul or in the attic, then let him declare that he's no longer rosh yeshiva and we'll find a substitute, perhaps someone better than he."

Reb Menakhem-Mendl didn't go to see Reb Avraham-Shaye. He was upset at having complained at all. What would he accomplish by complaining again? He would deprive the author of *The Vision of Avraham* of Torah study time, and he would also be considered a slanderer. But he would go to the rosh yeshiva and talk frankly with him.

Later that evening Reb Menakhem-Mendl sought out his friend. When he opened the door the principal's room was dark, and Tsemakh was lying on his bed fully dressed. A bluish night sheen glittered on his gaunt, pale face in strong contrast to his pitch-black, fully grown beard. Tsemakh sat up and swung his legs over the side of the bed.

"Why don't you have a light? Are you sick, God forbid?" Reb Menakhem-Mendl asked.

"I'm all right but the light disturbs me," Tsemakh answered coldly. Reb Menakhem-Mendl had left the door half open to let the light in from the adjoining room. He sat down in a chair near the doorway and reported what was happening in the yeshiva. For a while Tsemakh seemed stunned; then he murmured, "Has the entire yeshiva taken up the reading of these books?"

But he quickly fell back into his dispirited state. "I'm not in any condition now to do a thing."

"Then resign!" Reb Menakhem-Mendl leaped up. "I still don't know what's happened to you here. But no matter what it is, if you don't have the strength to lead the yeshiva, then resign!"

"Yes, yes, the yeshiva has to have a better leader than I." Tsemakh nodded despondently, like a Dekshne melancholiac.

"If you resign, they'll find another rosh yeshiva," Reb Menakhem-Mendl said, and he naïvely told Tsemakh Atlas about his talk with the rabbi's sons.

"They won't have to look long." Tsemakh raised his head and in the dim light of the adjoining room his eyes shone like coals. "I know how eager the rabbi's son and son-in-law are to take over my yeshiva. And what else did Sender Shishlevitzer and Hershl Zhvirer say about me?"

"No one was backbiting you at the rabbi's house, God forbid. On the contrary, the rabbi said that Reb Avraham-Shaye was your supporter. He won't let a speck of dust fall on you," Reb Menakhem-Mendl replied. But these words, blurted out in all candor, made matters worse.

"In other words, you admit that Sender Shishlevitzer and Hershl Zhvirer went to Reb Avraham-Shaye to talk ill of me and he defended me. I didn't realize until now that the author of *The Vision of Avraham* is such a close friend that he's become my advocate," Tsemakh said sarcastically, putting his hands between his trembling knees. "I know what my two former friends are up to! You can tell them for me that they won't be my heirs. I established this yeshiva. I've been the rosh yeshiva here, and I'll continue to be."

"By all means! Stay on as rosh yeshiva. All you have to do is come back to the yeshiva and deliver Musar talks and attend to the students," Reb Menakhem-Mendl said. But when he spoke again about the battle against the secular books, Tsemakh became dispirited again and repeated, "I'm not in any condition to do a thing."

"Then what will happen?" Reb Menakhem-Mendl asked.

"Nothing will happen," Tsemakh answered. "The students will read these silly stories until they get sick of them, and then they'll return to their Talmuds."

Short, slender Reb Menakhem-Mendl went along Synagogue Street to his quarters, his mind in dark disarray, as if the darkness of Tsemakh's room had penetrated his eyes and head. Besides Reb Menakhem-Mendl's troubles in the yeshiva, his wife always complained in her letters that she couldn't live alone any longer. He longed for his little son too, and lately it had been hell living in Reb Lippa-Yosse's house. Hannah-Leah quarreled with Yudel more than ever, and her father, Reb Lippa-Yosse, was always in a wild rage at his son-in-law. He kept shouting, "You won't get your way!" but what

Yudel wanted and what he wouldn't get was a mystery to Reb Menakhem-Mendl. In any event, he would not abandon the yeshiva to the winds and would not return to Vilna. He would continue teaching as long as students came to listen, and he would tell the townspeople that he had done his best against the plague of secular books. More than that he could not do.

Young wives sat on their porches wishing one another *mazel tov*. Hannah-Leah was pregnant again and was going around to her neighbors, wringing her hands: "My heart tells me that I'll have a boy this time and that Yudel is going to be the *mohel*." The women laughed at Hannah-Leah's fear that her shlimazel Yudel might hurt the child the way he made calves unkosher with his faulty slaughtering. The only one who didn't know why Reb Lippa-Yosse and his daughter were so vituperative toward the younger slaughterer was their lodger, Reb Menakhem-Mendl. Nor, of course, did he understand why the women on the porches giggled so much.

Gradually the village went to bed. The beth medresh lights were extinguished; the congregants dispersed after their studies. The windows seemed overcast with clouds of sorrow. Toward the end of the month of Av the Torah scholars usually came to the yeshiva in the evenings too, and the more diligent would remain till after midnight. But now the yeshiva was empty. Darkness crouched in all the corners. The students sat in their rooms or in the guest house reading. Instead of the chant of Torah learning sounding forth in the evenings, the sound of wanton laughter came from the bushes at the river's edge; every once in a while a girlish scream echoed. Couples from the library club were moving about down there like wild ducks in the marsh. The old tombstones on the other side of the river buried themselves deeper in the grass and darkness so as not to hear the secret whispering, the promiscuous kissing, the hungry murmurs. The marsh weeds that towered over the heads of the young couples also swayed feverishly; the water softly lapped the shore with muffled and tremulous desire.

After midnight the couples began to emerge from their hiding places. The boys and girls walked with arms around each other's waists or shoulders, heading for the market place. Ever since the library supporters had been kicked out of the beth medresh on the Sabbath of Consolation, the village had had a new byword, Reb

Hirshe Gordon's unintentional couplet when he ordered Dan Dunietz: "You're quoting the sages? First show me your fringes!" After midnight the library demons lined up opposite Reb Hirshe's house. Meyerke Podval gave a signal with his hand as if it were a sword, and the entire group bellowed out lustfully like a regiment on parade: "Blessed are you, Lord of Hosts, King of the Universe, who has sanctified us with his commandments and commanded us to wear the fringes."

"Fringes!" rang throughout the empty market place. "Fringes!" ricocheted between the houses, as if imps were playing there. A dusty breeze came by; it picked up the cry and carried the din over the town: "Fringes! Fringes!" The echo broke with a crack and spread to the other side of the wooden bridges—"Fringes! Fringes!"—as if the dead had awakened with a clamor: Resurrection had come and they wanted kosher ritual fringes.

Reb Hirshe Gordon's wife sat up in bed, drenched with perspiration. She waited for these wild noises every night and shook when she heard them. Reb Hirshe too sat up, choking with anger. He could not deal with these hidden sounds in the night. The heretics were throwing his own insult back at him: "You're quoting the sages? First show me your fringes!" This remark had reduced his status among the townspeople far more than his religious disputes ever had. Even the most pious congregants laughed at the foolish chant he had inadvertently blurted out when he scolded the rascal Dan Dunietz.

Reb Hirshe plucked at his beard, ground his teeth, and growled at his wife in the darkness, "It was your idea to have Baynish stay here all summer. In Kamenietz he could have been studying Torah, but all he does here is walk around with his dainty little walking stick."

Since his wife didn't want to irritate him further, she kept silent. People are right, she thought. He certainly is a difficult man. Baynish was the son of Hirshe's first wife, God rest her soul. Nevertheless, she had always treated her stepson as if he were her own child. She had told Hirshe that since Baynish had stayed on after Passover to see his venerable grandfather, the former rabbi of Valkenik, off to the Land of Israel, he ought to remain for the entire summer. Baynish was a delicate youth, his wife had said, weaker than the other yeshiva scholars who spent their vacation in Valkenik, and he should rest and gather strength. For once Hirshe had obeyed her—which was why he was upset with her now.

"Woman!" he shouted. "One must study Torah away from home, in want and distress, and then the Torah becomes dear and precious."

Tsharne lay in her room, her head buried in the pillow, crying. She loved her father very much and had always been proud that everyone in town respected him. Now suddenly everything had changed, and she was ashamed to go out on the street. Even when she visited a girl friend, the family there would beam as if they wanted to burst into laughter. No matter what topic a group of young people was discussing, they would begin with the remark, "You're quoting the sages? First show me your fringes!" Tsharne wept into her pillow and thought that she'd run away from Valkenik and go wherever her feet led her.

Her stepbrother Baynish, in bed in Reb Hirshe's library, couldn't sleep either. He was afraid his father might find the books hidden behind the bookcase. Even in the most devout rabbinic homes the young people were now reading whatever they liked, but he had to keep a wary eye. He got his books by meeting Meyerke Podval in the forest, and Meyerke had given his word of honor that no one would ever know. The next time they met, Baynish thought, he would ask the library club to stop their antics under his father's window. If they didn't he would stop borrowing Meyerke's books.

5

THE JEWISH VILLAGE of Dekshne had once had its own ritual slaughterer, a man who studied Mishna in the morning with the farmers and the stories in *Eyn Yaakov* in the evening. Then the slaughterer died, and the villagers couldn't find a replacement. Now, just as they went to Valkenik on Fridays for the bathhouse and for holiday services, they also sent their chickens to Valkenik to be slaughtered for their Friday night meals. But the Dekshners longed for a teacher who would study a chapter of *Eyn Yaakov* with them to keep them from being as depressed as their lodgers, the incurable melancholiacs.

One day the colonist Gavriel Levin came to Valkenik and told Reb Yisroel the tailor that he wanted to engage one of the yeshiva scholars as a teacher. Reb Yisroel advised him to speak to the bachelor Yoel Uzder. After considering the offer at length, Yoel Uzder finally declined it. He concluded that during the two-mile walk to the village and the two miles back, he would undoubtedly get his shoes, trousers, jacket, and hat dusty. It wouldn't pay. The tailor then advised Levin to talk to Sheeya Lipnishker. He was a prodigious scholar and a genius, though rather outlandish.

"The fact that this genius is rather wild doesn't scare me. Even keeping the madwoman Elke Kogan from New Sventsin in my house doesn't scare me."

Sheeya Lipnishker agreed at once. A two-mile hike was a joke to him, and he wasn't afraid of losing time from Torah study either, for on his way he would be able to review some Talmudic passages.

Sheeya wasn't as eager for the income as he was to teach Torah. A host of new interpretations on the Agada had gathered in his mind, and since he hadn't the patience to write them down, he wanted to unburden himself verbally. He soon saw that the farmers couldn't properly appreciate his accomplishments, but nevertheless he didn't shout and call them dunderheads or featherbrains, which was the way he treated the youngsters at the Valkenik yeshiva. Instead, he worked diligently, explaining the stories in *Eyn Yaakov* to his bearded old students as clearly and calmly as he could. Before long he was on friendly terms with the farmers and looked forward to the evenings in the little Dekshne shul where he tried to help his pupils comprehend one or another rabbinic saying. For their part the villagers didn't understand much of what the scholar had to say, but from the way he waved his arms, rolled his eyes, and bit his little black beard with his crooked teeth, they gathered that he was a gem of a scholar. Seeing that his mind was constantly ablaze, they stood in awe of him and disregarded his sloppy manner of dressing and the towel he wore around his neck instead of a shirt.

To avoid an extra trip to and from the village, Lipnishker stayed over in Dekshne from Monday through Wednesday, eating and sleeping in Gavriel Levin's tidy house. Levin was childless and was financially more secure than the other Dekshners. He owned more land and had two cows, as well as beehives. Moreover, the family of his woman patient from New Sventsin paid him a hundred and fifty zlotys a month.

Elke Kogan had fallen ill after her first confinement. When she didn't rant and rave, she radiated quiet joy and goodness. Her face glowing as if she were a beloved niece visiting from afar, she helped her landlady with all the household chores. Elke played like a child with the cat in the house and the dog outside, fondling and talking to the pets as if they were human. She reminded Gavriel Levin to give the horses hay and drive the cows out to pasture. While the landlady milked the cows in the barn, Elke would look on in delight, her hands folded on her apron. But when her husband, an exporter in New Sventsin, came with their little son to visit her, a radical change came over Elke. She would sidle off into a corner and gaze at her visitors in mute terror. And when her husband pushed the little boy closer to her, her whole body would begin to tremble; it was as if someone had brought her a horrible little beast that would suck the blood from her veins. The exporter would later complain to Levin, "Why did you write me that Elke is as normal as anyone?" and Levin would explain that he had written the truth; Elke had become as calm and healthy as his own wife. Once, just after Kogan and his son left, the good-natured patient became the wildest madwoman in the village. Because of her raging she had to be locked in a room with a barred window.

Elke then put her disheveled head against the grating and shrieked, "Take that bastard away from me. I don't want to have a child. It's not my child. I'm a virgin, a virgin. I'm not a whore." A few minutes later she whimpered, "My child, my little boy. Cutthroats have torn me away from my child." The other lunatics gathered around the window and watched Elke chewing at the grating. Some gaped silently, others laughed aloud, and some went wild themselves, and ran through the village roaring at the top of their lungs, "Take that screaming woman away! She's out of her mind!"

After raging for a couple of days, Elke quieted down and smiled out the window at the black dog who looked up at her with trusting pink-rimmed eyes. Unable to pat him, she stroked the iron bars of the grating. She began to laugh and talk to the madmen who wandered through the village streets, but they no longer paid any attention to her. Her landlord released her from captivity, and she was a quietly merry soul again, a small woman with great tresses under her kerchief, as kindly as a grandmother. A year later her husband and son came for another visit, and the cycle began once more. Then the husband stopped coming, and since according to Jewish law a divorce could not be granted to a madwoman, he sought permission from one hundred rabbis to marry again.

Even a worldly person visiting the village would never have guessed that the woman living in Gavriel Levin's house was ill. How much the more so Sheeya Lipnishker, who did not even look at women. But Elke did look at the young rabbi and saw how he bolted down his meals in a couple of minutes. She also heard him complaining to Levin that there weren't enough books in the Dekshne shul. He can't live without books, Elkele thought, delighted and enraptured. She put a pail of water, a bowl, and a copper pitcher in his room so that in the morning he could observe the mitzva of washing his hands as soon as he got up. And when Sheeya, as was his wont, stormed from one room to another, Elke made way for him and adjusted the kerchief on her head as she did on Friday nights when Levin recited the kiddush over the wine.

The lunatics would habitually stop every stranger and engage him in conversation. They stopped the yeshiva scholar too, and each one confided a family secret or complained about the wrong that the world had done him. Sheeya was afraid of the melancholiacs, and the colonists were always having to assuage his fears—the sick people wouldn't hurt a fly. Later on, just as they disregarded all the local people, the lunatics took no notice of Sheeya either. They would stand silently on either side of the long village street as the yeshiva scholar moved between them with the speed of a torrent flowing between banks overgrown with tangled, withered weeds.

Wolf Krishki was the only madman who continued to tag after Lipnishker. He was a rich man from a far-off Polish village who had a mania for never letting his bundle of tattered clothing—some of it decades old—out of his sight for a moment. Afraid someone might snatch a rag, he carried the huge bundle wherever he went: from one room to another inside the house—to the table where he ate and even to the bathroom—and of course he took it with him when he walked around outside or went to the beth medresh.

Krishki was a broad-shouldered man of middle height whose bright eyes twinkled roguishly under his overhanging black eyebrows. His mustache was as stiff as a brush and his beard had remained black all the years he had lived in Dekshne. Krishki was unlike the other mental patients, who were generally quiet and shadowy.

Whenever Sheeya Lipnishker left Gavriel Levin's house, Wolf Krishki would be waiting for him, his bundle of rags at his feet, to ask the question: "Why didn't you marry?" The prodigy would release his chewed beard from between his crooked teeth, stare at the questioner, and wonder: Indeed, why don't I marry? Wolf Krishki winked slyly. "How do you like Elkele? She's as vigorous as a warm little calf." The hundreds of Talmud pages he still had to review fluttered in the young scholar's mind and he wanted to let go at this blockhead for making him waste his time. But just then Wolf Krishki asked suspiciously, "You don't want to nab any of my clothes, do you?"

Sheeya Lipnishker remembered that he was talking to a sick person and held his peace. Wolf Krishki had asked him several times if Gavriel Levin and his wife were at home or if Elkele was all alone. Sheeya assumed that the madman was afraid Gavriel might steal something from his pile of rags, so he soothed Krishki by saying, "Levin and his wife are working in the fields and Elkele is all alone." Sheeya had seen the woman in the house and wondered why she spoke to the cat as if to a person: "You little lazybones, instead of waiting near holes and catching mice, you go off for strolls all day long."

After a while even the rag collector stopped waiting for Lipnishker, who was pleased that no one noticed him anymore. He was glad to spend day after day in the Dekshne beth medresh studying without interruptions. He also found a solution for the books he needed—he borrowed them from the Valkenik beth medresh and returned them after reading them.

Sheeya gradually formulated a plan. Instead of coming to Dekshne three days a week, he would settle in the village. He was wasting too much time at the Valkenik yeshiva; he couldn't chase the inquiring students away and he had to go to the yeshiva kitchen three times a day for his meals. On the first Monday in Elul, Sheeya came to speak to Levin about moving into Dekshne. But this happened to be a time when Elke was again raging in her locked room with the barred window, and when he heard her wild shrieks, chills ran down his spine.

Levin had never spoken to Lipnishker about Elke Kogan. He didn't want to make the yeshiva scholar apprehensive about living under the same roof with a lunatic. Now he had to tell the student about his patient and her madness. "For a year now she's been as calm and healthy as any normal person. Suddenly last Friday morning hysterical screams awakened my wife and me. We found Elke rolling on the ground, beating her fists on her belly and screeching, 'I don't want to have the bastard! I don't want to have a baby!' It turns out that Elke is pregnant—but who could have done this? Certainly not one of the older villagers, and surely not one of the demented living dead who have been here dozens of years. We can't get any information out of her. She remembers nothing except that she's pregnant. The only one she mentions by name—while she curses him—is her husband, and the last time he was here was more than a year ago."

Gavriel Levin had served in the Czar's army and kept the habit of wearing his cap at an angle. His height and build might have given the impression that he wasn't a scrupulously observant Jew, but people in Dekshne and Valkenik knew that Gavriel was honest and pious. His sole complaint against God was that he had no children, and this was the reason his face was always gloomy. Gavriel turned his head from side to side as though looking for the guilty party in his house. "Then who did it? There's no one left but me!" He pointed to himself with both hands and looked as dispirited and apathetic as a Dekshne melancholiac.

"A plague upon my enemies! Are you out of your mind?" his wife shouted, then became tongue-tied in the presence of Sheeya, who looked at the couple in silent terror.

That evening the ten Dekshne Jews were not in the mood to study *Eyn Yaakov.* Gavriel Levin and the other farmers sat around the table in the little beth medresh racking their brains over who might have done the pernicious deed. Unable to find a satisfactory answer, they demanded of their teacher, "Look here! You were often in that house when Levin and his wife were working in the fields. Did you ever see anyone coming in?" Neither Gavriel Levin nor the other Dekshners wanted to suspect the young teacher, and Lipnishker himself hadn't the faintest notion that he might possibly be accused of adultery with a madwoman. But no matter how hard he tried to recall, he couldn't remember. His astute, analytical Talmudic mind couldn't imagine that the mad rag collector, who always waited for him outside to ask if the Levins were at home, might have come to see Elke just as he, Sheeya, was leaving for the beth medresh.

The villagers sitting around the table in the shul argued at length about what should be done. Some felt that the entire matter should be given over to the Valkenik community council and that the pregnant woman should be taken to the regional hospital in Poviatov for an abortion. It would be better to report the matter voluntarily than stand in fear of an informer. Others thought the scandal should be hushed up and that everything should be done in secret to keep the sick woman from having her baby. If the Valkenik community council found out, they would send investigators and police and the matter would reach the woman's relatives, who would say, "If Dekshne can't even keep a sick woman from becoming pregnant, who knows what else could happen there?" The families would take their sick relatives home, and the village would be left without a livelihood. The farmers put their heads together around the table, bickering softly as though in fear of the beth medresh walls, while their teacher, the yeshiva student, listened silently.

Sheeya Lipnishker didn't sleep a wink that night because Elke, locked in her room, shrieked and raged without letup. On Tuesday morning Sheeya told Levin, "I'm going back to Valkenik. I was hired only for the summer months of Tammuz and Av. During Elul there may be bad weather, and it would be hard to walk such a distance. I would have stayed on because the weather is still good and I like the local people. I was even thinking about settling in Dekshne, because I'm losing too much time from Torah studies in Valkenik. But the waste of time here would be even greater now. I can't bear that lunatic's screaming, and at the moment the villagers have no intention of studying. That's why I'm going back to Valkenik."

This unexpected departure surprised Gavriel Levin. He was

distressed at the fact that the scholar, who for two months had lived in his house like a lord, was leaving him during a time of misfortune. Nevertheless, the farmer and his wife escorted the yeshiva scholar to the porch amid warm farewells. Sheeya walked down the steps, holding a bundle of books under his arm.

Suddenly they heard a wail. "My bridegroom, where are you going?" Elke Kogan called.

At which Sheeya Lipnishker bolted into the fields, running nonstop until he reached the Valkenik beth medresh. There he immediately threw himself into Talmud study, whose melody would drown out the lunatic's screams still resounding in his ears.

Reb Menakhem-Mendl sidled up to him and asked, "Why did you come back from Dekshne on Tuesday instead of Thursday?"

"The term's over," Sheeya grumbled. He didn't want to waste any time repeating the whole story, and as the Talmudic sage Resh Lokish had leaped from one river bank to another, Sheeya's crossed eyes leaped from one column of commentary to the other.

Reb Menakhem-Mendl felt that he had to pour out his heart, for as Proverbs states, "Heaviness in the heart of man maketh it stoop." "Lipnishker," he said, "our yeshiva is in ruins. The plague of reading forbidden books has infected our students and no one is making any attempt to stop it."

At noontime, when the beth medresh was usually crowded, only a few students—solitary stalks in an autumn cornfield—swayed over their Talmuds. For a moment the scholar's skewed eyes roved over the empty benches. Then suddenly, with a spurt of foam on his lips, he began to say things that Reb Menakhem-Mendl did not understand:

"What do they want of me? There are madmen here and madmen there. I had to run away from Dekshne because of a crazy married woman who's pregnant. And now the lunacy of heretical books has come through the walls of the Valkenik beth medresh. It's a crazy world, a world full of madmen."

And Sheeya Lipnishker began to sift through the Talmud like a man parched with thirst, sipping from a pail of water. Reb Menakhem-Mendl quietly slipped away from him, thinking enviously: That prodigy is lucky. He has no responsibility for the yeshiva.

6

MEYERKE PODVAL from Panashishok set his glance on the two oldest yeshiva scholars, Uzder and Lipnishker.

He had once caught up with Uzder during a stroll along the Meretshanke River bank and tried to persuade him that nowadays a man of marriageable age had to be well read. Yoel Uzder had frowned, making vertical furrows in his forehead, as he did when deliberating over whether to make a loan, and then replied, "Why don't you read these books for me and give me a brief summary of what's in them?"

"The main thing in these books is their style," Podval informed the yeshiva student. "It's not the plot. That's why you have to read for yourself, so your future bride will see how well educated you are."

"I'm not looking for a well-read modern-style bride," the ben Torah told him. "In fact, I consider that a drawback. You know what a duel is?" He turned stiffly to his would-be adviser.

"A duel!" Meyerke looked at the idler still mired in feudal romanticism. "A duel is two men shooting at each other with pistols or fighting over some wench with swords."

"See; even though I don't read them I know very well what goes on in your novels," Yoel called out triumphantly, and all the wrinkles in his forehead smoothed themselves out. "And you want me to take precious time from Torah studies to read about young people who stab each other like murderers over some female?"

What a fool! Meyerke thought. Even if he could convert the idiotic old bachelor into a reader of secular books, Uzder wouldn't leave the yeshiva any more than the young lodgers in the guest house were leaving. By now all Valkenik knew that the yeshiva lads were reading forbidden books; nevertheless, they were still warming the benches. If that Lipnishker genius could be hooked, *that* would be a victory. Since he was a bit of a madman and a fanatic, he would put all his diligence into secular books and cast off Torah studies. Valkenik would be turned upside down. But how did one get to him? Sheeya spent three days a week in Dekshne and the remaining four he sat in the Valkenik beth medresh from morning till late at night. Meyerke didn't want to enter the beth medresh in the presence of Reb Menakhem-Mendl and the congregants.

Meyerke saw Sheeya Lipnishker the morning he returned from Dekshne, racing like a locomotive from the yeshiva kitchen back to his studies. Meyerke decided to give chase. None of the other yeshiva students had finished breakfast, and the congregants had by now finished their prayers and left the beth medresh.

Podval remembered some pretty little Talmudic interpretations from the time when people were predicting that he would someday be known as the gaon from Panashishok. He demonstrated some of his Torah learning and, in a single response, resolved a problem from three different Talmudic tractates. Sheeya had grown accustomed to discussing Talmud with the vacationing yeshiva students from Mir, Kletzk, and Radun, but this Podval pilpulist didn't look like a ben Torah, and his mode of Talmudic reasoning was a ten-year-old's.

"You pipsqueak!" Sheeya shouted. "What are you babbling about?" and forthwith tore Podval's argument to shreds, as he might have torn the guts from a chicken with his crooked nails to see if it was kosher.

Podval pretended absolute astonishment. "Ahah! With a brilliant mind like yours, you could become a professor in no time. But first you need to acquire some worldly knowledge by reading secular books."

Sheeya's crossed eyes wavered and nearly bulged out of their sockets. Bent over his prayer stand with its Talmud folio, he poked his two forefingers into the instigator's ribs. "You, you, you! Now I know who made the Dekshne madwoman pregnant. *You* made her pregnant. If you can seduce yeshiva students into reading heretical books, you're capable of raping a betrothed girl on Yom Kippur! So you're the one who copulated with that crazy married woman. You're the corrupter! Troublemaker! You're the guilty one, damn you!" And Sheeya spat straight into his face.

Bewildered, Meyerke wiped the spit from his bespattered face and stared around in a daze as though looking for an iron bar to kill the lunatic scholar with. But his rage didn't blind him; he realized it didn't pay to come to blows. The yeshiva scholar was stronger and wilder then he.

"Just wait; you'll end up weeping," Meyerke muttered, and he left the beth medresh before the yeshiva students came back from breakfast.

He went through town, hands in his pockets, with measured stride, as if out for a stroll. No one would have guessed that his temples were pounding like hammers. How could he get even with that dog? If he and his pals bloodied Sheeya's eyes, broke his ribs, beat him to a pulp, it wouldn't be a bad thing. But if Meyerke told his friends what Lipnishker had done, they would laugh at him. Who asked you to quarrel with a bench warmer? Forget him! But it was not Meyerke's nature to forget. He had hated religious functionaries and fanatics from his boyhood in the Valkenik beth medresh, when he took his eating days with first one then another. He surely wouldn't forget what Lipnishker had done; he'd teach that scholar a lesson. He would have to calmly consider a course of action and not tell a soul that he had been spat upon.

All day long Meyerke wandered around, met friends, and paid visits. Everywhere he heard the same story: In Dekshne the mentally ill Elke Kogan from New Sventsin had become pregnant and no one knew who the father was. Meyerke Podval listened with pricked-up ears and realized why Lipnishker had yelled that if he could seduce yeshiva boys into reading secular books, he was surely the one who had impregnated the crazy Dekshne woman. Such logic was possible only in the twisted mind of a lice-ridden yeshiva scholar.

In the evening Meyerke went to visit the yeshiva boys in the guest house. "Which of you is ready to chuck the yeshiva?"

This time the students didn't run toward him happily, eager for new books. In fact, they looked hostile and asked with open suspicion, "Who spread the news that we're reading secular books all over Valkenik? Didn't we agree to keep it a secret?"

Meyerke Podval shrugged coldly. "I haven't the faintest idea who told. And it shouldn't bother you anyway. In a couple of weeks the semester will end, and you'll all go home. Next semester you'll stay home and go to work; you'll get an education, and you'll also show people that in a time of class struggle no one can stay on the other side of the barricades. What do you care if people in Valkenik know you're reading secular books?"

His friends from the library had warned Meyerke that his propaganda among the yeshiva boys would bring no results. Now he saw how right the library supporters had been. The boys in the guest house pounced on him. "We haven't even thought at all about not returning to the yeshiva next semester."

Melechke Vilner added, "And anyway, it's high time for us to stop reading these books. It's the beginning of the month of Elul now, and in Elul Navaredok tries to rise to higher degrees of spirituality."

Podbrodzer declared, "I'd read them even in Elul, but only if it was still an absolute secret. Since it has become public knowledge, it's not worth having our rosh yeshiva, Reb Menakhem-Mendl, cry so bitterly about our destroying the yeshiva—and all because of a few books."

"Things are getting more difficult," Araner called out. "Sheeya Lipnishker came back from Dekshne today because of something that happened where he'd been living, in Gavriel Levin's house. In the kitchen Sheeya made mincemeat of us, threatening to tear up every secular book he finds in our possession."

"Sheeya Lipnishker lived in Gavriel Levin's house in Dekshne?" Meyerke Podval's eyes darkened. "Why did he leave? What connection does he have with the pregnant madwoman?"

"Gavriel Levin and the other Dekshne residents are up to their ears in misfortune," Araner replied, "so they have no time to study now. No one knows who made the sick woman pregnant. What's the difference?" And all the students who slept in the guest house decided that for the present they wouldn't take any more new books.

"Fine; I'll stop in some other time to pick up the books you still have," Meyerke Podval said, and he rushed out of the guest house.

Soyeh-Etl was on the other side of the door with a broom in her hand. The cemetery caretaker, who had never been known to raise her voice, waved her broom and screeched, "Beat it, you swine, you filthy pig! You're leading Jewish children astray!"

Meyerke strode by her quickly. All he needed now was for people to learn that besides being spat upon by a yeshiva student, he had been threatened by the cemetery woman with her broom. He saw all his victories falling apart; what's more, his pals would laugh at him. But now events were taking a better turn. With one blow he would tear the entire yeshiva apart and teach that mad dog Lipnishker a lesson.

In the big rectangular library a dozen couples were listening to a lecture. They sat on a bench that ran along one of the long bare wooden walls, which had moss and grass in its crevices. Moshe Okun was on the stage speaking about the French Revolution: "People would have us believe that the French Revolution was fought and won in the National Convention, by the Montagnards headed by Danton and the deputies of the Jacobin clubs, led by Robespierre, both of whom defeated the Girondists. But the truth is that the French Revolution was given its impetus by the masses of the folk and by the communes in the Paris suburbs, led by the great tribune Marat, whom the bourgeois historians have falsely accused of cruelty. All this is clearly demonstrated by Pyotr Kropotkin, whose works can be found right here in the Valkenik Folk Library."

The young couples turned to the bookshelves where this Pyotr Kropotkin could be found and then looked back at Moshe Okun, whose eyes bulged like those of a fish on dry land. His audience wanted to leave for the river bank and the tall bulrushes, but the lecturer disregarded this and went on sarcastically about the bourgeois historians until Meyerke Podval entered and everyone turned to him as if to a redeemer.

"Listen to the latest! A local yeshiva student named Sheeya Lipnishker, who's mad as a hatter, was living in Dekshne during the summer and knocked up a madwoman."

The group had heard about the Dekshne incident but not that a yeshiva scholar had done the deed. "Is it true, Meyerke, or did you dream this up too?"

"This incident interests me about as much as last year's snow." Meyerke Podval laughed. "I'm just telling you the gossip in town. The Dekshne farmers are a bunch of fanatics. Nevertheless, they're sure that the yeshiva student impregnated Elke Kogan. He was teaching the farmers Torah and living in Gavriel Levin's house, where the sick woman boards."

The following morning people spoke of this at home and at the market place. A day earlier they had pitied the sick woman. People also commiserated with Gavriel Levin and the other Dekshne Jews who might lose their livelihood and have trouble with the authorities. But now everyone was so fascinated by the news that the prodigy, the yeshiva's most diligent and pious student, was apparently responsible that they forgot about the victims. The gossip about the perpetrator began as whispers and ended with loud, mocking remarks and sarcastic jokes. The pillars of the town wanted to wash their hands of the affair; glowering, they went to seek out Reb Hirshe Gordon.

"It's no news that a boor hates a scholar, or that a maskil can't stand a religious Jew," Reb Hirshe answered, his face shining like a brass lion. "Raise a rumpus in town—a ben Torah has been falsely accused."

Encouraged by Reb Hirshe's words, the shul Jews railed against the Jewish mudslingers, calling them worse than the anti-Semites. "Which one of the Dekshners said that the yeshiva student is guilty? And who in Valkenik heard it personally from a Dekshner?"

"When church bells ring, it must be a holiday," said the market peddlers, and a contingent of men headed for Dekshne.

Seeing a delegation from Valkenik going into Gavriel's house, the colonists realized that it concerned the pregnant madwoman and that the whole village was involved. They too went into their neighbor's house.

The Valkenik market people spoke with the familiarity of old pals. "How are you, Gavriel? Keep your chin up, Gavriel! What's new with Elke? Is she still ranting and raving?" Then the uninvited visitors sat down around the table as if they had gathered to make peace among good friends.

Levin wasn't pleased to have these visitors who were butting into other people's business. "Elke has no more strength to rage," he answered coldly.

A young man in leather-trimmed riding breeches planted his booted legs wide apart and said just as firmly, "Gavriel, people in Valkenik are quoting you as saying that this was done by the yeshiva student who lived in your house."

Levin jumped up, infuriated. "I never said that!"

Everyone at the table waited for him to continue, but he suddenly fell silent and looked in terror at the Dekshne farmers. They looked back at him apprehensively, as if the stranger had publicly expressed their secret torments.

"Gavriel, speak up!" the merchant cried, shoving his hands into his coat pockets.

Levin sensed the Valkenik men staring at him with gleaming eyes and repressed smiles at the corners of their mouths. For these vulgar boors it was logical to assume that if it wasn't the yeshiva scholar, then it was he, Gavriel. His wife was an old woman and Elkele, when she was quiet, was still an attractive, pleasant young woman. Levin again had an urge to get up and drive out the gang of visitors who had come to suck his blood. But he quickly changed his mind, afraid that people might indeed say that he himself had made his lodger pregnant.

"But I must admit"—Gavriel spread his hands—"I did think it strange that the yeshiva student left Dekshne as soon as the misfortune occurred. He said he couldn't stand her shouting. But who knows?"

The other Dekshne villagers tapped their sparse gray beards with their callused fingers, as if touching a wound that had healed, and looked down at the table. "One can tell right away that the young man is a great scholar," one of them said. "But there's one thing we don't understand. When Levin and his wife went out to the fields, the young rabbi remained at home. Why didn't he ever notice who was coming and going? When we asked him, he said he didn't know, and then the next morning he left town."

Gavriel's wife, a bent woman, all skin and bones, interrupted. "I don't know whether the young teacher is to blame. Still, there's something strange here. When Gavriel and I went out on the porch to see him off, Elke saw him through the bars of the window and shouted, 'My bridegroom, why are you running away?' "

"My friends, it's as plain as the palm of my hand that it's the yeshiva student's doing," said a Valkenik resident, displaying his shovel-like palm. The visiting delegation stood up. "Everything is perfectly clear."

They returned to Valkenik and reported that truth rises like oil on water. Almost everyone was entertained at the idea that the wild prodigy had had a secret love affair with the madwoman, and they made fun of the handful of bewildered congregants who refused to believe that Sheeya was guilty.

"I wish we had a pile of gold as big as the yeshiva scholar's *yetzer ha-ra*," said a member of the delegation. "What's the matter with him? Does he have a raisin for a soul?"

7

SHEEYA LIPNISHKER saw people pointing at him and shouting, "My bridegroom, why are you running away?" With his last ounce of strength he stumbled into the beth medresh and hid behind the Talmud. Why were people mocking him with the madwoman's words? Reb Menakhem-Mendl approached with lowered eyes and told him that the Valkenik rabbi wanted to see him at once. Sheeya Lipnishker noticed all the scholars in the beth medresh turning their heads to him as if Reb Menakhem-Mendl was their spokesman too. Although he had never had any dealings with the town rabbi, the prodigy felt a sense of foreboding.

"What does the rabbi want with me?" Sheeya asked, his voice and knees shaking.

"The rabbi himself will tell you," Reb Menakhem-Mendl mumbled. Sheeya followed him to Reb Mordekhai-Aaron Shapiro's house as if led to the slaughter.

In Elul the vacationing yeshiva students had returned to their schools and the rabbi's sons had left too. With his son and son-in-law away the rabbi was all the more incensed at himself for coming to a town brimming with controversy. Reb Hirshe Gordon had informed him that if he gave in to the town and didn't stand up for the falsely accused ben Torah, then the religious faction would wage war on him until he was forced to leave Valkenik.

Lipnishker's naïve innocence infuriated the rabbi even more; he sprang up seething, his body thin as a needle and his narrow shoulders and thick beard trembling with rage. "Are you so stupid that you don't know what people are saying about you all over town?" asked the Valkenik rabbi.

Finally Sheeya realized what he was suspected of. He burst into tears and began to pluck at his hair.

"Don't screech!" Reb Mordekhai-Aaron Shapiro clapped his hands over his ears. He despised a woman's tearing at her hair and detested this habit even more in a man. "I'm not suspecting you, and you don't have to justify yourself to me. On Sabbath morning I want you to stop the Torah reading and swear before the Torah scroll that you've been falsely accused. Even if you were the leading saint of the generation, according to Jewish law you must rid yourself of the slander leveled against you. Go talk to the congregants, to the masses, to the boors—but not to me, not to me." The rabbi trembled and made faces.

"Reb Sheeya, no true ben Torah suspects you, God forbid," Reb Menakhem-Mendl added with an anguished face, his voice breaking. "But to keep the town from listening to the slanderers and to avoid a terrible desecration of God's name, tomorrow morning you should swear before the entire congregation that you are completely blameless. As the Torah says: 'Ye shall be clean before the Lord and Israel.' That's what I would do."

The conversation in the rabbi's home occurred on Thursday. Sheeya waited impatiently for the next morning. Panting and drenched with perspiration, he began to stop congregants in the synagogue courtyard and weep that he was a victim of trumped-up charges. An older man heard him out with closed eyes, pounding his cane on the cobblestones. "Scandalous, scandalous! The slanderers must be uprooted from our midst." Another man modestly ducked his head and said he didn't want to get involved. A third just wanted to know all the details and then went on, frowning, without saying a word, as befitted a judge who had to weight all the facts before issuing a decision. The yeshiva students, seeing the prodigy running after the congregants and humiliating himself, turned away in shame. Among themselves they spoke of leaving the yeshiva before the end of the term.

Sheeya wandered about the courtyard with the befuddled look of one of the Dekshne melancholiacs. He didn't dare go into the beth medresh and wouldn't go to the kitchen for his breakfast. When he saw a ben Torah passing by, he would step aside, afraid and submissive, as if he had already been excommunicated. He felt that he had forgotten everything he knew—it seemed that even the Torah wanted to steer clear of him until his innocence was established.

Meyerke Podval from Panashishok approached Lipnishker. He had heard that the yeshiva student would swear in the beth medresh that he was innocent. Meyerke didn't like that. If the townspeople saw the cockeyed, sloppy-looking yeshiva student swearing before the Torah, they would believe him. Meyerke winked to the scholar to follow him and Sheeya Lipnishker came docilely.

"You see, even though you abused and insulted me, I'm still your friend." Podval stopped near the Cold Shul, next to a ditch full of nettles. "The religious functionaries, the congregants, and the yeshiva students believe everything that's being said about you, but my friends and I don't believe it. But what thanks do I get? You attacked me for trying to persuade you to read secular books."

"Forgive me," Sheeya pleaded, touched to the point of tears that the youth didn't believe the false accusations against him.

"I forgive you completely, right here and now," Meyerke said after the fashion of yeshiva students who ask forgiveness of one another before Rosh Hashana. But his half-closed eyes glittered with hatred. He wanted to see the mad prodigy squirm. "Now you tell me, have you any sense? I wanted to make you a professor, but you preferred to remain a dirty yeshiva student, a lice-ridden recluse whose underwear shows and whose ritual fringes are filthy. Now you tell me, are you intelligent?"

"No, I'm not intelligent." Lipnishker trembled with fear that the youth would think ill of him.

"Well, it's your good luck that you're a moron. If you weren't a moron, I'd have taken your head off for spitting in my face. Now listen to the advice of someone who *is* bright. Don't go proclaiming your innocence before the Sabbath worshipers. No one will believe you. Wherever you turn, people will call you an adulterer. They'll drag you to the door and everyone will step on you. They may even tie you up and hand you over to the gentile authorities and have you locked up for years, maybe even for life. Do you know the penalty for being involved with a woman of unsound mind and making her pregnant? You ought to run away while there's time—in fact, right now. Leave town and let them all kiss your behind. A prodigy like you will be honored and welcomed at every yeshiva."

"If I run away, it will be a terrible desecration of God's name. People will say that a ben Torah was involved with a married woman and ran away from the punishment. That's why I'm going to stay, and with the Torah in my hands I'll swear that I had nothing to do with her. They'll believe me," Sheeya murmured, his teeth chattering.

"They won't believe you and you know it. That's why you're so scared." Meyerke laughed.

"Then I'll martyr myself for the sake of God." Lipnishker's big crossed eyes quivered.

"You're crazy! Dekshne's the proper place for you. I can't understand how even a loony would lie down with a bedraggled, lice-ridden yeshiva student like you. You stink!" Meyerke spat out. "Just wait. You'll be sorry you didn't listen to me." Meyerke Podval shook a fist at him and went away.

Perhaps I *should* run away, Sheeya thought. His eyes darted this way and that. Then he suddenly leaped back. From the low, half-opened door of the women's gallery Reb Tsemakh Atlas was eying him as if on the lookout to keep him from escaping.

That morning the yeshiva supporter Reb Yisroel had spoken to the principal. "The students have taken to reading secular books," he said, angrier than ever, "and you're not doing anything about it. People have besmirched the name of our finest student, a young prodigy, a saint—and you, you haven't said a word! Afterward, Tsemakh sat in the women's gallery of the Cold Shul asking himself how long he could remain silent. Suddenly he heard voices in the weed-covered yard into which Vova Barbitoler had recently stumbled while looking for the entrance to the women's gallery. Tsemakh looked out the window and saw a stranger talking to Sheeya Lipnishker, who looked terror stricken. Tsemakh approached the half-open door and listened to the conversation.

As soon as Meyerke Podval left, Tsemakh went out to Lipnishker. "Who was that young man? Why was he trying to talk you into running away, and why did he insult you?"

"Rabbi, have pity on me!" The scholar fell to his knees, wailing. Tsemakh drew him into the women's gallery, sat him down on a chair, and again asked him about Meyerke Podval.

"The other day he tried to persuade me to read secular books and I called him a corrupter and spat in his face. Now he's been advising me to run away." Sheeya began to shiver again, as if with fever. "I won't run away, rabbi. I'll martyr myself for the sake of God, rabbi."

Hitherto, Lipnishker had not deigned to take notice of his rosh yeshiva. He felt that even as a youngster he had known more Talmud than Tsemakh Atlas knew now; moreover, he hadn't the slightest respect for a Musar lecturer. But now he huddled up to the principal and called him "rabbi."

"Don't be afraid," Tsemakh said soothingly. "You *should* speak to the congregation tomorrow morning at Sabbath services. People will listen to you and believe you." Tsemakh did not leave Sheeya on his own, but took him to supper at Reb Yisroel's house, where everyone fed and consoled him. Tsemakh himself, however, was inconsolable. He had planted a vineyard and let evil beasts trample it.

Feeling and looking like a mourner who could not recite the Kaddish because the corpse was not yet buried, Sheeya Lipnishker stood in the beth medresh the following morning, flanked by Reb Tsemakh Atlas and Reb Menakhem-Mendl. He waited for the Torah reading to end so that he could go up to the pulpit. All three waited silently, but the congregants were impatient, unwilling to hear the yeshiva student. One faction didn't want Sheeya to speak because they wanted to spite the fanatics and Reb Hirshe Gordon, who wanted him to be whitewashed by swearing in the presence of the holy Torah. The other faction didn't want to see Sheeya Lipnishker crying and screaming that he was free of sin, as if they were back in the Middle Ages when a community could put a man into the pillory, sentence him to be whipped, even excommunicate him. They held that the High Holy Days were approaching, and if Sheeya has indeed sinned, then let him repent. Beyond that it was none of their concern. But what worried the third and largest faction was that the youth's remarks would spark an uproar, and another Sabbath would be ruined. Therefore, as soon as the man who chanted the Haftora finished the blessings, dozens of congregants cried out to the cantor, "Take the Torah scrolls!" and everyone continued with the service. The first to slip out of the beth medresh was Reb Menakhem-Mendl Segal. Sheeya Lipnishker, wild-eyed and tongue-tied, shuffled after him. The last to leave was Tsemakh—who backed out as if unable to tear his glance away from the bent, swaying backs piously immersed in the Silent Devotion.

The prayers had ended, and the congregation could have gone home peacefully to eat their cholent. Nevertheless, they remained in their places. Some of the congregants regretted not giving the scholar the opportunity to justify himself; others regretted having deprived themselves of a free show.

Reb Hirshe Gordon went up to the rabbi and shook his finger at him. "You shouldn't have let them take the Torah scrolls back to the Ark until the yeshiva scholar had had a chance to speak, and afterward *you* should have spoken and warned them that you would excommunicate anyone who repeated the slander. But you didn't do it because you were afraid. As far as I'm concerned, you're no longer the Valkenik rabbi."

"What do you want of me?" Reb Mordekhai-Aaron Shapiro writhed as though threatened by sticks, his watery eyes spraying anger. "I believe the youth is innocent, but how can I keep others' mouths shut? The fact is that he *did* live in the same house with the sick woman, and, as the Talmud says, anyone can be suspected of lewd behavior."

Reb Hirshe had not greeted the rabbi when he came in and didn't wish him Good Sabbath when he departed. He went back to his seat on the other side of the eastern wall and, his face steaming with rage, told his brother-in-law, "Instead of demanding that the persecuted student be given permission to speak, you and your faction kept quiet. You won't be forgiven for this. There's still a God in this world."

"What have you got against me?" Eltzik Bloch touched his heart and then stretched out both hands to reckon on his fingers. "When the Miadle rabbi delivered a sermon this past winter, you sat in your seat near the Holy Ark and purposely snored out loud for the entire beth medresh to see and hear what you think of a Mizrachi rabbi. Weeks later, when the Misagoleh rabbi preached—he's not from the Mizrachi party and he's considered a gaon—you interrupted his talk ten times to show that he was no scholar and that he wasn't worthy of holding our rabbinic post. And then a couple of weeks ago, on the Sabbath of Consolation, when a local youth, Dan Dunietz of the Tarbut School, was visiting in town, you didn't let *him* speak, and that prompted a fight in the beth medresh. The fact remains that everyone has the right to complain that the prodigy wasn't given permission to talk—except you!"

The congregants were delighted with Eltzik's clever retort, but they hid their smiles in the wrinkles of their bearded faces and behind their mustaches. The worshipers put their tallises into the drawers of their prayer stands and said amiably, "Indeed, it's a pity about Sheeya. Even if he did sin, it's obvious he wants to repent. But the sick woman and the Dekshne farmers who may lose their income over this incident deserve even more pity."

Sroleyzer the bricklayer removed his tallis too, turning his oxlike head from side to side. He wanted no more to do with cowardly congregants and young heretics, but he was fuming about the wrong that had just been done. He blew his nose resoundingly and bellowed like a trumpet, "Fellow Jews, listen to me. Everyone knows I'm a demon and therefore have good intuitions. When the poor lad stood by the pulpit steps waiting for permission to say a few words, I didn't take my eyes off him. And I tell you he's as innocent as a dove. If not, you can chop off my head." Sroleyzer ran his finger across his throat. "This trumped-up charge against the poor boy was started"—and he pointed—"by that bastard. By him and no one else. Don't worry, fellow Jews. You can believe me."

The congregants turned to see whom Sroleyzer had singled out, and there was Meyerke Podval from Panashishok standing behind the pulpit. When Lipnishker and the two rosh yeshivas left the beth medresh, the youths from the library club and the fire brigade had also dispersed, disappointed that there wouldn't be a commotion this Sabbath. Only Meyerke had remained, and now he smiled at the bricklayer with cold contempt. He didn't want to dignify him with an answer. The worshipers thought Sroleyzer was babbling because he was still angry at Meyerke for scratching his face during the Sabbath of Consolation fight. Not even Reb Hirshe Gordon took Sroleyzer's accusation seriously.

This time Reb Hirshe left the beth medresh without his usual entourage. He felt a surge of hatred toward those pseudozealots. Valkenik had become an evil town, a center of idol worship in which a Jew was forbidden to live.

Ambling along a few feet behind Reb Hirshe was Meyerke Podval, smiling through his half-closed eyes as if he knew that Gordon wanted to tell him something. Normally Reb Hirshe wouldn't even have looked at him, but now he didn't want that Bolshevik to consider himself the victor.

"Listen, you bedraggled jailbird! You persuaded the yeshiva boys to read secular books, and you and your pack of guttersnipes howl under my window at night. I want you to know that it won't do you any good. As long as I live in Valkenik, the community won't give you one penny to buy books. And there's another thing I'm glad about. When you were still a little worm and local congregants treated you to eating days because you were an orphan and studied in the beth medresh, I predicted what would become of you, and I never let you cross my threshold."

"But you see, it didn't do you any good," Meyerke replied with perfect composure, his hands in his pockets. "Not only the local yeshiva boys, but even your one and only son, Baynish, the grandson of the former Valkenik rabbi, a student in the Kamenietz yeshiva—Baynish is also borrowing books from the library, and he hides them behind your bookcase."

Meyerke slowly strolled on with a calm smile and a relaxed stride. But it was all a pretense. He couldn't bear to be reminded of the years when he'd studied alone in the beth medresh and the local Jews supported him. His consolation, however, was that he had repaid Hirshe Gordon. That son of his had demanded that they stop calling under his father's window during the night; otherwise, he would stop borrowing books. But soon Baynish would be yelling in his cutthroat father's house even louder than the library supporters had yelled under Hirshe Gordon's window.

8

AFTER THEIR SABBATH CHOLENT LUNCH the townspeople closed their doors and lay down for a nap. No one saw or heard what was happening in Hirshe Gordon's house. There, no cholent was eaten. Although it was the Sabbath, Reb Hirshe had moved the bookcase and found a thick tome entitled *A History of the World*. Full of pictures of strange animals, it advanced heretical notions on the very first page—that the world had not begun with the six days of creation, but millions of years ago. It was with this thick tome that Reb Hirshe beat his thin, sickly only son's head, blow after blow without letup. Baynish, doubled over, endured the beating without crying out; he merely moaned. He knew that Valkenik must not know what was happening in his home. Reb Hirshe's wife and daughter too pressed fists into their mouths to stifle their shrieks. Their horrified eyes filled with tears and looked with dread at the two hands holding the hard book which rose and fell like an iron mortar over Baynish's bent body until he collapsed, his hands and feet outstretched.

Gordon's wife and daughter rushed to the beaten youth and protected him with their bodies. "Father, you'll kill him!" Tsharne cried.

"Hirshe, he's bleeding!"

The two women had to restrain Reb Hirshe, who was trembling as if he'd been hit with a bullet.

While his wife and daughter were trying to revive Baynish, Reb Hirshe locked himself in a distant room for a couple of hours. Later he straightened his clothes, smoothed his disheveled beard, wiped his face, and went out onto the street. He strolled along with Sabbath calm, hands behind his back, as though after a pleasant nap. But instead of going to the beth medresh for the Afternoon Service, he went to the women's gallery of the Cold Shul and met the person he sought.

Ever since the winter, Tsemakh had avoided Gordon because he couldn't stand his obduracy and didn't trust his zealousness. But now a broken man sat before him, tears streaming from his eyes.

"If my son had died today, I would have had the strength not to cry on the Sabbath, but what happened to me today is even worse." Reb Hirshe looked down at his spread fingers as if incredulous that his hands had beaten his only son till the blood ran. His voice shaking, he told Tsemakh how Meyerke Podval had lured Baynish into reading heretical books.

"And today this very same Meyerke Podval told me that my son had hidden borrowed secular books behind my bookcase. In Kamenietz, Baynish was among the best students. The rosh yeshiva wrote me that Baynish would be a great sage in Israel. Now he has come home and fallen into the devil's hands. And that blackguard Meyerke Podval is even bragging that it was he who seduced the yeshiva boys into reading secular books so that the yeshiva would disintegrate. Sroleyzer the bricklayer said in the beth medresh today that he'd stake his life on the fact that the false accusation against Sheeya Lipnishker stems from Meyerke Podval too. I don't know that Sroleyzer's suspicion has a basis in fact. Why should Meyerke do that? But his best friends wouldn't deny that that bastard, may he fry in hell, is capable of doing such a foul deed. And it's all your fault. You, the yeshiva principal, sat behind locked doors, like the people of Jericho, while the plague of reading secular books infected your students. And you didn't even come out of your hiding place when the finest student in your yeshiva was falsely accused."

But when I do come out of my hiding place, Tsemakh thought, Valkenik will shudder and tremble as never before. He wanted to rein in his anger so that when it exploded it would be all the more forceful. Hence, he made a special effort to speak calmly and soberly, as if altogether unmoved by Reb Hirshe's tears.

"While Reb Menakhem-Mendl and I stood next to Lipnishker at services this morning, that same Meyerke Podval stood behind the pulpit looking like someone who has committed a terribly wicked deed and is overjoyed with his success. Sheeya Lipnishker told me that Meyerke had recently tried to talk him into reading secular books and that in response he spat in his face. Yesterday that troublemaker urged Lipnishker to run away. It's logical to assume that Meyerke Podval initiated the frame-up and then tried to frighten him into leaving town, just as he lured your son into reading secular books and then informed on him."

"Then in that case things aren't too bad, because for a frame-up like that he can rot in jail." Reb Hirshe beamed with the joy of vengeance. But then his face turned dark with anger and pain once more. "I've known him since he was a little worm and I prided myself on knowing him through and through. But it seems that you know him better. Still, you were the one who let him bring such destruction upon your yeshiva."

"You're right; it's my fault and mine alone. But now we have to think what to do next. An outright battle with Meyerke won't be worthwhile. First of all, he's a contemptible good-for-nothing, a buffoon, a smelly little creature. Second, if we have him put in jail, he'll say that we informed on a Jewish lad. Third, we might bring misfortune on the Dekshne Jews, who don't want the police to know about their pregnant, sick woman. And besides, this corrupter isn't alone. He has supporters. The evil has to be uprooted from our midst. The library should be burned down."

The principal didn't wait for Reb Hirshe Gordon's answer. He paced back and forth along the length of the women's gallery, then returned and began pounding his fists on his prayer stand.

"I won't keep silent over the wrong that was done to Sheeya Lipnishker! I'll demand restitution for his humiliation. Burn all the books!"

The whites of his eyes gleamed and his eyes flashed as he paced and spoke without stopping, as if wanting to saw through the barred windows of the women's gallery with his sharp voice.

"As much as my heart pains me for the wronged Lipnishker, it hurts me even more for the mocked truth, the humiliated law. I never thought a congregation of Jews would refuse to permit an accused person to defend himself! I couldn't imagine such a thing happening. When I saw it, I was dumbstruck. I felt my heart bursting, my mind crumbling away, but I couldn't say a word. And perhaps it was a godsend that I couldn't open my mouth. Those bearded Hamans wouldn't have let me talk, just as they didn't let Lipnishker talk. Or perhaps they might have listened and laughed. They would have gone into a wild rage had it been proved to them that Meyerke Podval of Panashishok had concocted all this and made the false accusation against Lipnishker. They were scared to death that if they let the ben Torah talk, they would have to decide he was telling the truth, for words of truth are recognizable. But those Hamans in their Sabbath prayer shawls didn't want the ben Torah to be declared innocent. They *want* him to be guilty."

"Why should a townful of Jews want a ben Torah to have sinned with a sick married woman?" Reb Hirshe stared at the principal pacing in the long, narrow gallery.

"Because they're jealous of him." Tsemakh stopped for a moment in mid-stride. For many weeks the shadows of the Cold Shul had chilled him like ice; in his mind a cemetery silence reigned. Now he was stirring out of his numbness and choking with almost drunken rage, thrilling to the released wrath that boiled over in him.

"The Valkenik townspeople want the ben Torah to be the transgressor because they begrudge his being a prodigy, a diligent scholar, a saintly man. They can't bear having to show respect for him, and they won't forgive him for it. They even envy him his habit of going around in rags and tatters and his refusing to enjoy the pleasures of this world. They're also deeply resentful that he doesn't care if they consider him a wild man. And above all, they begrudge him his world to come. They have perfect faith in the world to come and Sheeya Lipnishker has prepared a share in that world for himself. And what a share! The Jews of Valkenik have provided Lipnishker with a crumb of bread and a hard cot because to their merchants' way of thinking it was a good investment. They'd become partners in his Torah and would get a piece of the Wild Ox, a slice of the Leviathan, a golden chair in the Garden of Eden! But now they're celebrating the seven days of the great feast. The prodigy has committed a grievous sin, and, what's more, he's an even greater sinner than they. He has been held up to contempt and ridicule because the married woman is a lunatic. And, in addition to that, they can hate Lipnishker because, instead of providing them with a share of the next world for the crumbs they've given him, it turns out that he has deceived them. So they don't have to support the yeshiva scholars any longer. They don't have to bear the expenses, and that's the most important thing of all. That's what they were waiting for!" Tsemakh pounded his fist on the prayer stand for so long that he felt his head whirling. He sat down, but his lips continued mumbling feverishly, "Incredible! Unbelievable!"

Even though Reb Hirshe had often said the library should be burned down, he really hadn't meant it. But the rosh yeshiva does, he thought. Apparently Reb Tsemakh doesn't realize what might come of it. In any case, he was speaking in a wild delirium. But Reb Hirshe's bitterness toward the library demons who had driven him to beat his only son so brutally overcame his fear of consequences.

"How do you intend to carry out your plan?" he asked. "The books are locked in the library. Would you go there at night, break the lock, put the books into sacks, and take them to your lodgings and burn them?"

"I haven't thought about that yet," the rosh yeshiva replied.

"And you won't come up with anything workable when you do. The only recourse is to put Sroleyzer the bricklayer in charge of the job," Reb Hirshe said, watching Tsemakh's face from behind his glasses.

Tsemakh's face darkened. He didn't like the thought of having a fence and kidnaper as a partner. Sroleyzer had, after all, helped the woman from Argentina and her brothers in Vilna take Hertzke Barbitoler away. But on the other hand he had no alternative. A man was needed who could break locks and work in the dark.

"I agree," Tsemakh ground out after long deliberation. "The bricklayer doesn't live decently, but he did stand up for Lipnishker, and for that alone he's better than the other Valkenik congregants."

"If he agrees, Sroleyzer will want to be paid well, and he'll make us promise that no one will know who did it. I'll pay him, but you'll have to promise him that no matter what happens you won't mention any names," Reb Hirshe said carefully.

"I'll take the responsibility," Tsemakh answered just as carefully.

"If people find out that you're responsible, you'll have to leave town," Reb Hirshe went on. Then, astonished, he fell silent. The principal was looking at him, face shining, as if overjoyed at the threat that he might have to leave Valkenik. "And if you don't care about yourself," Reb Hirshe said after a moment, "just remember that this can jeopardize the yeshiva. I'm explaining this to you now so that you won't have any complaints against me later."

"Things can't get any worse than they are." Tsemakh jumped up again. "A saintly young prodigy has been falsely accused. The other yeshiva students aren't coming to classes. They're reading secular books or just wasting time, and the townspeople are beginning to say that the yeshiva should get no further support. Something's got to be done. As Moses declared, 'Whosoever is for the Lord should join me.' The true scholars among the yeshiva boys will keep on studying, and the true believers among the villagers will continue to support the yeshiva—and as for the rest, let them fall by the wayside. But, Reb Hirshe, if you're afraid, we'd better call the whole thing off."

"You're a stranger in Valkenik," Reb Hirshe Gordon replied sadly. It won't make any difference to you if you have to leave town. But I've lived here all my life, and my family is here—I don't want the whole village against me. In shul this morning I noticed that one can't even depend on the pious congregants. But all the same, if they find out that I was the one who sentenced the filthy books to burning—well, let them find out. I don't believe any more that my son will grow up to be an honest, faithful Jew. Baynish will grow up to be a Meyerke Podval from Panashishok. Now I must mourn seven days for my only living son as I mourned for his dead mother of blessed memory." And Reb Hirshe Gordon wept again—hot tears that ran down his cheeks and hid in his beard as if ashamed of falling on the Sabbath.

9

THE FOREST was empty. When the vacationing students returned to their yeshivas for Elul, the minyan in the forest shul was canceled. Reb Avraham-Shaye Kosover prayed with the manager's minyan at the cardboard factory. The worshipers were laborers who barely eked out a living from the woods and the factory together—and the factory work was as onerous as drawing pitch from the pine trees. Even when they chanted aloud from their prayer books, their thoughts and feelings were muted; these men were always tired and careworn. Local news didn't interest them; they didn't like to talk at all. Chaikl hadn't been to the village for conversation either; his father had ordered him to visit less often, to avoid scenes with the landlady's daughter. That was why no one in the vacationing rabbi's cottage knew about the storm in Valkenik over the Lipnishker incident.

Day by day Chaikl spent less and less time studying Talmud with the rabbi. He roamed about in the forest and taught himself to blow a twisted, golden-yellow, honey-clear, ram's horn. The silver-bearded man from Reb Shaulke's beth medresh in Vilna who blew the shofar always had difficulty making clear sounds at shofar-blowing time on Rosh Hashana. Chaikl dreamed that he was this man's substitute and that his shofar sounded as clear as a bell. The worshipers, tallises over their heads, gazed at him in astonishment. His mother looked at him through the little curtain in the women's gallery. But more than his fantasy of blowing the shofar in a crowded beth medresh, Chaikl was entranced by the echoes his shofar made in the empty forest.

Chaikl practiced the three types of shofar calls: *tekiah*, a lone blast; *teruah*, three short sounds; and *shevarim*, nine quick blasts.

He blew the *tekiah* once; the echo resounded for a long, long time, stretching out through the forest until finally silence reigned again and the green outbranching thickness hovered with suspended breath. He blew *shevarim*, imagining that in this green and secret place he had awakened a monster, half man, half beast, who had lain here in hiding for generations and now was answering him with a primordial mouth. This monster, unable to speak with human tongue, replied to him with heart-rending cries. *Teruah!* Gay, frivolous sounds leaped down from the branches, crept out of the bushes, and ran around like barefoot imps. "Happy is the nation that knows the *teruah* sounds!" Chaikl sang with the Rosh Hashana melody and began blowing anew with all his strength, melting with joy, intoxicated with the echoes. He heard the sounds leaping from place to place. It seemed to him that the swaying trees ecstatically recited the prayer after the blowing of the shofar. Then gradually the resounding echoes vanished and Chaikl was overwhelmed by a mysterious silence.

The tender, nostalgic, almost-autumnal sunshine trembled and played on the spires of the tall pines. Chaikl thought the dark green trees looked sad; they longed for the yeshiva students who had pressed their foreheads to their trunks while reciting the Afternoon Service. Chaikl waded up to his knees in the tall ferns, now no longer green but yellow. He lingered in a spot thick with withered pine needles and dried cones, then went into a cleared section of the forest, with felled trees sawed into lumber, where he sniffed the moist aroma of rain-soaked sawdust. Then he went back into the thicket and saw an unfurled carpet of silvery moss, here and there turned rust-red. Suddenly there was a flash of autumn-blossoming lilac, and he imagined he had discovered a secret lake that mirrored a violet sky in the undergrowth. As he went on, he saw a section of the forest floor dotted with colorful mushrooms; they looked like a troop of dwarfs in broad-brimmed hats. Poisonous, he thought—then let out a whoop of joy.

At the foot of a huge tree grew the king of mushrooms—three truffles with stiff brown heads and thick stems; they looked like three heroic statues. Chaikl knew that the gentile housekeeper at the rabbi's cottage would be very grateful to him for these truffles. She would sauté them and make an entire meal of them. But he felt it would be a pity to pluck these sturdy miniature trees. He wiped away a clinging veil of cobwebs from his damp face and thought of the saying in the *Ethics of the Fathers:* "Whosoever breaks off his Torah study to say, 'How lovely is this tree' places himself in peril." No matter how this statement was interpreted or glossed over, he still couldn't understand how a Talmudic sage could have said it.

Chaikl's amazement at the forest and everything in it never ceased. For instance, the old, low-branching oak on the hill opposite the rabbi's cottage: it had countless elbows and spreading hands and fingerlike twigs and millions of leaves. Depending on the angle of sunlight on its notched leaves, the oak always looked different. In late fall it would blaze with colors, become a pillar of fire. Its trunk was huge. Its centuries-old roots crept out of the ground onto the little hill, as if weary of remaining in one place all these years. And if one considered that in this huge forest surrounding Valkenik there were probably hundreds of thousands of trees, evergreen and deciduous, and every kind of bush and weed, and all sorts of birds, animals, and insects—one could live one's whole life in the Valkenik woods and see new things every day. But if he were to tell this to Reb Avraham-Shaye, he would reply, "Sitting in the shade of one tree in the heat of the day is enough for me."

Chaikl looked around him. Where had he wandered to? He had reached the bridge to the village.

He stopped for a minute and hesitated. Should he turn back or not? Since he was already at the bridge, he decided to go on to the village and see how his father was. Chaikl put the twisted shofar into his shirt pocket and thought: The rabbi is upset because I'm idling more than studying. But instead of castigating him, the rabbi punned and made jokes with him. Chaikl told his teacher, "The shofar-blowing is going well. I'll blow it in your beth medresh on Rosh Hashana if you wish."

Without looking up from his book the rabbi calmly answered, "The man who blows the shofar in the Poplaver beth medresh is an honest man and a diligent scholar. No matter how busy he is in his shop, he runs off to study whenever he has a spare moment. Why should you waste so much time just learning to blow the shofar well? You want a congregation to rise in your presence because you're a Torah scholar. People don't rise in honor of someone who blows the shofar, no matter how well he does it."

Chaikl proceeded along Synagogue Street, heading down the hill to Freyda Vorobey's house. But the synagogue courtyard was swarming with people, and he walked over to have a look. In the midst of the tumultuous crowd stood Sheeya Lipnishker. He was pale and he gaped skyward like someone saved from a death sentence at the last minute. Since Chaikl knew nothing about Sheeya's trouble, it took him a long time to understand what was happening.

The Dekshne farmer Gavriel Levin was speaking: "For more than thirty years now, everyone in Dekshne and Valkenik has known Wolf Krishki and his mania for carrying his bundle of old clothes around because he's terrified of someone's stealing it. Yesterday morning he ran into my house shouting, 'Your patient is a thief. She stole a velvet waistcoat of mine.' He ranted and raved and kept trying to break into the room where Elke has been locked up since she became pregnant. I asked Wolf Krishki, 'How could Elke have stolen your waistcoat?' and Krishki waved his fists and shouted, 'It's she, it's she! She's a promiscuous bitch and she stole from me.' I finally began to realize what had happened; I couldn't believe a madman would accuse himself falsely, but Wolf Krishki is in his late sixties, after all. Anyway, I unlocked Elke's room and went in with the rag collector. Elke was tired and hoarse from screaming day and night, and she had been quiet for the past few days. But as soon as she saw the rag man come in, she started screaming again. 'Help! He's a demon, a devil! I don't want to have a bastard by a devil!' And Wolf Krishki stamped his feet and said that she'd enticed him into her room while we were working in the fields and had stolen his velvet waistcoat."

Gavriel Levin pointed his finger at a couple of the Valkenik merchants. "You're the guilty ones! You came to Dekshne to tell me it was the yeshiva student who had made my lodger pregnant."

"We're perfectly innocent," the merchants answered. "We heard that the Dekshners were saying they suspected the yeshiva student and we went to the village to find out if it was true."

"Yes, that *was* the way it looked." Gavriel Levin's wife spoke up. "Elke Kogan didn't love her husband, and maybe that's why she went crazy after giving birth. When her husband and son came to Dekshne she was terrified of them, like a frightened animal. She liked the yeshiva scholar even though he was sloppy and had a beard. She always stared at him with her hands folded and her face shining. And when the misfortune occurred, she shouted after him, 'My bridegroom, why are you running away?' Who could have known?" Gavriel's wife concluded. "Elke didn't remember who had made her pregnant until we let the rag collector into her room."

"But rabbi, it's your fault too," one of the Dekshne farmers said, approaching Lipnishker. All the colonists had come to town with Gavriel Levin because they wanted to apologize to the yeshiva scholar. "We asked you if you'd seen anyone coming into the Levin house and you said no. Why didn't you tell us you saw Wolf Krishki around sometimes? You have the reputation of being able to tie all the Talmudic tractates together in one interpretation, quicker and better than a woodsman ties logs onto a raft on the river. Couldn't your sharp brain tie the madman Wolf Krishki to Elke Kogan? Didn't it ever cross your mind?"

"No, it never crossed my mind," Sheeya Lipnishker gasped, still looking up in gratitude to the Divine Providence who had saved him. "It's true that the sick man with his bundle of old clothes used to stop me and ask if the owners were at home or out in the fields, but it never occurred to me to suspect Wolf Krishki either before or afterward. I must admit that I was ready to do myself harm, but I didn't do it because then everyone would surely have said I was the guilty one. I might have disregarded what people would say and taken my life anyway, just to be rid of all these troubles, but I didn't want to commit suicide because I didn't want to lose my share in the world to come."

10

ONCE AGAIN Yosef Varshever took to wearing his light topcoat with its turned-up velvet collar as he had before his wedding. Pale, with blue circles under his eyes, he sat in Reb Avraham-Shaye's sun-flooded room, his thin hands and small chin shivering with cold as if he were outside on a chill wintry day.

"Reb Tsemakh Atlas has spread it around that I break my word," Yosef Varshever was saying, "because I didn't marry the yeshiva kitchen girl. But Reb Tsemakh himself broke an engagement to a girl even though he had signed a contract. And he doesn't get along well with his wife, either; she's in Lomzhe and he's in Valkenik. What right does he have to inform on others, especially when I was never formally engaged to the cook and never promised her anything? What is your decision? Will you give me a letter of recommendation to the Yeshiva Council so that I can be sent abroad as a fund raiser?"

Knowing that he was alive by the grace of God to study Torah and hence obligated to rest and guard his health, Reb Avraham-Shaye Kosover had developed the ability to ignore things that would cause him anguish. He had often heard hints about the rosh yeshiva's troubled family life, but he hadn't wanted to know more about it. Suddenly his heart turned against the principal. Yesterday evening Reb Avraham-Shaye had sat up till late at night—the tip of his nose pale, his lips dry—listening to Chaikl's account of the Sheeya Lipnishker frame-up. He realized that Reb Menakhem-Mendl had not come to him for advice or help because he knew from experience that the rabbi would side with Tsemakh Atlas. Reb Avraham-Shaye felt a pang of guilt. He himself did nothing for the yeshiva, but he was preventing the dismissal of the man who stood on the sidelines while his beth medresh was being destroyed.

"Why did Reb Tsemakh Atlas break his first engagement? And why isn't his wife with him?" asked the author of *The Vision of Avraham*.

Gedalya Zondak's son-in-law jerked forward, beside himself with anger, and said, "That tattletale Reb Tsemakh Atlas is much more practical than I. He realized early on that his prospective father-in-law wouldn't pay him the promised dowry and that he could get a prettier bride. So he married a free-thinking beauty who was richer. First he followed her ways and then, when he needed to lord it over students again, he left her. I didn't leave my wife a couple of months after my wedding. Will you give me a letter of recommendation?"

But from the sharp flash in Reb Avraham-Shaye's eyes, Yosef realized that he had not yet convinced him; he added tearfully, "My boor of a father-in-law says that if I can't become a religious functionary, i should become a merchant. Lord of the Universe, I'm not a murderer like Cain, but like him I say, 'My punishment is greater than I can bear.' And are people forbidden to trust me just because I didn't marry the kitchen maid?"

"I don't understand why being a traveling fund raiser is better than being a shopkeeper. An emissary is rarely at home, and you've just married." Reb Avraham-Shaye spoke softly so as not to excite the young man even more.

"A fund raiser comes home for the festivals, like Azriel Weinstock, the son-in-law of the local slaughterer. He's also an emissary for a big yeshiva," Yosef replied, his thin, bony knees trembling nervously in his narrow trousers.

"You shouldn't imitate anyone. Everyone should go his own way, but the Torah has to be the guide." Reb Avraham-Shaye went over and lay down on his cot. Frowning, he spoke in a cold, stern voice. "I know nothing about the income or expenses of the yeshivas of Mir, Kletzk, and Radun. It would therefore be downright foolish for me to suddenly intervene in money matters and write letters to get a new person hired. In any case, it's a hard way to earn a living and not an honorable one, unless it's done solely for the sake of heaven. There is no lack of traveling emissaries—they all go to the same places and compete among one another—and often the result is a desecration of God's name. Moreover, you have to be an expert at collecting money. A man who is shy, too gentle, or too excitable can't accomplish very much. One failure is enough to make the institution that sent him out dismiss him at once. Besides, no yeshiva would send out an inexperienced emissary. And according to the law, a young man must not seek a livelihood that separates him from his wife."

Yosef Varshever was somewhat aware of all this. Even if they hired him, could he be sure they would send him to Amsterdam or London, like Azriel Weinstock? They might assign him to beg for money in the poorest villages of Lithuania. Azriel Weinstock wasn't living in clover either. Never mind that he was sly enough to act innocent—if you spat in his face, he'd say it was raining—he'd still had to stay at home after Passover because of a quarrel with the yeshiva he worked for, and he might have to stop traveling altogether.

"So, then, it looks like I'll have to become a merchant—a

shopkeeper—as my father-in-law wants me to be." Yosef looked as if he were about to cry.

"I've already told you that I don't see why being a shopkeeper is worse than being a public servant." Reb Avraham-Shaye rose from the cot to bid farewell to his visitor and wish him a happy and healthy new year.

During the private talk in the rabbi's room, Chaikl had had to wander about in the courtyard. Finally Yosef Varshever left, and Chaikl gazed after him contemptuously. As a youth Yosef Varshever had minced along rubbing his chin into his velvet collar. Now he walked with hunched shoulders and coughed nervously.

At three that afternoon another guest arrived. Chaikl spotted Yoel Uzder from the veranda and said to himself, "The Sedate Mind has come!" At the beginning of the summer, people in the yeshiva had debated over why Reb Avraham-Shaye had taken Chaikl Vilner as his pupil. Yoel Uzder had replied, "It's quite simple. Reb Avraham-Shaye Kosover has to have an assistant—a youngster to sleep in his room and carry his towel to the river." Sheeya Lipnishker's view was even more acerbic: "Never mind Reb Avraham-Shaye's intentions and never mind whose pupil Chaikl Vilner is—he's still a complete ignoramus! He doesn't even know five hundred pages of the Talmud by heart." Since he had recently disparaged Chaikl Vilner in public, Yoel Uzder now called him Reb Chaikl and begged him to ask his teacher's permission for a consultation on a very confidential matter.

When Yoel was seated in Reb Avraham-Shaye's room, he frowned his vertical frown for a long while, as he did when considering a loan. Finally he decided to reveal the secret. "When I visited you after Lag B'Omer, you asked me why I hadn't married. So now, in mid-Elul, I've come to answer that question. I'm about to become engaged to a Valkenik girl, the cook at the yeshiva. No one in town knows yet, and if they find out, everyone will be amazed. Even the bride and her mother didn't want to believe me because they'd had a bitter experience with another ben Torah. Since the bespoken girl's mother is a poor widow, discussions about the size of the dowry or the number of years of free board would be superfluous. And there's certainly nothing to talk about as far as family lineage is concerned.

Nevertheless, after thinking about it for several months, I've come to the conclusion that it would be a good thing."

"Is this the same girl who's supposed to have been Varshever's fiancée?" Reb Avraham-Shaye asked.

"Varshever's was the younger of the two sisters; mine is the older. I wouldn't take the younger before the older," Yoel Uzder answered, amazed at Reb Avraham-Shaye's knowledge.

Reb Avraham-Shaye, on the other hand, was amazed at something else. "I've heard that you haven't married because you're afraid you might be deceived. Why are you suddenly taking the daughter of a poor widow from an undistinguished family? It seems to me that a ben Torah must think about status to some extent because he himself is not a wage earner, and parentage is as important as the person herself."

"Of course I think money and familial lineage are important too," the old bachelor replied, "as long as I know that I'm not being deceived. But in most cases people who marry do get deceived. For example, instead of taking the cook's younger daughter, Yosef Varshever married the rich Gedalya Zondak's daughter—and that marriage has failed miserably. Even Reb Tsemakh Atlas once had to break an engagement. And as careful as I've been, I once had to break an engagement too."

"What's going on here?" Reb Avraham-Shaye's face flamed with anger and embarrassment. "Is it possible that yeshiva scholars who talk all the time about self-sacrifice for God and friends do not realize how much desecration of God's name, how much humiliation and anguish they cause by breaking an engagement? Yosef Varshever broke one, Reb Tsemakh broke one, and you too?"

"My fiancée was a bit deaf," Yoel justified himself. "Why didn't I notice this earlier? Because I don't hear too well at a distance myself, so it took me a while to find out that my fiancée had a defect. What's more, Reb Tsemakh's situation and that of Yosef Varshever are not alike. There's just no comparison. People say that the rosh yeshiva learned after the contract was signed that his father-in-law wouldn't give him the dowry or the few years of free board that would have enabled him to study—and that the man was simply a very difficult person. Reb Tsemakh was even less successful with his second match, even though his wife is wealthy and has other qualifications." Yoel Uzder paused. "In any case, I've been eating in the yeshiva kitchen for almost a year now, so I know that my betrothed is a quiet dove who feels she's second best because her younger sister is more popular. But the fact that the Valkenik boys aren't attracted to her is not a flaw in my eyes, but an attribute. I've saved some money and she doesn't seem to be a spendthrift, so after the wedding, God willing, I'll continue my studies in a yeshiva for married students, accompanied by my wife, may she live and be well. And if I can't do that, I'll open up a shop in Valkenik and become a merchant."

Reb Avraham-Shaye smiled; his cheeks bloomed and his eyes shone. If he hadn't been so ashamed to display his feelings, he'd have kissed Yoel Uzder for his candor and integrity. He escorted the future groom to the gate and pressed his hand.

"If you marry or sign the engagement contract before I go back to Vilna, I'd like to come to the celebration."

On his way back to the village Yoel Uzder walked with his usual measured stride. He was perspiring in his stiff hat and double-breasted jacket with its shoulder pads. He frowned again, his throat swelling with strain. Why had Reb Avraham-Shaye invited himself to the engagement ceremony? "For two reasons," Yoel sang out gaily. "One, the author of *The Vision of Avraham* wants to come to my engagement to do me honor; and two, he wants to see if I have chosen well."

11

WHEN IT COMES TO MAKING A MATCH, Reb Avraham-Shaye thought after Yoel Uzder had gone, very few yeshiva students are careful not to humiliate a Jewish girl. That evening he did not study alone or with his pupil. He went to bed early but couldn't sleep. His usual ability to dismiss a thought that pained him was of no avail this time. The two young visitors earlier that day, and his thoughts about his imminent return to Vilna for Rosh Hashana, forced him to reflect on his difficult life at home. Here at the resort only his sister knew why he grew more dejected and withdrawn day by day, but Reb Avraham-Shaye didn't discuss the matter even with her.

Because he'd had heart trouble even as a youngster and because the doctors hadn't expected him to live, his family had considered every day of his life a miracle. As he grew older his parents, both from rabbinic families, began considering a proper match for him. In addition to his heart condition, the youth was also extraordinarily pious. Finding a bride for a young man like him was always difficult, especially if the family sought a girl who would also be a provider, enabling him to continue Torah studies. The bride-to-be his family found was indeed expert in business, pious, good-natured, and devoted. But immediately after the engagement his family concluded that they had made a mistake. The fiancée wasn't merely several years older than the twenty-year-old bridegroom, as they had been told; she was almost twice his age. Moreover, she came from a rather ordinary family, and her father didn't possess even a third of the promised dowry. Reb Avraham-Shaye's family asked him to return the engagement contract but he pounded his fist on the table: he would not humiliate a Jewish maid. If she was indeed that much older, then her humiliation would be all the greater. And so they married.

The morning after the wedding, his bride donned a big heavy marriage wig and began calling her husband "my old man." Yudis toiled in the shop and was constantly concerned about his health. She never dreamed of asking why she had to work so hard and be a poor cloth merchant when great yeshivas were inviting her husband to be their principal. When Reb Avraham-Shaye came to help her during a market day, she would tell him to return to the beth medresh. Yudis wanted him to sit and study and let her wait on him. Instead of delighting in her husband's growing reputation, she complained angrily to his intimates that his fame was taking him away from her. Once when a respected visitor said, "Rebbetsin, do you at least realize that Reb Avraham-Shaye is a world-famous gaon?" Yudis quickly wiped the smile of joy from her lips and responded, "We're poor plain people, thank God for that. The main thing is that my old man is healthy." But when a woman customer would prattle, "I hear that your husband is a fine scholar," Yudis would shriek, "I hate fishwives, especially a boot-licking fishwife. Didn't you come here to buy cloth for a dress? Buy it and go in good health!"

Reb Avraham-Shaye gradually grew accustomed to his wife's boisterous, uncouth ways, but not to the way she dealt with people. He wasn't eager to have guests, though he received them graciously and sometimes considered it his duty to give advice or make a rabbinic decision. But the rebbetsin wouldn't let visitors approach him. If her husband insisted, she would slam the door so loudly after the guest's departure that Reb Avraham-Shaye would tremble and say, "He'll think you could hardly wait to get rid of him. Don't do that any more." Once her textile wholesaler came to her and said softly, "I can't wait any longer. I have to pay taxes and I'm actually cutting my profits to the bone. I know your husband's a saint and so you'll pay the . . ." The creditor didn't have a chance to finish because Yudis shrieked at him, "Who's asking you if my husband is a saint? Get out of here! Get out!"

"What are you afraid of?" Reb Avraham-Shaye implored her. "Why do you carry on like that if someone says I'm a saint? Let them say it. They won't cast an evil eye on me by saying it."

On the other hand, Yudis would welcome a Torah scholar as a Sabbath guest. She would continually remind him to eat and not be ashamed to help himself. And while she was welcoming him, she would bang the plates, clack her heels, and incessantly ask which dishes he liked, how his wife cooked, and if his children were a joy to him. Reb Avraham-Shaye's face would burn with anguish, and after the guest had gone he would plead with her, "Couldn't you see that our guest was in delicate health? He may have a weak stomach and can't eat much. But because you were so insistent, the man didn't want to insult you and ate more than he should have. Another thing, don't ask a guest too many questions about his wife and children. Perhaps his children don't give him any pleasure, and if you ask the same question over and over again, you may force him to lie or even drive him to tears."

Yudis, however, had neither the ability nor the patience to be so perspicacious and careful. "If you're ashamed of me," she replied, "don't invite any more guests for the Sabbath."

On another occasion, when he again asked her to be more affable with visitors, Yudis exploded, "I know your family didn't want you to go through with the marriage. You married me out of pity. You never loved me the way a man loves a woman."

To give him a respite from his valorous spouse, the rabbi's sister Hadassah stayed at the summer cottage with him until the eve of Rosh Hashana. But as the day for returning home drew near, Reb Avraham-Shaye would sigh more frequently and think: Too late. He was too old to regret not wanting to humiliate a Jewish girl in his youth. In her own way Yudis was a saintly woman, even though it was very difficult for him to live with her and he still felt no great fondness for her. Each time he heard about a ben Torah who had broken a match, he shuddered. From his own experience he knew why this was happening among scholars. Marriage brokers arranged the matches, and bride and groom had very few meetings before the engagement. It took time to discover that one's fiancée was ill suited or that her family's financial condition was not sound. But the justification used by an average youth could not be used by a Musarist. Was Reb Tsemakh Atlas a money man? Would Reb Tsemakh Atlas break an engagement for fear he wouldn't be paid his dowry?

Reb Avraham-Shaye didn't hear himself moaning aloud. Chaikl awoke from a light sleep and blurted out, "What's the matter, rabbi?" He always thought of Reb Avraham-Shaye as "rabbi" but had never before addressed him that way. Chaikl assumed that Reb Avraham-Shaye wouldn't be pleased to hear this even from his own pupil.

"It's nothing. The *yetzer ha-ra* is warning me that if I fall asleep, I might oversleep the time for reciting the Shma Yisroel." Reb Avraham-Shaye chuckled softly and told the story about a man who had come to a rabbi with a question: "What's to be done, rabbi? I can't sleep a wink all night out of fear that I may miss the time for reciting the Shma." The rabbi answered, "Your *yetzer ha-ra* is keeping you awake at night so you'll fall asleep in the morning and miss getting up for morning prayers. That's the *yetzer ha-ra*'s Shma!" And the rabbi ordered the man to stop reciting the bedtime Shma altogether until his fear went away. "The moral of the tale," said Reb Avraham-Shaye, "is that in matters pertaining to heaven, just as in matters pertaining to earth, we have to live according to preset laws. If one is overzealous in sacrificing oneself for another person and does so at an inappropriate place, one may very well turn cruel when compassion and pity are required."

Reb Avraham-Shaye fell silent and his thoughts again returned to Reb Tsemakh Atlas, who had terminated a match because of money. Chaikl couldn't go back to sleep either. No matter what kind of story Reb Avraham-Shaye tells, he thought, there's always a moral to it—and somehow that makes me very gloomy.

Reb Avraham-Shaye was lying on his back. His beard, golden blond by day, sparkled with gray and silver in a net of cold moonbeams, like the bark of an aspen tree. Through the window the wind blew clusters of wilted leaves, redolent with a damp autumnal fragrance. Chaikl inhaled the fresh raw wind and wished the room were filled with a whirlwind of twisting, turning leaves, but he was also afraid the rabbi might catch cold.

Chaikl got up and closed the window, then went back to bed and said to his teacher, "Ever since the vacationers went home and left the summer cottages empty, I've been thinking every night before I go to sleep that the forest is sad at being all alone. It doesn't know what to do with itself."

Reb Avraham-Shaye was silent for a long time. Then he answered with a smile in his voice, "You're even more imaginative than I thought. You often say things that sound like my little nephew Berele, but nevertheless you've toned down and have become more mannerly."

Gray clouds stretched across the sky. The room grew dark. Then the clouds dispersed, and in the light of the emerging full moon Chaikl saw the trees on the hill across the way. They were like giants with upraised hands. A stampede of clouds came again, looking like watery creatures with enormous heads. They floated from one end of the world to the other, bringing secrets to Him who sat on His throne in the celestial heights.

"As you told me last night, Chaikl, the people of both Valkenik and Dekshne deny that they started the rumor about Lipnishker. It seems logical that the townspeople wouldn't falsely accuse a saintly scholar, and even the village Jews wouldn't talk that way about a man who came to teach them Torah. But on the other hand, there's no doubt that somebody did this with malicious intent. Have you heard who it might be?"

"On the way back from visiting my father I went to the yeshiva and heard that everyone suspects the head of the library, a former ben Torah who talked the yeshiva boys into reading secular books."

"After tomorrow morning's lesson, go into town and find out what's been happening." Reb Avraham-Shaye fluffed up his pillow in the hope that it would help him fall asleep. "Since there are forces in Valkenik working against the yeshiva, I'm afraid we haven't seen the end of this."

Chaikl laughed and began chattering briskly, as if it were midday. "Yoel Uzder is nicknamed 'the Sedate Mind.' A year ago last winter Yosef Varshever borrowed one and a half zlotys from him which he still hasn't repaid. Yoel Uzder maintains that Varshever borrowed the money without intending to pay it back, just as he never had any intention of marrying Leitshe the cook, pockmarked Gitl's daughter." The pupil prattled on but Reb Avraham-Shaye was silent, as if he were already asleep. Varshever, he reflected, should not be put into a position where he might be tempted; he should not be trusted with other people's money, especially yeshiva funds. But Yoel Uzder was honest and upright. A smile flitted across Reb Avraham-Shaye's tightly closed eyelids, a sign that there was still light behind them, just as the sky is blue and clear above a bank of clouds.

12

SROLEYZER THE BRICKLAYER undertook the job of burning the forbidden books. Saturday night after Havdala, Reb Hirshe Gordon gave him an advance payment.

Early Sunday morning, Tsemakh could not sit still. He longed for company. However, he noticed the opposite of what he had expected.

A holiday mood reigned in Valkenik. Everyone was delighted at the Dekshne farmers' glad news that the yeshiva scholar was absolutely innocent. All day Sunday and Monday the men stood in the synagogue courtyard, faces glowing, discussing the miracle. The women wiped their eyes, overjoyed that the Almighty had saved the saintly man. "We ought to fall down at his feet and beg for forgiveness. We ought to blow the dust off the chair he sits on."

In the beth medresh the younger students surrounded the prodigy, patting his back and consoling him. This time he didn't chase them away, and he kept turning toward the Holy Ark to thank the Creator for helping him in his hour of need. Reb Menakhem-Mendl bustled about, beaming, driving his students to the Talmud. "Enough; you've wasted enough time." He didn't want to take notice of Reb Tsemakh Atlas. The students didn't speak to him either, because they had sensed that he no longer cared about the yeshiva.

Confident that Sroleyzer had already done the deed at the library and that it was too late to change his mind, Tsemakh raged silently, feeling increasing contempt for all those who supported Lipnishker today, whereas they'd been openly hostile toward him yesterday.

The local people were saying that the frame-up against the yeshiva scholar had been concocted by Meyerke Podval of Panashishok. The congregants asked the library supporters, "How is that troublemaker Meyerke any better than an anti-Semite who stirs up the blood libel?" His friends looked for Meyerke, but there was no trace of him. He didn't come out of hiding until Tuesday, whereupon the youths met him and said harshly, "We suspected you the night you came and told us the news about Dekshne. Now we want to debate the subject of whether we can use immoral means in the fight against the common enemy." The spokesman, naturally, was Moshe Okun, the beanpole with the dangling paws, cadaverous face, and cold, bulging eyes.

"Fine, you raggle-taggle intellectuals," Meyerke replied, obviously still angry at his failure to destroy the yeshiva. "I'll come and debate tonight." Since the librarian hadn't shown up Sunday or Monday, the library remained closed. The empty shelves were first noticed on Tuesday night when the building was opened for the debate. The group stared silently and blankly at Meyerke; for a long while he couldn't comprehend what had happened either. Then he had an idea.

"The enemy isn't as finicky in his means as you raggle-taggle intellectuals. Come; I'll show you who did this."

Sheeya Lipnishker was once again studying diligently, and so were the students. Sheeya's ordeal and his saintliness had dampened their desire for secular books. Regretting all the time they had wasted with nonsense, the yeshiva boys sat elbow to elbow, swaying over the Talmuds. The congregants also chanted along sweetly, swaying over their holy books; as Rosh Hashana approached, Jews left their little shops more often and spent more time in the beth medresh.

Suddenly the library gang burst in. Meyerke Podval stormed in first, followed by all the other youths, like a pack of wolves jumping a fence and heading for a flock of huddled lambs.

Meyerke Podval stopped next to Sheeya Lipnishker. "He's the one who did it," he panted.

The students and congregants formed a protective ring around the prodigy and listened as Meyerke cited evidence that Lipnishker had taken the books from the library. "After he returned from Dekshne, he threatened the younger students in the yeshiva kitchen, saying that he would tear up the forbidden books they were reading. And since he was later accused of the crime with the Dekshne woman, he stole the books to have his revenge."

Tsemakh, who had not left the yeshiva for the past two days, saw the look of anguish returning to the persecuted ben Torah's face.

Reb Menakhem-Mendl made a disparaging gesture. "How could Lipnishker alone have carried out an entire library?"

To which Meyerke Podval responded, "You helped him! You were the one who dragged the books the yeshiva boys were reading out of their boxes. You—and that mad scholar!" Protected by friends and older congregants, Sheeya looked toward the Holy Ark with a mute cry: Whence cometh my help?

"Where are the books?" the library group shouted. "Did you hide them or tear them up? Speak up, fanatic, or we'll tear you to pieces!"

Tsemakh, in his corner, wondered why no one was pointing at him.

"Watch the door," Meyerke Podval shouted to his friends, "Don't let any of these students out. I'm going to get the rabbi." He left with two of his colleagues.

The youths surrounded the doorway and blocked the students' path. The congregants around Lipnishker shrugged and returned to their books. But Reb Menakhem-Mendl and ten brave young students didn't leave Sheeya. Artisans and shopkeepers began to stream into the beth medresh for the Evening Service, and word of the new scandal quickly spread through Valkenik.

When Kreyndl Vorobey came home that evening, she said exultantly, "It's the yeshiva boys again!"—and reported what had happened. Reb Shlomo-Motte had noticed that Kreyndl's anger at Chaikl made her increasingly angry and acerbic toward the yeshiva boys, but this time the old maskil also flared up against the rabbinic establishment and, leaning on his ivory-headed cane, left for the beth medresh.

Just then Chaikl arrived from the forest and heard the uproar in the beth medresh from Synagogue Street. He went in and found his father standing behind the pulpit. Reb Shlomo-Motte looked down to the corner of the eastern wall. There stood the principal, looking like a deaf mute who sees a commotion around him but doesn't comprehend it.

Meyerke and his troop returned with the rabbi. From Reb Mordekhai-Aaron Shapiro's hunched shoulders and pious grimaces one might have thought that he had come to eulogize a great saint and that the black-decked coffin containing the deceased already rested on the pulpit table. In his heart the rabbi again cursed the day he had left Shishlevitz and chosen a village where there were new disturbances every day, but outwardly he proceeded through the crowd with the doleful ecstasy of a preacher famous for his ability to weep. He approached the prodigy and began questioning him about the missing library.

Sheeya Lipnishker burst into tears, as he had during his first ordeal. The irascible rabbi immediately lost his temper. "What kind of shlimazel are you? Wherever there's trouble, you're in the midst of it."

Then he turned to the library supporters. "Are you stupid or just crazy?" he yelled. "Aren't the persecutions he's already suffered enough for you?" Then he pushed his way to his seat next to the Holy Ark, determined not to intervene any further.

The older congregants caught the rabbi's words and also attacked Meyerke. "You vicious sinner! The Dekshne frame-up didn't satisfy you, did it? Now you're starting a new one."

Moshe Okun nodded once, a sign that one had to deal fairly, even with an opponent. "He's religious—let him swear he didn't touch the books."

The crowd shouted its approval. "That's right! Let him swear before the open Holy Ark, in the presence of the Torah scroll, that he's not guilty. During the Dekshne incident he wanted to swear, but they wouldn't let him. Now we'll let him, and everyone will believe him."

Sheeya seized the back of the bench with both hands to keep himself from being dragged to the Holy Ark. "I will not swear," Sheeya said, still weeping. "Before, I was prepared to take an oath so I wouldn't be suspected of sinning with a married woman. But since one must not take an oath even for the sake of the truth, Divine Providence came to my aid and I wasn't allowed near the Torah scrolls. Do you expect me now to take an oath, this time just because of some filthy books? I didn't touch those heretical books. I don't even know where the library is, but I won't take an oath over those silly storybooks under any circumstances."

Meyerke Podval, the former yeshiva student, understood Sheeya's point and smiled slyly. But since the library group hadn't studied Torah, they crowed: "Aha! If the scholar isn't taking an oath, that shows he did it." Even some of the Valkenik Jews didn't understand why Sheeya refused to swear. Like a ship listing in a storm, the entire beth medresh bent to the side of the library crowd. Young people shouted, "Of course he did it!" and old people groaned, "What misery! What a misfortune! Since the yeshiva came to town we haven't had a day of peace."

With the weekday curtain over the Holy Ark, the bare tables, and the worshipers in their work clothes, the dim room looked like a crowded fairground. The Jews of Valkenik knew that Sabbath was the day for controversies in shul. On the Sabbath everyone had time, people were rested, and for a day they put aside their concerns about livelihood. But everyone was annoyed by this feud on an ordinary Tuesday night in the month of Elul, while the scent of autumn rains hovered outside and the wind blew at one's neck and worries gnawed at one's mind.

A young man beat his breast with a bony fist and screeched, "My money; my blood; my books! I don't give a damn about that madwoman from Dekshne, but I pay monthly dues at the library and my greatest joy in life is to read a book on the Sabbath. Now they've taken that away from me. I don't care if the world turns upside down. Those books have got to be found!"

"For doing such a thing the yeshiva boys' veins ought to be

pulled out one by one, measured by the yard, and thrown to the dogs," an older man with a trim mustache sang out pleasantly, eyes sparkling.

"Call the police!" another yelled. "If this pack of God's thieves can steal books, we can inform on them and have them locked up."

"We don't need the police. We'll kill them ourselves. We'll break their ribs and crack their skulls," the library group answered, and they lunged toward the students.

Tsemakh saw the library youths tearing the Talmud out of the yeshiva students' hands and yelling, "You took our books; we'll take yours!" A tall youth grabbed Reb Menakhem-Mendl by the beard and shouted at him, "Where are the books, you old goat? I'll cripple you." Reb Menakhem-Mendl, his face pale, looked at the young man and kept silent. Meanwhile, Meyerke Podval and his gang were besieging Lipnishker, who was protecting himself with his prayer stand and shuddering.

Tsemakh sauntered out of his corner, both hands outstretched; he shoved Meyerke Podval to one side and the roughneck who had hold of Reb Menakhem-Mendl to another. The principal's height and distraught look momentarily confused the group. His face looked like a sharpened ax. "Don't you dare lift a hand!" he roared, and went up the steps of the Holy Ark. The tumult in the beth medresh subsided into a restrained murmur, and finally there was silence.

Then Tsemakh Atlas called out loudly, "I did it. Not Sheeya Lipnishker and not Reb Menakhem-Mendl. None of the Torah scholars had anything to do with it. No one even knew that I took the books out of the library and burned them."

A cool wind blew through the beth medresh. It was as though the silence had turned to ice, covered the walls, frozen the chandeliers. Faces lengthened in astonishment. The first to recover from the shock was Meyerke Podval.

"Who helped you? You couldn't have done it by yourself. Where did you burn the books? Tell us where and how you burned the books."

The principal was silent. Tsemakh's pale face and his black eyes like two open cellars made the crowd feel ill at ease. The worshipers exchanged glances, wondering if he was sane. Reb Yisroel the tailor approached the Holy Ark, his head and his white beard trembling.

"You're just trying to take the blame, Reb Tsemakh. You didn't do it."

Cries of support came from the crowd. "He wants to save the culprit, so he's putting the blame on himself."

"I swear I did it, and I wouldn't swear falsely! I did it because the library had become the source of evil here, a den of iniquity for all the heretical youths." The principal pointed his long hand at Meyerke Podval. "This sinner and corrupter lured the younger yeshiva boys into reading secular books and then made false charges against Lipnishker because he had repulsed him. I said to myself: I'm going to pluck out the evil by the roots. The truly pious and upright people here will rejoice, and those who support that spoiled brat from Panashishok can rise up and stone me."

"But he still hasn't said who helped him." Meyerke laughed brazenly. "I'll tell you who helped him. It was Hirshe Gordon! Hirshe Gordon has always said that the library should be burned down. But even his one and only son Baynish secretly borrowed books from me until his father found out. I know he found out. So he teamed up with the yeshiva principal to steal the books and burn them."

The congregation looked around the beth medresh. Indeed, Reb Hirshe Gordon hadn't shown up for the Evening Service. As the folk saying went, the cat knew she'd licked the cream—the guilty party wasn't there. Tsemakh came down the steps from the Holy Ark and the congregation began to seethe again. The principal was a stranger in Valkenik, yet he lorded over them as if he were at home.

"Well, what do you say about your Reb Tsemakh Atlas now?" Reb Shlomo-Motte turned to his son. "As soon as I got here and took one look at him, I saw that burning a library befitted him. That's the end of the Valkenik yeshiva."

Despite Chaikl's anger at his father for his remarks about Reb Tsemakh, he realized that Reb Shlomo-Motte had predicted correctly.

"Beginning tomorrow morning," one of the library supporters told the congregation, "there will be a twenty-four-hour guard at the door of the beth medresh to keep the yeshiva students out. Hirshe Gordon won't be permitted to come to pray either, not in midweek and not on the Sabbath. What's more, we're going to picket his textile shop so that not one customer will set foot in it."

13

A DELEGATION from Valkenik consisting of Reb Mordekhai-Aaron Shapiro, Reb Menakhem-Mendl Segal, Reb Yisroel the tailor, and Eltzik Bloch was sitting at the table in the courtyard of Reb Avraham-Shaye's cottage. Chaikl looked through the window and saw how agitated the rabbi was: he had left his visitors and was pacing in the yard. He walked back and forth, hands folded on his chest, head back, as if longing for cold raindrops from the cloudy sky to cool his thoughts. Actually, the rabbi was musing, there was nothing to think over. His visitors had told him that virtually all of Valkenik sided with the young people who were keeping the yeshiva students out of the beth medresh. There was only one solution. Nevertheless, Reb Avraham-Shaye wanted to calm down and delay his response for a while lest his visitors think that his decision was made in haste or anger. He also wanted to understand why the principal had propounded the idea and committed the deed. But he could come to no conclusion about that and, instead of calming down, grew more agitated.

He went back to the table with quick steps and told the visitors, "Chase him away. That's my advice and my position. Tell him that he is no longer the rosh yeshiva and that he must leave Valkenik at once." The author of *The Vision of Avraham* turned to Reb Yisroel. "And you tell him that he can no longer live in your house. Give him a day to pack and move out."

The Valkenik rabbi was quick to approve. "But I'm not sure," he added, "that this won't lead to an even worse quarrel. Some of the congregation still side with Tsemakh Atlas. Wouldn't it be better to talk things over with him peaceably and advise him to leave for his own good? Besides, there's no guarantee that those devils from the library will let the yeshiva boys into the beth medresh even if the rosh yeshiva *is* driven off. They're demanding new books."

Reb Avraham-Shaye blushed, as he always did when he heard someone voicing opinions that weren't honestly felt. The Valkenik rabbi, Reb Avraham-Shaye thought, was the first to speak out against Reb Tsemakh at the beginning of the summer. The rabbi ought at least not pretend to be a compassionate man now.

"Indeed, the community *should* replace the destroyed library," Reb Avraham-Shaye replied. "Such measures must not be taken against nonbelievers nowadays; it only increases the hatred and obstinacy of the freethinkers. If new books are bought and the person responsible for the fire leaves town, the library group will leave the yeshiva students alone."

Reb Menakhem-Mendl and Reb Yisroel were dejected; they realized that Reb Avraham-Shaye wanted to save the yeshiva, but they didn't have the heart to dismiss the founder of the school. Even the Mizrachi leader Eltzik Bloch wasn't overjoyed at Reb Avraham-Shaye's decision, even though the principal's deed was altogether improper. "Everyone says that my brother-in-law, Reb Hirshe Gordon, had a hand in the fire and that he won't let any new books be bought," Eltzik Bloch said.

"Public opinion is against him, and there's no need to consult him," Reb Avraham-Shaye cut in sharply.

"Reb Hirshe Gordon has said publicly that as far as he's concerned I'm no longer the Valkenik rabbinic authority." Reb Mordekhai-Aaron groaned, plucking a hair from his beard. "Assuming the principal leaves," he asked plaintively, "who will help Reb Menakham-Mendl run the yeshiva? Surely he can't manage it all alone."

Knowing that the Valkenik rabbi wanted to place his son or son-in-law in the yeshiva, Reb Avraham-Shaye shrugged impatiently. "Who says that Valkenik has to have a Navaredker yeshiva with a principal who delivers Musar talks? The older scholars have no business remaining here at all. Lipnishker should be told to go, and the sooner the better. After all his anguish and humiliation here, Valkenik is no longer the place for him. Valkenik should have a preparatory yeshiva for beginners and for those in the first stages of independent study—and for such a school you already have a rosh yeshiva, Reb Menakhem-Mendl. Incidentally, it's high time the community brought Reb Menakhem-Mendl's family to Valkenik. He'll teach the more advanced students, and Yoel Uzder could teach the younger pupils. He's an honest, pious man and a great scholar, and he's just become engaged to the older daughter of the widow who cooks for the yeshiva. Very few Torah scholars would have taken such a poor bride. Yoel Uzder, then, should remain in the yeshiva and teach the youngest students. This would also be a way to compensate the widow for the disgrace she suffered when another ben Torah backed out of the match he had made with her younger daughter. And with her son-in-law teaching in the yeshiva, the cook would treat the students as if they were her own children."

The Valkenik rabbi drummed his fingers on the handle of his cane. His watery eyes flashed. Neither my son nor my son-in-law, he thought, but Yoel Uzder. Reb Mordekhai-Aaron Shapiro chewed the edge of his beard until he had chewed up and swallowed his anger. He didn't want to argue on this point in the presence of the other men.

The next moment Reb Avraham-Shaye suddenly put an end to the conversation. "If the honorable gathering will excuse me, I can't spend any more time with you. My health won't permit it." And he quickly went up on the porch of his cottage.

The visitors realized how upset their host must be, not to escort them to the gate. The first to make his way across the courtyard was Reb Mordekhai-Aaron Shapiro, waving the cane he was holding behind his bent back. Reb Avraham-Shaye speaks with such authority! he thought. Who does he think he is, Maimonides? Moreover, Reb Mordekhai-Aaron had to listen to Eltzik Bloch's asinine musings and remain silent.

"No doubt about it," Eltzik Bloch was saying enthusiastically, "Reb Avraham-Shaye is a distinguished man. You can see that he doesn't like those wild fanatics. But our vacationing rabbi is also a decent man. Did you hear what he said? According to him the library books should be replaced."

Behind them walked Reb Menakhem-Mendl, who was extremely depressed. It was certainly high time for his wife and little son to come to Valkenik, but God was his witness that he didn't want to prosper at the expense of his old friend's downfall.

Reb Yisroel the tailor trailed behind them all. His head and beard were quivering and his eyes were full of tears. He and his wife had come to love their lodger like a flesh-and-blood son. Reb Tsemakh had always been exceptionally gentle and kind to them. He never made any demands and constantly expressed his gratitude for everything. Living under the same roof with him wasn't very cheerful, since he was always deep in somber thought, but by the same token how on earth could he have suddenly done a thing like burning the library? And how, Reb Yisroel thought, can I bring myself to tell Tsemakh to leave?

"I told them to send him away!" Reb Avraham-Shaye shouted as he entered the house, and he immediately went to lie down in his room. His sister Hadassah had been looking through her bedroom window, watching the commotion in the courtyard. Now she entered her brother's room and bent over him anxiously. Chaikl too looked on in fright as the rabbi gasped for breath. His brows, his chin, the corners of his mouth, and his mustache were trembling.

The rest of that day and the next morning Reb Avraham-Shaye lay huddled on his cot. He looked into a holy book, but did not see the script before his eyes. Downhearted because the rabbi had ordered the principal to be sent away, Chaikl dolefully waited for the day he would return to Vilna. He was sick of the fading forest and the overcast sky. Milk-white mists rose lazily, followed by gray autumn clouds that slowly crawled up the sky. Suddenly a thick, slanting rain began. It cut the air like a scythe and then stopped at once. Even when no rain was falling, the trees—a smear of darkness—oozed huge leaden drops, sighing silently. Even if the sky clears, Chaikl thought, the summer is over.

Thursday at noon Reb Avraham-Shaye's sister came into his room, bent over him, and whispered. He shivered and replied aloud, "No, tell him I can't see him." When Hadassah hesitated in confusion, Reb Avraham-Shaye shouted to Chaikl, "Tell the rosh yeshiva I can't receive him. Go tell him right now!" Chaikl, not daring to say a word, left the rabbi's room. Hadassah followed and went directly into the children's bedroom.

Reb Tsemakh Atlas was standing just outside the front door, looking like an impatient creditor made to wait at the threshold. "The rabbi can't see you now," Chaikl stammered.

The principal looked at him in astonishment, as if incredulous that the Vilna youth had the nerve to transmit such a reply. He pushed Chaikl aside and entered the house.

In spite of the weather Chaikl turned up the collar of his jacket and left for the village. He was deeply angry with the rabbi for having forced him to tell Reb Tsemakh what his own sister, the mistress of the house, had lacked the courage to say.

Tsemakh had expected the Valkenik Jews to oppose him, but he hadn't expected the Valkenik rabbi to inform him—and with such a pitying look, too—that Reb Avraham-Shaye had ordered him to leave town forthwith. His landlord Reb Yisroel groaned out similar tidings, and his friend Reb Menakhem-Mendl avoided him altogether. Tsemakh saw that his support among the few congregants who had sided with him was crumbling. But he didn't want to leave Valkenik rejected by everyone. At the beginning of the summer Reb Avraham-Shaye had quietly thrust him aside from the yeshiva, and now, to top it off, he was ordering him sent away. Before he left, he wanted to tell that saint a thing or two!

Reb Avraham-Shaye's unwillingness to receive him irritated him even more, and he tore into the rabbi's room with a shout: "You've ordered me driven out of my yeshiva, but you're afraid to face me. I've been more devoted to Torah than those who write new Talmudic interpretations and listen to the world singing their praises from a far-off corner. Who appointed you my judge? And how could you possibly have rendered judgment before you heard me out?" Tsemakh sat down on the bench opposite the scholar as if to show how little he cared that he was an uninvited and unwelcome guest.

The rabbi did not hide his displeasure. His face sad, he answered coldly and slowly, "Your burning the library books has led to a desecration of God's name and has also placed the yeshiva in great danger."

"I burned the books because the freethinkers had spread the poison of heresy among the yeshiva students and falsely accused Sheeya Lipnishker," Tsemakh said, his hands gripping the bench between his outspread knees.

"You used a fire to stop the students from reading secular books and to demonstrate Lipnishker's innocence?" Reb Avraham-Shaye stood up, his eyes smoldering. "First of all, you should have gone to the village where the incident occurred and investigated on the spot. If you had done that, perhaps the real culprit would have been discovered a few days earlier, and you wouldn't have had to burn the books. But you didn't go to the village, and you didn't even conduct an investigation in Valkenik. First you completely neglected the yeshiva for a long time; you went into seclusion as if you were about to receive a new Torah. Then you suddenly jumped up and burned the books. And finally you heroically admitted before the Holy Ark that you had done the deed—you, the leader and rosh yeshiva. That's why I don't believe you did this to keep the Torah students from reading secular books or to defend Lipnishker. The actions of a truly zealous believer will cause sanctification and not desecration of God's name."

Tsemakh watched Reb Avraham-Shaye pacing around the room. Indeed, he thought, frowning, why hadn't he gone to Dekshne to investigate the matter? Then he replied, "I didn't need proof that Lipnishker was innocent. After one look at the poor boy, anyone would have come to that conclusion. But the Valkenik congregation *wanted* Lipnishker to be guilty. They wanted him to be the sinner because they begrudge him his Torah and his saintliness. That's why they didn't let him talk Sabbath morning in the beth medresh."

"Nothing of the sort! They didn't let him speak because they were afraid it would drag out the service and their cholent would get cold." Reb Avraham-Shaye laughed and continued pacing. "The Musarists' method of imputing who knows how much evil to all man's thoughts and deeds is false from beginning to end."

The rabbi's criticism stung Tsemakh like nettles. He replied, "I have no respect for the crowd either, for the mass that moves back and forth capriciously, now with one side, now with another. Still, I wouldn't accuse a congregation of Jews of not wanting to listen to a persecuted man because they consider a warm cholent more important than the truth. I don't have *that* much contempt for people. But I demand as much from others as I demand from myself. The chicken that's unkosher for me is also unkosher for others."

"The way of the Torah is to be strict with oneself and lenient with others," Reb Avraham-Shaye interrupted him.

"And I believe that just as we mustn't demand *more* of others than of ourselves, we can't demand *less* of them than of ourselves." Tsemakh leaped up, blocking Reb Avraham-Shaye's path at the doorway. "If an upright man doesn't insist that his friend be upright, he shows his lack of concern for his friend. He is smugly delighting only in himself and his own good deeds."

Reb Avraham-Shaye let his path be blocked. Just as he would not respond to some lout in the market place, he did not reply to Tsemakh. Tsemakh knew that any Torah scholar who heard him talking this way to Reb Avraham-Shaye Kosover would say he was unworthy of being a rosh yeshiva. As far as the library was concerned, he realized that he had failed miserably; he should have left Valkenik months ago, and spared himself the ignominy of having to leave with everyone considering him a malefactor. But Reb Avraham-Shaye Kosover also wanted to show him that his entire way of life was false, that his thoughts were twisted and his acts foolish. Tsemakh let his anger drag him down like a whirlpool. He seated himself on the bench at the table and pointed at Reb Avraham-Shaye, who had stopped in the middle of the room, half facing him and listening.

14

"YOU COMPLAINED that I neglected the yeshiva and spent a long time in seclusion, as if preparing myself to receive a new Torah. Well, that's your way of making fun of me. But it was you who drove me to my seclusion. It was you who drove me from the yeshiva. When I first visited you, you said I shouldn't give any more Musar talks because they might lead the students to heresy. And while I sat in forced seclusion in the women's gallery of the Cold Shul, I thought of another recluse who voluntarily and joyfully hides from people. And that freewill recluse, that hidden, holy, pure man teaches Torah solely for its own sake; he prays with his head toward heaven and thinks high-flown thoughts like an angel. Why should he pursue honor that might flee from him when he can flee from honor and have honor pursue him? He dwells in his summer cottage, knowing full well that beyond the forest the entire world sings his praises because he doesn't intervene in controversies, speaks no evil of others, and doesn't assume the role of a leader. He knows that he loses nothing by being easygoing. And so he becomes an even greater saint and an even more humble man. He is severe with himself but lenient with others. He knows how popular one becomes by being strict with oneself and lenient with others. He speaks out against evil but doesn't single out the evil-doer—and that lets everyone assume that the saint isn't referring to *him*. Everyone kowtows to that lover of peace and pursuer thereof because no one can stand a contentious man who, besides having a penchant for quarrels, is also on occasion a bewildered soul. Yes, one must admit that because of the never-ending battle against falsehood, one's rationality and common sense go awry. But the saintly gaon who lives behind the forest never founders on that problem. He immediately gauges public opinion and decides that the principal should be expelled because that's what the town rabbi wants, that's what the congregants want, and that's what the masses want."

"It's not true!" Reb Avraham-Shaye's lips were white. "I'm not interested in pleasing the local rabbi or the Valkenik congregants. But I realized that as long as you remain in town, the library faction will harass the yeshiva. So I ordered you to be dismissed to preserve a place of Torah learning. Your trouble is that you're too full of Navaredker distrust. You always look for the taint of ulterior motive, the sin of selfishness. But the Omniscient and the Torah trust man more than a Navaredker Musarnik. The rabbi can decide for his rebbetsin whether her Sabbath chicken is kosher nor not, and the Torah doesn't suspect a conflict of interest and hence lenience. A rabbinic judge is even permitted to sit in judgment in a dispute involving a man he likes and another he dislikes. As long as there is no suspicion of bribery or of open hatred on the judge's part toward one of the litigants, the Torah trusts him to deliver an honest decision. But if we see Satan in everything and everyone, and if we live with the assumption that man must not trust himself or his friends, then we nullify every judgment and every court of law, even the great Sanhedrin. By so doing we destroy the order of the whole world. It's as if we're living in a fog. You don't see your neighbor; you don't see your own threshold; you don't even see yourself. And you, Reb

Tsemakh—your entire existence has been built upon presumption of guilt. When Lipnishker wasn't permitted to talk, your interpretation was that an entire congregation of Jews wanted a ben Torah to have committed the sin of adultery. You say that I'm a recluse to gain popular esteem and that I ordered you dismissed from the yeshiva to impress your opponents. Well, as Scripture states, let my soul be to all as dust—but in regard to the yeshiva, I realize more than ever that you must not deliver any Musar talks, precisely because your style and language please the youngsters. I often hear you talking through Chaikl; he is still more your pupil than mine. I have also heard from Chaikl the exhortations you've recently delivered. When you were here at the beginning of the summer, I advised you to be more prudent in your talks to the students. And what did you do? You withdrew from the yeshiva altogether and stopped looking after the students because it was beneath your dignity to be prudent. You are a terribly proud man, Reb Tsemakh."

Reb Avraham-Shaye fell silent for a moment. He gazed sternly at his fingertips, as was his habit when he was upset. Then he approached Tsemakh Atlas and, head bent, said as if sharing a confidence, "You may continue telling me everything you think of me and say anything that's on your mind. Meanwhile, let me ask you a question about your home life. I don't usually ask personal questions, but tell me, why did you leave home? Couldn't you get along with your wife? Or was there another reason?"

"You want to know if I also had quarrels in Lomzhe? Yes, in Lomzhe too! I became a partner in my wife's family's store and couldn't bear the hypocrisy of the middle-class merchants' world. Our worst battle was over an orphan housemaid who was made pregnant by my older brother-in-law's son. My wife's family wanted to get rid of the maid—they wanted to send her away to have her baby in a gentile village. I defended the orphan, and things became so ugly that I had to leave home. If I didn't act correctly and according to the law, tell me, and I'll return to Lomzhe and reconcile with my brothers-in-law, and I'll feel good, very good!"

"You were right, not your brothers-in-law. But you should not have left home." Reb Avraham-Shaye was silent again, weighing the facts he had just learned. Then his face flamed and his eyes pierced Reb Tsemakh. "I don't understand you. At home you fought for a suffering orphan. And Chaikl told me that you also stood up to the drunken Vova Barbitoler when he humiliated his wife before the congregation and that this sparked the bitter enmity between you. In Valkenik you rebuffed a ben Torah for breaking his promise to the yeshiva cook and marrying a richer girl. And yet you too broke off a match over a dowry."

His head spinning, Reb Avraham-Shaye went back to his cot to rest. Tsemakh realized that Yosef Varshever had been here complaining about him and that Reb Avraham-Shaye had listened to even that miserable creature's complaints against him.

"Suppose *you* had found out after your engagement that your father-in-law wasn't going to give you the promised dowry, and that, moreover, the bride wasn't suitable either; would *you* have married the girl?"

"I did," Reb Avraham-Shaye said, his lips dry. He had never before discussed his difficult home life with anyone. Now, however, he felt that he must talk. But since he didn't have the strength to tell exactly how he had been deceived, he merely mumbled, "After the engagement I too discovered that the match wasn't right for me and that it would cause me lifelong suffering. That's precisely what happened, and I'm still suffering—but I'm not sorry that I didn't humiliate a Jewish girl, and I don't regret marrying her."

Reb Avraham-Shaye lay huddled on his side. Tsemakh Atlas bent over him, silent. He felt a paralysis in his feet, knees, abdomen. He sensed that if he didn't leave at once, the paralysis would reach his chest and stop his heart. He went to the door, watching his footsteps as if testing his feet.

At the doorway he heard Reb Avraham-Shaye's voice pleading, "I tried to protect you as long as I could from the people in Valkenik and also from the Vilna tobacco merchant. He spent a night here, and I persuaded him not to cause you any humiliation. But now I think it would be better for you to leave; better for the yeshiva and better for you. Go home."

Tsemakh did not reply. He went out, took two strides, and stopped in the middle of the courtyard. Large raindrops splashed noisily on the bare table and the two long, narrow benches. A shudder ran through him. He imagined that the bright raindrops on the table were from Dvorele Namiot's eyes, tear-filled as they had been when he went into her shop in Amdur and told her he was leaving. Tsemakh stood still and felt his coat becoming drenched with raindrops . . . from Dvorele's eyes. . . .

Reb Avraham-Shaye's sister watched him through the window, then went out on the porch with an umbrella and smiled amiably at him. Instead of returning for the umbrella, Tsemakh left the courtyard, but when he crossed the path to the forest, he stopped again. Heavy drops fell from the pine trees, sounding like sobs—like a dejected heart freeing itself of choking sighs. In the gloomy silence a pine cone occasionally thudded to the ground and a handful of needles dropped from a branch. A long-legged bird with a stiff tail fluttered from tree to tree. Erect and wide-eyed, Tsemakh listened to the stillness of the thick autumnal woods as if waiting for an echo.

Chaikl came up the path from the village, chilled, soaked, and vexed that he had dragged himself off to town and back in such bad weather. A shiver of fear ran through him as he saw the tall, black-bearded principal, looking like a forest sorcerer who has suddenly made himself visible.

"Vilner, today I discovered that Reb Avraham-Shaye is an even greater man than he is thought to be. But as I've already told you, he is not the teacher for you. Go to a yeshiva." Reb Tsemakh strode on, and Chaikl silently watched him disappear among the trees.

When Tsemakh emerged from the thicket, night was falling. At the point where the forest ended—near the bridge and the first group of houses—a fluttering shadow approached. It was a woman—Ronya. From her window she had seen him on his way to the forest at noontime and had realized at once where he was going, because her family had talked about the principal whom Reb Avraham-Shaye had ordered dismissed. Shortly thereafter, Ronya had left the house and hid behind a clump of trees until she saw him returning, whereupon she ran to him, crying, "Tsemakh!" And although he remembered that she was a married woman and that he had moved out of her father's house because they were a temptation and a danger for each other, he could not push her away.

"Go home; you shouldn't be seen with me," he implored, looking with anguish at her small, tear-stained face encircled by a kerchief.

"I don't want you to leave." Ronya pressed against him. "I'll be happier if you stay in Valkenik, even though you haven't visited us once since you moved into the tailor's house—not even to see how my children are. You never came," she sobbed. "Why did you have to do that to the library and make enemies of everyone? I know what a pure and proud man you are. Pure and proud and good."

Tsemakh knew he shouldn't permit such intimacy, but he longed for the sympathy of at least one living soul. His beard touched her wet cheek; his voice sighed with the sadness of an autumn wind among dying leaves.

"Don't say I'm pure and good. I'm a lost soul." He looked about in despair, as if he regretted that he had tormented himself to overcome his desire and now wanted to lie down with her on the soaked earth. Her small palms pressing his chest, eyes half closed and lips parted, Ronya too sank into a mute, pained ecstasy, as if waiting to claim her lost happiness. Soon his powerful arms would lift her and put her down somewhere, anywhere, even on the wet grass—if only he would warm her frozen limbs and make her sleep. Tsemakh felt the numbness in his body melting. A sweet intoxication dizzied his brain. The temptation was returning. He gasped a final farewell and almost ran toward the village. He knew that Ronya was still standing at the edge of the forest, watching him with her tear-stained face. But as in Amdur, when he had told Dvorele Namiot that he was leaving and had left quickly, trying not to see her tear-filled eyes, now too he was afraid to turn around.

15

ON FRIDAY MORNING the rosh yeshiva disappeared. Carrying a small bundle under his arm, he left his room, thanked his landlord and landlady for their hospitality, and departed before they could say a word. He said good-bye to no one else, and he left most of his possessions behind. None of the local carters took him to the station.

The memory of the tall, black-bearded principal walking across the empty fields to the train station with his bundle under his arm remained with the villagers for a long time.

After Tsemakh's disappearance the library group disbanded the guard in front of the beth medresh, and the yeshiva students resumed their praying and studying. But the library demons still forbade Reb Hirshe Gordon to enter the beth medresh and kept their pickets in front of his shop in the market place. Jews didn't try to go in, and the peasants were afraid of being attacked. The pickets knew that Hirshe Gordon wouldn't ask the police for help—he didn't want to be called an informer. Local residents were openly delighted at his downfall; it was as if they were getting revenge for all the years that everyone had made obeisance to him. Even the congregants in his ultrareligious faction spurned him.

Reb Hirshe had not expected to be barred from the beth medresh. Moreover, he was becoming impoverished. Soon he'd be bankrupt. The townspeople stood around his store encouraging the youths who prevented customers from entering: "Serves him right! He burned the books we bought with our hard-earned pennies. Let him pay for it now. When it hurts his pocketbook, he'll realize what he's done." But Reb Hirshe's worst hell was at home. His wife was silent; she looked pale and apathetic. His daughter Tsharne came to meals with red, bleary eyes and was ashamed to show her face outside. Baynish wouldn't leave the house either, and he coughed as if his father had damaged his lungs. When Baynish coughed, Hirshe saw his wife and daughter staring at him as if he were a monster; they were delighted that all of Valkenik was against him. "As the Prophet says, 'A man's enemies are the men of his own house,' " he muttered to himself. If things went on this way, he'd have to run away to Valkenik too.

Reb Hirshe went to Sroleyzer for advice. "How can I get rid of that boycott? Did you by any chance save any of the books?"

The bricklayer looked at him coldly and said, "If you double what you paid me to take the books away, I'll take them all back to the library. Not a page will be missing." Reb Hirshe assumed that the fence was pouring salt on his wounds, but Sroleyzer wasn't joking. He spoke plainly, and he meant business.

When the bricklayer found the key that fit the library lock and dragged the books off in bags to burn them in his brick oven, he had decided at the last minute: No rush! Starting trouble with those leftist brats wasn't the same as leading a cow out of somebody's barn. The gang might very well send him out of his house feet first. Keeping the merchandise in the bags for a while would be better. If anyone discovered that he was the culprit, he'd return the books willingly and wash his hands of the affair. He'd decide what to do only when he was sure he wasn't under suspicion.

As it turned out, not even the young crooks in his gang who watched him carefully suspected he'd had a hand in the business. The bricklayer had coolly watched the uproar in town and had thought of a profitable venture. Why should he burn the books when he could take a few at a time to Vilna and sell them to a book dealer? Then Sroleyzer examined the stolen merchandise and was stunned. Every flyleaf and every tenth page was stamped in large letters with a big round seal: The Folk Library of Valkenik. Well, that finished that. No bookseller would touch this merchandise. Burning was the only solution. But that was no good either. People would ask why smoke was drifting up to the sky from his oven. Sroleyzer had forgotten that he'd stood up for the honor of the holy Torah and that on the Sabbath of Consolation, he'd had a bloody fight with the heretics. Now he wanted to suggest to them that if they gave him adequate compensation for his trouble, he would look for the lost books. But on the other hand, how could he be sure the library group would pay him for his labors? And if he fleeced Hirshe Gordon, people would say that he couldn't be trusted. But when Reb Hirshe came crying for help of his own accord, Sroleyzer realized that he could be a nice fellow and at the same time earn a pretty penny. Reb Hirshe would pay through the nose.

The bricklayer went up and down the village spreading the word that he had saved the library and telling how he had done it. "One Saturday night Reb Hirshe Gordon rushes into my place all in a stew and says that he and the principal, that chap with the turned-in eyes like the Angel of Death, want the library burned. I saw right away that I was dealing with a couple of loonies. If I had refused them, they would've hired a gentile or started the fire themselves. So I pretended to agree and took the books from the library, thinking that I'd return them when the fuss was over."

Overjoyed at finding the lost books, the library youths clapped the fence on the back and raised him onto their shoulders like a rabbi on Simkhas Torah. "Music! Music! We'll return the books to our library with music." The only unhappy person was the librarian, Meyerke Podval of Panashishok. He would have believed anything except that Sroleyzer, that underworld character, had had a hand in the theft. The pickets were removed from Reb Hirshe Gordon's shop, and he was allowed to go to the beth medresh. But no one paid any attention to him. He had lost his prestige.

Eltzik Bloch rushed to the vacation cottage to tell Reb Avraham-Shaye that the yeshiva's existence was assured for the coming semester. Reb Tsemakh's involvement with the bricklayer had astonished Eltzik Bloch more than Reb Hirshe Gordon's participation. Had Reb Tsemakh Atlas banded together with a gangster to uphold the honor of the Torah? Since the day when the rosh yeshiva had visited him, Reb Avraham-Shaye had been ill—he even prayed in bed. As Eltzik Bloch spoke, Reb Avraham-Shaye sat up, his tallis over his shoulders and his eyes becoming sharper behind his glasses. Even after Eltzik Bloch's departure, Reb Avraham-Shaye's eyes blazed with anger. His voice cracking, he told Chaikl, who was suffering in silence for the principal:

"People like Reb Hirshe Gordon make local rabbis weep bitter tears. Reb Hirshe Gordon doesn't stop to wonder if his zealousness stems from anger or envy. And the Musarnik Tsemakh Atlas, who negates even self-sacrifice if it has a trace of ulterior motive, cooperated with Reb Hirshe Gordon. Well, at least Reb Hirshe is a scholar and a distinguished townsman. But how could a yeshiva principal have joined hands with someone who makes a living from thievery? Reb Tsemakh thinks he has to tell everyone the whole truth even if he has to quarrel with everyone. No man can live entirely without friends. And he who rails against good people because he can't tolerate their minor sins will end up befriending people who do great wrongs. Therefore Reb Tsemakh teamed up with the leader of a group that uses brute strength and even knives."

Chaikl imagined that the rabbi, with his curly beard and pointed nose, wrapped in his tallis and wearing his high skullcap, looked like some big bird in a tree. Even though his birdlike countenance seemed calmer and happier than Tsemakh's, he was in fact much stricter and more severe than the principal. Chaikl couldn't forget Reb Tsemakh's parting words: "Reb Avraham-Shaye is an even greater man than he is thought to be, but he is not the teacher for you." Chaikl had reported this to his father when Reb Shlomo-Motte was in the horse-drawn wagon on his way to the Valkenik station. The old Hewbrew teacher had turned to his son. "In that, you see, the mad Musarnik is right. He knows you better than your present teacher." Just then Freyda Vorobey had stuck her head out the window to wish her lodger a good trip. She was ashamed to go out to say good-bye in person because her only pair of shoes was worn out.

After his father's departure, Chaikl had no further reason to go to town. He even got sick of wandering about in the forest blowing the shofar. And so, bored to death, he sat in the cottage looking out the window as if it were a prison. Low-lying clouds swept by one after another. Occasionally a spurt of rain came, but stopped at once, never developing into a storm. On such wet and gloomy fall days the rabbi's sister didn't like staying at the cottage either, but she had to wait for her brother to become strong enough for the trip home.

On Sabbath morning a week before Rosh Hashana, Reb Avraham-Shaye went to pray with the manager's minyan at the cardboard factory. That night, after Havdola at home, he announced that he would go to the Valkenik beth medresh for the first penitential prayers. He put on a heavy overcoat and knee-length rubber boots and carried his cane. Chaikl brought an umbrella. They left the courtyard at ten-thirty, assuming that even if the walk to town took an hour, they would arrive at the beth medresh half an hour before the penitential prayers began at midnight.

16

IT WAS WINDY AND DARK OUTSIDE, but there was no rain. To keep from losing their way in the dark, the rabbi and his pupil took the wide dirt road that ran along the edge of the wall of trees rather than the forest path. They had gone a good part of the way when suddenly it began to thunder. Lightning stripped bare a chunk of sky, showing clouds pushing one another like huge fierce beasts. Increasing thunder came roaring down like boulders. Bolts of lightning flashed through the clouds every few seconds, and the whole forest was reflected in the blazing sky. A heavy, biting rain plunged down on them. Chaikl opened the umbrella over the rabbi's head, and the rain soaked through the stretched cloth at once.

"The people at the morning minyan said they would go to town for the penitential prayers, so we must go too, lest people say that we disregard the concept of praying with a congregation," Reb Avraham-Shaye murmured as he sought shelter under the trees. But the rain drenched him even through the thick pine needles, and, afraid that a bolt of lightning might strike a nearby trunk, he returned to the road. Chaikl held on to the wind-whipped umbrella with both hands. The metal supports bent, and the iron tips tore through the silk. The rain gushed in on their faces. Suddenly a lightning bolt, like a flying green snake, struck almost above their heads, and Chaikl, terror stricken, let go of the umbrella. At that moment the wind swooped it up and carried it off like a huge black bat.

"The umbrella has become a rag. It's not worth looking for. Let's go back," Chaikl panted, soaked and dripping.

"We're closer to town than to the cottage and the wind is letting up. It will stop soon," Reb Avraham-Shaye answered, lost in sad thought as if all were still and sunny around him and he were looking for an overgrown grave in the cemetery. Another flash of cold light came, and Chaikl saw his teacher standing in the rain with closed eyes, bowed submissively over his cane. It seemed to Chaikl that Reb Tsemakh too was still standing in the woods and that he had prayed for a storm when Reb Avraham-Shaye went to the first penitential prayers. Reb Avraham-Shaye knew this and received the heavenly decree with love.

The rain gradually slackened, and though lightning still cut across the sky, it was a creature that grimaced strangely with its gigantic merry face and contorted its eyes and lips, but could not scream. Teacher and pupil inched along, their sodden clothing as heavy as lead. Just after they crossed the bridge, another downpour began—heavier than before, stubborn as an overburdened heart that refuses consolation and weeps unendingly—but in the village they could find shelter from the rain. Two rows of houses stretched on both sides of the road, and strips of light edged through the shuttered windows; the residents had gone to the penitential prayers and left the lights on for their return home. Chaikl headed toward one of the houses to wait out the new thunderstorm, and Reb Avraham-Shaye followed.

In the darkness neither of them noticed that they had come to the Valkenik slaughterer's porch. From holes in the roof long jets of water poured down on them. Chaikl took his teacher by the hand and led him into the entryway. They made their way through scattered, rotting straw and inhaled a warm, moldy odor compounded of scalded milk and washed diapers. The door to the lighted room was ajar, and from the entryway they could clearly hear two women talking in the adjoining dining room. Since the men had gone to the penitential prayers and the children were asleep, the two sisters, Ronya and Hannah-Leah, spoke freely.

"Yes, I've been in love with the principal from the time he moved into our house. I've never met such a fine soul, such a heroic man," Ronya said, raising her voice. "He was always proud and sad. His head was lowered, but his shoulders were straight, never bowed or hunched. And when he looked at me, I felt a warmth all over my body. During the winter nights a year ago, when he spent all his time in the beth medresh, I would warm up his supper and wait in the passageway to the kitchen, watching unnoticed as he ate. But when he realized that I was watching, he stopped coming late at night, and I cried because he wouldn't let me serve him."

"Ronya, you've gone crazy," her older sister said softly, her voice shaking. "You're Reb Lippa-Yosse the slaughterer's daughter; you're a married woman and the mother of little children. What sort of madness has taken hold of you? I saw what was going on inside you, even though you didn't say a word to me. That's why I thanked God when Tsemakh moved to the tailor's house. You yourself said that he didn't even come to visit us all the time he was living at the tailor's and that you rarely saw him, so why are you complaining because he's left town?"

"As long as I knew he was here I felt good, even though he didn't visit us. Now my life has become empty." Ronya burst into tears that seemed to echo the autumn rain outside. "It's lucky that my husband isn't at home. I couldn't bear to look at Azriel now. I always see

Tsemakh before my eyes. What a comparison—Tsemakh and Azriel!" She burst into bitter laughter. "My darling husband, the father of my children, an emissary for the yeshiva, has a mistress. Everyone in town knows that he plays around with women abroad, and Father has gathered this too. Father says nothing, but I see him looking at me and hear him moaning over my misfortune. But Tsemakh, that beautiful, heroic man, is faithful to his wife. I know this better than anyone. I know even better than his own wife how honest and how faithful he is to her. She's a clever woman, his wife, and beautiful too, but I hate her. When she came here last winter, I liked her. Perhaps deep down I didn't like her then either, but I forced myself to like her. I thought she had come to settle down here—and who am I, a stranger . . . I wanted Tsemakh to have a beautiful, intelligent wife, a woman who was devoted to him. But when she left him here to fend for himself and went back to her rich family, I began to hate her and think of her as a pampered beauty. Now the victory is hers. Now he has gone back to her in defeat. She loves him—I saw that she loves him—but still she didn't want to tear herself away from a comfortable life and be the wife of a poor, small-town yeshiva principal. I hate her! Why does she deserve a man like that? Why?"

"You'll wake the kids with your yelling. Talk quietly," Hannah-Leah pleaded. "You know how I suffer because of my shlimazel. Still, before God and man Yudel is my husband and the father of my children. But you; the dybbuk's come into you, God save us. We're on the threshold of the Days of Awe; tonight the first penitential prayers are being said. Your old father is crying his eyes out, praying for a good year, and you have such sinful thoughts. Don't stain your young years with sin."

"My young years are wasted anyway, so I don't care if I stain them with sin. The day before he left I saw him passing on his way to the forest. I realized he was going to see that harsh rabbi who ordered him dismissed from the yeshiva and driven out of town, and I went to the woods and waited till he came back. I pressed close to him without caring what he thought of me. Let him think ill of me; let him think I'm dreadful. But there was such sadness and goodness of heart in his gaze, I'll remember it to my dying day. But he remained faithful to himself; he pulled away from me and ran."

"The devil take my enemies! God help us all! Someone could have seen you. Maybe you *were* seen! You're a lunatic!" Hannah-Leah clapped her hands. "You've changed. You don't resemble my little sister Ronya any more. You used to giggle with embarrassment when a man looked at you; you blushed like a little girl. Now you've become shameless. What did you see in him? What people say is true: he's a mad Musarnik. Did you ever in your life hear of a yeshiva principal hiring a thief and a fence to burn books? No wonder the vacationing rabbi ordered him dismissed from the yeshiva and evicted from his lodgings. Our father, and our boarder Reb Menakhem-Mendl, and all the good people in town consider Reb Avraham-Shaye a wise and holy man. They say that if the principal hadn't been turned out, there wouldn't be a yeshiva in Valkenik by now. Perhaps the principal isn't a bad man, but he's reckless. I'm sure he doesn't get along with his wife either, because he's hotheaded."

"What does the vacationing rabbi—or any of you—know about Tsemakh?" Ronya asked, her voice cracking, hoarse from weeping. "Does the rabbi know that Tsemakh invited my sweet husband to teach in the yeshiva? Azriel told us this when he was at home for Passover. He couldn't understand why the principal wanted to engage him. Even you and Father didn't realize why Tsemakh had done this. But I understood that he wanted to hire my husband, and even give him some of his own wages, so that Azriel would stop traipsing around and I wouldn't be alone. I like him despite his rage and his wanting to burn the books. He couldn't keep silent when the scoffers from the library framed Lipnishker. And I even like him for the way he left town carrying his own bundle. I like everything about him." Ronya began sobbing again, as if the well of her tears had been replenished with the autumn rains. "Who is that rabbi who had such a noble, gentle man driven out? And if he is indeed such a great saint, as people say, he should have known that he was ruining my life."

Throughout all this Reb Avraham-Shaye stood with bowed head, listening. Hearing the last words, he slipped out of the entryway and stepped off the porch into the rain. Chaikl followed, but he wasn't aware of getting drenched until minutes later, because he was so intoxicated by the strange, sweet sadness Ronya's words had evoked in him. He wouldn't have been able to resist temptation with Ronya, he thought, and this made him ashamed in the presence of the rabbi. Yet he was glad the rabbi had heard the stringent criticism of him for having driven the principal away.

They turned into Synagogue Street and went toward the beth medresh, which lighted their way with the misty glow of all its lamps. Through the windows they saw a large congregation. Their heads were raised, and their tears and moans gradually increased in volume. The penitential prayers had begun, but Reb Avraham-Shaye chose to remain in the courtyard.

As the ice-cold water poured down from his hat brim onto his face, he repeated with stifled sobs the words of the *baal tefilla* who was standing before the Holy Ark, "Cast us not away from you, and remove not your holy spirit from among us."

Chaikl was much affected by the downpour and the darkness, the men weeping in the beth medresh, the rabbi's tears here, and Ronya's in her house. He shivered with cold, dampness, and despair, but he clenched his teeth and kept still. He felt that the rabbi's compassion for the woman was greater than his anger with her for desiring a man not her husband. In his mind's eye Chaikl saw Reb Tsemakh's shadow still roving about in the slaughterer's house, in the Cold Shul, and in the forest opposite the rabbi's cottage; he imagined that Reb Tsemakh too was praying in this great storm, this incessant downpour. "Cast us not away from you, and remove not your holy spirit from among us."

17

TSEMAKH ARRIVED in Amdur, near Grodno, still carrying his bundle under his arm. He stood on the narrow street, the only one in town, and gazed at the semicircle of houses as if he had come to the second semicircle of his life. Reb Avraham-Shaye had sent him to Amdur. The rabbi had charged that he, who demanded honesty from everyone and came to the defense of humiliated women, had himself broken a match and humiliated a Jewish girl over a dowry. Tsemakh was therefore going to Lomzhe via Amdur to learn what had happened to Dvorele Namiot, after which he planned to return to his wife and try once more to lead a quiet middle-class life.

He found the inn where he had stayed two years ago. Tsemakh reminded the innkeeper who he was and asked for a room. The owner, Reb Yaakov-Yitzhok, a man with a large elf-locked beard and tufts of hair in his ears, lifted his shoulders piously and asked, "Have you come again to found a yeshiva?"

"I'm no longer establishing yeshivas." Tsemakh smiled sadly. "I've come to find out about Reb Falk Namiot's daughter. We were once engaged, remember? Has she married?"

When the innkeeper opened his toothless mouth, his mustache looked like tangled weeds at the mouth of a cave. He coughed several times and croaked inaudibly, as if waiting for the questioner to forget what he had asked.

"Did she marry or is she still a maid? Tell me," Tsemakh demanded, feeling a pressure in his chest.

"How should I know?" Reb Yaakov-Yitzhok blinked foolishly. "We heard that later on you married in Lomzhe, so you're apparently either divorced or a widower now, God forbid, and you're trying to rearrange that match."

"I'm neither widowed nor divorced." Tsemakh felt a stab in his heart. He was not divorced from a woman—but a whole town had expelled him. "I made a good match, but my life has become miserable, and that's my punishment for having shamed my first fiancée. I came to apologize to her, and I'm prepared to compensate her father. But first I must know whether she is married."

The innkeeper blinked even more furiously and bleated, "I don't know what's happening at Falk Namiot's. And anyway, it's strange that it took you so long to remember to apologize to your ex-fiancée. Did you see her in a dream?" The innkeeper suddenly went into raptures. "Ay-ay-ay!" he cried, smacking his lips. "What a preacher you were. If you preach again, the beth medresh will be overcrowded. But don't ask any more about Namiot or his daughter, because everyone will think it's very strange. And now, if you'll excuse me, I'm very busy." And the innkeeper hurriedly left the room.

In a town this size, how could the innkeeper not know whether Falk Namiot's daughter is married? Tsemakh wondered. Evidently something has happened there that the man doesn't want to discuss. Tsemakh had to sit down. The ceiling and the walls were spinning before his eyes. He ought to go to an Amdur family that didn't know him and calmly ask about the grocery woman, Dvorele Namiot. That was the only way he would hear the truth. But Tsemakh felt that he could neither play games nor wait another moment. He had to know everything now. He decided to disregard the difficulties and go to Namiot's house. He hurried out of the inn to avoid having regrets. Tsemakh recalled the disagreeable silence in Namiot's house, but had forgotten what it looked like from the outside. He wandered about in front of the row of houses, unable to recognize Falk Namiot's. Local people watched him from the porches and the shops, evidently aware of who Tsemakh was and whom he was seeking. A little girl wearing her mother's kerchief and big, unlaced shoes stood between two puddles of water and gazed inquisitively at the stranger.

"Do you know where Reb Falk Namiot lives?" Tsemakh asked her.

"Right there! That's where that old cutthroat lives." The little girl pointed to a house and jumped away.

The house was shuttered and the door closed. Falk Namiot has surely gone to Grodno, as he did two years ago after the engagement ceremony, Tsemakh thought happily, breathing freely now. He wanted to go back to the inn, but from all sides men and women were signaling that Namiot was at home. Their expressionless faces and finger pointing seemed to block his way. That was the moment it struck him that Dvorele Namiot had not yet married. He didn't know why he was so sure of this, but he held onto this thought to save himself from a more ominous doubt. Tsemakh rapped several times on the locked door, still hoping that no one would respond. Soon he heard footfalls.

A voice that sounded like a dry well asked, "Who's knocking?" In the doorway stood Falk Namiot, looking as he had two years ago: a long, gaunt face, slits of eyes surrounded by a net of wrinkles, a tuft of moss on his throat in place of a beard, and a bare, pointed chin.

With enormous effort Tsemakh squeezed a few words from his constricted vocal cords. "I was once engaged to your daughter. I'm Dvorele's fiancé, Tsemakh Atlas." For a minute the man looked at him dully. His eyes opened wide, his jaw trembled. Tsemakh repeated who he was and said, "I've come to apologize to you and your daughter for the suffering I've caused you. I'm also prepared to compensate you for the grief and humiliation . . ."

"Murderer!" Falk Namiot shouted with all his might. He ran out into the street and began to scream, "Look who's come! Her former fiancé! My daughter's murderer has come! He's come to apologize, he says. My Dvorele has lain in the earth a year and a half. And *now* he comes to apologize to us. That murderer doesn't even know she's dead. That he caused her death."

The old people in Amdur remembered a plague and they remembered that a wedding had once been held in the cemetery. The destruction of the Great War was fresh in everyone's memory. The village had lost people in the postwar pogroms when a new regime took over, and they remembered those who were slaughtered in the village lanes during peacetime. But never before had the Jewish settlement in Amdur witnessed such a sad and bizarre scene.

When Tsemakh heard that his former fiancée was dead, he lay down in front of her house and pressed his face into the soft autumnal earth. Falk Namiot stepped over the long, outstretched body, went into his house, and locked the door behind him. People gathered around the handsome man, begging him to rise. But he didn't move or reply. The local people stood there—dispirited, mute, paralyzed.

Falk Namiot emerged from his house with a thick walking stick under his arm, on his way to the Afternoon Service. Seeing that Tsemakh was still lying in front of his door, Namiot stepped over him as if he were a carpet. Tsemakh rose, his face and beard smeared with mud, and blocked Namiot's path. "Please forgive me," he said. Falk Namiot whipped the walking stick from under his arm and waved it over the head of the petitioner, who stood with arms slack, waiting for the death blow. But Namiot had concluded that it wouldn't be wise to kill a man, so he spat in his face and went to pray.

Tsemakh followed at a distance, then stopped outside the shul as if forbidden to enter a holy place. People gathered in knots nearby and watched; they didn't dare talk to Tsemakh. He didn't say a word either.

After prayers Falk Namiot left the beth medresh, and Tsemakh blocked his path once more. "Please forgive me." Shaking with rage,

Namiot growled and began beating Tsemakh's head with both fists. The onlookers pounced on Namiot, but Tsemakh Atlas pushed them away and waited for his opponent to continue hitting him. Falk Namiot picked up his stick and ran home, shouting, "I'll never forgive that murderer."

Tsemakh returned to the inn; the townspeople followed. He sat in a chair in the middle of the room, surrounded by the local congregants. "You're not responsible for Dvorele's death," they consoled him. "She was always sickly. She suddenly fell ill around Passover, six months after you left, and died soon afterward."

The old Talmud teacher who had suggested the match with Dvorele was also at the inn. "He was within his rights to change his mind," he called out. "After the engagement ceremony, everyone told me that the future father-in-law would renege on the dowry and the promised years of free board. I was heartbroken that I had unwittingly helped to deceive a ben Torah, and when the financé later returned the engagement contract, I felt a stone fall from my heart, even though it cost me my matchmaker's commission."

His nostrils and beard sprinkled with yellow snuff, the old teacher sneezed, attesting to the truth of his statement, and said, "It's not unusual for engaged couples to call off the match. It happens every day. People don't die from that. Dvorele died because she was sick."

The innkeeper, Reb Yaakov-Yitzhok, who had once quietly described the father of the bride-to-be to her fiancé, now spoke aloud for all to hear. "Falk Namiot is a murderer, a cutthroat. He tormented his wife to death and beat his sons with that thick walking stick until they were grown, whereupon they fled to Grodno. They never come to Amdur, and they don't let him cross their thresholds when he's in Grodno. They came only for their sister's funeral and then immediately returned. They didn't even spend the seven-day period of mourning with their father. The sons realized that he had tormented Dvorele just as he had their mother. What burns Namiot up most of all is the fact that he couldn't marry again. There was a Cossack of a woman who was dying for his money and waiting for him to marry his daughter off. But when his daughter's match was broken off, the woman spat on Namiot's hard head and set up a wedding canopy with someone else. That—more than anything else—is what's really eating him."

Tsemakh hadn't forgotten that after the engagement ceremony the innkeeper had whispered into his ear that his fiancée was depressed and submissive because her father kept her terrorized. Dvorele was somewhat sickly, Tsemakh mused, and when he broke off with her, the father must have tormented her even more because she was preventing his marriage. She must have suffered a lot and wept quietly as the life seeped out of her. Thinking this, Tsemakh shuddered and then sat as if petrified. People tried in vain to change the subject. The old Talmud teacher asked him, "Did you succeed in establishing a yeshiva in another town?" "And how is your wife and her family?" the innkeeper wanted to know. Tsemakh couldn't speak; he stared at the walls before him. The innkeeper motioned to the people in the room, and they slowly slipped out. Tsemakh continued gazing at the wall as if expecting a secret door to open soon and lead him to Dvorele Namiot's grocery. Now he understood why Dvorele had looked at him with such tearful eyes when he bade her farewell. She was bidding him farewell forever, for all eternity. She had known that he wouldn't return to her and that she would die.

18

THE CLOUDS ROSE from the cemetery like thick black smoke from hell. "He's lying on her grave," people whispered, their eyes full of tears. Amdur had hardly taken notice of Dvorele during her lifetime and had forgotten her at once after her death. But the conduct of her ex-fiancé now awoke their compassion for that sweet, gentle girl who had been cut down so young. They did not blame Tsemakh Atlas, however. "How could he have known that her father would snuff the life out of her?" the local residents said to each other, and cursed Falk Namiot.

Tsemakh lay on a damp mound of earth covered with half-withered weeds and felt that his heart was sinking into the grave. The wind whistled in his ears, pulled at his clothes, and leaped over his head like a wild animal playing with a human skull. Memories and fantasies wafted through his mind like wisps of fog. She would have been a good, faithful wife, he thought. "Tsemakh, eat your food," she would have said. "Don't spend so much time in the shop. Go to the beth medresh." If he had been a salesman in her grocery, he wouldn't have fought with the customers as he had in the Stupels' big store. In fact he wouldn't have had to be a shopkeeper at all. Dvorele would have agreed to his becoming a yeshiva principal in a village, and he would have spent his entire life there in tranquil Torah study. Such a kindly, pious soul inspires her husband to become a different person too.

Tsemakh tried to recall all her gestures and her manner of speaking. He remembered only her smooth, upswept hair and gray eyes and the smile that was occasionally childlike and occasionally very old. He had seen her only two or three times and exchanged very few words with her. Tsemakh had thought of Dvorele for a long time after leaving Amdur, and had been sorry for having humiliated her. But it had never occurred to him that her father would torment her to the point where she might die of sorrow and longing. But then he had gradually forgotten his first fiancée. During the summer in Valkenik he hadn't even dreamed of her, as if she had known in the other world that he had put her out of his mind. But now she sensed his recall of her and smiled gloomily as she had in the shop when he bade her farewell. Dvorele was not angry with him; she even forgave him. A person with such sad and kindly eyes could only forgive. But he did not forgive himself. He would never forgive himself.

Tsemakh felt himself dozing off as he listened to the whining wind that was covering him with dry leaves. Suddenly his tense body shivered with joy: a woman turned her head fetchingly; her cheeks reddened and dimples appeared. Tsemakh knew that she was smiling happily at her children because Tsemakh sat opposite her at the table. He tore himself away from the mound of earth and fled the cemetery. He didn't want to dream about Ronya on his fiancée's grave. Ronya too was a humiliated woman and he felt sorry for her, but still she was no Dvorele Namiot. No strange man would ever have been a temptation for Dvorele. She would have consented for her husband to become a recluse in a village or a fund raiser whom she would see only once every six months. How happily she would have awaited his arrival on a holiday! Woe unto him that he hadn't understood this before!

On his third day in Amdur, Tsemakh was again lying in front of Falk Namiot's house; Namiot had bolted the door and wouldn't set foot outside. He merely looked out the window once in a while with an expression of satisfied vengeance on his long, wrinkled face. The townspeople watched the young rabbi rolling in the mud and thought they would go out of their minds. Neither kind words nor angry shouts could bring him to his feet. After trying both, they charged into their rabbi's house: "Why are you watching so calmly while that old dog is sucking the life out of a Torah scholar?"

The Amdur rabbi, Reb Borukh Rubin, had a paunch under his silken gaberdine and a cold, scholarly gaze behind his gold-rimmed glasses. He was obsessed with what was appropriate and inappropriate for a rabbinical scholar. When Tsemakh had come to establish a yeshiva in Amdur two years ago, the rabbi had taken a dislike to him for his Navaredker sermons and for his hasty betrothal to Falk Namiot's daughter. Rabbi Rubin now grimaced with even greater distaste at the vulgar way the Navaredker Musarnik was doing penance. Rabbinic circles and the yeshiva world of Lithuania were already buzzing about the Valkenik principal who had ordered a library to be burned and was subsequently run out of town. The Amdur rabbi wanted nothing to do with such an impetuous and contentious man. But to prevent further desecration of God's name and to keep people from remarking that he was backbiting a persecuted Torah scholar, he didn't tell his congregation about the Valkenik incident.

"When a ben Torah comes to a town, it's common courtesy for him to visit the rabbi first to discuss Torah and to explain why he's here. Our visitor hasn't done that." Reb Borukh Rubin calmly smoothed every little hair of his softly curled beard over his neat collar. "Nevertheless," the rabbi told the congregants, "if you can manage to bring Reb Falk Namiot into the rabbinic courtroom, I'm prepared to persuade him to forgive the ex-fiancé."

The crowd surged to where Tsemakh was still lying on the ground. "Get up, Reb Tsemakh!" Dozens of hands raised him up. The people began pounding on Namiot's bolted door and calling into his windows. "You enemy of Israel! The rabbi wants you! You'll be excommunicated. We'll tear your house down. We'll smoke you out like a wolf from a cave." To show him that they meant it, they found a log and began ramming it into the locked door.

Falk Namiot ran out with a cry, tearing his hair. "It was because of that murderer that my one and only daughter departed this world."

Nevertheless, he let himself be pushed by the crowd to the rabbi's house, and Tsemakh trailed along.

In the rabbi's house the congregants shouted at Dvorele's father, "You're still sending matchmakers around to find you a young wife. Who'd want to marry a man with a heart of stone?"

"Then I won't marry, but I won't forgive that murderer," Namiot answered.

The crowd lunged at him, fists flying. "Usurer! Skinflint! No one in town will pay back a penny—not the interest and not the principal. Do you hear, you bloodsucker?"

For a moment Namiot blinked his narrow eyes in fright, then he remembered the notes and the security he held from every debtor. The threats were idle. Namiot didn't reply to them. He was as mute as a blunt ax set into a knotty log. Seeing that they could do nothing with him, the people spat in disgust.

When complete silence had descended, the rabbi turned to Tsemakh. "According to the law, you must ask for forgiveness three times in the presence of three witnesses. If the other man refuses to forgive, you have no further obligation. By what you've done, you've more than fulfilled the requirements according to the law."

"I don't want to get rid of the obligation. I'm going to stretch out in front of his threshold for weeks or months, until he forgives me."

The townsmen were terror stricken at the scenes in store for them. Namiot too shuddered in fear, realizing that he might be buried alive in his house. If that murderer stayed in Amdur and persisted in his outlandish behavior, then he, Namiot, wouldn't be able to show his face outdoors to collect his debts. For that reason he suddenly shouted for all to hear, "I forgive that murderer and I don't want any compensation, not a penny—but on condition that he leave Amdur today!"

"He's forgiven you," everyone shouted happily, as if Tsemakh had become engaged again and they were wishing him *mazel tov*.

For a moment all the faces of the crowd blended before Tsemakh's eyes. A moment later every face became three, as though he were seeing the crowd in cracked mirrors. People spoke to him, waving their hands, but he seemed to be deaf, as if he were standing by the wheels of a water mill that drowned out everyone's voice.

"Really? He's forgiven me?" His eyes burned with the despair of a sick man who awakens from a nightmare and sees that reality is even worse. The congregants exchanged suspicious glances; they wondered if he was sane. Then gradually the crowd left the rabbi's house, and only Reb Borukh Rubin and Reb Tsemakh Atlas sat at the table.

The Amdur rabbi considered himself the overfastidious man described in the Talmud: one whose life is made miserable because every unclean thing and every act of unrefined behavior disgusts him and makes him ill. Reb Borukh Rubin pulled at his long white fingers as though milking them and spoke with cold fury.

"According to the law, no one is obliged to stretch himself out on the ground to seek forgiveness. A Torah scholar must not do this even if he wants to. That's the decision handed down in the *Mishna Berura* in the name of the great medieval rabbis. As I've said, one must ask for forgiveness three times from a living person in the presence of three witnesses. A dead man must be asked for forgiveness in the presence of a minyan. But it's unheard of for a married man and a Torah scholar to lie down on the grave of his former fiancée and stay there all day. When Falk Namiot saw you rolling on the ground, he decided it was a good time to take revenge. If you had behaved in a more refined manner, as a Torah scholar should, you could have spared yourself both your own humiliation and the humiliation of the Torah. And what's more, Namiot would have forgiven you sooner."

"I didn't intend to force a pardon out of Falk Namiot. Even if he had forgiven me with all his heart, I still haven't forgiven myself. I was seeking the humiliation, not the forgiveness. And I wanted the humiliation to last as long as possible," Tsemakh said with an angry wrinkle at the corner of his mouth. He was impatient with those who had witnessed his humiliation, and he felt contempt for all of them. Before the astonished Amdur rabbi could reply, Tsemakh got up and left the house.

He went to the inn to pick up his bundle, then stopped for a minute at Namiot's home. The door was bolted and the windows shuttered;

all was blind and mute as a ruin. From all sides the townspeople watched him, afraid he might lie down at the door again. But Tsemakh strode away. Stretching out in the mud once more would have made him a buffoon in his own eyes, like Vova Barbitoler with his door-to-door begging. Tsemakh had recalled Reb Avraham-Shaye's remark that he was a terribly proud man. He had rolled in the Amdur mud to break this pride. But, Tsemakh thought, a man cannot change his character with one act of self-abnegation. In Navaredok he had learned that one must toil a lifetime to change one's character. Oh, Tsemakh Lomzher, he told himself, you'll have to roam about and suffer torments much longer before your heart breaks and you can liken yourself to the Psalmist, who says, "A broken and contrite heart, O God, you will not despise."

19

SLAVA'S HUSBAND returned home, and silence suddenly came over the spacious rooms of the Stupels' residence. At about nine in the morning, while the two sisters-in-law, Hannah and Freida, whispered in the kitchen, their husbands awaited their brother-in-law in Volodya Stupel's living room.

Volodya had become more paunchy and lazy; he dozed and yawned whole evenings away in his deep, soft easy chair. A couple of times each evening he would good-humoredly call to his wife—"Madame Stupel?"—but he had nothing else to say. Hannah knew that her husband simply wanted to know if she was at home so he could calmly continue listening to the monotonous tick-tock of his collection of large and small clocks. To avoid disturbing his repose, Volodya had even stopped worrying about Slava's troubled family life and the recent decline of his business. Last night, sitting beside his wife, he had been entranced by her big body and rosy face—still peaches and cream. Hannah too had grown accustomed to the silence of the clean, empty rooms and no longer sighed with yearning for a child. But this morning the tranquillity had suddenly vanished. Volodya sat as if on hot coals. Who could know what ill wind had brought that Musarnik back?

The older Stupel brother, Naum, had become more excitable; he shouted constantly both at home and in the store because no one paid attention to his orders. Now he recalled the troubles that his only son Lolla had caused him. And Slava's husband was responsible for that! He should have been destroyed root and branch rather than permitted in this house. After Tsemakh took up for Stasya, the kitchen maid whom Lolla seduced, Lolla had moved to Bialystok, ostensibly to gain business experience. But in fact he was roistering there at his father's expense, because his Uncle Volodya wouldn't let him set foot in the store. Naum was about to fume that he was an equal partner in the store and needed no one's permission to employ his son. Just then the two women looked in from the kitchen with questioning eyes.

Volodya rose. "It's time to go down to the store. If there had been good news, Slava would have come in to announce it."

Tsemakh was sitting in his old room, his coat on and his bundle on the floor, as if he had merely dropped in for a while. Slava sat near him, hanging on his every word. Although he looked at her, she felt that he did not see her. When he told her about the Valkenik library, she smiled to herself. All along she had been waiting for him to have a fight with the supporters of his yeshiva. But the Amdur affair made her shudder, and Tsemakh's disheveled appearance made her ask herself: Was this her husband? Perhaps she too had become an old woman in a marriage wig.

In the light of the gray autumn day Slava's smooth forehead shone dimly. Her high neck emerged full and warm from her sweater. The blond hair falling over her right temple was thick and heavy. Her cheeks were as smooth and rosy as ever; the whites of her eyes were bluish and her teeth gleamed between her fresh lips as if she had just bitten into a ripe pomegranate whose winy juice had sprayed her mouth. As far as Slava was concerned, the fact that Tsemakh's first fiancée had come to such a bitter end, should have made him glad that his wife was alive and sitting beside him. But Tsemakh looked like a man who'd been swimming for hours in icy water and finally reaches a deserted island where he can pause just to catch his breath before casting off for a distant shore.

"I've come to give you a divorce because I want to go out into the world and become a wanderer. Now that I have discovered that I was the cause of Dvorele's death, I can't lead a family life."

Hearing this, Slava felt ashamed for still clinging to him. He had never been able to treat her tenderly; nevertheless, she had always admired him for his strength and his unique personality. But now he was a broken, groaning man.

"You can't forgive yourself for what you did to the Amdur girl, but you can forgive yourself for what you've done to me. You don't care about me," Slava said, frowning.

"That's why I want to set you free—so that I won't be to blame for your ruined life too," he said.

"Is it the wrong you've committed against your first fiancée that you can't forget, or is it she herself whom you can't forget?" Slava asked.

"When I found out about Dvorele Namiot's death," Tsemakh replied as if confiding in a sister, "I suddenly realized that she had been destined to be my wife." Tsemakh looked like a mourner consoling himself by remembering what an honest, pious, and good person the deceased had been. "She had a shy smile and light gray eyes. I'll never forget the look on her face when we said good-bye. It was the look of a person who bids farewell to life. She sensed then that she would die of sorrow and yearning, but I didn't sense it."

Slava listened, her eyes blazing with azure fire. Doesn't he know, she thought, that a man shouldn't speak that way to his wife about a former fiancée? Or does he know it and not care? And how lovingly and longingly he speaks about her! Under that overgrown beard and earlocks he can still be loving and devoted. To others, but not to me.

"Yes, if you had married the Amdur girl, you wouldn't have left her. You left me because you missed her. But then again, maybe you would have left her too. . . . Yes, I'm sure you would have left her! You talk about her so passionately because she died; you can't feel that way about a living person. That's the kind of character you have. But just as your feelings of regret can't resurrect her, you can't resurrect my ruined life with a divorce. I'll think about accepting a divorce—perhaps I won't consent to it at all."

"What do you want of me?" He stretched out his hands pleadingly.

"You're still young. You'll marry someone suitable and be happy with him."

Indeed, what *did* she want of him? Nor did she know what she wanted of herself, her family, her friends. During their brief time together Tsemakh had poisoned her heart with contempt toward ordinary people. No one pleased her any more. "I don't know what I want of you," she said after thinking a long time, and she burst out laughing. Then came a torrent of words. "You're behaving like a stranger in your own house. Let me have your clothes bundle—I'll put it with the dirty laundry. Now go wash, eat, and lie down to rest. You ought to see my brothers and sisters-in-law too, or do you want me to call them in here? Don't you want to know about Stasya? In Valkenik you criticized me for not knowing where she is, and now you're not even asking about her!" Slava walked around him in her tight skirt and low-heeled slippers and told him joyfully, "Stasya and her child are living in a nearby village with Jews."

Tsemakh nodded sadly. "I defended the maid because she's an orphan—but Dvorele was also an orphan, and that I didn't want to remember. Stasya and her child are alive, thank God, but Dvorele Namiot lies in the grave."

Slava sat down opposite him. She put her hands on his knees and tried to speak calmly, soberly. "The Amdur Jews told you that Dvorele Namiot had always been sickly. Why do you want to persuade yourself that you're to blame and assume a punishment for a sin you didn't commit?"

"You're clever and gentle." A faint smile reached Tsemakh's sad eyes. "When I stood up for the pregnant maid, you didn't throw it up to me that I had behaved even worse toward my fiancée."

From his praising her and blaming only himself, Slava saw how much he had changed. She also noticed that he was affecting the characteristics of old age. He *wanted* to become a broken old man. Tsemakh retrieved his bundle from the floor and stood up.

"You probably know that my Aunt Tsertele died and that Uncle Ziml is alone. I'll stay with him until you make up your mind about the divorce, and then I'll be able to leave." In his disheveled clothes and with his bundle, Tsemakh looked like a battered wanderer.

Toward evening, when Volodya left the store and came up for supper, Slava went to his apartment. "You know," she said gaily,

"Tsemakh wants to stay at his Uncle Ziml's." She even cavorted around the room from table to table, winding Volodya's clocks, as if bent on irritating him. Volodya looked at his sister, his face aflame. Hannah too was silent, annoyed that Slava was pretending to be cheerful.

Suddenly Slava became serious and reported everything that Tsemakh had told her about his experiences in Amdur. "Now he wants to divorce me."

The story about the dead fiancée struck terror to the heart of the pious Hannah, as if at midnight she had passed a beth medresh full of the dead. But Volodya merely shrugged his broad, brick-wall shoulders.

"I thought I knew your husband, but I realize I still don't know him. He'll always dig up new ways to ruin your life and his. If he's offering you a divorce, grab it with both hands."

Slava didn't reply; an embarrassed smile flitted over her face. She went slowly back to her rooms, leaving behind a subtle, gentle fragrance like that of pale flowers at twilight.

Volodya didn't enjoy his supper that night. He twisted and turned in his deep easy chair; he didn't know where to put his huge paunch. After two hours of silence, he could no longer restrain himself, and he asked his wife, "Look, after all, you're a woman. Can you tell me what my sister sees in that wild Musarnik?"

Hannah blushed as if she were confessing a sin. "I'll tell you the truth. I didn't properly appreciate Slava before. All along I thought of her as frivolous. Others still think she's a breeze in the field, superficial, a wild nanny goat. But she's just the opposite: very serious and devoted. No matter what you say about her husband, he's still not an ordinary man. Slava won't divorce him because none of her other acquaintances pleases her as much as he. Anyway, that in my humble opinion is what I think." And Hannah looked apprehensively at Volodya, fearing that he might shout that she was a village woman, a pious cat, a kosher cow.

20

THE ACTOR HERMAN YOFFE, a tall man with hair silvering at his temples, smiled gaily at everyone. He had kind eyes and a soft mouth that enjoyed talking, laughing, and chewing. At the beginning of the theatrical season, he and a troupe of actors had left Warsaw to tour the larger towns. The actors disbanded on the way, and Herman Yoffe toured the provinces alone, presenting solo recitations and character roles from previous productions. His one-man show was a success in Lomzhe, and the local people engaged him to direct a play. During rehearsals with the amateurs of the Lomzhe Dramatic Theater he would always ask: "Is there a fine family in town with whom one can spend a free evening?" Soon, through a friend they had in common, he became acquainted with Slava Atlas. With his experienced eye he saw that she wasn't a provincial cow. Slava liked him too, for his kind, clever eyes and his homy but not overbearing demeanor. She knew that Lomzhers considered her marriage to the scholar Tsemakh Atlas the caprice of a rich, spoiled only daughter; sooner or later they would get divorced. Slava kept up appearances and invited the actor only with other guests, but her fascination with his anecdotes about the theater and people smitten with it quickly faded. Nevertheless, she was still fond of him for his sharp wit and even more for his silence. While others spoke and he listened, his face took on the sadness of a perpetual wanderer whose profession it was to entertain others. Tonight Slava was to go to Herman Yoffe's new performance. She knew he was waiting for her and—if only for a few hours—she wanted to forget her morning talk with Tsemakh.

The light wool of her pale green dress and her jacket with its two-piece, tie-looped collar gave her figure a soft and supple appearance. Her wavy hair tumbled over her temples, her long neck gleamed beneath her round chin, her eyes swam in a moist, blue sheen. Her coat and purse were on a chair, and a pair of little boots gazed up at her from the floor like two kittens. But at the last minute, just before she put on her coat, she decided she wasn't in the mood for dramatic recitations. And it wasn't proper to be seen in the theater when it was known in town that her husband, the yeshiva principal, had returned. Slava remained on the sofa in her favorite position, feet folded beneath her. After sitting thus for fifteen minutes, cozy and warm, she was glad she hadn't gone. Now she could examine her own mind and refresh her thoughts with memories of meetings with people.

Volodya always said that some of his friends were much nicer and more intelligent than her Musarnik. Therefore, Slava had befriended the grain merchant Feivl Sokolvsky, a man of medium height with a heavy tread and a head thrust forward like an ox butting its horns. He had a wild shock of hair, a low, wrinkled forehead, small, narrow eyes, and wide palms with short fingers. Sokolovsky was so preoccupied with business that he hadn't had time to marry; he also loved to tell how wary he was of deception. "Gentlemen, I don't let myself be fooled! Once when I was buying cloth for a coat, the salesman whispered an exorbitant price into my ear. So I told him, 'Who are you trying to fool? Look me straight in the eye!' " While Sokolovsky spoke, Slava laughed continually, as if charmed by his cleverness. Herman Yoffe would wink at Slava. He knew she was laughing at the merchant's foolish story. But if Volodya was present, he would move restlessly in his chair, irritated.

Later, Volodya reproached his sister. "I told you that some of my merchant friends are much nicer and more intelligent than your Musarnik. So, just to spite me, you singled out an idiot. If Sokolovsky catches on that you're laughing at him, he'll become my blood enemy."

From the shaded floor lamp a thin circle of light fell on the table. Outside in the darkness an electric light swung on a wire. Beneath it swayed the dark green crown of a tree, dotted with wet yellow leaves. A network of light and shadows from the street moved through the room and shimmered on the dark brown wallpaper. Slava looked out and thought: Just as the tree can't shake off all its leaves until the height of autumn, I can't shake off all the memories of those few happy months with Tsemakh right after the wedding. Who among her new friends could take his place? Perhaps the Hebrew teacher Zevulun Halperin.

Evening Hebrew courses for young women had been introduced in Lomzhe. Slava attended the lectures to recall the Hebrew she had studied in her girlhood at the Bialystok *Gymnasium.* Instead of finding the lessons attractive, she found the teacher attractive, and he became a frequent visitor in her home. Zevulun Halperin had thin, transparent hands and a rather long, slender face and jutting jaw. His flat chin had a blue gleam from frequent shaves with dull razor blades. Unshaven, his stubble looked like needles. When Slava served tea on the evenings he came to call, he was almost always silent, smiling only with his broad lips. He was apparently uncomfortable with the actor and the grain merchant, his rivals for the beautiful young woman.

The wind outside abated, and the tree huddled toward the window like the drooping head of a tired man. Slava too was weary of thinking. Volodya said that she had purposely chosen a group of shlimazels so that her Musarnik would stand out as finer and more handsome. Indeed, when she compared Tsemakh with her other friends, all her stored-up bitterness against him vanished like smoke. Why should she accept a divorce from him? He would give her freedom any time she wanted it so as not to have another sin on his conscience. Tsemakh always remembered everything he had done in his life, while others forgot their deeds the next morning. He had got it into his head that he had to suffer punishment because of his dead fiancée. So no matter how repulsive it was to her, she would have to wait until he got this new madness out of his system. Slava was pleased that Tsemakh had gone to live with his uncle. She didn't want to see him depressed and despairing. She still wanted to remember him the way he had looked after their wedding a year and a half ago, in the spring, when they would both look out at the budding tree by the window.

21

THERE WAS NO LONGER A HOUSEWIFE to dust the furniture at Reb Ziml's. On the cracked old chest of drawers stood the family photographs, ancient ancestors covered with cobwebs that hung from brows and beards and marriage wigs. The gray mirror in the cold parlor was frosted over with cold dew. Throughout the week the green-mold-encrusted candlesticks that the widower lit on Friday before sundown stood on the dining-room table. Scattered pieces of challa remained there from Sabbath to Sabbath. Reb Ziml knew when it was Sabbath and when it was weekday; he knew the time for prayers, but he prayed as if his lips were not his own, and he put on tefillin as if his hands were not his own. He had become an altogether different person. Instead of looking up at the ceiling, as his old habit had been, he constantly looked down, as if still looking for his short, roly-poly Tsertele. Every day one or another of his daughters-in-law came to cook a meal for him and reproached him for eating so little. Reb Ziml didn't reply and gazed out the gray window in amazement. He didn't know whether it was always twilight outside or whether he was just imagining it.

Tsemakh moved into his uncle's house so quietly that he seemed to slip in barefoot. He described his experiences, and his uncle listened, head lowered, as if he'd known that everything would happen exactly as it had. But Reb Ziml remained silent all evening. His nephew served himself, then lay down to sleep in the cold parlor. He had slept there when he returned from Amdur the first time, crestfallen over his broken engagement to Dvorele Namiot, and his Aunt Tsertele had covered him with her warm shawl. And now both were gone—his Aunt Tsertele and Dvorele Namiot. "Death is preferable to life," he said, groaning. "I've lived enough."

The next morning in the low-ceilinged room two tall, melancholy men prayed, wrapped in their prayer shawls, standing apart from each other, enveloped in a long, rapt silence. The nephew looked up at the ceiling, the uncle down at the ground.

After the Silent Devotion they turned to each other and Reb Ziml said with an otherworldly voice, "The children want me to sell the house and move in with them. They don't understand that while I live here, I still feel united with their mother. She's in every corner, and she's angry with me for neglecting everything in the house. The only thing I do is wind up the wall clock every night. As long as the clock works, I feel that our life together is still going on. By staying on here I feel that I'm apologizing to Tsertele for my fantasies of leaving home and becoming a recluse. She pretended to laugh at these wild ideas, but it really annoyed her. I know this, and I can't forgive myself for having caused her grief."

"Uncle, you only *wanted* to leave home, but I actually left. And now I must go again. I'm sick of living, Uncle; I've ruined my life because of arrogance." Tsemakh wrapped himself in the tallis as if he were shivering with cold.

"And how can you be sure, Tsemakh, that what you're about to do now doesn't stem from arrogance?"

"I'm leaving home for the second time now to extirpate pride from myself. The bramble of pride grows in every pore of my body. To rid myself of this bramble I have to wander about in the world as an animal singed by fire rolls on the ground, rubbing his burned skin in sand and stone. Do you understand, Uncle? I have always felt that a man must constantly tell himself and others the entire truth. Then I was punished, and I realized that by fighting day in and day out for small truths, one misses the larger truths. And that way a man is not as honest as he thinks. A pure-hearted man of compassion lives his life better than I have lived mine."

Reb Ziml tucked his hands into his sleeves; his sparse gray beard came to a twisted point like a bent hook. His words too came out crooked and pointed, mocking and angry.

"Since you realize that you should have been more pure-hearted and compassionate, why are you leaving your wife again?"

Trembling with fear, Tsemakh looked at his uncle as if suspecting him of hiding a sharpened slaughtering knife in his sleeve. But Reb

Ziml again looked like a mute golem, as if he hadn't remembered asking the question. Tsemakh looked down at his long legs and explained why they would have to tramp the roads.

"My first fiancée will always stand between Slava and me—that's why I want to give her a divorce. But she doesn't want a divorce, and I have to leave home for her own good, so as not to destroy her with my mourning."

That night Volodya came and addressed the wall to avoid looking at his brother-in-law's despicable countenance. "Listen, Tsemakh, as far as my sister's misfortune is concerned, it's my fault more than anyone else's. It was I who introduced you into our house and thereby brought grief upon our entire family. But it seems that you have the capacity to drive other people crazy too. My little sister doesn't want to accept a divorce from you. So what can I do?"

Volodya took a purse stuffed with money out of his pocket. "Slava doesn't want you to come to say good-bye. But, in any case, she's giving you a couple of hundred zlotys so that you won't have to depend on the charity of strangers," he said, panting and gasping. Instead of money, he'd have preferred giving that Musarnik a blow in the ribs.

"I won't take the money," Tsemakh said without hesitation. "That's precisely what I want to do—depend on the charity of strangers."

The flour merchant raised his eyes and gazed at his brother-in-law. He had never heard of a man wanting to be a beggar. Then he could contain himself no longer and burst out laughing. His belly began to shake; his broad, perspiring face turned red, puffed up with the strain of not spitting right into that Musarnik's face. He chuckled, wiped his brow, and in his heart cursed his brother-in-law: perhaps God will have pity, and he'll die a miserable death on the road.

Tsemakh was silent and numb, as if he hadn't heard one peal of the flour merchant's laughter but saw only the long road ahead of him. In the other room Uncle Ziml stood, his arms tucked into his sleeves. He stared silently down at the moldy candlesticks, as if he had returned from a distant journey to an eternally sad, gloomy, and wintry Sabbath twilight.

PART III

1

A YEAR LATER Reb Shlomo-Motte lay on his deathbed, looking up at the low ceiling with its unplastered, cracked beams blackened with soot and covered with gray spider webs. The mortally ill Hebrew teacher breathed with difficulty, like the bellows in the front room that the landlord had rented to a blacksmith. Water oozed from the sick man's swollen feet. To turn him over, his wife and son needed the blacksmith's help. The ailing man cried out in pain and begged not to be moved. He never once took his glance from the shelves of books; he was bidding them farewell. Heavy as a log and lying on his back as though nailed to the bed, he occasionally turned his head to his son and with great effort repeated, "Are you going to sit in the beth medresh while your mother slaves for you?"

Chaikl did not reply. He saw that his father awaited the Angel of Death.

During his final moments Reb Shlomo-Motte raised his head and, with his last strength, rattled to his wife, "Bury me as soon as you can—tomorrow morning—so that your Sabbath will be a day of rest."

Reb Shlomo-Motte died that day—Thursday evening. He was laid out on straw on the ground in the front room, covered with a black cloth. He was surrounded by boxes of tools and scrap iron, a mechanized saw, a vise attached to the workbench, heavy hammers, an anvil on a block of wood, a bin full of coal, and bellows with a turreted, rusty tin cover. The blacksmiths were idling in the courtyard in front of the dusty windows of the smithy like pious laborers during the intermediate days of Passover or Sukkos. Women peddlers came into the smithy, wringing their hands. They asked the dead man to intercede for them and consoled the widow. "He's well off now; he has overcome it." They lit big memorial candles around the deceased. Two hired psalms sayers chanted one verse after another for the dead man.

Vella the fruit peddler sat on a low stool and spoke to her husband, "Shlomo-Motte, don't be angry at me for keeping you in a room without fresh air and light." And then she turned to Chaikl. "And you, my son," she pleaded, "don't be angry with me for not paying enough attention to your father." It seemed to Chaikl that his father wanted to say something to his mother but that he was forbidden to talk because he was dead. So he merely listened and wept beneath his black covering.

Night fell. Neighbors from the street and the courtyard stopped coming in. Vella swayed silently on her low stool, exhausted with weeping. The psalms sayers lowered their heads into their tangled beards and dozed. Total silence reigned in the soot-filled workshop. The half-burned memorial lights around the corpse melted. The wicks sputtered and the little flames quivered as if suffocating in the surrounding darkness.

Chaikl heard the silence of the steel tools. He imagined that the saws and files were apologizing to the dead man for the screeching din that had drowned out his talk when he was alive and his groans on his deathbed. Chaikl felt a shudder running down his spine; his breath froze. He had the sudden notion that now, while his mother and the psalms sayers were dozing, his father would throw the black garment from over his head and angrily reproach him: "Are you going to sit in the beth medresh while your mother slaves for you?" At that instant the street door opened, and from the darkness Vova Barbitoler barged in, dead drunk.

After seeing Reb Avraham-Shaye in Valkenik, Vova had returned to Vilna and tried to resume his tobacco business. But the wholesalers and customers had lost their confidence in him. So he began to sell ritual fringes again. He also continued to collect bread and challa for his Free Bread Society—for impoverished townsmen and for himself as well. But Vova had become a docile pauper. He no longer frequented the tavern and didn't stop to talk with old acquaintances. He hadn't even paid a sick call on his old friend Reb Shlomo-Motte. Therefore, Vova's sudden rolling into the house cast a fear upon the widow and her son. The psalms sayers, awake now, saw that the man was intoxicated.

Vova slapped one hand against the other and sang out cheerfully, "Reb Shlomo-Motte the teacher is dead. Dead, indeed! The pious congregants of Reb Shaulke's beth medresh won't come to his funeral because he's an old maskil and because he was a friend to me, a bigamist. And now these respectable congregants and the Vilna rabbis can't wait to get rid of me too. But they won't get rid of me that quickly. To spite them I'm going to live and live until I outlive that piece of corruption, Confrada."

Vova swayed on his crooked legs, and the words rolled off his tongue heavy as stones. "Once, over a glass of whisky at the tavern, Reb Shlomo-Motte cleverly advised me to send Confrada a divorce. That saint in the summer cottage—the one who's called after his book, *The Vision of Avraham*—tried to talk me into this too. And when I returned to Vilna from Valkenik, I thought about sending that piece of corruption that twelve-line bill of divorce. But I just couldn't make myself do it. My guts got all knotted up. On top of all my other troubles and humiliations, why should I send Confrada a divorce so she could legally live with her Argentine husband? I did well, Reb Shlomo-Motte, not listening to you!" Vova screamed to the covered corpse. Then he turned to Chaikl.

"Your teacher Reb Avraham-Shaye blessed me by saying that if I repent, I'll be helped. And I believe your teacher. I believe in his blessing that if I send Confrada a divorce, I'll be a merchant again, and my bastard Hertzke in Argentina will remember that I'm his father. But I'd rather be a pauper, even a beggar, and I'd rather have my bastard not want to know me than set his darling mama free. In Valkenik Confrada laughed at me. She didn't need my divorce, she said. But she was laughing through tears, because she knows that according to Jewish law, the children by her Argentine husband are bastards! And the older she gets, the more pious she gets, that promiscuous slut! She wants to die a saint. Lately her brothers have been trying again to persuade me to send her a divorce. Her brothers, those thieves from Novogorod, pretend to be doing this on their own. But I know it's their sister who keeps pestering them, that old whore . . . Why are you staring at me with those wicked eyes of yours?"

"Don't humiliate my father! Don't humiliate a dead man!" Chaikl pleaded with tears in his voice. "This is not the time for such stories."

"Now is *just* the time!" Vova screeched, his eyes bulging. "I'm not humiliating your father. You humiliated him—remember?—when you raised a prayer stand at me, your father's old friend, in Reb Shaulke's beth medresh, and then when you helped that crazy Musarnik kidnap my Hertzke. I've heard that that crazy Musarnik Tsemakh Atlas has come to a bitter end. Reb Avraham-Shaye chased him out of the yeshiva and drove him out of town. Your teacher is a miracle worker. But your father didn't believe that he was a miracle worker; even now, dead as he is, your father doesn't believe that your teacher is a miracle worker. And you, Chaikl, you'll grow up to be a heretic like your father."

Vella managed to jump up and stand between Vova Barbitoler and her son, who leaped at the drunkard with fists flying.

"Control yourself! Don't shame your father," his mother said, holding on to Chaikl. Grieved that her learned, white-bearded husband was lying on the ground amid scrap iron and was even being called a heretic, Vella sank down on her low stool and began sobbing softly. Chaikl wept too and fled into the rear room of the smithy so as not to see Vova raging.

The sleepy, wrinkled-faced psalms sayers added, "It's unheard of to come dead drunk and make a scene in a house where a dead man lies. It seems you haven't considered that you'll die too."

"Not before Confrada drops dead!" Vova laughed, as if to spite the Angel of Death. His tongue turning and twisting, he spoke thickly, "It'd be a relief for me to close my eyes forever. But I dare not die before Confrada so that she won't rejoice at my death."

"He's a lunatic." One of the psalms sayers shrugged. " 'Happy are they that are upright in the way, who walk in the law of the Lord.' " He continued chanting from the point where he and his friend had stopped before dozing off. But before the other psalms sayer could recite the next verse, Vova Barbitoler continued:

" 'Happy are they that keep his testimonies, that seek him with the whole heart.' " And he began bawling as if a dybbuk were gnawing at him. "Oh, dear God, how I envy the upright! Jews like that don't know how well off they are. They bear the heavy yoke of life submissively. They eat their meager meals quietly and pray with devotion. They store up great credit for the world to come. They even enjoy a little bit of this world. But I get no joy out of life, even though I know that I have to thank and praise the Almighty that that woman ran away from me. I remember how much shame and disgrace she caused me during the brief time we were together. If she hadn't run away from me, grass would be growing on my grave today. Nevertheless, I still can't forget what she's done to me, and I'll struggle with her till the day she dies. She'll just *have* to drop dead before I do."

The effect of the alcohol gradually dissipated into perspiration and tears. Vova opened his eyes as if from a faint and saw the dead man lying among boxes of tools, his head next to a bellows full of extinguished coals.

"Is this where Reb Shlomo-Motte had to spend his old age?" Vova Barbitoler shook his head sadly and apologized to the widow for his conduct. "When I heard that my only old friend was gone, I felt even more heartbroken and had to go to a tavern before I came here."

The door of the rear room of the smithy was slightly ajar, and Chaikl, half asleep, saw what was happening in the workshop: his mother swayed on her low stool; Vova Barbitoler stood in mournful silence, leaning against the ladder by the wall; and the psalms sayers sat with heads lowered, also silent. It seemed that everyone had lost his tongue, awaiting the dead man's imminent awakening.

The funeral was held on Friday morning, a week before Rosh Hashana. The sunny Elul day was dry and cool. Old friends who lived with their children or in old-age homes came to pay their last respects: maskilim of a previous generation with small, trimmed beards, yellowed rubber collars, and frayed caps. They accompanied the coffin to the Zaretche Bridge, leaning on canes and taking short steps, but their feeble feet could no longer carry them up the Zaretche Hill. The shopkeepers from Butchers Street too stopped at the bridge and returned to their shops, rushing to their preholiday business. A few courtyard neighbors and women peddlers who competed with Vella but respected her husband walked behind the humble wagon hitched to one horse. Some of the poorer congregants of Reb Shaulke's beth medresh also followed along. The scholars and well-to-do pious congregants did not come to the funeral, as Vova Barbitoler had correctly predicted. He himself walked behind the coffin all the way. But Chaikl was so stunned by grief, shame, and anger that Reb Avraham-Shaye had not come to the funeral, he wasn't aware what was happening around him. In the cemetery's purification chamber—where the corpse lay in a white shroud like a snow-covered oak—when Vella wailed to her son, "Say good-bye to your father," anger at his teacher constricted Chaikl's heart with pain, and he clenched his teeth in silence.

He realized that Reb Avraham-Shaye had not come to the funeral because his father had been a maskil. I'll never forgive him for this! Chaikl thought. Nevertheless, when he returned to his studies at the end of the seven days of mourning, he said nothing to the rabbi just because it hurt him so deeply. He sensed that the humiliation had seeped into his bones and had become calcified there. He had often thought that the hotheaded and belligerent Reb Tsemakh Atlas was in reality much less strict and demanding than Reb Avraham-Shaye Kosover, who studied Torah for its own sake—entirely for its own sake. Chaikl began to be more tolerant of the former tobacco merchant, too. Vova Barbitoler either forgot or pretended to forget the old grudge he bore Reb Shlomo-Motte's son and often went up to him in Reb Shaulke's beth medresh and repeated the same remark, "Your father didn't achieve in his lifetime what he'd set out to achieve, and I feel that I won't either. I have a hunch that that woman in Argentina will outlive me."

Indeed, Vova Barbitoler died two months after Reb Shlomo-Motte. On a cold, windy day at the end of Kislev, he collapsed in the middle of the street while carrying a large basket filled with pieces of bread he had collected for impoverished townsmen and for himself. By the time people bent over him he was already dead, and the scattered bread on the cobblestones seemed to mourn him.

Vova had a big, tumultuous funeral. Paying their last respects were the trustees and teachers from the various Talmud Torahs where, during his good years, he had donated ritual fringes for the orphans, and impoverished townsmen who had clandestinely accepted gifts from his Free Bread Society since the time he himself had become poverty stricken. Most of the mourners, however, were customers at the tavern he had frequented—young toughs from Butchers Street and the surrounding lanes.

"He was a good man," the crowd said, reviling the rich men and the Vilna rabbis for not coming to Reb Vova's funeral and for not begging his pardon for having sucked his blood for years over his refusal to divorce the Argentinian woman. The people of the street said loudly to each other, "He did well not kowtowing to them! There's a man for you!" Melechke's mother, Zelda the tinsmith's wife, and her three daughters all walked in a row behind the coffin and wept over the deceased as if he were a flesh-and-blood father. "He made a man out of our Melechke. He gave him ritual fringes. Since then our Melechke has studied at a yeshiva and will become a rabbi, a gaon, and a saint."

Vova Barbitoler's son and daughter from his first wife walked along saddened and embarrassed. They felt that it was not proper for everyone to be still talking about his second wife, Confrada, at their father's funeral. Vova's third wife, Mindl, looked even more befuddled and lost. She pulled her kerchief down to her eyes and dared not mourn her husband aloud. Mindl huddled close to Reb Shlomo-Motte's widow, who led her by the arm like a sister. In so doing Vella continually turned around to see if her Chaikl had left the funeral procession, God forbid. After all, Reb Vova—God rest his soul—had hired a teacher and ordered a suit for him.

When the dead man was being garbed in the shroud and his friends entered the purification chamber to remove him, they were left dumfounded. Vova's teeth were bared, and he seemed to be laughing, just as his son Hertzke had laughed, baring *his* teeth. The young taverngoers went from the purification chamber to the cemetery delighted. "The tobacco merchant is happy even in his death, because he prevailed in his battles against all his enemies and didn't divorce that shrew in Argentina!" The more refined mourners groaned in distress at the unruly folk who were praising the deceased for deeds which, out of respect for him, ought not be remembered.

Vella the fruit peddler sighed and told her son, "One can say that what a man wishes for himself during his lifetime, he gets after his death. Reb Vova made such a fuss about that woman from Argentina that everyone talks about her as if she were his wife. But Mindl, who was a faithful wife and suffered so much from him—God spare us—Mindl is thrust aside, a stranger at her own husband's funeral."

Reb Avraham-Shaye too, in his corner in the Poplaver beth medresh, heard people talking about Vova Barbitoler's funeral. The next morning when Chaikl came for his lesson, the rabbi asked, "What are you, a professional mourner? It takes time from Torah learning. And besides, weren't you and the tobacco merchant at odds?"

Chaikl was waiting for this moment to square accounts for the insult to his father. "I was sure that you too would come to Vova Barbitoler's funeral. After all, in Valkenik you bedded him down in your room."

Reb Avraham-Shaye pushed his little Talmud folio closer to his smiling eyes. "In Valkenik I wanted to save you from the tobacco merchant's blows and Reb Tsemakh from humiliation. That's why I let him sleep in my room. Moreover, I also thought he would obey me and send the woman in Argentina a divorce. But he didn't do this—and so a ben Torah must not go to the funeral of a man who humiliated the Torah."

"Of course, according to your outlook, Vova Barbitoler didn't behave the way he should have," Chaikl replied quickly and angrily. "But if you had watched while a man was lowered into his grave and covered with earth, you wouldn't ask if he followed the Code of Law and had enough faith in Torah scholars."

Chaikl immediately regretted his remarks. He saw the rabbi's myopic eyes assiduously scanning the page with its minute Rashi script. With his little Talmud Reb Avraham-Shaye sought to cover his face, which was twitching with barely restrained tears. He hunched over as if afraid of the pupil who had reproached him for forgetting compassion on account of his zealousness for the law.

2

REB AVRAHAM-SHAYE KOSOVER lived in a two-room basement apartment opposite the Zaretche Market, on the side of the Vilenke River Bridge. One entered the rebbetsin's textile shop and from there a glass-windowed door led to the living quarters. The long, dark, narrow room that the childless couple shared was made even more bleak by pedestrians who continually passed by the one low window. At the back of the room stood two beds blocked by a large wardrobe. In the front was a round drop-leaf table with one leaf up, and several chairs, with a sofa against one wall and several bookcases against the other.

In the winter, during his mourning period for his father, Chaikl crossed the Vilenke River Bridge every day and went to the Poplaver beth medresh, where Reb Avraham-Shaye prayed, for instruction. On Friday nights Chaikl went to the rabbi's home.

After lighting the Sabbath candles and eating a meager meal, Vella the fruit peddler would fall into bed in her clothes, dead tired from toiling until fifteen minutes before sundown. When his mother fell asleep, Chaikl would be alone in their room, listening to the silent shadows on the walls. Cobwebs hung from the split wooden beams overhead. The little scarlet flames of the Sabbath candles in their copper candlesticks burned with a workaday sadness. Opposite the table stood his father's books, which seemed to him like faded inscriptions on tombstones. Chaikl wasn't drawn to his books of philosophy from Spain, Mendelssohn's German Bible written in Hebrew characters, or the flowery Hebrew works of the Lithuanian maskilim. He put on his heavy winter coat and left for the rabbi's house.

Wherever Chaikl set foot outside, he was assaulted by a seductive world. On the broad boulevard, he was dazzled by the electric lights above the theaters' display windows. He looked at girls wearing high, shiny boots and furs, sprinkled with coruscating snow crystals. He also looked in amazement at groups of youths. Weren't they ashamed to laugh so loudly in the middle of the street? But when he entered the rabbi's house, a shimmering, secretive light embraced him in a sweet warmth and silence.

Chaikl was not particularly enthralled by the Tractate Kiddushin, which deals with a man who marries a woman and doesn't specify to her that he is consecrating her in marriage. After studying for half an hour, he wanted to talk, especially since on the Sabbath it was a mitzva not to exert oneself. Even the Talmudic sages interspersed their legal discussions with anecdotes and folklore to keep their heads from bursting. But Chaikl was still perturbed by the old problem:

"What have you got against Navaredok and Musar? The fundamental principle of Navaredok is the battle against self-interest. They hold that man should do good deeds without the slightest ulterior motive. Now isn't that a lofty trait?"

"Your very wish to talk about ulterior motives has a blatant ulterior motive—you don't want to exert yourself to ponder the Mishna." Reb Avraham-Shaye sighed. Nevertheless, he let himself be drawn into a discussion about good traits. "It's cruel and stupid to criticize someone who looks out for his own interests. Since this trait is inherent in every human being, a man can seek advantage for himself as long as he doesn't hurt anyone else. And this surely applies to someone who seeks recognition and good friends by helping a friend, a neighbor, a stranger—a person like that is even thought of as a man of high moral attainment. Just as we sympathize with the one who receives charity, so must we recognize the one who gives. Just as we don't reproach a needy man for thanking his benefactor, so we must not cast stones at the benefactor who seeks gratitude."

After dozing in her bed behind the wardrobe, Reb Avraham-Shaye's wife rose to serve tea. Chaikl liked the rebbetsin Yudis. He thought of her as a good, down-to-earth, hard-working woman like his mother. But he noticed that her every move made the rabbi suffer: the way she gulped tea, the way she clacked her heels when she walked, and especially the way she spoke. The rabbi had told Yudis to prepare for a guest for the Sabbath, but the visitor had gone elsewhere.

The rebbetsin took quick sips of the hot tea, puffed out her thick, scalded lips, and said in her masculine voice, "Who does that privileged character, that genius, that saint think he is, planning to come for the Sabbath and then not showing up? Nicer people than he used to polish my father's boots. I got up in the middle of the night to prepare a meal for that new Maimonides, and now I have to dump it into the slops for the dogs and pigs in the market place. I'd like to know how he sniffed out in advance that my meals wouldn't suit him? I wish I could be sure of better days, as I'm sure he's a big, wide man with a fat paunch and a hefty unmentionable to sit on. I'll bet he wears an expensive gaberdine and soft leather boots. He probably has a broad beard and a thick black mustache, and a pair of heavy eyebrows—in short, he must be a very imposing chap. But if you look closely, you'll see that he's got sly eyes and a sneaky face. You can tell that he's lazy, a glutton, and likes to drink, and he gives his wife a hard time at home; her life is misery with him. So this rabbinic individual got cold feet when he suspected that he might not be able to stuff his guts in Reb Avraham-Shaye's house. And what's more, it'd be torture for him to drag himself up the Zaretche Hill. He might even crunch his hat going into the low-ceilinged house of the poverty-stricken textile merchant. That pig; that swine!"

Eighteen-year-old Chaikl just managed to restrain himself from shouting with joy, he was so entertained at the rebbetsin's market lingo. Yudis prepared another glass of tea for herself and cooled it by pouring it from the glass to the saucer. But she could not cool her rage.

"Can you possibly tell me what kind of person our guest is?" she shouted at her husband. "I don't want to know his name—just tell me what he does. Is he a rabbi? A yeshiva principal? Or is he merely a two-legged plague?"

"What difference does it make who he is and what he does?" Reb Avraham-Shaye snapped, raising his voice. "A man was supposed to come to have a Sabbath meal with us and then he went somewhere that was perhaps more convenient; or perhaps he went to a relative. If you had his interest in mind, you ought to be pleased. If it doesn't bother me, why should it bother you?"

The rebbetsin nodded to Chaikl as if asking: Well, doesn't one need a constitution of steel to take all this? Then she went behind the wardrobe to make her bed. The rabbi and his pupil were alone again, enveloped by the mysterious and awe-inspiring flames of the still-unextinguished Sabbath candles. Reb Avraham-Shaye laughed congenially, as if his previous outburst had been mere pretense. "That's the way people are. At first they supposedly do everything for someone who needs their help. But should he refuse their help, the benefactors get furious. During the Grace After Meals we recite: 'We pray to you, O God, let us never come to need the help and gifts of flesh-and-blood men.' While saying this we must bear in mind and hope that no one becomes dependent on us either. From this we learn that the adherents of Musar are not entirely incorrect when they demand good deeds without ulterior motives. But for a man of flesh and blood to do good deeds solely out of the pure goodness of his heart, he must be a man who lacks nothing. A rich man of this sort can only be one for whom Torah wisdom is the joy of his life. Only the man of faith can be that wealthy."

Chaikl saw that even when the rabbi discussed non-Torah matters, even when he drank tea and ate biscuits, his mustache moved with modest piety as if he were whispering a prayer. And how different was his way of speaking from a Musarnik's! Reb Tsemakh Atlas always spoke about people's faults and deprecated the freethinkers. Reb Avraham-Shaye didn't say that the secularists were bad—they simply couldn't comprehend the good fortune of the pious. The man of faith isn't one who hopes that his will may prevail—that's a man of pride, Reb Avraham-Shaye declared. A true believer is one who is confident that no matter what happens, it is all for his good. As the Talmud says: Everything that the All-Merciful does is for the good. The maskilim and the freethinkers laugh and say: Our earth is a speck of dust compared to the stars and constellations. Doesn't the Creator have anything else to do but watch over Yankel the shoemaker who lives in a cellar on Poplave Street? The man of faith, however, knows that he has all of the Creator for himself alone, as every child has all of his father for himself. The believer also gets infinite joy out of life because he sees the wonder, the riddle, the hidden secrets of creation everywhere and in everything. How much godly wisdom and divine love toward man is found in a pair of hands! Take for example a baby's little fingers—how they stretch, flex, touch, fondle. And is there any greater mystery, any hidden wonder more profound than an open eye? The black pupil is set into the white of the eye and is protected from above and below with lashes that prevent a speck of dust from entering. How much charm and beauty and thought radiate from a human eye. But because during the day we see dozens, hundreds of eyes, and because people often look at one another with suspicion and hatred, they forget to thank the Creator for making man with a pair of such miraculous eyes.

Chaikl spent the night at the rabbi's home and lay awake on the sofa in the dark room for a long time. Through the crevices of the shuttered windows a bluish light seeped in and trembled on the bookshelves. Passers-by crunched the snow. From far off came a loud laugh—and then the echo of a long, piercing cry, its strange reverberation seeming to come from the moon. Thoughts crept like patches of fog into Chaikl's sleepy head. He had often noticed the rabbi's delight when his sister's son tweaked his nose or squeezed his beard with his soft little fingers. That was why Reb Avraham-Shaye said that a baby's little fingers were a great miracle. Chaikl had heard that Yudis was so much older than the rabbi at their wedding, she could no longer bear children. The rebbetsin herself had confided to Chaikl, "My old man suffers because he can't have a son. When no one hears, he groans, and every groan of his pierces me like a needle . . . Now you must swear that you won't tell the rabbi a word of what I've said." Chaikl had agreed. "My saintly husband," she had said, "is always afraid I might tell someone, God forbid, about our bad fortune." Chaikl was then plagued by a problem: If it's true, as Reb Avraham-Shaye says, that a believer is pleased with everything that happens to him, then the rabbi must be glad that he doesn't have a child. . . .

At dawn a whispering awakened Chaikl. The rabbi stood bent over him, already wrapped in his tallis. "Do you want to come to the beth medresh with me?" Within a few minutes Chaikl was dressed and helping the rabbi put on his overcoat. Outside it was still dark. The snow-covered street was empty except for the lone Polish policeman standing on the corner, banging one boot against the other to keep warm. White vapor came out of his mouth and gathered around his mustache. He knew the rabbi and amiably wished him good morning.

The Poplaver beth medresh was large and airy, like the Vilna railroad terminal. Because of its size it couldn't be heated in the winter, so prayers were conducted in a smaller adjoining room. Even this room was chilly on an early Sabbath morning. But the first worshiper, Reb Avraham-Shaye, didn't feel the cold. He draped the tallis over his head and at once immersed himself in quiet, ecstatic prayer. Gazing at him, Chaikl recalled what the rabbi had recently told him about prayer: "There are those who don't understand how a man can recite the same prayers all his life. The worldly people maintain that even a poet who sings his own songs must continually produce new ones. Those who don't pray themselves can't imagine that when a Jew recites a psalm with all his heart, the ancient poem becomes the worshiper's own brand-new poem, just as all of creation is made new daily for the man of faith. Every sensitive man has a day in his life when he awakes and looks at the sun as if he had never seen it before. Of course no one dreams that a new sun would actually materialize before his eyes. Similarly, new prayers aren't necessary for the person who prays with all his heart and soul."

During his summer vacation the rabbi also prays at dawn like an angel, Chaikl thought. Summer or winter, day or night, makes no difference to him. He doesn't even sense any great difference between a Sabbath and a weekday. How did he get into this state? Certainly not by striving for it. He was *born* an angel. He rose in the middle of the night; it was winter and a gloomy rain was falling. Another person in his position would feel neglected and forgotten by the whole world. But he felt that he was with his Creator, who awaited his awakening. And around him there was as much tranquillity as if the Messianic Sabbath had already begun. Reb Avraham-Shaye felt that the entire world should consist of such reclusive people as he. No one should complain; everyone should bear the yoke and be concerned only with spiritual things. The rabbi's inner world had its own secret life; it was a world of eternal dawn and awesome silence, akin to the eve of Resurrection, when those that dwell in dust await the sound of the great shofar, to awake and rise from the grave.

But Chaikl's guilt toward his dead father increased along with his amazement at and enchantment with the rabbi's life as a hidden saint. He saw before his eyes the wintry nights in Reb Shaulke's beth medresh: a minyan of Jews sat around the table reviewing a page of Talmud. Old men sat by the stove studying laws and Midrash, two by two. These angry fanatics, Chaikl thought, squabble, cough, and wheeze until they doze off. The wicks of the melting candles sprayed wax and sputtered as though angry at the congregants' snoring. Occasionally the old men joked and nudged each other with their elbows, having good-natured fun. But they all avoided Reb Shlomo-Motte and sarcastically parodied the Psalm's verse, "blessed is he who considers the poor," by calling him "the unconsidering poor man" because he, the pauper, dared to be a maskil. Therefore Chaikl's father sat in a corner as if in a deep, vaulted cave, and his mild, sad glance spoke of a hard, unsuccessful life. Nevertheless, he did not regret his path, which was diametrically opposite to that of Reb Avraham-Shaye's. Chaikl knew that his father had departed the world true to the outlook of his youth: that the chosen person must not isolate himself from the people, and that Jews must not isolate themselves from the world.

3

AT TWENTY Chaikl still had childish lips, dreamy eyes, and a pale, round, moonlike face. But his body and the way he moved and walked reminded one of a strong-shouldered young porter, solid as lead. Although he studied diligently and tried to acquire the traits of a yeshiva scholar, the merry stories of the boys and girls of Butchers Street confounded his nights and days. Exhausted by forbidden desires, he went about in a gloomy stupor, feverish with lust even when he stood over the Talmud. The rabbi sensed his pupil's hidden urges and toiled with him at Torah to save him from temptations; but Chaikl was also reading secular books, which stoked his imagination even more. Occasionally he cast himself into his studies, and the rabbi radiated joy. But then, gradually, the forbidden books and his passion for girls would get the upper hand again.

Chaikl had missed the sharp comments of the Musarists ever since he stopped studying with Reb Tsemakh Atlas. For the month of Elul he went to the Navaredkers in Nareva, where he stayed until after Sukkos and then returned to Vilna for the winter. The emptiness of the big Poplaver beth medresh, where he foundered in a little corner, oppressed him even more. However, his consolation was that being at home with his mother was preferable to living in deprivation away from home and going about hairy and disheveled, with insufficient food and sleep, and constantly eyed by those who suspected him of reading forbidden books.

When Elul came again, Chaikl struggled every morning after prayers with the shofar sounds, which reminded him that the Days of Awe were approaching—and he felt himself drawn to Nareva. On Rosh Hashana Chaikl piously swayed in Reb Shaulke's beth medresh. But the *yetzer ha-ra*, his evil inclination, teased him. During the Ten Days of Repentance he had burned with impure desire more than at any other time. In the midst of the lesson the rabbi suddenly asked him why he wasn't going to Nareva for Yom Kippur.

"As a matter of fact, I've been thinking about it." Chaikl wiped the perspiration from his brow, exhausted by the struggle within himself.

"If you leave early tomorrow morning, you'll get to Nareva before Kol Nidrei." And before Chaikl had a chance to consider it, Reb Avraham-Shaye had already pressed his hand. "Go, and God be with you."

It was as if the rabbi were bidding him farewell, not just for the Days of Awe, but for the entire winter. Chaikl had sensed on earlier occasions that Reb Avraham-Shaye regretted having taken him as a pupil, but he didn't want to remain in Nareva for a whole term. The night before Yom Kippur he tossed in bed, trying to decide. The cries of people and of the roosters and hens from the poultry shop in the courtyard lasted until midnight. The women besieged the butcher shops, buying live fowls for the sacrificial ceremony and slaughtered ones for the final meal before the fast. Chaikl pulled the quilt up over his head and tried to fall asleep. Suddenly his mother, carrying a kerosene lamp, shone the light in his face.

"I know what's troubling you. You're uneasy because you're drawn to the yeshiva just as you were last year. But when you get there, you're drawn back to your home and to your teacher in the Poplaver beth medresh. Lately you're studying less and less. You shuffle around aimlessly, or you read books all night and a good part of the day. I've been hearing a lot of praise about your becoming a great rabbi—but I just hope you'll at least be a good Jew. Go to the yeshiva for Yom Kippur and Sukkos."

Chaikl sat up in bed. "If I go to Nareva, I'll stay there all winter. That's what the rabbi wants, and I want to study in a yeshiva too. It's very gloomy here in Vilna with no friends my age. And isn't it time for you to stop supporting me with your fruit baskets?"

"You silly child! That's exactly why I'm slaving—so that I can support you." Vella laughed at him and wiped her eyes at the same time. "But if you and your teacher both say you'd be better off in the yeshiva, then do stay all winter. If you're studying in Nareva, I'll be much happier here in Vilna than I am now watching you mope around. It's all or nothing with you. Once you didn't trust me to keep a kosher home and wanted to know where I bought our meat—and now I'm afraid you may take your hat off along with your ritual fringes. I'd rather have all than nothing."

At dawn on the eve of Yom Kippur, Chaikl packed and departed. Tired from his sleepless night, he dozed off in the corner of the car and woke up only momentarily when the conductor asked for his ticket. Before his sleepy eyes flitted villages, forests, wells, and herds of cows led by cowherds in broad hats. Everything moved in reverse, in a quick, dizzying dance, as if the closer he came to the Musar school, the faster the world was running away from him.

He arrived in Nareva two hours before Kol Nidrei and went to the house where he had stayed the year before. The landlady clapped her hands in surprise.

"Look who's come!" she cried to her family. By now none of her other yeshiva lodgers were at home. Chaikl quickly donned his holiday clothes and went to the yeshiva kitchen. On the way there he imagined the surprise on his friends' faces at seeing him, but only one of his fellow Torah scholars was in the kitchen. Everyone else had already eaten the pre-fast meal and gone off to the yeshiva. The one who was still in the kitchen eating without appetite, was Moshe Chayit Lohoysker, a youth with a long neck and face and thick, prickly hair like bristles. His high, narrow forehead was always wrinkled as if he were trying to recall something. His cloudy eyes seemed to be doubly magnified behind his thick glasses. When he was talking to someone, he would look over the other person's shoulder as if a clown were mimicking him behind his back.

From his visit to Nareva a year ago Chaikl knew that Moshe Chayit Lohoysker was one of the group of students that Tsemakh Atlas had brought over from Russia and taught before he was married. Lohoysker had once been a seeker, but during the past couple of years he had strayed from the path, and his friends who had remained pious avoided him. Now he came to the yeshiva kitchen to eat and spent the rest of his time lolling in his room, reading in the town library, or roaming around alone in the woods and fields near Nareva. When he became disgusted with this kind of life, he would return to the beth medresh and approach a group discussing Musar. But as soon as he put his ear into the circle, everyone fell silent. Lohoysker had a reputation as a mocker, which was why he was now sitting in the kitchen in gloomy solitude. He was delighted to see the Vilna latecomer, and after eating they went together to the yeshiva for Kol Nidrei.

On the narrow Nareva lanes the people had locked their houses and were hurrying to the shuls, the men carrying their heavy tallis bags under their arms. Since on Yom Kippur one was forbidden to wear leather-soled shoes, they shuffled over the sharp cobblestones in rubber overshoes. On street corners friends shook hands and wished each other a good year. Women in silk shawls, their High Holiday prayer books wrapped in white kerchiefs, stopped to greet neighbors, kissing and sobbing. Children followed their parents, wide-eyed and silent, earnest at the awesome hour. Even Lohoysker strolled along quietly, enthralled by the Yom Kippur mood, while Chaikl Vilner could hardly wait to see his yeshiva friends again.

Suddenly the lane was inundated with a throng of Musarniks. The Nareva rosh yeshiva, Reb Simkha Feinerman, was accompanied by his associates: principals of little yeshivas in the surrounding villages; young rabbis; administrators who provided food, clothing, and lodging for the students; older scholars who worked with the younger ones to rid them of their bad traits—all of them Navaredker workers and thinkers who could not only see and hear but perceive and comprehend. They were on their way to Kol Nidrei from Reb Simkha's house, where they had eaten the last meal before the fast. In their billowing gaberdines and long ritual fringes, faces glowing and beards and earlocks disheveled, they looked like a flock of blackbirds that had invaded the narrow lanes. Lohoysker turned away, but Vilner stopped happily near the passers-by, waiting for them to greet him.

When Reb Simkha Feinerman saw Lohoysker, his face turned red with anger. Then, with a look mingling surprise and terror, he stared at Chaikl and quickly strode by. Another man passed them walking behind the rosh yeshiva; his eyes gleamed fervently as if he had already chanted Kol Nidrei. A third measured Lohoysker and Vilner with a sharp glance; a fourth shrugged. Most stormed by as if the two youths were not even there.

Chaikl felt as if all life had gone out of his fingers. He tried to make a fist in vain. Lohoysker was pale, but he laughed slyly. "Now you're finished, Vilner. They've seen you walking with me."

A year ago Lohoysker had been disliked, Chaikl recalled, but he hadn't been treated as if he were under the ban or as if anyone accompanying him were to be ostracized too. Enraged and humiliated at the chilly reception, Chaikl muttered, "I'm not afraid of anyone, and I'll make friends with whomever I choose."

"We'll see about that." Moshe Chayit Lohoysker laughed again, with a choked sob.

4

THE NAVAREDKER yeshiva in Nareva didn't have its own building. The students prayed and studied in Hannah-Hayke's beth medresh on Bialystok Street, and other worshipers gathered in its side room. On Sabbath and festivals, when the beth medresh was crowded, the students used a hall in the community building. In honor of the multitude that had assembled for the Days of Awe, the community offered its largest hall. Reb Simkha Feinerman stood at the eastern wall, next to the small Holy Ark that had been brought in, and watched the rows of youths passing before him. They paced swiftly from one end of the beth medresh to the other, each at the heels of his neighbor, then turned quickly on their heels and dashed back. Thus long rows of youths linked and intertwined. Faces blazed, eyes glowed, the air was charged with fire. There was good reason today for the Navaredker boast that Torah fervor made their Musar room so hot that if a bird flew in, it would get burned. All year long they studied Musar aloud and shouted to spur themselves to ecstasy. But before Kol Nidrei they did not deafen themselves with screams. Everyone studied in a soft murmur and took spiritual stock of himself: What is man's duty in this world, why does he live here, and what does he bring to the Day of Judgment?

Chaikl Vilner and Lohoysker sat down on a bench next to the door in the dimly lighted room and contemplated the crowd. The oldest yeshiva scholar, Zundl Konotoper, whom Chaikl remembered from a year ago, still hadn't married. Although his thick beard had grown even longer, he was still wearing a youth's short jacket. Every time Konotoper went to see a prospective bride he trimmed his beard, much to the astonishment of the beth medresh: without his thick locks his face looked no larger than a dried fig. As soon as the match came to naught, he would let his beard grow long and curly again. Now he was running back and forth holding a little book, humming to himself as if his beard had grown into his throat and gagged his leonine voice. When he approached Chaikl Vilner and Lohoysker, he shouted a verse from Isaiah: "Turn ye unto Him against whom you have deeply rebelled, O Children of Israel!" And then he quickly turned, as if seeing the open gates of hell at the feet of the two recalcitrant youths.

Behind Zundl Konotoper ran Reb Simkha Feinerman's oldest son. He had the flaxen hair of a peasant lad, long earlocks tucked behind his ears, full, rosy cheeks, and bright, darting eyes. In his screechy little voice he threw Zundl Konotoper's verse at Chaikl: " 'Turn ye unto Him against whom you have deeply rebelled, O Children of Israel!' You've gone astray, Vilner! Repent, Vilner!" And he rushed off after Konotoper like a colt after a horse.

Yankl Poltaver was a powerful, broad-shouldered young man. He had a strong chin, a well-modeled nose, and fiery brown eyes. When his landlady's younger sister looked at him, things would fall from her hands; his eyes burned her to the quick. Yankl Poltaver knew that he was handsome but laughed it off. The philosophy of Navaredok was that when a student has improved himself to the point where he can do without collar and tie, then he can wear them. But Yankl's view was entirely different, and he told his Bar Mitzva–age pupils: "Once and for all you must tear the world out of yourselves!" Now he thrust himself into the throng of Torah scholars swiftly, as if a fire had broken out in the building and he wanted to save himself first. The closer he came to Chaikl Vilner and Moshe Chayit Lohoysker, the wider he spread his arms—it seemed that he intended to seize them both and crush them. Suddenly he clapped one palm against the other. "The most important thing in man's life is to perfect his character. If he doesn't, then what purpose is there to his life?" And he immediately turned back like a hurricane, a thunderburst, a waterfall cascading down a mountainside. Reb Simkha Feinerman's son dashed out from behind him and clapped his hands too. "The most important thing in man's life is to perfect his character. If you aren't doing that, Vilner, why are you living in this world?" And he quickly followed Yankl Poltaver away.

Bilgrayer waddled broadly and calmly back and forth. He had a big paunch, pomaded yellow hair, a pockmarked face, a fleshy nose, and large, crooked teeth. Bilgrayer was a scholar of repute. He shook quotations from Maimonides out of his sleeve and was often contemptuous of the Musarniks. The Nareva elders complained to the rosh yeshiva that Bilgrayer had the best lodging and a larger allowance than anyone else, but the rosh yeshiva replied that he couldn't help it. Opponents of Navaredok always charged that not a page of Talmud was studied in Nareva; they emphasized only Musar. Therefore, a Bilgrayer was needed as proof that only in Nareva could one excel in learning. Bilgrayer knew his own strength and looked at everyone with provocative disdain. Now too he stood next to Chaikl Vilner with belly out and hands in his pockets. From under his upturned hat a shock of greasy yellow hair fell over his forehead. In his fleshy face and calm demeanor there was something of the hoodlum casually sizing up his opponent before starting a fight.

Chaikl heard Butchers Street within him, urging him to give back as good as he got. The humiliation he had suffered today boiled over in him and he stood up, but Bilgrayer passed by calmly. From behind him the rosh yeshiva's son swam by again. He waddled up to Chaikl, belly out, and even imitated Bilgrayer's style of speech. "Ask me twelve Talmudic questions, Vilner, and I'll solve them all—with one reply. Were you busy with Torah studies, or were you loafing around in Vilna, the way Lohoysker does here?"

For a moment Chaikl wanted to seize the little jokester by the throat, but he restrained himself in time. Everyone would laugh at him; whoever starts a fight with a child is a child himself. He looked around for his friends from a year ago and saw them sitting on a bench on the other side of the hall. They were reading Musar books, apparently immersed in gloom. Chaikl felt that they were annoyed with him for appearing with Lohoysker the moment he came to town and that was why they were keeping their distance.

"See that tall chap with the tallis over his head?" Moshe Chayit poked him with his elbow and pointed to a man facing the wall. "That's your former principal from Valkenik, Tsemakh Atlas, the one who dragged me here from Russia when I was a kid." Lohoysker breathed heavily, as if his lungs were stuffed with sand.

In the yeshivas of Lithuania there had been much talk about a Navaredker Musarnik who had wanted to burn down a library in one village and had rolled in the mud in another to gain forgiveness from his former fiancée's father. People knew that he was wandering from place to place. Yet when Chaikl had come to Nareva in Elul a year ago and asked about his Valkenik principal, no one had known exactly where he was. In midsummer, however, he had suddenly appeared in Nareva, and after lengthy deliberation Reb Simkha had decided that Tsemakh Lomzher would not cause trouble any more. He had suffered enough; he was a true penitent.

A resounding bang on the table announced that Kol Nidrei was beginning. The line of Musarniks who a moment earlier had been racing from wall to wall crumbled in a flash. They pressed forward to their seats, faces ecstatic, each one finding his place more with his outstretched hands than with his glassy eyes.

After Kol Nidrei someone pounded the table again to announce that the rosh yeshiva would talk. Tall, thin, red-bearded Reb Simkha Feinerman stretched his arms out from under his tallis like an eagle flapping its powerful wings before flight. He leaned his elbows on the prayer stand and began speaking calmly in a loud, clear voice so as to be heard in every corner of the hall. His subject was repentance.

"In honor of the Day of Judgment every ben Torah must promise himself to become a better person. But the first condition for becoming better is to have good friends. Even our father Abraham was deprived of the spirit of prophecy during the time he was in the company of his nephew, Lot. Only when Lot left him and went to the place which had attracted him all along, Sodom, did prophecy return to Abraham."

The Musar students knew that the speaker could address a crowded beth medresh yet direct his remarks to one young man. Nevertheless, Chaikl refused to believe that Reb Simkha Feinerman would speak to such a large congregation with just him in mind. But Lohoysker whispered into his ear, "Well, you've lived to see the day! Now you know why the Divine Presence of Navaredok doesn't rest on you. You're palling around with the drunkard, Lot. You were caught in the company of a man of Sodom."

Lohoysker's vicious remark disgusted Chaikl. "I didn't catch the last train before Kol Nidrei to hear your interpretations of the rosh yeshiva's talk." Lohoysker fell silent and looked toward the door as though wanting to escape but afraid of going out into the dark by himself.

Reb Simkha stopped and swayed in silence for a long time. His long, narrow red-gold beard hung over the prayer stand like the festive curtain that covered the Holy Ark on holidays. The room was filled with a charged, tense atmosphere. A yellowish mist covered the light bulbs, seemingly darkened by the exhaled heat of the scholars who awaited the stormy outburst—the rosh yeshiva's exhortation for spiritual awakening. The students covered their eyes with their hands as if reciting the Shma Yisroel, so as not to feel ashamed in case they wanted to cry. Reb Simkha began with a plaintive melody, and the crowd accompanied his remarks with a subdued hum.

"My teachers and colleagues, the Prophet Isaiah states, 'The wicked are like the troubled sea, for it cannot rest, and its waters cast up mire and dirt.' The stirred-up waves in the sea think that they can go farther up the shore than previous waves. But no wave has yet succeeded in going farther than the place assigned to the sea during the Six Days of Creation. The stormy waters cast up only dregs and silt. No matter how much a man exerts himself to achieve more than his predecessor, no one has yet left this world having achieved half of what he wanted. The Midrash states that the path of repentance too may be compared to the sea. As the sea is open to all, so is the way to repentance constantly open to all. But woe unto the man who flees danger on land to save himself at sea—and then drowns. Woe unto him who stumbles on his way to repentance. He needs a new Yom Kippur to atone for the previous one."

The yeshiva students felt as if their clothes were being singed from all sides. Everyone moved closer to Reb Simkha and stood with wrinkled brow and glazed eyes. Permeated by the all-encompassing, electrifying hum that accompanied his plaintive melody, Reb Simkha soared even higher.

"My teachers and colleagues, no matter how much we do for a person, we do nothing for him if we disregard his world to come. No matter how great our sacrifice for a friend, we give him nothing if we don't give him eternity. If we can't console an anguished man that eternal life will be the reward for his suffering, with what then *can* we console him?

"My teachers and colleagues, the Old Man of Navaredok, Reb Yosef-Yoizl Hurwitz, always said that the worst sentence for a person is to be unable to renounce his own nature. But if a person tries hard to overcome his innate evil traits, heaven also comes to his aid. So let us ask for heavenly help in the words of the prayer: 'Our Father, our King, destroy the evil decree against us,' " the rosh yeshiva cried out, and the words were repeated by the entire congregation like thunder reverberating on a mountain where every abyss, ravine, and slope echoed the sounds a hundredfold.

"My teachers and colleagues"—Reb Simkha's voice was heard again, and the other voices began to recede and vanish as crumbling thunder dwindles into the distance—"We believe with perfect faith that the world is sustained by virtue of the saintly man—and we, we want to be saints. But at first glance some of us might think: Is it possible? *I* slave away to achieve perfection, *I* walk about disheveled and hungry, and the world that is sustained through me even makes fun of my ritual fringes! But whoever thinks thus is surely not one of the saints because of whom the world is sustained. The Talmud tells us about the sage Rabbi Hanania ben Dosa: 'Every day a heavenly voice is heard saying: "The entire world is sustained because of my son, Hanania, yet one measure of carob suffices Hanania from one Sabbath eve to the next." ' The true man of perfection is satisfied with a pot of dried carob from one Sabbath eve to the next. He demands nothing and even lovingly accepts the humiliation of the world which is sustained on account of him. And so, my dear friends, with the strength of a vast multitude, let us come at least one step closer to the presence of Rabbi Hanina ben Dosa in Paradise. Now, in this hour of mercy, when the heavenly gate is open, let us pray once more for divine help: 'Our Father, our King, let us repent fully before you!' "

The exhortation had ended but the storm raged on. The walls on all four sides of the room were empty. The students had gradually moved from their places and gathered around Reb Simkha's prayer stand. Chaikl found himself locked in on all sides by the students who had previously snubbed or chastised him. Teeth clenched, Zundl Konotoper hummed along, his razor-sharp voice seemingly flaying strips of his own skin. His humming fused with Yankl Poltaver's cries of "Ay-ay-ay." Poltaver was shouting as if he despaired of repentance for his sins. A young scholar aimed his childish whining heavenward, pleading like a fledgling in first flight who has just managed to reach the nearest tree but can't grasp a twig with its claws.

Moshe Chayit Lohoysker stood alone near the exit, gazing off toward the corner where the tall figure of Reb Tsemakh Atlas was also standing by himself. Facing the wall, tallis over his head, he screamed with the mute, prolonged scream of a drowning man: "Our Father, our King, let us repent fully before you!"

5

LOHOYSKER AND CHAIKL VILNER were the first to leave after the Evening Service. Prayers had concluded earlier in other shuls. Beside an open window of an empty, lighted beth medresh one old man in tallis and white linen robe was still reciting Psalms. The lane the two youths were walking in looked like a narrow, twisting path between tombstones, and the voice of the old man sounded funereal. Glad that Vilner had no choice but to remain in his company, Lohoysker invited him to his room.

"I'll go, but why is everyone giving you the cold shoulder? What have you done this year?" Chaikl asked, striding ahead quickly.

"I haven't become any more of a heretic this year than last," Moshe Chayit responded cheerfully. "I've just stopped being careful. When I eat in the yeshiva kitchen, I don't mince words—I tell them what I think of the Navaredker bench warmers. That's why the older Musar students asked the rosh yeshiva to expel me. But Reb Simkha Feinerman has his own calculations: it doesn't pay. Since I'm from Russia and can't cross the Soviet border to go back home, I have to stay in Nareva. Reb Simkha is afraid people in town might say that the Navaredkers took a son away from his parents and then abandoned him. Still, Zundl Konotoper and his bunch are trying to get their way. They claim that I'm ruining the younger students. But now that Tsemakh Lomzher has returned to Nareva, he won't let them touch me." Moshe Chayit stopped in the street and explained, waving his hands.

"When Lomzher fled into the world and left me in the yeshiva, I was still very pious. Now that he's returned, supposedly a penitent, and discovered that I've left the religious way, he blames himself for my following in his footsteps. So he begs the rosh yeshiva not to drive me away. Perhaps I'll repent, he says. He tells me about his failures, hoping I'll realize that, as the Torah says, sin lurks at the door, and one mustn't put one's foot out into the world."

"Reb Tsemakh stood up for someone who scoffs at Musar?" Chaikl asked in amazement. "This means that he really has changed."

But Moshe Chayit wasn't at all moved by the principal's solicitude. In fact, hatred sprayed from him: "Aside from the fact that Tsemakh Lomzher broke an engagement with one girl and married another, who knows how many other women he's slept with? People say his wife loves him with all her heart. Actually, why *does* she love that hairy, hook-beaked beanpole? Maybe he charmed the beauty with stories about how he kidnaped children from their parents in Russia and dragged them over the border into Poland. Despite his success with women, he still doesn't enjoy life. Thoughts of repentance have overwhelmed that kidnaper and sensualist like ants, and they bite him. Oho, how they bite him! An hour after morning prayers and breakfast, when all the students are already sitting over their Talmuds, he is still wrapped in his tallis and tefillin, facing the wall and whispering: 'O Master of the Universe, if only she'd appear to me in a dream so that I could ask her forgiveness. But she doesn't appear in a dream, and I can't forget her. O Master of the Universe, ask her to forgive me, and tell me in her name: I have forgiven!'"

Chaikl Vilner felt a pressure in his chest. He wanted to cry. His heart was wrenched with pity for the suffering principal and with disgust at Lohoysker. "He's the saint and you're the fiend. Envy is positively pouring out of you. You're jealous that he was more successful than you."

Moshe Chayit laughed and hunched his head into his shoulders as if afraid that the enraged Vilner might slap him. "Of course it's envy talking, rotten envy. But it's not my fault that his first fiancée died and he went back too late to ask her forgiveness. So he came here and consoled himself that he has other merits stored up in the Almighty's record book. He kidnaped children from their parents and made them into yeshiva students. On his way here he thought: The presence of Moshe Chayit Lohoysker, a rabbi's son, will stand me in good stead so that my dead fiancée won't torment me so. But when he came to Nareva, he saw that this rabbi's son was no longer in the grave where he had thrown and abandoned him. The truth is, I'm still lying in that Navaredker grave, but I'm lying there without the Musar spirit. So Lomzher complains that neither the dead Amdur fiancée nor the living student Lohoysker gives him any peace. Do you want me to remain a lice-ridden scholar so that tired sensualist who's supposedly become a penitent can put his soul at rest?"

"Then leave the yeshiva! Who's keeping you here?" Chaikl cried, quickening his pace.

"Come inside and I'll tell you what's keeping me here." Lohoysker stopped in front of a house with narrow, crooked steps. Chaikl followed, annoyed with himself. Reb Simkha Feinerman and his friends had turned away from him because they met him with a young man who had been ostracized by the yeshiva. Therefore, to spite them all, he had sat next to this ostracized youth throughout the service, and he had left with Lohoysker to show the yeshiva people that they didn't faze him. But that sort of behavior, Chaikl realized, was childish.

Moshe Chayit opened the door to his room. "The landlord and his wife live at the other end of the corridor, and they're a pair of deaf old imbeciles besides. We can talk loudly or even scream to our hearts' content." The two walked into a thick, foul darkness that had the moldy smell of old clothes rotting in a cellar. A red eye suddenly glowed on the ceiling—a small bulb.

"You turn on lights during Yom Kippur? Let me out of here!" Chaikl yelled.

"Forgot! Completely forgot!" Moshe Chayit slapped the side of his head but made no attempt to hide his oily, clownish smile. "On the other hand, do you really believe that hellfires are kindled because an electric light is turned on in here? Sit down, Vilner," he said, quickly and ingratiatingly, like a lonely person thrilled at suddenly seeing an unexpected guest.

The room was narrow and small. An iron cot with a frayed blanket on it and a shabby, round-bellied old dresser strewn with tattered books were against one wall and a wardrobe covered the other. Under the only window in the room stood a little table and chair.

"Anyone who violates Yom Kippur and still comes to eat in the yeshiva kitchen every day is absolutely shameless, and I don't want to spend a minute with you. But I'd like to hear you explain why you're not leaving the yeshiva," Chaikl said, sitting down on the chair.

"I don't have anywhere else to go." Moshe Chayit sat down on the bed. Now he looked tired and sad, like someone who'd spent all day looking for a loan and come home that night empty-handed. "Do you expect me to learn a trade at the age of twenty-two? I couldn't even have done it earlier. Don't forget, I'm a rabbi's son. From my father, the rabbi of Lohoysk, I inherited a love for arguing, not strength to work with my hands. Tsemakh Lomzher wasn't the only one who poisoned my heart—my grandfather and father did the same thing. On the eve of every new month, when a lesser Yom Kippur is celebrated, my grandfather, the old rabbi of Lohoysk, beat his breast in contrition while he recited the great confession of Rabbenu Nissim. It goes without saying, of course, that when Yom Kippur came, my grandfather looked for more transgressions. He assumed that he had sinned according to the abc's, and he beat his breast for sins alphabetically. In his will he stated that his body was to be dragged over the ground, then picked up and thrown down. Stones were to be placed on his heart and his chest hair singed. He wanted to undergo all the death penalties described in the Torah. And my father, the younger rabbi of Lohoysk, beat his breast the same way. He too thought he had committed the most despicable sins. And so they drummed it into my head and heart that I'm a sinner too."

"You're raving! You're out of your mind!" Chaikl squirmed on the chair. He felt a cramp in his stomach. "On the one hand, you turn on the light on the holiest day of the year. On the other, you tell me you feel that you're a sinner because your father and grandfather beat their breasts in contrition."

"Right! That's just it." Moshe Chayit Lohoysker nearly choked with excitement. "Yes, I violate Yom Kippur and I deny everything—Navaredok, Torah, even God. Still, I feel that I'm a sinner. I often lie here on my cot dreaming of everything that's forbidden. Then suddenly, right here in this hole I'm buried in, I see my parents and grandfather. 'All you think of is stuffing your guts and drinking,' my grandfather shouts. 'A glutton and swiller won't think twice about stealing as long as he can stuff his belly.' And my father groans, 'Don't think of girls, my son. Think of being a religious Jew.' Then my mother cries out, 'My child, you're lying in bed with your head uncovered.' So my heart constricts with pity for my parents. My head becomes as heavy as a stone from being in bed without a yarmulke. The hair on my skin pricks me for going around without ritual fringes. I inherited the need to beat my breast in contrition from my father and grandfather. They never hit or beat me—my Hebrew teacher did that." Moshe Chayit grimaced with disgust, as if damp, slippery bugs were crawling over his naked body. He slid up on his bed until his back touched the wall and began to talk about the Lohoysk Hebrew teacher.

"He wasn't one of your greasy little Jews with a matted beard, copper-colored nails like a ritual slaughterer's, and the eyes of the Angel of Death. Actually, he was a tall, broad-shouldered, rather serene man with a tidy beard, neat clothes, and a luxuriant black mustache. He was also an expert at the Bible and a master of Hebrew grammar. When a boy did something wrong, the teacher didn't grab his whip and tell him to undress. On the contrary, he would fix his big bright eyes on the pupil and gaze at him in a friendly way. Then he would calmly stroke his thick mustache with his thumb and even more calmly take out a cute little notebook with a little string between the pages. Then, with a sharp pencil, he would jot down in his round, clear handwriting how many lashes were due So-and-So. Friday was punishment day, and he enjoyed this as much as going to the bath. He locked the door and covered the windows; you could hear a pin drop. Then he delivered a sermon to the students. He would begin with a verse from the weekly portion of the Torah and conclude by listing every student's sins. Only then did he get to work. He whipped the pupils slowly and with obvious pleasure, counting the way the High Priest of the Holy Temple counted during the ancient service—one and one, one and two. . . . He involved the students in his work, too. A couple of youngsters who would get their due later on helped him out. It seems that the pleasure of seeing others being whipped can be stronger than the pain and shame of being beaten yourself. The parents weren't supposed to know about this, and the youngsters kept the secret. And it was worthwhile. Everyone knew that you could loaf and fool around all week—but on Friday your rear end belonged to the teacher.

"Naturally, the moral of the tale isn't exactly applicable to the story itself. My teacher was a calm, voluptuous sadist, while Tsemakh Lomzher is a wild, fiery one. Tsemakh beat me with his Musar whip while my stupid friends—the ones who avoid me now—piously nodded their calves' heads in agreement." Moshe Chayit looked at the door as if afraid that someone might be listening on the other side. "By the time Tsemakh Lomzher returned to the yeshiva, he had his fill of all pleasures, while my worldliness is artificial, my impudence contrived. When I try to get close to a girl, I feel that she's laughing at me. Perhaps she really is laughing. . . . Sexual lust is driving me crazy."

"Get married," Chaikl said.

"It won't help!" Lohoysker sounded delighted to be punishing himself. "If I were to take a wife and not have holy matters in mind during marital relations—if copulation wasn't performed with holiness and purity like an ecstatic Silent Devotion and my sole intent was physical pleasure—then my seed would be a rotten seed, and my future child would have the blood of a bastard flowing in his veins. Violating Yom Kippur doesn't frighten me; being an atheist doesn't frighten me; I revile everything that's sacred. I'm an instigator, a blasphemer, a Jeroboam who sins and corrupts others—but I'm afraid to get married. The dybbuks of all the Musarniks of generations past have come into me, shouting their eternal shout: 'It's forbidden! It's forbidden!' That's why I hate the Navaredkers so . . ."

"You're a lunatic! You're obsessed with Navaredok!" Chaikl backed away from Lohoysker as if frogs were leaping from the youth's pockets.

"Right; I'm obsessed with Navaredok." Moshe Chayit gave a soft, provocative laugh. "The *Code of Law* and the Musar books emphasize the same thing. In essence, nothing is permitted if there's no holy intent in it. Every pleasure is a slice of something forbidden, a piece of pork fat. You're still faring well so far. You come to Nareva for just a few weeks and then run back home. You told me last year that in Vilna you live on a street lined with butcher shops. Looking at your face one can tell that you live on a fleshy, this-worldly street and that the fleshy, this-worldly street lives in you. But sooner or later the Torah of Navaredok will settle into your bones and your life. And then the Musarnik in you will close the kosher butcher shops and only the nonkosher ones will be inside you. You'll enjoy only what's forbidden, because nothing is permissible. And then, like me, you won't enjoy anything but sinning. . . ."

Lohoysker's mouth dropped open; his face grew long. His bespectacled eyes stared at the door. Chaikl jumped up, turned toward the doorway, and saw Reb Tsemakh Atlas.

6

THE PENITENT, as he was called in the yeshiva, entered the little room. His beard had spots of gray now, his coal-black eyes had become deeper and sadder, but his carriage was still stiff and erect. To keep Tsemakh from sitting down, Moshe Chayit jumped up from the cot and went to sit on the only chair. Then he took off his glasses and held them up to the lamp, contemplating the points of light dancing on the polished lenses. He tried to look undisturbed, but his jaw was trembling and he had an angry frown. Chaikl was shaken too, and he listened to the Valkenik principal in a daze.

"Lohoysker, have pity on your parents," Tsemakh pleaded. "They cried bitterly when they bade you good-bye. Nevertheless, they let you go to save you from growing up to be a member of the Yevsektsiya, the Jewish section of the Communist Party in Russia, and a heretic toward the God of Israel. Just imagine how much the rabbi of Lohoysk would suffer if he heard that his son had strayed from the true path."

"I know that if it weren't for you, my parents wouldn't have sent me into a life of wandering away from home." Lohoysker's teeth chattered as if he had just stepped out of ice-cold water. "Perhaps you'd already decided to leave the yeshiva while you were in Russia, but that still didn't prevent you from luring me away from my home and dragging me off to Poland."

"That's not true. It wasn't until later that I stumbled—and my punishment is greater than I can bear! But when I saved you for Torah, I had sacred purposes in mind. All the students I saved from becoming addicted to communism stayed with Torah—except you, the rabbi's son, who has fallen into evil ways and even corrupts others." Reb Tsemakh cast a quick glance at Chaikl.

"In Russia you promised parents that you'd watch over their children," Lohoysker answered, an angry smile on his pouting lips, "but in fact you completely neglected them. When you went out into the world and married well, you never thought of sending a new garment to the Lohoysk rabbi's son or any other smuggled-in student so that he needn't rot in his old rags. In his exhortation Reb Simkha blubbered that the world is sustained by the saint who demands nothing of the world. Perhaps Rabbi Hanania ben Dosa was satisfied with a pot of dried carob. But just as I don't want to make myself miserable with dried carob—and I'll do without Rabbi Hanania's portion in Paradise, thank you—in the same way, the other Navaredkers, try as they might, can't deny themselves a bit of worldly pleasure. They're jealous of the yeshiva students at Mir, Kletzk, and Radun because they get better lodging, a bigger allowance, and new clothes. 'Ay-ay-ay! Our Father, our King,' the seekers pray. 'We'll give up bread and new clothes!' they yell to high heaven. They want to, but they cannot!" Moshe Chayit pointed at the floor as if a subterranean prison full of Musarniks were down there. "No matter how many times a day the seekers bury themselves and assert that man has come into this world to provide himself and others with eternal life, they still can't renounce worldly pleasure before they step into eternal life." Moshe Chayit looked up toward the ceiling as if there were cells full of Navaredker prisoners above him too. "I know a kidnaper who claims he gave his life for the Torah. Still, he didn't want to deny himself a few years of plenty by free-loading at his brother-in-laws' house, and because of that he broke off a match. Isn't that so, Reb Tsemakh?"

Terror stricken, Chaikl looked at Tsemakh Atlas standing in the middle of the little room, head down, submitting to this abuse.

"You're a disrespectful, big-mouthed hoodlum with the heart of a gangster. If I'd known earlier what sort of a person you are, I wouldn't have left the beth medresh with you," Chaikl berated Lohoysker.

But the latter, hands in his pockets, answered mockingly, "You're angry because you were seen with me, and you're afraid they'll ostracize you too. You won't be able to continue last year's conversations, and the Navaredkers won't fall into calflike raptures because of your profound ideas. After all, you've come here to talk, not to listen. You don't want to know the truth about yourself—and which one of these local bench warmers has enough sense to tell you the truth? I'm the only Musarnik who understands the soul's strengths. That's why I'm telling you, Vilner, that you're an impetuous, confused moron. You get stirred up too easily, but above all, you're a dreamer. You swim around in fantasies, and you don't want the mists to dissipate. You're afraid someone might burn you with an idea and drive away all your flights of fancy. That's why you're so incensed against me—because I tell you more than you want to know, more than you can bear to hear. But you won't always be blind. What you've learned about self-awareness won't let you stay blind. You see, Vilner, what an expert I am in psychology? I actually have the divine spirit to predict the future. This way I'm showing my former group leader how thoroughly I mastered his method of creeping into someone's heart and guts. Now imagine how much I suffered while he cut me to pieces and I assumed that everything he said was God's holy truth."

"I cut myself to pieces even more. And if you're imitating me, then repent as I have done," Tsemakh Atlas said.

Moshe Chayit jumped toward him and shouted into his face, "I don't believe in your repentance! And it was *you* who taught me not to believe anyone. 'Lohoysker, Lohoysker,' you shouted at me, 'are you weighing your good deeds on the balance scale of the Torah? If a grain of selfishness clings to the scale where you weigh your good deeds, then you're giving false weight. Lohoysker, Lohoysker,' you shouted at me, 'you can keep all the mitzvas and customs, but if you have an ulterior motive, then in the next world they'll present you with a bagful of your wormy mitzvas. Lohoysker, Lohoysker,' you shouted at me, 'if you see someone standing with a tallis over his head, swaying with eyes glazed with piety, watch him—watch him carefully to see if the impure flame of sly expediency isn't burning in those pious, glassy eyes. Watch him to see if his sighing and groaning and clutching at his heart isn't just a Purim masquerade. Watch the penitent carefully too, because, for the sensualist, crying and repenting is also a kind of lust.' That's what you'd yell in our group sessions and in our private talks late at night. And I was a good student! If you had come back from the secular world starving for worldly pleasures, perhaps I would have had greater faith in your repentance. But you came back satiated with pleasures—that's why I don't trust your repentance. You want me to sacrifice myself for you just so your professed regret should be heard in heaven? Oh, no! I won't sacrifice myself for you!"

"I'm not asking you to sacrifice yourself for me. I'm just warning you that someday you'll have regrets as I do."

"That's when I'll become a penitent. Meanwhile, I want to try doing what you've done," Moshe Chayit answered, pale and exhausted by the quarrel. "I know I don't have the courage to make the first step out into the world, but I can't and I don't want to become religious again."

Shoulders sagging, Tsemakh went to the door; but he immediately straightened up and turned to Lohoysker. He pointed a long finger at him and spoke with a muffled voice, as if from a cellar. "Remember, you'll regret it! As soon as you enter the turmoil of the world, you'll see that good and evil do not stem from the Almighty. A man does everything with his own hands. If you give in once, you'll continue to give in more and more as time goes by, like a glutton with a stretched belly. The choice is yours only the first time, when you don't know the hidden qualities of the transgression. If you let yourself be lured in and slip just once, you'll continue to stumble until you break all your bones—like me. Then you'll see for yourself that sin and punishment are intertwined, and you'll become a penitent. But the life of a penitent is as bitter as gall, because he wonders constantly how he went astray and realizes that with just a bit of effort to overcome his lusts, he could have avoided the anguish of regrets. Such thoughts can drive one mad. If one of the wishes of a freethinker isn't fulfilled, he doesn't assume that everything has a cause and effect and that he is at fault. But since you studied Musar, you will assume that you and you alone are solely responsible, which is the way I think. I'm warning you in time, you'll regret it!"

"You're lying! It hasn't crossed my mind at all that you're responsible for anything. You've become a supposed penitent because by nature you're an adventure seeker." Moshe Chayit stood on tiptoe, craning his neck up to the tall Reb Tsemakh. "In Russia you waged war against members of the Yevsektsiya, the Jewish Communists. In Poland you ran around from town to town like a cyclone, establishing new yeshivas. When you had nowhere to go and had to stay in Nareva, you were bored to death. You needed intense experiences. So you had no choice but to get rid of the storm of rage inside you by tormenting the students you brought over from Russia. Finally you got so tired of sitting and studying that you pulled yourself together and went out to stir up the world. Your greatest stroke of good fortune was finding out that your first fiancée had died. You rolled in the mud in Amdur supposedly to gain forgiveness from her father, but what you really wanted was to stir up the world even more. That's why you became a wanderer and made a reputation for yourself as a penitent. I don't know how long you'll last in your new role, because your heart is still desolate. It keeps pushing you to look for adventures. You're not the zealous extremist the Musarniks think you are—you're simply an adventurer!"

A mild smile flitted on Tsemakh's lips as he looked wistfully at his impudent student. Then he turned and went to the door, accompanied by Chaikl.

"It's not hard to be a Musarnik a couple of weeks a year," Lohoysker taunted Vilner. "How long are you staying? Till after Sukkos as you did a year ago? Or are you leaving right after Yom Kippur this time?"

"This time I've come for the whole winter," said Chaikl, and he quickened his pace to catch up with Reb Tsemakh.

Both strode along the dark little lanes in silence until they came to a corner illuminated by a lantern.

"I didn't think Lohoysker had such a big mouth," Chaikl apologized.

"But I did. I know him and I know that his bitterness poisons his common sense," Reb Tsemakh said softly, swaying, as if he'd dozed off on his feet, in the street light's chiaroscuro. "And when you get angry, Vilner, you have no self-restraint either. At least that's the way you used to be in Valkenik. Perhaps you've changed."

The two walked on until they came to the courtyard of the community building where the yeshiva people prayed during the high holidays. Near the large windows of the empty, light-filled hall, a few students swayed over Musar books like lone cornstalks bending in the wind of late autumn.

Reb Tsemakh had decided to go to the yeshiva and study all night. He put his hand on Chaikl's shoulder. "The Nareva rosh yeshiva knows that you studied with me in Valkenik. Tonight after the Evening Service he asked me why you're befriending a heretic like Lohoysker. I answered that you're basically an honest person, and you trust everyone who offers you his friendship." Tsemakh fell silent for a moment but soon shook off his dreamlike apathy and gave Chaikl a strange Musar lecture. "We haven't seen each other for about three years. During this period I've come to the conclusion that compassion is the foundation of belief. For a person who isn't compassionate—even his belief in God is a kind of idol worship . . . Go and get some rest, Vilner. Tomorrow will be a hard day of prayer and fasting. One must not be cruel toward oneself either."

Exhausted from so many experiences in the brief twenty-four hours since he had left home, Chaikl barely managed to drag his feet back to his lodging. The rosh yeshiva had changed completely, he thought. Lohoysker had reviled him, and he hadn't protested. Lohoysker knows he no longer belongs to the yeshiva, Chaikl thought, and that he's afraid to leave. But I still don't know where my place is—whether in the yeshiva or in the world. Am I a freethinker or a religious, he wondered, or like some kind of amphibious creature? He would have to stay in Nareva for a term to clarify for himself exactly where his place was.

7

THERE WAS A MUSARIST SAYING: As Yom Kippur goes, so goes Simkhas Torah. At the conclusion of Simkhas Torah, everyone went to Reb Simkha Feinerman's home. The entryway served as the women's section. The extended table was set with small jugs of sparkling sweet wine and plates of apples as red as the cheeks of the women. Among the young women wearing fashionable little caps, decorated hats, and nicely combed marriage wigs, there were also unmarried girls with black, blond, or red hair curled to the nape of the neck and held with colorful combs. These were the prospective brides whom the rebbetsins of the Navaredker scholars had brought to Nareva. These girls from middle-class homes continually turned, adjusted their braids, and fanned their overheated faces with snow-white lace kerchiefs. They looked about in confusion, somewhat frightened. The young rebbetsins sought out bridegrooms for them with knowing glances, but the pious students barely sniffed into the women's section. If a ben Torah wanted to go outside, he passed through with lowered head. The only one who wandered about freely was Bilgrayer, with his greasy, yellow shock of hair and his large, wide-spaced teeth. On his pockmarked face with its broad, fleshy nose one could see a connoisseur's contempt, the impudence of a practical man. He knew all the available rabbinic matches with the same expertise that he knew the most difficult passages in commentaries to the *Code of Law*. Bilgrayer was looking for a wealthy father-in-law with an important rabbinic chair to be inherited. As for the "monument"—as he sarcastically referred to the bride—it went without saying that she had to be pleasant looking, though not necessarily a beauty. He found no one in the women's section at Reb Simkha Feinerman's home, absolutely no one. Nevertheless, he roamed about because he was bored with the pious-eyed Musarniks who kept to themselves in the other room even on Simkhas Torah.

The other room was filled with beards, yarmulkes, and gaberdines. Young Navaredker students and the older scholars had surrounded a visitor, a Nareva youth studying in Mir who had come home for Sukkos. He too had come to Reb Simkha's for the postholiday festivity. The Navaredkers pounced on him like wolves, mercilessly flaying him with their tongues and controverting his every remark. Most skillful at this was Zundl Konotoper. He shouted with his leonine voice and shook his beard like Samson with his locks. Seeing that they wanted to tear him to pieces like a herring, the visitor innocently asked, "Which Talmudic tractate did you study in Nareva this past term?"

"*Kesuvos*," Konotoper answered drily and immediately lost his lion's voice. He knew that in a scholarly discussion, he would be lost.

"We studied *Kesuvos* in Mir this past semester too. We spent weeks just on one part." The youth cited a passage and wondered why Maimonides had ruled contrariwise. "Go ahead; let's see how you sharp-tongued Navaredkers can solve this difficult passage in Maimonides."

Just then Bilgrayer came back into the room. Hands in his pockets, the scholar bent over the table, pressing his huge belly against the short, thin Konotoper, who became mute, head down, crushed by the fleshy weight on him. Bilgrayer told the visitor that his question was no question at all. "In fact, it's blown up out of nothing."

"What do you mean, blown up out of nothing?" Bilgrayer's contempt made the Nareva youth, who studied at the Mir yeshiva, angrier than all the other Navaredkers' barbed remarks. A minute later both scholars were on their feet, gesticulating like windmills. The visitor was beside himself in his effort to prove that Nareva was perverting the plain and simple interpretation. But Bilgrayer refuted all of Mir's original interpretation. "Even Reb Joseph Caro himself, in his commentary on Maimonides' *Mishne Torah*, didn't understand Maimonides' remark . . ." Then he looked around. The two scholars were alone. The Musarniks had vanished, grumbling like wild beasts with a tasty kill snatched from their mouths.

"Who would you want to compete with here? This gang? All they know is how to throw themselves around during prayers and scream 'Ay-ay-ay,' " Bilgrayer said, laughing.

"True enough." The visitor nodded. He saw that the speaker was indeed a scholar. "When did you have time to accomplish all this?"

"While they're shouting over their Musar books, I sit and study." Bilgrayer stretched his thick upper lip over his big teeth.

"But you still haven't answered the original question." The visitor frowned.

"Is that all you have to worry about? This isn't the time to argue over a difficult passage in Maimonides." Bilgrayer went on to ask the youth, "How much of an allowance do you get in Mir? And what is your news about marriages? Famous rabbis and rich men don't come to the Navaredkers in Nareva looking for a bridegroom. Assistant synagogue caretakers come here to find a bargain for spinster daughters."

Hands folded behind his back, Reb Simkha Feinerman strode from room to room. His face was rosy and fresh, his golden-red beard gleamed, his light blue eyes sparkled. Wherever he appeared a path was immediately made for him through the crush. As he entered the middle room, which was crowded with young people, his glance fell on Chaikl Vilner, who, during the summer vacation, had swum and done the breast stroke better than any of the students who went swimming with him. Reb Simkha's eyes gleamed with mischief. He looked around, then waggishly sneaked up to Vilner.

All through Sukkos, Chaikl's former friends had kept away from him. Hence he sat amid the festive throng, sadly musing that he had begun poorly in Nareva and would have to return home. Once again Chaikl saw himself sitting alone like a golem in the large Poplaver beth medresh in Vilna. Suddenly he felt a sharp, painful tweak in the muscle of his right arm. He whirled, incensed, ready to punish the impudent brat who had pinched him like a little schoolboy. But the yeshiva boys were singing and dancing ecstatically; they weren't even looking at him. Who could have done it?

Only Reb Simkha Feinerman, who had just passed, was looking at him. There was a cheerful smile on his face, but at the same time he tugged at his mustache in vexation, as if to say, You're a rascal, and you deserve to be whipped. But deep down I like a youngster who's a rascal. Chaikl felt a stone rolling off his heart, as if with that pinch Reb Simkha had opened up a blister. He pushed his way through the crowd to the rosh yeshiva and said, "This coming winter I want to study in Nareva. My teacher, Reb Avraham-Shaye Kosover, also wants me to stay here."

After a lengthy silence Reb Simkha said coldly, "Well . . ." Then he added more amiably, "If that's what Reb Avraham-Shaye wants, we'll see." Then, unexpectedly, he laughed and slyly winked a blue eye. Apparently he was pleased that Vilner had accepted a painful tweak in silence. A moment later he became serious again, slowly stroking his long, narrow beard until he reached the tip. "Actually, you can draw Torah learning from Reb Avraham-Shaye like water from a well, but your teacher wants you to be in an environment of worthwhile friends." Reb Simkha ended the conversation, and the newly accepted pupil understood the hint that he should no longer befriend Lohoysker.

At one gesture from the rosh yeshiva, Chaikl was immediately surrounded by his friends of a year ago. Yankl Poltaver, handsome, powerful, and wild as a young horse in the steppes, reconciled himself with Vilner by reciting a couplet: "Take criticism, heed fault; if not, you're lost, foolish colt." Zundl Konotoper grabbed Chaikl with both hands. "Come, Vilner, let's dance to the tune, 'Purify our hearts to worship You in truth!' "

Yeshiva students, sprawling in chairs in the corners, exhausted by the last dance, now stood up again and joined hands. Zundl Konotoper led the chain into the room where Bilgrayer and the visitor from Mir were still talking. Yankl Poltaver seized both of them with his iron hands, and soon the paunchy yellow-haired Bilgrayer and the Mir scholar with his rubber collar and sheep's eyes were also whirling in the dance, looking like two wood chips in a storm. Konotoper led the chain from room to room and caught all the youths and children in his net. The line grew and snaked its way through the corridors and rooms until it came to the women's anteroom.

The rich men's daughters who had come to look at prospective husbands were sitting there in boredom. Not one young man had even showed his face. Seeing the entering scholar-dancers, the girls perked up and began to blush. Bilgrayer danced by, belly out, shoulders back. His half-closed eyes looked disparagingly at the prospective brides of Nareva, as if he were glancing through a pamphlet written by a man who traveled around peddling his book full of folksy homilies that lacked deep learning. Yankl Poltaver raged behind Bilgrayer, stamping his feet as if they were ice picks and singing right into the women's faces. Those geese didn't intimidate *him*. But the Nareva brides, for their part, weren't intimidated either. They knew that although Yankl Poltaver was pretty as a picture, he was a savage and had no thought of getting married. Bilgrayer *did* think of marriage, and he was a sedate person too. He had a reputation as a great scholar, and indeed one could see that he was clever. He wanted to be gilded with money even though he had a face like a monkey. The girls didn't even glance at the yeshiva student from Mir. He had been born in Nareva and was known as a mediocre scholar. His deliberate gait and his way of nodding like a bearded goat clearly showed how clever he was. Therefore the rich girls looked further, some with furtive glances, some with sugar-sweet smiles. Helping them in their quest were the young rebbetsins, experts in the art of matchmaking. But as time passed the Nareva girls became angry: the young men were dancing with closed eyes and weren't even facing their way.

In one of the empty rooms Tsemakh Atlas sat on a sofa, breathing heavily. He was oppressed by the thought that his inability to participate in the joy of the Torah was a sign that he was not yet a full-fledged believer. Who knew whether his regret and repentance were sincere? Perhaps Lohoysker was right not to believe in his repentance. Among the empty bottles on the table Tsemakh saw one half full of whisky. There were small whisky tumblers and some soda glasses next to the bottle. He filled a soda glass with whisky and downed it with one gulp before anyone could come into the room. He was ashamed of himself for drinking like a drunkard, but he wanted to feel happier even if he had to force himself. He felt as if his throat, his insides, were on fire; his mind was numb, like a cold, empty anteroom closed off for the winter. The dancing line of yeshiva students serpentined into the room, and this time Tsemakh let himself be dragged into it. His feet were stiff, his eyes dim; he felt pin pricks in his temples. The scholars danced into the women's room again, and the chain broke into a circle within a circle. The youths put their arms around one another's shoulders, still dancing and singing.

Head and shoulders above the group, like the lean and melancholy King Saul, Tsemakh Atlas stood among the interwoven dancers and swayed along with them like a torn door hanging on a hinge. Knowing the story of his life, the women didn't take their eyes off him. They stopped chattering and whispering. The penitent's tall, manly stature, aquiline nose, and black eyes, where the whisky was already sparkling, brought a surge of warmth to the young women's throats. Their faces changed color. Tsemakh noticed the impression he had made, and his eyes glowed. His teeth flashed behind his grown beard. He straightened up, tense-limbed, and inhaled deeply. Suddenly he remembered something, shivered, and shut his eyes for a moment.

During his years of wandering he had often thought that by the time the engagement contract was signed, he had already taken a dislike to his first fiancée. He had looked at the local girls and had seen that many of them were prettier than Dvorele Namiot and that they were interested in him too. He ought not to be impressed now, because his regret at the match had begun with his looking at the women's table, and that had made him return the engagement contract. Now too, some of the women looked at him with pert eyes, lips curved as if mocking his self-torments and reclusiveness. Again he was enchanted, as he had been long ago, by the moist, flashing eyes, the tight, well-filled blouses, the girls' braided hair, and the young women's smooth white foreheads. Soon, he felt, he'd burst out with a demoniacal laugh at why he had renounced everything that makes life sweet. He had been standing with one foot on the throat of his *yetzer ha-ra*, and now the *yetzer ha-ra* had grabbed him by the throat again. Moshe Chayit considered him a person who thirsted for adventures, but above all he was obviously not yet sure there was a God. Only a man who does not believe that there is another world could lust so keenly for the pleasures of this one.

Weeks later people in Nareva were still talking about the scene at the rosh yeshiva's house during the Simkhas Torah celebration. The penitent had torn open his shirt, rumpled his earlocks, thrown off his frock coat, rolled up the sleeves, then put the coat on again inside out. To evoke more laughter from the women he had pulled the tails of his gaberdine over his head and begun to swirl and spin furiously, until his long woolen ritual fringes puffed up like a balloon. The dancers retreated to the sides of the room, and he alone remained in the middle—a whirlwind of hands and feet.

The astonished women exchanged glances of revulsion and fear. They would have fled the house, but they saw the other yeshiva scholars calmly standing by, clapping their hands and singing. The Nareva youth who studied at Mir shrugged his shoulders, however, and Bilgrayer grimaced with disgust. But this did not satisfy the penitent; he apparently wanted to nauseate everyone. He opened his shirt wider, made crazy faces, and gave wild, hoarse cries. Now the women began to giggle softly; then they burst into loud laughter, screaming until the tears ran. They poked one another with their elbows, doubled over, covering their faces with their hands, afraid their cheeks might drop off.

"Is he drunk or has he gone mad?"

Chaikl knew that in Navaredok such an antic was called "making naught of oneself." When a Musar scholar felt that the *yetzer ha-ra* had overcome him and was dragging him to sin, he purposely aroused disgust so that worldly people would laugh at him and push him away, thereby keeping their filthy material world at arm's length. This was why the Navaredker yeshiva people had calmly surrounded him, clapping in rhythm. Chaikl, however, burned with shame.

Grieved at seeing his Valkenik principal humiliating himself, he pushed his way up to him and pleaded, "Reb Tsemakh, what are you doing? It's a desecration of God's name!"

Pale and perspiring, beard disheveled and wet, Tsemakh stopped for a moment and opened his large, bemused eyes. He embraced Chaikl, pressed him close, and whispered in a broken, tearful voice, "Sing 'Purify our hearts' with me!" Then he resumed dancing, but his weak legs stumbled. Thereupon his former pupils rushed over to him, followed by other youths. Hands were again placed on shoulders and feet stamped the floor.

"When young people smoke on the street on the Sabbath, it's a desecration of God's name. But when the street laughs at yeshiva scholars, it's a sanctification of God's name," Zundl Konotoper shouted to Chaikl Vilner.

"Sometimes one reaches higher heights through dancing than through confession!" another scholar called out.

"One must know how to study Musar in ecstasy while dancing and through dancing!" cried a third.

"Once and for all, one must tear the world from oneself!" Yankl Poltaver thundered, and he stormed into the center of the crowd. Reb Simkha Feinerman emerged from the inner room and joined the singing. The aspiring brides stopped laughing, the young rebbetsins clapped their hands, and the men sang louder and louder in rising ecstasy, repeating, "Purify our hearts, purify our hearts to worship You, to worship You in truth."

8

YANKL POLTAVER, one of Reb Tsemakh's oldest students, had a reputation among the Navaredkers. When he rushed off to morning prayers, he took off his coat outside the beth medresh and the coat flew in ahead of him, fluttering in the air, looking for a place to land. After prayers Yankl would grab the first coat he could lay hands on, drag it over the floor by the collar, and put it on three blocks away. The next morning a friend would complain that Yankl had run off with his new coat. Yankl would return it at once, but the complainer was dumbstruck. In one day the garment had become as wrinkled and dirty as if dragged from a garbage can.

If a little yeshiva had to be founded somewhere, and Yankl was chosen, he would dress up so elegantly that he was hardly recognizable. He remembered exactly which one of the older scholars had a nice suit, who had a pair of brown shoes, who had shirts and ties. A

Musarnik would be ashamed not to lend a garment, especially since Yankl might claim that while others collected clothes to look at prospective brides and thought only of themselves, he was working for the public good. They would lend him the clothes with heavy hearts, very much afraid he would return them as rags. An hour before his departure, Poltaver would show himself in the beth medresh all decked out, even down to a pair of pressed-suede gloves. He would walk among the benches calmly rehearsing a sedate demeanor for the village he was about to visit. No choice; among the well-to-do he had to wear a tie and collar, like a nag tied into his horse collar, or a wooden manikin dressed in the latest fashion and displayed in the window to attract customers. When Yankl worried about having no money for a train ticket, he would mull over his condition for a few minutes and then come to the conclusion that lacking a ticket was an even loftier spiritual degree, for here was an instance when one had to depend upon absolute faith. On the train Yankl wouldn't hide under a bench, but instead moved like a wind from car to car until he met the conductor face to face. Then he would shrug his shoulders, as if he had already shown him the ticket ten times, and give the conductor such a scathing glance that he would back off respectfully for the young nobleman with the handsome, arrogant appearance.

Yankl would return from his trip in tatters but crowned with victory. The yeshiva was always established, and he always brought back bags of potatoes, flour and grits, a tub of fish, sometimes even money for the big yeshiva in Nareva. Thus Nareva tolerated his antics and privately the rosh yeshiva even enjoyed them. During the past summer, however, he had pulled a bit of mischief which embarrassed the yeshiva and for which Reb Simkha had to reprimand him: "This is not the way!"

In the summer, when the vacationers came for their rest in the woods around Nareva, Poltaver arrived for a few days' visit with his friends. Anyone else would have settled into a hammock and swung slowly, or leafed through a sacred text and dozed a bit. Not Yankl. He clambered up to the top of a tall pine, hooked his powerful legs over a branch, and hung head down like a huge pine cone. Holding on to his yarmulke with both hands, he began preaching Musar with a voice that reverberated through the entire forest: "The most important thing in man's life is to perfect his character. If he doesn't, then what purpose is there to his life?" The tired vacationers, men with weak nerves and women with puffy stomachs, began to scream, "We can't bear to watch!" and only then did Yankl come down, quick and nimble as a squirrel. He couldn't make amends for this prank and had to leave the resort. Nareva simmered with the story, which prompted the heretic Moshe Chayit Lohoysker to sermonize in the yeshiva kitchen.

"There's the whole Musar teaching for you! Hanging upside down over an abyss and holding on to your yarmulke with both hands to keep it from falling off! Yankl Poltaver is certainly a born savage, but he also had Tsemakh Lomzher as a teacher, and he's the one who gave his stamp of approval to such wild behavior." As usual the Torah scholars did not respond, so as not to open the door for further abuse. But they looked at one another in horror. What impudence! Lohoysker never set foot in the yeshiva, yet he came to the kitchen to eat and had the nerve to mock a group that didn't let him starve.

Yankl Poltaver was by now leading a group of Bar Mitzva boys taking their first steps toward independent study. Yankl's favorite aspect of the Navaredok teaching was going out on bold missions that showed one wasn't intimidated by the world. "It's no use, friends, no use," he told his students. "Our conduct doesn't enrage the world any more. There must be perpetual war between the beth medresh and the street as there was between the Children of Israel and Amalek. We must remember that just as the Jews couldn't have survived among the nations of the world without a separate Torah, so the Navaredkers couldn't have survived among Jews without a special code of behavior, without its Torah, its teachings. We have to prepare ourselves for many trials in life and learn in time how to overcome these trials. Where else will a Navaredker get the strength not to be ashamed to put on tefillin in a train while onlookers snicker and whinny like horses? And after he marries and becomes a small-town yeshiva principal, who will encourage him not to be intimidated by the local rabbi and the townspeople? Not to mention the fact that the Navaredker, poor soul, may himself become a rabbi, woe unto him! From where will he draw the strength to tell a rebellious congregant the truth to his face? For this, studying the Talmud and even studying Musar is not enough. We have to get into the habit of brushing the world away from us and holding it in absolute contempt. But, friends, things are too quiet for us here."

After such a lecture Yankl's group would scatter to various corners and study Musar enthusiastically for fifteen minutes. Then they fanned out over the streets of Nareva, their ritual fringes down to their ankles, wearing yarmulkes instead of caps—for the entire world to laugh at them. And indeed Nareva did laugh. Nareva considered itself a miniature Paris because its young men and women wore the latest fashions. There were also unions in town, and when the young Musarniks appeared in the streets in their strange garb, workers shouted after them: "Parasites! Freeloaders!" Seamstresses who worked at home or in factories left their boy friends for a moment and dashed in among the scholars, who huddled against one another, lost and bewildered. The girls knew that a yeshiva boy wasn't permitted to touch a strange woman, so they laughed at these fanatics and purposely grabbed their hands. Just then Yankl Poltaver would materialize. He had been following all along so that the students wouldn't be alone in the outside world. He rushed at the impudent young women and sent them sprawling like tomatoes tumbling out of a basket. Disheveled and rumpled, the girls gazed at the handsome young man who had pushed them in all directions. To avoid ridicule and derision in their turn, they retreated with their escorts.

After such a victory, Yankl Poltaver would send his pupils out on a mission that demanded even more courage. They would go into a pharmacy and innocently ask the pharmacist for kerosene, matches, boxes of nails, or some other nonpharmaceutical item. The pharmacist would be puzzled; he didn't know whether the young Musarniks were crazy or were just teasing him.

The other senior yeshiva scholars looked askance at such goings-on, and Moshe Chayit Lohoysker had something else to talk about in the yeshiva kitchen.

"What would Yankl have done if the Nareva pharmacist *had* had kerosene, matches, and nails? And what would Yankl have done if people on the street hadn't laughed at his boys with their dangling ritual fringes? The whole Navaredker mission would have come to naught. Yankl and the other bench warmers are confident that the world's only worry is planning how to catch these lunatic yeshiva boys in its net. The world needs you fellows like it needs a hole in the head."

At the beginning of the term the seekers who constantly worked at improving their character were caught up in the ferment of studies. Yankl, however, never opened a Talmud, and his pupils followed his example. For half a day they screamed in the Musar meditation room, and in the other half they wandered around in Nareva doing things that emphasized their contempt for the secular world. They came to the yeshiva only to hear an older scholar calmly lecture two younger students who walked at either side of him like lambs rubbing against the shepherd's legs. Then Yankl would fly through the beth medresh like a storm, accompanied by his group. Stepping on everyone's feet, they waved their hands and shouted, "Once and for all we have to pluck the world from out of our midst. Of course, it's better when one doesn't let the world come in in the first place, for then you spare yourself the headache of tearing it out later!"

The older scholars complained to the rosh yeshiva that Yankl Poltaver wasn't letting his students spend time with other Musar scholars. Reb Simkha replied with a sparkle in his eye, "Reb Tsemakh Lomzher in his time also ran a separate school within our beth medresh. Now the pupil is following in his teacher's footsteps." Reb Simkha Feinerman evidently didn't fear Poltaver's competition—hence he didn't persecute him as he had the Lomzher years ago.

At the beginning of the winter, when Chaikl Vilner was already considered a student of the Nareva yeshiva, another Vilner entered. It was Melechke. During his three years at the Valkenik yeshiva under Reb Menakhem-Mendl Segal's tutelage he had made excellent progress. Melechke, now fourteen, had also grown taller, but his small, rosy face was still childishly round. According to his age, he was made a member of Yankl Poltaver's group, but he noticed at once that compared to the other students, he was a veritable Talmudic sage. For his part, Yankl Poltaver decided that a spoiled brat, proud and stubborn, had been added to his group. Yankl burst out laughing. If he could with a snap of his fingers persuade a little village to establish a yeshiva, couldn't he convince a Vilna youngster? He dragged Melechke off to a corner and started in: "Just as the saintly Mordekhai wasn't intimidated by the wicked Haman and didn't bow down to him, so too a ben Torah must not be intimidated by the world."

Melechke Vilner hunched his little shoulders. "No comparison," he said. "Our sages of blessed memory say that an idol hung on Haman's chest. That's why Mordekhai refused to bow down to him. But what's the sense of going through Nareva's streets with ritual fringes dangling for everyone to laugh at?" Melechke continued, "True, for a while in Valkenik and in Vilna I too walked around with my ritual fringes hanging out. But now that I can study a page of Talmud with the commentaries on my own, I no longer believe in doing things to spite people on the street."

"Then you're talking just like a Mir yeshiva student, or even a Kletzker," Reb Yankl fumed. "If that's the case, you shouldn't have come to Nareva. Here among the Navaredkers in Nareva you have to keep up the Musar spirit."

"I came from a little yeshiva to study in a great yeshiva," Melechke answered drily. Still, he couldn't overcome his old habit and tears welled up in his eyes. "Maybe you're right. Maybe I should have gone to the Chafetz Chaim's yeshiva in Radun."

Hearing such words, the group leader clutched at his head. "Why don't you come right out and say you want to commit suicide, God forbid? Wanting to change Nareva for Radun is like wanting to take a knife and stab yourself."

The youngster bit his rosy lips and stood his ground. "I didn't come to Nareva to participate in crazy antics to get the local people to laugh at me. I want to hear the rosh yeshiva's Talmud interpretations and I want to come up with my own."

"So you want to make your own interpretations?" Reb Yankl cried, and he began to take the impudent student to task. "The Prophet Micah says that Israel will be as numerous as 'showers on the grass,' and the Vilna Gaon comments that Torah is like rain. When rain falls on fruit trees, the fruit grows; when it falls on thorns, the thorns grow. You, Melechke Vilner, probably think that everything can be justified with a simple little interpretation—and that everything can be twisted with a tortuous argument. You're probably aspiring to be the big shot in Nareva that you used to be in the Valkenik yeshiva and in your mother's house in Vilna. Instead of seeing your own flaws, you see flaws among friends who sanctify the name of God. . . ."

At this point Melechke burst into tears, and Yankl Poltaver had to stop. That spoiled brat might possibly run and join those sheepish students of the Chafetz Chaim's yeshiva in Radun, and then the Nareva rosh yeshiva would complain, "You're driving our students away." Yankl backed down at once: "All right, if that's what you want, you can spend day and night stuffing yourself full of Talmud commentary." But he was thinking: I'll make that pampered only son go through such contortions while he's learning to break his own will that the very earth will reel.

9

FOR A LONG TIME the Nareva townspeople had muttered against the Navaredkers who had occupied Hannah-Hayke's beth medresh on Bialystok Street. The Musarniks, they claimed, had pounded their fists into the prayer stands until they broke them. All the holy texts were tattered and torn. No matter when one entered the beth medresh, the Musarniks were in the middle of lectures or in the middle of running back and forth. When did they sit down and study Talmud? During the Silent Devotion they shrieked and writhed like epileptics. And why were the youngsters so melancholy?

Gradually, however, the townspeople had seen that the Musarniks also had many good attributes. They were gentle youths, pious and good-hearted. All week long meager meals sufficed them; they rarely saw a piece of fish or a sliver of meat in the yeshiva kitchen. They walked about in tatters and slept on hard, uncomfortable beds. Nevertheless, they never complained. Finally the congregants in Hannah-Hayke's beth medresh concluded that they should be glad the scholars sat in their holy place and that the sound of Torah studies was never interrupted.

Only the trustee of the Free Loan Society, Zushe Sulkes, would not make peace with the Musarniks. Zushe Sulkes had inherited his seat in Hannah-Hayke's beth medresh from his father. But there, at his own prayer stand, a yeshiva student would sit and trim his nails and then slice some wood from the prayer stand and throw it into the fire along with the parings. Often Sulkes would find a bundle of dirty laundry inside the prayer stand—some yeshiva student had left it there after coming back from the bathhouse. But no matter how much Zushe Sulkes ranted, the Musarniks did as they pleased, though they held their tongues at his complaints. Reb Simkha Feinerman had told them, "Be very careful; I don't want that man as an enemy." Even Yankl Poltaver bit his lips and said nothing.

The group leader and his students were sitting in the smaller study room of Hannah-Hayke's beth medresh when the trustee Sulkes arrived, the silver chain of his pocket watch dangling across his waistcoat and a ring of keys in his hand. Twice a week the Free Loan Society permitted women to pay off their debts and get new loans, and at those times Zushe Sulkes evicted the young Musarniks and their leader. Yankl Poltaver immediately gestured to his pupils to follow him into the beth medresh itself. But he kept returning every ten minutes with another excuse. Once he supposedly came for a book; another time he looked around as though one of his students were missing; the third time he made straight for the trustee.

"Reb Zuse Shulkes, will you be here much longer?"

The trustee's bluish face turned beet-red. "I've told you many times that my name isn't Reb Zuse Shulkes but Reb Zushe Sulkes. I spell my first name with a 'sh' and my surname with an 's' and not vice versa."

Poltaver shrugged. "What's the difference whether it's 'sh' or 's,' as long as you know that I mean you? My group and I need this room, and we're waiting for you to finish with the loans."

Yankl didn't really need the smaller room that urgently, but the way the trustee sucked the blood from poor women made his blood boil. As the women passed through the large study hall to the smaller one where the trustee sat, they stood for a while in the darkness behind the pulpit. Wrapped in winter shawls and wearing heavy felt boots, the peddlers listened to the sweet sound of Torah and felt the ice in their hearts melting, as if they were warming their frozen hands and cracked fingers over fire pots. They envied the mothers of the yeshiva boys. How lucky they were to raise precious children who provided joy for this world and would sustain them in the next. But the peddlers couldn't allow themselves the luxury of standing in the men's section and watching the youths swaying over their Talmuds. Sighing and heavyhearted, they went to see the trustee in the other room as if on their way to an irascible nobleman.

Sulkes sat at the table looking only at the fingers that pushed coins toward him. When a woman brought the weekly payment in full, he took it without saying a word, marked the sum in a book, and placed the few zlotys in the iron cash box on the table. When he saw trembling, wrinkled fingers counting out a smaller sum than he had expected, he raised his head slightly and told the woman, "Next time you come for a loan, I'll only give you half, because you're only repaying half." But when Sulkes heard a terror-stricken voice begging him for a new loan to pay an installment of the previous free loan, he raised his head all the way, eyes gleaming coldly.

"I'm not sending good money after bad. As long as you don't repay your old debt, you won't get a penny."

The rejected woman was submissively silent; the other women were afraid to speak up for their friend. They merely exchanged glances, and their eyes seemed to say: Better a bitter leaf from God's tree than all of man's sweetness. Yankl Poltaver heard Sulkes' remark and barely managed to restrain himself. The trustee gave him a sidelong glance and wondered why Yankl was floating in and out of the room. Was he looking for a bride among these old women? Or a prospective mother-in-law?

Poltaver stormed into the beth medresh and ran up to a couple of old congregants who were studying together. "Couldn't you find a gentler soul for that job? Just look at the way your trustee treats poor women who can't meet their payments. What's the matter—can't he afford to pay it out of his own pocket?" the yeshiva scholar asked angrily.

"But according to the law it must be paid, especially since it's an unsecured loan," one of the old men retorted.

"If someone doesn't have the money, he doesn't have to pay it," Poltaver snapped, and he explained how the system worked among the Navaredker Musarniks.

"When someone lends money to a friend, the lender immediately considers the loan a gift. That way, if the latter can't repay it, it's not considered theft. When a person borrows, he must remember to repay the loan; but when he lends, he must assume that the borrower can't repay it." Then Reb Yankl ran through the beth medresh to find his pupils. He wanted to lead them into the side room and show them the kindheartedness of a worldly Jew. The two old men looked on and shook their heads. The candle they held to light up the small, thick Rashi script of their holy text trembled between their fingers. "It's just as our holy sages say," one of them remarked. "Happy is he who gives to charity and woe unto him who must distribute it. Sulkes was chosen trustee of the Free Loan Society precisely because he's strict and unrelenting."

Zushe Sulkes had invited Melechke Vilner for Sabbath meals. He told the congregants, "Among the wild Musarniks this little youngster feels like a lamb among wolves. His neat way of dressing, his gentle way of speaking, and his quiet studying off in a corner lets you see at a glance that he's made of velvet and silk. I treat him like my own child."

When Yankl Poltaver was told about the trustee's boast, he was furious. He couldn't imagine a pupil from his group spending the Sabbath in that bloodsucker's home, and he offered Melechke a Sabbath elsewhere. But Melechke stubbornly hunched his head into his thin little shoulders. "I haven't got a thing against the trustee," he said. "Besides the fine Sabbath, Reb Zushe Sulkes has even invited me for the Saturday night meal."

"You still don't want to try to achieve a higher level of spirituality? Are you still spending your days toiling away at Talmud and commentaries?" Yankl seared him with his dark brown eyes, his stony chin perspiring.

"People say that even Reb Tsemakh Atlas regrets not having sat and studied," Melechke muttered nasally to express his contempt, giving the group leader a meaningful look as if warning him that Yankl too would regret not having toiled over Talmud and commentaries. Poltaver was dumfounded by the child's impertinence, but he concluded that either Melechke Vilner would become a true Navaredker seeker once and for all or he would bounce him out of the group like a piece of rubber. Yankl's hatred of the trustee grew, and he didn't have to wait long to show his feelings.

All the women peddlers were wringing their hands before Reb Zushe Sulkes. "You have to lend us some money so that we can buy merchandise. When we have merchandise, we'll be able to pay back our old debt and the new one. But if you have no pity on us, we'll be forced to jump off the bridge."

As usual, the trustee was saying, "Until you pay up your old debts, I won't make any new loans. One of the scholars told me that according to the Torah, one must not lend money to people who you know won't repay it."

"You're lying! You're the cruel one, not the Torah!" came a shout, and Yankl Poltaver pushed his way to the trustee among the crowd of women and said to his face, "The people who contribute to the Free Loan Society don't set conditions that flay the skin of the needy. You're not giving them your own money."

"True; true. Where there's Torah, there's wisdom," the women agreed.

"You insolent slanderer! Are you telling me how to do my job? I'm going to chase you and your gang out of the beth medresh like a pack of dogs. And as for you, you fishwives, you're not going to get a penny!" Shrieking, Sulkes locked the account books into the heavy cash box. Then he put the iron money box under his arm and left.

The women surrounded the yeshiva student and complained, "You shouldn't have butted in. Perhaps we could have persuaded him. Now it's hopeless." Some of them said angrily, "Every Friday we donate fish, meat, and challa for the yeshiva. And if we don't have any merchandise, the yeshiva people will go hungry too."

"Navaredok rises to greatness when it goes hungry," Reb Yankl answered, and realized at once that he wasn't speaking to his students now. He soothed the poor women: "The trustee will be made to give in by fair means or foul."

"Then do it by fair means. Butter him up if you have to," the peddlers pleaded and shuffled away, disconsolate. How could the young rabbi help them when he himself went around in rags and was hotheaded besides?

Yankl stayed in the dim room and worried. To land in a village and establish a little yeshiva against the will of the rabbi and the leading townspeople was not a difficult task for him. Consequently, he surely wasn't going to be intimidated by that heartless trustee. But the rosh yeshiva wouldn't permit him to start anything with Zushe Sulkes and his backers for fear they might drive the yeshiva out of Hannah-Hayke's beth medresh. Perhaps he shouldn't have interfered. The next day, though, Poltaver saw that it was divinely ordained that he wage war with the trustee.

In the midst of the commotion of the start of the winter term, Reb Simkha Feinerman had to prepare for a journey instead of planning Talmud lectures. The Navaredker Beth Yosef centers in Lithuania, Polesia, Volhyn, and Poland were always complaining to the Yeshiva Council that they were getting a much smaller share of subsidy than the yeshivas of Mir, Radun, Kletzk, and Kamenietz. Because of this, Reb Simkha had to go to a meeting in Vilna and leave the yeshiva under the care of his close associates, chief among whom was Zundl Konotoper. Yankl Poltaver was overjoyed: he had no fear at all of these people, especially Zundl Konotoper. By the time the rosh yeshiva returned, the battle with that skinflint trustee would be over.

10

TO TEACH the rebellious women a lesson, Zushe Sulkes did not come to the study room for the Free Loan Society on Monday evening. The women found Yankl and his pupils there instead.

"What's going to happen, rabbi?" they wailed, surrounding him.

"Everything's going to be all right," he answered proudly. "Go to the trustee's shop tomorrow evening and make all the trouble you can. We'll be there too," he said, pointing to his group. As soon as the women left, he told his pupils, "Tomorrow we will say afternoon prayers at Zushe Sulkes' grocery." He turned to Melechke Vilner. "Will you join us?"

"God forbid!" said Melechke, trembling.

"I realize you don't want to oppose the man whom you'll be eating with on the Sabbath." Reb Yankl sighed with regret as if he'd seen a rabbi taking a bribe during a rabbinic judgment, and the other members of Yankl's group glared at Melechke.

On Tuesday night women wearing heavy jackets with aprons tied over them streamed to the trustee's grocery—and there they encountered an amazed crowd staring at a strange sight.

Every few minutes the front door would open and Zushe Sulkes would tumble a yeshiva boy out into the freshly fallen snow. Each boy picked himself up and stood at the store doorway, mumbling, his face as ecstatic as if he were immersed in the Silent Devotion and dared not break off. Soon the door opened once more and another bundle flew out—a youth with curly earlocks. That instant the first boy tore into the grocery again, and as the shopkeeper sought to block his path, the second boy slipped in.

"Jews, help! I've been invaded by locusts!" Sulkes shouted.

The crowd outside pushed its way in and saw half a dozen youngsters scattered in the corners, swaying in prayer. A burly onlooker grabbed two of the yeshiva boys by their collars and shook them. "What sort of crazy antics are you up to? You'll soon be flying like pancakes!"

The student said not a word in reply, but the broad-shouldered, hard-chinned yeshiva scholar came to their support.

"Don't lay a hand on them!" Yankl Poltaver ordered, his nostrils steaming as if he were an overheated horse. The onlooker was delighted; he was happier dealing with an adult.

"And just who are you?" he demanded.

At which the women shouted at him, "Your hands will wither if you touch the young rabbi who's trying to help us." And then the women told the crowd how the trustee was sucking their blood.

"I've been entrusted by the Free Loan Society to give loans without interest but not to squander the money. You won't get your way." Zushe Sulkes jangled the coins in his pocket and shouted to the yeshiva boys, "You think you're students? You're a bunch of Bolsheviks, that's what you are! I'm going to call the police!"

But the women outshouted him. "You're going to put Jewish children into gentile hands? We hope you end up a beggar."

The burly man was now on the side of the yeshiva students. "If you denounce Jewish children who study the holy Torah," he said pleasantly, "you may be carried out of here feet first in a wet sheet. I'm not guaranteeing that it won't happen to you."

Sulkes was terrified, but he attempted banter even though it was obvious that he was near apoplexy: "The Musarniks want to stay in my shop and sway? Let them stay and sway. I've got plenty of patience."

Facing the wall, the yeshiva boys continued their prayers, which were as long as those of Yom Kippur. Finally they took the three steps backward that signaled the end of the Silent Devotion, turned their heads to all sides, and spat. "Don't worry," Yankl Poltaver told the shopkeeper. "Tomorrow they'll come back for the Afternoon Service. And the day after tomorrow too—until you either give in or give up the trusteeship."

The yeshiva students went out onto the street accompanied by the crowd. The women were confident that Sulkes would no longer wage war against the children. Motherly faces shone with joy. "God bless them! We thank God and our young scholars." The men too were amazed at the young Musarniks who'd had no fear of the trustee. Yankl Poltaver's pupils said little; they merely shrugged and answered in surprise, "You expect us to be intimidated by some little shopkeeper?"

The following morning half of Nareva went to Sulkes' grocery to see what would happen. But the trustee was thumbing his nose at them all—he didn't open the store. He kept it closed the next day, and he visited the leading congregants and asked, "Do I deserve humiliation and financial loss just because I won't let community funds be squandered?"

But Yankl Poltaver wasn't silent either. He sent the women to the congregants to moan and plead while he himself took his students to the older Jews who studied in the beth medresh. He showed them how that Haman had twisted one ben Torah's leg, another's hand had nearly been broken, the face of a third lad scratched, a fourth had been beaten, and the ritual fringes of a fifth had been torn.

"Scandalous! Scandalous!" The old men smacked their gums. "The trustee doesn't really care about Free Loan Society funds being used up. He just gets pleasure out of refusing."

Seeing that he had supporters among the congregants, Yankl Poltaver summoned his group into the study room where Sulkes had previously sat.

"Well, what have you got to say now?" Reb Yankl turned to Melechke. "While your friends are sacrificing themselves for the glory of God, you're hiding there behind that big Vilna Talmud."

Melechke was silent. He saw everyone looking at him as if he were some vile, creeping thing. Reb Yankl, swaying, asked his students, "What was mighty Samson's sin? After all, the Bible tells us explicitly that Heaven wanted Samson to have dealings with the gentile Delilah to enable him to take revenge later upon the Philistines. So what was his sin?"

"Because Samson *himself* wanted to have dealings with the gentile Delilah and not because Heaven had ordained it," shouted the flock of holy lambs.

"The plague of self-interest led the most powerful man in the world astray," the group leader explained to Melechke. "This point is clearly stated in *Man's Spiritual Attainment*, by Reb Yosef-Yoizl, the Old Man of Navaredok, of blessed memory. In our beth medresh even a babe in arms knows this. But you, Melechke Vilner, you don't know this because you haven't studied *Man's Spiritual Attainment*. You study Talmud with all the rabbinic commentaries and you memorize the commentaries. So now, Vilner, you see how we've proved you wrong. Your friends are waging a holy war, but you're afraid of the trustee because you eat at his house on the Sabbath. And if that's the case, admit it publicly and let the beth medresh know the entire truth once and for all."

"All right," Melechke answered, choking back the tears. "So people won't say I'm afraid of losing my Sabbath meals, I'll do what everyone else does."

On Friday evening Zushe Sulkes came to the beth medresh to pray and found his seat at the eastern wall surrounded by the same group that had besieged his grocery.

"Are the Bolsheviks confiscating my father's seat too?" he shouted.

To which Yankl Poltaver retorted, "They want to redeem a father in the other world from a son who is wicked in this world."

Sulkes saw that even the old men of Hannah-Hayke's beth medresh were against him: "You made these little yeshiva boys black and blue. They're limping and their faces are swollen."

The young Musarniks stood there purposely not complaining so that people would pity them all the more, Sulkes thought. The group leader too wasn't talking about his beaten pupils, but about the poor women peddlers. "This Sabbath they won't have any challa, fish, or meat because you wouldn't give them any loans. In the next world they're going to reproach you: Is that how you treat widows and orphans?"

Thinking of Judgment Day, the old men trembled and said heatedly, "No one has asked the trustee to flay the skin of poor people who can't repay loans right away."

Sulkes consoled himself with the thought that on Friday evening only the doddering old idlers came to prayers, but on Sabbath morning the well-to-do congregants would be there, and they would side with him. He stepped toward his prayer stand and stood there dumbstruck, noticing for the first time that among the youngsters around his seat was the little scholar who ate in his house each Sabbath. There he stood, pious-faced, hunched into himself, ostensibly an onlooker. It was clear, however, that he too was part of the group. Sulkes was so depressed by this that he no longer wanted to win; he felt as if his own son had been summoned as a false witness against him. He raised both hands as if warding off blows and called out, "I'm saying this for all to hear: I hereby resign as trustee of the Free Loan Society. I'll return the keys after the Sabbath. Now let me go to my seat."

Just because Sulkes had announced this without words of abuse and in a broken voice, regret began to gnaw at the old men's beards for having permitted a man to be humiliated. Even the *baal tefilla* in the pulpit chanted the prayers inaugurating the Sabbath in a voice full of shame and chagrin. Yankl Poltaver winked to his pupils to follow him to the community building where the yeshiva students prayed on the Sabbaths and holidays when Hannah-Hayke's beth medresh was crowded.

"And where will I eat on the Sabbath?" Melechke asked softly.

"You'll still eat at that bloodsucker Sulkes' house. I'm sure he didn't notice you. After all, you hid behind your friends' backs," Reb Yankl answered, and Melechke prayed to God that Reb Zushe Sulkes had indeed not seen him. Poltaver strode forth from his group, gloom-ridden, not at all pleased with his victory. He expected the older Musarniks to pounce on him, and he was already preparing his answers.

On Sabbath morning the well-to-do, influential congregants of the eastern wall who didn't attend services on weekdays pleaded with Sulkes not to resign as trustee. Wrinkled, his shoulders sagging, Sulkes replied, "Even if you beg me on your knees, I'll have nothing more to do with the Free Loan Society or with the women. And I'll be spared having to fight with the Musarniks too."

That night, when the yeshiva students returned to the beth medresh from the community building, they were met by the influential congregants who sat at the eastern wall. Their verbal barrage sounded like Sulkes'.

"You Bolsheviks! Don't set foot in our holy place again. If you don't leave voluntarily, we'll hire some of the carters to break every bone in your bodies."

The older yeshiva scholars knew that threats and actual expulsion were miles apart. But they knew too that there would be trouble, and that Reb Simkha Feinerman would not forgive them for permitting such a situation to develop. Zundl Konotoper and other yeshiva leaders surrounded Poltaver.

"You're ruining the Nareva yeshiva. Go to Mezeritch!"

Realizing that he had brought on misfortune, Yankl replied brazenly, "I've long considered going to Mezeritch with my pupils. There one can find true Navaredkers who maintain the spirit of Musar throughout the year, not just for the Days of Awe."

Zundl Konotoper knew very well that Reb Simkha loved a crowded beth medresh. He did not want Mezeritch to outstrip Nareva in number of Torah scholars, especially because Mezeritch was also a Navaredker yeshiva. And Yankl Poltaver's students would surely follow him, because they were devoted to him heart and soul.

Zundl restrained his anger and tried to speak in a friendly way. "The fundamental principle of Musar is to reform oneself. You've begun by attempting to reform the world. How can a Musarnik interfere with a shul congregation?"

"Indeed, one can't reform the world," Yankl said in a passion, "if one isn't perfect. But one can't become perfect if one doesn't stand up for the wronged. And this is the first time I've heard that a Musarnik shouldn't interfere when a cruel person is tormenting poor women. We'd be in pretty sad shape if goodness of heart were reserved only for our fellow Musarniks."

"The women will be able to take care of themselves as they've done up till now, but if we're driven from the beth medresh, we'll have nowhere to go!" Konotoper could no longer hold back his anger and shouted even more loudly, "Who gave you permission to put our students into the trustee's grocery and block his way to his seat in the beth medresh?"

"The booklets of Reb Yosef-Yoizl Hurwitz, the Old Man of Navaredok," Yankl snapped. "And I learned it during our group sessions with Reb Tsemakh Lomzher."

"Aha! Why didn't you say so?" Zundl Konotoper's thick beard trembled, and his small, penetrating eyes grew even tinier and narrower. "Admit straight out that you're aping your former teacher and not following our rabbi, Reb Yosef-Yoizl, of blessed memory. Our mentor's remarks and books taught us that it isn't so much the deed that counts as the acts around the deed. But all you know to do is to rage and go wild—even the lesson of Reb Tsemakh Atlas' experience hasn't affected you."

Konotoper and the other yeshiva leaders went over and surrounded the penitent. "Can't you do something to restrain your former pupil? Since you've come back to Nareva, Moshe Chayit Lohoysker has become more of a spiteful wretch and Yankl Potlaver more of a savage."

"Poltaver has even less respect for me than for you. And as far as Lohoysker is concerned, I certainly don't have any influence over him," Reb Tsemakh answered. His voice and eyes were so full of sorrow that the older scholars regretted having turned to him.

Morning prayers and breakfast were over and the students were swaying over their Talmuds. The benches were crowded; the students sat elbow to elbow. It was so crowded that individual voices could hardly be heard. Outside, winter reigned; the windows were closed. The Talmud chants bounced off the walls like a waterfall from a stony crag. Reb Tsemakh had not yet eaten breakfast. In his tallis and tefillin he stood in a corner by the eastern wall perusing a book, one elbow on the prayer stand. Suddenly a warm glow came into his eyes. A smile crept out from behind his mustache—Melechke Vilner had suddenly appeared next to his prayer stand. Whenever the former Valkenik rosh yeshiva saw his little pupil, he recalled the night he had found him dozing over his Talmud in the Valkenik beth medresh, carried him to his lodgings, and put him to bed. But as soon as the yeshiva's youngest student began to speak, Tsemakh's smile slowly vanished.

"Reb Yankl the group leader," Melechke declared, "pestered me to join the others in the group to stop the trustee from sitting in his seat in the beth medresh. And then Reb Yankl urged me to go to that same trustee for my Sabbath meals, as I did a week ago and two weeks ago. Then, when I went for the Friday night meal, Reb Zushe Sulkes was in the middle of Kiddush. He actually broke off in the middle of the Kiddush, grabbed me by the collar, and kicked me out of the house with a curse. 'Go to hell,' he said, 'with all the other Musarniks.' I feel so bad that now I'm not even ashamed to have the Talmud students see me crying like a little boy." Melechke rubbed his tearful eyes with his fists and sobbed. "It's your fault, Reb Tsemakh. Back in Vilna you talked me into going to Valkenik to study in the little Navaredker yeshiva. And that's why this winter I came to the big Navaredker yeshiva in Nareva. But if I had studied in Radun or Kamenietz, I wouldn't have had to join a group and be subjected to so much suffering."

Bent over his prayer stand, Tsemakh stroked Melechke's tear-stained face with his broad palm, as he used to do in Valkenik. "If you hadn't come with me to the little yeshiva in Valkenik, you might not have remained with Torah. I'll see to it that you have an even better Sabbath in someone else's home."

Melechke's tears turned to anger. "I'm not going to eat at anybody's house," he replied, "neither on weekdays nor on Sabbaths. I want to eat in the yeshiva kitchen like my fellow townsman Chaikl Vilner. And I don't want to waste entire days listening to Musar talks either. And if I don't get what I want, I'm going to leave for another yeshiva."

As soon as Melechke had gone, Tsemakh Atlas looked around the beth medresh until he spotted Yankl Poltaver standing alone behind the pulpit. Yankl appeared to be in a bad mood; he must be troubled because he had lost the war with the trustee and had even been censured by the yeshiva.

"What's happening to you, Poltaver?" Tsemakh asked. "First you persuade a young student to help drive the trustee away from his seat in shul and then you send him to that same trustee for his Sabbath meal so that he will be kicked out." Tsemakh spread his hands in amazement.

"Why not? Melechke Vilner's going to the trustee's house on Sabbath was an act of spiritual courage," Yankl answered, frowning, his eyes angry. "Our Talmudic sages went out into the market place wearing their tefillin at a time when it was certain death to do so—when the Romans, may their names be blotted out, used to torture people to death for that. At the very least we ought not be afraid to let our ritual fringes show or be intimidated by laughter and derision from people on the street."

"You're saying this to me?" Tsemakh gazed at him with even more astonishment.

"I'm just reminding you of your own words when we sat together in your group." Yankl seized his coat from among a batch of garments draped over the pulpit railing. "What you taught me, I teach my students; but that Melechke Vilner from your Valkenik yeshiva had the gall to tell me that he regretted having studied Musar instead of Talmud and commentary. And Zundl Konotoper says I'm just imitating you. So it turns out that both the younger and older students are denying your teachings. And what's more, now you yourself are reproaching me for behaving the way you've taught me to behave." Yankl shoved his feet into either his or someone else's muddy galoshes and stormed out of the beth medresh.

11

REUVEN RATNER was Reb Tsemakh's oldest student. He excelled in learning, in character traits, and in singing. When he chanted a melody, his eyes would fill with tears; when he expressed an idea, he would open and close his long, thin fingers as if touching the thought with his hands. When another person spoke, he would listen with such bright eyes that their glow could have warmed one's hands. Only when Moshe Chayit Lohoysker sermonized in the kitchen at mealtime would Reuven Retner smile with contempt and commiseration—he pitied a friend who had gone astray. This drove Lohoysker to distraction, and he would begin to speak like a spiteful apostate. Then Ratner would cease smiling and begin tugging at his big earlocks as if warning them not to hear such blasphemies.

Though Reuven Ratner was an excellent scholar, he had no luck at marriage. Prospective in-laws were fond of him, but the brides usually thought of what their girl friends would say, and girls didn't like a young man with high, sharp shoulders, puffy cheeks, and nostrils as large as a Tatar's. Just lately another fine match had been proposed to him. He appealed to the girl's parents, but the girl herself was reluctant. So Reuven Ratner sat dejectedly over the Talmud, studying without enthusiasm. He didn't want to discuss this with his friends, but he had talked with Reb Tsemakh a couple of times about his lack of success and always concluded with the remark, "Perhaps I should be glad I'm not lucky with matches. That way I'm exposed to less temptation." But the conversations made Reb Tsemakh Atlas feel guilty at not being able to explain to himself why prospective brides had not rejected him.

Another student, Shimshl Kupishker, who had grown up to be a mindless fanatic, troubled Tsemakh even more. Shimshl took to fasts and self-afflictions and was always running to plunge himself into the ritual bath. At first he had maintained a self-imposed silence only during Elul, but now he was silent for weeks at a time, even in midyear. The only sounds that came from his dry lips were ceaseless mumbled incantations to ward off impurity. Shimshl was slightly built. He had watery, wide-set little eyes, a pointed yellow beard, and faded ritual fringes that hung down over his knees. Kupishker ate like a bird, and the rosh yeshiva was afraid he would get sick. Reb Simkha pleaded with him to take a walk every day and to talk with the congregants and engage in some non-Torah conversations.

But Shimshl Kupishker murmured, "I don't have any time. I still haven't completed the section on sacrifices, and I've fallen behind on my daily portion of Psalms. And besides, I have to run off to the ritual bath because of a nocturnal emission."

"Repentance through self-affliction is the common man's way," Reb Simkha told him. "A ben Torah atones for his sins by studying. That was the way of the Vilna Gaon and his pupils. Self-torment can cause more harm than good in the service of the Creator, especially nowadays, as the generations become weaker."

But Shimshl Kupishker didn't hear what people were telling him. His lips moved swiftly, and in his watery little eyes one could see his fear of imps, devils, and she-demons.

"At first I thought he was a fool, but even a fool has some sense when it comes to his own needs. I've come to the conclusion that Kupishker is just plain crazy," Lohoysker declared in the kitchen, defiling the humble table with malicious snickering. "Even the Angel of Death himself won't be able to bite into Kupishker, because every mortal knows that while one is praying or studying, the Angel of Death cannot take a soul—and Shimshl Kupishker is constantly in the midst of saying and praying, praying and saying. Nevertheless, I admit that I like that maniac. Our Torah of life is indeed a Torah of self-abnegation. So either you follow Kupishker's path and deny yourself everything, or you follow my path and deny yourself nothing. The two of us are the most consistent Navaredkers, in contrast to our former group leader Tsemakh Lomzher—who's a weakling and a hypocrite. When he left the path of Torah, he didn't really leave it all the way; and now that he's back, ostensibly as a penitent, he hasn't come back all the way and refuses to become completely pious like that lunatic Kupishker."

After hearing such words from Lohoysker in the yeshiva kitchen, some of the students ran to Reb Tsemakh with the cry: "Why don't you let that heretic be driven away?"

Looking exhausted, as if his entire life journey up to now had been made on foot, Reb Tsemakh Atlas answered, "As long as Lohoysker is considered a student at the yeshiva, he still keeps himself from doing certain things. If he were driven away, he'd tumble down to the nether depths of hell." In the penitent's eyes a black melancholy burned, and his beard hung slack as though it had been slaughtered.

"Don't you understand, my friends, that Lohoysker is hoping to be chased away? He has often said that he's afraid of going out into the world because he can't earn a living and doesn't know how to behave among nonreligious people. That's why he *wants* to be driven from the yeshiva—so that he'll have no choice but to leave and thus publicly violate God's commandments."

Tsemakh sought the root of his students' perverted ways and found it in himself. The more he suffered, the more he told himself that the entire world was made up of mirrors that showed man his own life. But the greatest cause of his anguish was Daniel Homler, the youngest of his Russian students.

In the early years, the Nareva rosh yeshiva had affectionately called him Daniel the greatly beloved, after the biblical Daniel. When Danielke Homler first came to the yeshiva, he was still in short pants and had a pair of full, freckled cheeks that begged to be pinched. He was from a wealthy home where Yiddish was not spoken, and it took him a long time to get rid of the rolled Russian "r." But he worked at it until the "r" softened somewhat, as if a brook were babbling in his throat. From his merchant family he had inherited a passion for bookkeeping. Just because he was from a rich home, he tried harder than others to be a Navaredker seeker and toiled at self-improvement: he would offer his share of meat at mealtime, a well-lighted corner in the beth medresh, or even a garment to a friend. But he was infuriated if anybody took something of his without his knowledge. His cheeks flamed, he coughed, and paced back and forth in his room. Even though the taker justified himself and Daniel smiled and said, "It's perfectly all right, perfectly all right," the "r's" came out hard as stones. He had behaved that way when he was in Tsemakh Lomzher's group, and during the past two years he had become increasingly unfriendly.

The Musarists set great store by the commentary to the statement in the *Ethics of the Fathers* that he who says "What's mine is mine and what's yours is yours" is one of the evil men of Sodom. Even someone who was not attempting to increase his spirituality would not get angry when a roommate took his coat without asking permission. But Daniel Homler no longer hid his annoyance when, on Friday afternoon, a roommate would take some shoe polish from Daniel's box to clean his shoes or a piece of soap to wash with in honor of the Sabbath. Daniel suspected his friends of using his towel; he kept an eye out to see whether someone might have worn his second pair of shoes, which he stored under his bed. Finally he was no longer ashamed of his anger when someone took a piece of bread from his little shelf in the kitchen pantry. If a lodger came home late at night from the Musar meditation room, Daniel would be irritable the next morning. Even though he hadn't had to get up to open the door for the late-comer, Daniel would complain that his sleep had been interrupted. Only two years ago he would have given his portion of meat to a friend; now at mealtimes he looked around sharply to see if he was given a smaller piece than others.

"What's happened to him?" friends asked, and Lohoysker the troublemaker answered, "What's happened to him? He's become what he's been all along! The Navaredkers think that man can break his habits. It's easier for man to break down than to break his habits. And coming to the surface in Homler one can see the merchant father and bookkeeper with his philosophy of what's mine is mine and what's yours is yours. If I didn't know that the Bolsheviks rule Russia and that my father is a beggar there now, I'd hate Reb Tsemakh Lomzher like poison for having torn me away from home."

"Your piece of bad luck is that *you're* not under Bolshevik rule. You would have become a commissar there, with a pistol at your side," Yankl Poltaver shouted from across the table.

"I couldn't have been a pistol-toting commissar, but our group leader, Tsemakh Lomzher, and you, his ape—both of you would surely have been commissars in Russia," Lohoysker answered.

Later, the youths reproached Poltaver. "Why did you start anything with that gypsy? The best punishment for him is to ignore him."

Once, in the middle of the night, Daniel Homler began to writhe in pain. He was taken to the hospital, where the doctors diagnosed appendicitis and ordered immediate surgery. The yeshiva students recited Psalms before an open Holy Ark and the operation was successful. But there were complications later, and Daniel had to remain hospitalized. At first the hospital nurses took care of him, but his illness was lengthy and the yeshiva had to pay three separate bills: for a bed in the ward, for doctors and medicines, and for nursing care.

Reb Simkha, deciding that the nurses weren't necessary, assembled Homler's friends and told them, "Now you don't have to go looking for someone to be good to. Now you can help your friend and write *that* down in your list of good deeds accomplished."

Shifts of yeshiva students stood by at Daniel Homler's bedside. They learned how to change his sheets, give him his medicine on time, and help him to the bathroom. But Daniel Homler was capricious. He was angry all the time, complaining that he wasn't being tended. Insulted by his behavior, the students found excuses not to stand their shifts. The strong-as-iron Yankl Poltaver groaned that he himself wasn't in the best of health. Reuven Ratner, head drawn in between his pointed shoulders, gave the excuse that he was in negotiations with a matchmaker and prospective in-laws. Shimshl Kupishker mumbled that he couldn't spare that much time away from the service of God. Others who lived with Homler and especially disliked him for his miserliness said openly, "As long as it's a matter of saving money, the yeshiva must make an effort to collect the necessary funds."

These complaints reached Reb Simkha. His response came in his Sabbath night talk to the entire yeshiva.

"Helping a friend is doubly significant, for it is both material and spiritual help. If he is cut off from the beth medresh and can't participate in studies, he should be cheered up with words of Torah to keep him from falling into despair, God forbid." In the darkness preceding the Evening Service, Reb Simkha couldn't catch his listeners' eyes. But the students around his prayer stand knew very well what he meant and that whoever thought he was being singled out—then it was indeed he at whom the words were directed.

"If a Musarnik doesn't help a friend," Reb Simkha continued, "then all his remarks about sacrificing oneself for another are no more than pretty words. Deeds are what count, not theory."

The students frowned in displeasure. They resumed their visits, but they didn't hide the fact that they considered them a torment. "I'd rather go all over Nareva collecting bread and potatoes for the yeshiva kitchen," Yankl Poltaver said, "or get eating days and rooms for the younger students." Reuven Ratner moaned that he himself was prepared to pay for a nurse for Daniel Homler. Shimshl Kupishker had to immerse himself in Musar and contemplate the torments of the wicked in hell before he could bring himself to visit the sick boy again.

The yeshiva students returned from the hospital even more outraged and ashamed. "When a nurse in a cap, a white uniform, and flat white shoes comes into the ward," Yankl Poltaver observed, "Daniel gives her a sugar-sweet smile. His eyes shine and get damp, even though a minute earlier his face was full of despair or anger. How attached he is to those white geese!" Yankl Poltaver continued. "He knows each of them by name. If one of them happens to stop by his bed and asks him how he is, it's obvious that he considers it a great stroke of luck. But as soon as the nurse leaves, his face becomes more sour than ever, and he glares at the friend taking care of him." Kupishker added that Daniel Homler would often tell him, "I'm embarrassed before the doctors when you wear these long, filthy ritual fringes." And Reuven Ratner asserted, "I once had the nerve to tell him that these sisters of mercy don't faze me—they take good money for their mercy. At this he flew into a rage and said, 'I don't care a bit why the nurses do it, as long as they do it well. And besides, they like one patient more and another less, even though everyone pays the same amount. This proves that even the nurses don't do everything just for money.' "

"It sounds as if Homler's fond of the world. It may be the hospital world of the sick, but it's still the world," said Yankl Poltaver, venting his thoughts in the yeshiva kitchen.

"You bench warmers are so naïve! Moshe Chayit Lohoysker interrupted. "It's the nurses he likes. What if they do wear white uniforms? Aren't they women?"

The yeshiva boys exchanged confused glances. Granted that while Daniel Homler lay in fever and pain, one would not expect him to think of modesty; but since the fever had abated and the pain subsided, wasn't he ashamed before strange young women, especially since his body was so emaciated? Seeing that the boys were entirely befuddled, Moshe Chayit burst out laughing.

"If you really understood people and didn't get your knowledge of them from *The Duties of the Heart* and your Talmudic interpretations, you'd realize that that's precisely what Daniel Homler wants. He *wants* girls in white uniforms to touch his shriveled body, to caress and pamper him, dress him and undress him, feed him like a baby with a little spoon, and even take him to the bathroom."

The Musarists sprang up in disgust, as if they'd suddenly noticed they had made a blessing over wormy bread.

"Lohoysker, the father of defilement, debases everything on the table with his filthy mouth," one student said indignantly.

Another yelled, "That skeptic is putting his own thoughts into Daniel Homler's mind. As the saying goes, 'finding fault with others for your own defects.' "

"That heretic has no freethinking friends to talk to," a third outshouted him, "so he elbows in among yeshiva students."

The scholars' excitement and their abuse of Lohoysker in the kitchen came to Reb Simkha Feinerman's ears, which turned even redder than his beard. It was he, after all, who had nicknamed Daniel Homler Daniel the greatly beloved. Had Daniel fallen into a state of such unhealthy lust that he wanted strange women to be near him? This time Reb Simkha didn't make use of a sermon, and he didn't keep his stare inward lest someone suspect he was being singled out. This time Reb Simkha pointed directly at the scholars.

"Each one of you looked for an excuse not to go—and when you finally did go, you went with hatred in your hearts. The patient sensed your hatred; hence, hired women please him more than his friends."

The students kept silent out of respect for their rosh yeshiva. They realized that he was blaming them more than he really intended to.

After deliberating privately, Reb Simkha came to the conclusion that Homler should be brought back to a room with a more homelike atmosphere. A doctor would visit him from time to time, and his friends would tend him.

Zundl Konotoper brought this message to the hospital and returned at once with the patient's answer: "I'm going to fight with all the strength I have not to be transferred to a private home, because I'll die there, and the yeshiva wants me to die."

"Has he gone mad?" Reb Simkha asked in alarm, running his fingers through his long beard once more until he came to its tip and to the conclusion: "If the sick youth has taken it into his head that we want to do away with him, God forbid, we must not remove him from the hospital now. We'll have to pressure Homler's friends to visit him again, no matter how much suffering it causes them."

12

REB DUBER LIFSCHITZ —who had once gone with Zundl Konotoper to visit Tsemakh in Lomzhe to bring him back to the correct path—had not changed at all. Duber still maintained that the purpose of his life was to spread the teachings of Navaredok. His short, stiff beard was still afraid to grow without his consent, and Reb Duber gave no consent to anything physical. But the circumstances of his life had changed. Because of a dispute with the rabbi and the leading congregants, he had been obliged to leave his little yeshiva in Narevke, a village near Nareva. Immediately after Sukkos he came to the main yeshiva and asked that a place of Torah be established in another village, where he and his family and some of his students would settle.

"At the beginning of the term, none of our students want to go anywhere. They want to listen to new Talmud interpretations and study," Reb Simkha said, standing in a corner by the eastern wall, shifting his weight from one foot to another. "On the other hand, we have the double responsibility of preparing lessons and of providing subsistence for so many yeshiva scholars, may their number increase. That's why at this time we can't release the older scholars who help us run the beth medresh."

"Which means that I have to stay in Nareva and sit on my hands till someone takes pity on me," Reb Duber snapped.

"In the meantime, we have no one to send. We'll see—perhaps around Purim time, when the study schedule in the yeshiva is more relaxed." Reb Simkha Feinerman looked somewhat aloof and cold, so that the Narevke principal would remember that he was speaking to the rosh yeshiva of Nareva.

Reb Duber Lifschitz no longer doubted that Reb Simkha was playing politics with him. The Nareva center had always wanted to demolish Narevke: Nareva was delighted that Narevke was going under. Reb Duber's two-way battle against the rabbi of Narevke and the rosh yeshiva of Nareva had his head whirling.

Duber Lifschitz also tried to talk to the penitent. "Once upon a time, Reb Tsemakh, you used to set the world afire. Why don't you go out and find a village for me? I'm not an expert at such matters."

"If I were to leave, I'd go to establish a yeshiva, and then I might not be able to return or even want to return, and that has already happened to me once." Tsemakh drew the tallis higher over his head, to put a boundary between him and the world.

Reb Duber Lifschitz fumed silently, thinking: A true penitent would have been overjoyed at the privilege of establishing a new place of Torah learning, and he wouldn't have been so afraid of leaving the beth medresh for a short time. Which means that the outside world still has a powerful attraction for Reb Tsemakh Lomzher. Reb Duber became despondent. Even if he found a couple of students to make the trip, who knew whether they would find a village, and who knew how long he would have to wait before he could take his family there? Meanwhile, they were stranded in Narevke; the yeshiva that he had expended so much energy upon was falling apart; and he was totally superfluous here in Nareva.

When the time came for Reb Simkha to go to the Vilna meeting, he spoke to Duber Lifschitz in an entirely different fashion.

"Reb Duber, you and Zundl Konotoper must assemble Daniel Homler's friends and persuade them to take care of him again. Logically, Tsemakh Lomzher would be the one to deal with them, since Daniel Homler and his friends used to be in Lomzher's group of seekers. But Reb Tsemakh says he's not in the mood to talk to them now, and they wouldn't listen anyway. Nevertheless, he's agreed to be there if someone else does the talking. In short, you'll be the main speaker, and something good may come of it for you too. But don't overshoot the mark, Reb Duber, because if you go too far, you'll end up with too little," Reb Simkha quipped, and Reb Duber Lifschitz still didn't know where he stood. Being entrusted with the group of students should mean that the Nareva yeshiva wasn't playing politics with him. But on the other hand, this in itself could be politics. Reb Simkha had hinted that some good might come of this for him, but actually he had promised nothing.

After Reb Simkha's departure for the Vilna gathering of the Yeshiva Council and after Yankl Poltaver's dispute with Sulkes, Zundl Konotoper, the acting rosh yeshiva, quickly decided to call the group together. "And while we're demanding to know why they're not taking care of Homler, we'll also take Poltaver to pieces. We'll skin him alive!" Zundl roared in his lion's voice.

Reb Duber Lifschitz shuddered. "God forbid! Yankl Poltaver does great things for others." Reb Duber knew that if there was one person he could count on to go out and find him a village, it was Yankl Poltaver.

After the Evening Service, the group met in the study room of the beth medresh. Everyone knew there was no need to hurry. The talk would last till dawn. Reb Duber Lifschitz and Zundl Konotoper sat at the head of the table—the former as head of the group, the latter as his assistant. The students sat along both sides of the table and Reb Tsemakh Atlas was at the other end. The dusty, yellowish light of the bulb above their heads played on the leather spines of the books on the shelves. The light, which cast mysterious, changing shades of gold, served to obscure the hairy faces of those gathered around the table. All were immersed in silence, as was customary before a Musar talk: no words were spoken for a long while so that everyone could divest himself of materiality and concentrate on higher things.

Duber and Zundl swayed back and forth energetically. When

Duber moved forward, hitting his chest at the table edge, Zundl surged the other way. On the wall their shadows imitated them, like two giants standing on swings and betting who could swing higher to the sky. Reb Duber threw an angry sidelong glance at the boys who refused to tend a sick friend and to go out to establish a new place of Torah studies because they didn't want to give up their warm beds and regular meals. Reuven Ratner was said to be always among the first to help others, but lately he had become depressed because he couldn't arrange a good match. What was he looking for? A bride who wore high heels? Then let him take a serving girl. And anyway, what would he be missing? Troubles with his wife and children. Reb Duber laughed to himself, musing that Zundl Konotoper was smarter than everyone else for not having married yet. But Shimshl Kupishker was—he was sorry to say it—a fool. With his eyes constantly glued to the prayer book, how could he ever find time for human relationships? Shimshl's former teacher, Tsemakh Lomzher, had left him midway, so he had strayed off into the cemetery, talking to the dead as if he were superstitious.

Reb Duber glanced at Chaikl Vilner and became even more depressed. Vilner was neither studying Talmud nor learning Musar. He was always talking with the students and always looking into every corner. What was he looking at, and what did he see there? To top it off, his Valkenik principal, Reb Tsemakh Atlas, proudly said that he was excellent at faultfinding. And Reb Simkha considered him very special because he was a pupil of Reb Avraham-Shaye Kosover. I don't see a thing in him, Reb Duber thought. I'd chase him out of here. Reb Duber twisted his little beard into a stiff point and narrowed his eyes. Chaikl Vilner spoke in the Navaredker idiom and was an expert at delivering Musar talks. Nevertheless, the smell of heresy wafted from him like herring from a herring merchant even in his Sabbath clothes. The only one here with a fine character, Duber thought, was Yankl Poltaver, even though he was capable of wild antics, like his former mentor Tsemakh Lomzher years ago. Duber didn't know how to extricate himself from the silence that had taken hold of him. It was as if he'd gone astray in a bend in a river full of slime and seaweed, where one could neither stand up nor swim. Finally he turned to someone he didn't wish to see at all—Pultusker the Hasid.

Reb Duber believed that Musar and Hasidism were like a double-faced shadow on the wall, or the two-headed eagle of the Russian Czar. Reb Duber particularly despised Pultusker the Hasid. Why did his earlocks jiggle out of his little cap like two barefoot peasant lads? Why were his boots so neatly polished? It was no accident. If someone's mind was on polished boots, it wasn't set on the service of God. While everyone else in the kitchen took the advice of the *Ethics of the Fathers* and discussed Torah matters while eating, lest enjoying the meager meal be considered idol worship, Pultusker chewed away posthaste. Like a donkey chomping into his sack of oats until he had shoveled it all in, he never lifted his head from the plate. And that was exactly the way he studied. He sipped the Talmud without commentaries, waved his hands about like a windmill, pilpulized, and threw sand into everyone's eyes. Everything in him was pure delusion, deception. The yeshiva students usually finished reciting the weekday Silent Devotion in five or ten minutes, but it took Pultusker either one second or half an hour. And the more he swayed, the less devotion there was to his prayer. Even a blind man could see that. Now too he was swaying piously, but no matter how ecstatic he seemed or how much he groaned, everyone knew he didn't mean it. Receiving a smaller allowance than others or a smaller piece of meat than he thought he deserved irritated him. He was vexed at not getting the room he wanted, and moreover, he had been assigned a dark corner in the beth medresh. Not being assigned to a group was the only thing that didn't upset him. Then, suddenly, Zundl Konotoper had driven Pultusker into the study room like a chicken into the slaughterhouse. Everyone knew that this was precisely what the Hasid thought. Once he had specifically declared for the entire beth medresh to hear, "At Musarnik group discussions, the students are inspected just the way a rabbi tears a chicken's guts apart with his nails to see if there's a needle there."

Reb Duber began to shout, unexpectedly and without preamble, as though to test his voice, "I've heard people say, Pultusker, that you claim that among the Musarniks, melancholy grows like hair under the armpits. So I ask you—why are you so happy?"

"Me?" Pultusker clapped his hands to his heart. "I never said that."

"And why are you squabbling with Orsher and Bobroysker over a place to sit? We are taught: 'It is not the place that honors the man, but the man that honors the place,' " Zundl Konotoper whooped at him.

"Me? That's been my seat for a long time." Pultusker blinked, looking petulant, wondering why he happened to be chosen as the first victim. Then he began to tell a long story: "Orsher took my place, so I had to bump Bobroysker. Then Bobroysker bumped me back, so I had to bump Orsher again."

"We're not interested. You should have given in just *because* it's been your seat for a long time. Not taking something that belongs to someone else is no accomplishment. That's why the Torah tells us, 'Do not steal,' " the big-bearded, sharp-eyed Konotoper bellowed. Then the Narevke principal with the little beard and the slaughtering-knife eyes shouted louder, "This isn't one of your little Hasidic shuls where the boys throw wet towels at each other and children address old men as if they were their equals. This is Navaredok!"

The Hasid jerked forward, gesticulated wildly, and said angrily, "I'm completely innocent." But before he could disentangle himself, Reb Duber Lifschitz swayed once more and cut him to the quick with one question, like an experienced hunter on horseback who hits a bird in mid-flight with his arrow.

"Have you been infected with the plague of reading newspapers too?"

"All I read is the anti-Zionist religious paper from Warsaw," Pultusker protested, almost in tears, but the group leader was no longer paying attention. With a sidelong glance Duber contemplated Vilner again: What was he doing among pious yeshiva students? His kind was deadly poison for a beth medresh. One had to be as wary of him as of fire. He devoured everything with his eyes. And whose fault was it that he was here? It was Reb Simkha's. He was the one who had favored Vilner.

Reb Duber began softly, as though arguing with himself. "The author of *The Path of the Upright* tells us that people forget their most common responsibilities. That's why Musarniks sit together—to remind one another of what everyone knows but has forgotten. Old Jews with white beards, world-renowned scholars, and saints like Reb Israel Salanter, the founder of the Musar movement, his friends and pupils whose teachings sustain us—none was ashamed to reveal his faults to his friends. So we certainly shouldn't be ashamed, for as long as a man is aware of his faults, he can still be helped. But the sort of person who doesn't know what his fault is—or, on the contrary, makes an attribute of it—is lost forever. *That's* the unmistakable sign of a Musarnik—he is a connoisseur of himself and starts with himself."

Duber Lifschitz chewed the tip of his beard and made faces as if the hairs between his lips tasted bitter. Then he resumed swaying. "So, then, what were we talking about, friends? That a man must first of all begin with his own faults. That's what we were talking about, friends. So, then, I'll start with myself and let you be my judges." As he began to speak about his controversy in Narevke, a network of wrinkles formed on his face. "I couldn't bear having the rabbi and the congregants tell me how to run the yeshiva. The Jews of Narevke, on the other hand, couldn't bear my interfering with local affairs. Should I have looked on and kept silent when men who shaved their beards and desecrated the Sabbath ran the affairs of the community? Or when a vulgar boor of a rich man turned up his nose at the foul odor in the beth medresh from the yeshiva boys who slept there? Shouldn't I have given that ignoramus his due? I didn't start an argument for the sake of my own honor—I did it for the sake of heaven—and I shouldn't back away even now. On the other hand, I'm used to teaching my students, and while I'm here in Nareva, I'm not doing a thing. To put it bluntly, my family in Narevke is going hungry, and the yeshiva there is falling apart. I ought to return to Narevke and become reconciled with my opponents. But what would my students say? Could I tell them to live on faith while I kowtow to a congregant who donates bread and herring to the yeshiva? My students would consider me a liar and do just the opposite of what I teach them. In brief, my situation is like that of a rooster in a pile of cotton: he crawls out with one leg and becomes more entangled with the other. I'd like to hear from a group of God-fearing youths how we can resolve the problem."

The listeners knew how the problem should be resolved. A couple of older students should be sent to Narevke to keep the little yeshiva going and another village should be found for Reb Duber. But since the students were unwilling to go, they remained silent.

Reb Duber, infuriated now, castigated them. "A diligent scholar is always in a rush. The day is short and there is much work to do, he says. He wants to show that he can swallow the entire Torah and come up with all the new interpretations. But if he remembered that he stems from a putrid drop, he would also remember that others will come after him. What will remain for them if he monopolizes all the new interpretations? This question is even more appropriate to Navaredker Musarniks. They risked their very lives to tear a Jewish child away from the Yevsektsiya. How is it possible that today, when one's life is not in danger, no one wants to do anything for the dissemination of Torah?" Reb Duber Lifschitz stretched his head toward Reb Tsemakh Atlas to show him that the remarks were directed at him too.

"The answer is," Reb Duber chanted, "that we've become weaker just *because* we're no longer called upon to risk our lives. There is a kind of person whose criterion of great and small is not the mitzva, the good deed in itself, or the sin in itself. If the effort involved in overcoming his *yetzer ha-ra* is spectacular enough to endanger his health or shorten his life, then he won't give in. The greatest danger is underestimating the small temptation. It is easier to resist a great temptation that demands a concentration of all our faculties to overcome it once and for all than to deal with small temptations day in and day out." Duber Lifschitz groaned and fell silent. I've come to teach and have been taught, he mused. Not only Tsemakh Lomzher but I too found it easier to risk my life as a youth in Russia than to withstand small mundane worries now.

The group leader's assistant was red with anger. "What does all this mean?" Zundl Konotoper demanded. "I've remained a bachelor, and my only joy in life is to teach children to become men of fine character. I forget about myself. The rosh yeshiva is happy that he has a helper, so he's in no hurry to arrange a marriage for me and never even asks if I need money for a new suit. But if Musarniks won't go to look after a sick friend, then the end of the world has come, and we must close the Musar school like a shopkeeper who's gone bankrupt." With piercing eyes Zundl Konotoper looked around for a victim, and he too chose Pultusker, who had been the previous scapegoat. Bored to death with this melancholy talk, the Hasid had twice managed to escape to the toilet. He stayed away as long as possible, and when he returned, he took his time drying his hands and, eyes shut tight, reciting the proper blessing with utter devotion.

"You plaster saint, we know you!" Konotoper shouted at him. "Hasidim think that their rebbe fulfills their religious obligation—he climbs up to heaven for them. But Musarniks know that the Torah is every man's duty. Every man must do everything himself." Warmed up now, Zundl turned upon Yankl Poltaver. "Was anyone more of a wild savage than Ishmael? The Torah itself calls him that. Our sages of blessed memory tell us that he boasted to his brother Isaac, '*You* were circumcised on the eighth day, and *I* let myself be cut when I was thirteen years old.' To which Isaac responded, 'Should the Almighty wish it, I'm prepared to sacrifice my life.' And indeed he proved this when Abraham bound him for the sacrifice. The moral of this tale is that the wild savage lunges at everyone and always boasts that his battles are for the sake of heaven. But the truly religious and honest man is calm and gentle. When necessary, he offers to sacrifice his life. And if not, he sits in silence."

Yankl Poltaver squirmed in his seat as if the bench beneath him were smoldering. He waited for the assistant group leader to speak to him without allusion, in straightforward fashion, and then he would reply. Oh, how he would reply! Reb Duber Lifschitz didn't want a quarrel with Yankl Poltaver, the only group member who occasionally went out to establish a village yeshiva. Therefore, Reb Duber interrupted the incensed Konotoper and went on talking about the patient in the hospital.

"Daniel Homler's friends maintain that he has become grouchy and capricious, an ingrate. That's exactly what the freethinkers want—they don't want to be burdened by favor seekers. If they help someone, he has to look like a poor wretch to boot. If he's the kind that has recently fallen into poverty and has no intention of demeaning himself, then he can die of hunger! It's no wonder, then, that the nonbelievers have no patience with the sick and needy. After all, they don't believe in a God who is also merciful to them. But how can yeshiva students possibly be insensitive to the fact that one must do good? I've seen much during this futile life of mine." Reb Duber nodded sadly, recalling how much he had suffered from the Narevke do-gooders. "There are even jealous people who masquerade as men of compassion. Confronted with the successful and talented man, they feel discomfited. So, with candles in hand, they go out looking for the shlimazel. Such two-faced men of compassion constantly sigh that the world is vanity of vanities and that only the little bit of good they do keeps them alive."

In a stillness that radiated heaviness of heart, like a pale halo in a fog, Tsemakh Atlas sat with head bent, listening. He knew that Reb

Duber's remarks gave vent to his own resentments and complaints. Nevertheless, with all of Reb Duber's trials and failures, he remained a whole person. He had quarreled with a rabbi and a congregation—not with the Torah. And he had never abandoned the correct path and thus been obligated to become a penitent. For the penitent was a man whose life was pieced together out of shards and chips like a broken earthenware pot.

13

THE DOOR OPENED quickly and Moshe Chayit Lohoysker came into the room. He looked as if he had just left and was now returning. His appearance caused a silent tumult. The boys sat open-mouthed; the two group leaders stopped swaying and looked toward Reb Tsemakh Lomzher, who maintained his despondent silence. Tsemakh knew that if not for his presence, Lohoysker wouldn't have had the nerve or the desire to come.

Moshe Chayit at once found a seat between Reuven Ratner and Shimshl Kupishker. Both turned away from him, but he pretended not to notice their surprise and agitation. But the group soon recovered; everyone silently agreed not to take notice of the uninvited guest or be upset by him.

Reb Duber shut his eyes in contemplative ecstasy for a while and then resumed, "What were we talking about, friends? About the difference between the worldly nonbelievers and the men of Torah. That's what we were talking about, friends. At first glance the man who renounces pleasures cannot be kind and tender because he is continually preoccupied with the most difficult task, the battle with the *yetzer ha-ra*. Therefore, the spiritual man is by nature severe, while the person dedicated to material things seems to be happy, generous, good-natured. Then why should the sensualist treat others badly when he treats himself so well? But, actually, the goodness of the worldly man is superficial, because on his march toward satisfaction of his lust, he'll trample everything that stands in his way. At best, the sensualist can be good-natured after he has satisfied himself for a while. But a good-natured person still isn't a good person, just as wisecracks aren't wisdom. Indeed, the recluse who wages a bitter lifelong war with the *yetzer ha-ra* is the one who will wholeheartedly offer help where the Torah commands him to help. He doesn't give in. The man who has a certain goal in mind and is calculating by nature won't give in to others without being calculating. The spiritual man knows how to give, where and when it is necessary. He learns this trait from the Almighty Himself, as it is written: 'As He is merciful, so shall ye be merciful.' Did you want to say something, Vilner?" Duber Lifschitz turned to Chaikl and the little wrinkles around his eyes became as hard as rope.

"No, I didn't want to say a thing," Chaikl answered, but nevertheless blurted out, "What you're saying, then, is that with the exception of Torah believers, the whole world is made up of wicked people."

"Of course the whole world is made up of wicked people!" Zundl Konotoper roared, looking accusingly at Reb Tsemakh Atlas, who had not explained this to his Valkenik pupil.

Chaikl Vilner hated being shouted at. He immediately replied, "It's impossible for a man to crawl out of his skin and do good without the slightest self-interest. Even if the doer of good seeks neither honor nor reciprocation because someone else helped him, and doesn't think of future favors, his help is a way of expressing his gratitude for the good fortune that *he* wasn't afflicted with his friend's trouble. He may help another person because he's afraid; that is, he wants to bribe fate so the same thing won't happen to him. Or he may help the victim so that afterwards he can calmly enjoy life. There are also people who by their very nature can't be stingy, and they will give anyone what he asks for. So it's clear from this that you can always find an ulterior motive that drives man to do good."

Chaikl had hardly finished before Reb Duber Lifschitz flared, "Just what do you mean when you say that the doer of good helps another because he's afraid, so as to bribe fate? How can a believer express such an idea? Instead of talking about Divine Providence, you talk about fate. From your remarks it seems that fate is some evil beast we have to feed regularly so that it won't attack and devour us. Phoo! These words give off an odor of filthy heresy, like medicines in a sick man's room. And now for that bright idea that some people by nature can't be stingy! Are we talking about the wicked? Or about profligates and wastrels? We're talking about adherents of Musar and spiritual men!"

Chaikl recalled similar talks with his Valkenik principal. And now Reb Tsemakh was sitting in silence as if behind a cloud; the longer he remained silent, the larger the cloud around him grew. Instead of Reb Tsemakh, Reb Duber Lifschitz was speaking again about man, as if nothing else existed. Chaikl couldn't forget the Valkenik woods and the three rivers that flowed together behind the town. At their juncture the naked eye could see their diverse hues. One was greenish blue, another leaden gray, the third translucent yellow. At the point where the three met, one could feel warm and cold currents. The vacationing yeshiva students in Valkenik never noticed this. Reb Tsemakh had no feeling at all for beauty—neither for the beauty of a tree nor for the Holy Ark hand-carved out of a tree. Reb Avraham-Shaye too had often answered Chaikl's questions about why he didn't go into raptures over the forest: "I can't manage to do everything." Reb Avraham-Shaye devoted his entire life to Talmud and commentaries. The Musarniks burrowed into the attributes of man's soul. Only Chaikl thought that the world writ large was bigger and more interesting than man, who was a world writ small.

Chaikl turned his attention back to the talk. Reuven Ratner was speaking now. As was his habit, he raised his thin shoulders and moved his fingers as though he were touching the words. "Human beings belong to that lonely family that dwells in darkness and in the shadow of death. Perhaps a happy prince once came into this world, but no one ever left this world a happy prince. On the other hand, man is the crown of creation, created in the image of God. With his good or bad behavior he either improves or ruins all of creation. Consequently, this puts an awesome responsibility on him—because if he has an impure intent in the service of God or while helping a friend, he can destroy worlds."

The group leader Reb Duber Lifschitz made faces and squirmed in his seat. He wanted to yell: Reuven Ratner is speaking like a Kabbalist, but still he doesn't want to take care of a sick friend or go out and establish a new place for Torah studies. But one couldn't be that harsh with Ratner, for he was one of the best students and had connections with marriage brokers. Incensed at these pretty words,

Reb Duber nevertheless held his tongue, and the others were silent too. Perhaps because no one said a word, Chaikl Vilner spoke up again, although he could never understand what had prompted him to do it.

"Man is not the crown of creation, and the world was not created for him. Man is even more profound and interesting if we look at him as a part of creation and not as its ultimate purpose. He is just a little room in that great structure of creation, and we must get to know the entire structure. That's why we should realize that the little room precedes the objects placed in it. That is, the very fact of man's creation and his habits precede his direction in life. Hearing birds singing makes a man feel better, because birdsong reminds him that last night's bad dreams and the new day's worries are not eternal. Even if he doesn't think of it, man senses that creation didn't begin with him and won't end with him. He knows that birds generally have a shorter life span and are more vulnerable, but nevertheless they sing. This perception gladdens mortal man's heart. He shouldn't regard himself as the center of all existence and should understand that he can't know himself if he doesn't know the world around him."

The students sat with wrinkled brows and hostile faces, though in private talks with Chaikl Vilner they would listen to even more biting, heretical remarks. Konotoper's small, pointed eyes drilled through Chaikl, and Reb Duber Lifschitz stared at him from under arched brows before he replied.

"You say that a man can't know himself if he doesn't know the world around him. Musarniks assert precisely the opposite. A man can't know the world if he doesn't know himself. The foundation of Musar is: Know yourself!"

"Socrates counseled, 'Man, know thyself,' thousands of years before the Navaredker Musarniks," Moshe Chayit Lohoysker suddenly leaped into the discussion with murder in his eyes.

"Well, yes, the Greek philosopher, Socrates, Plato's student," Reb Duber said contemptuously over his shoulder, as if warning the students not to bother turning their heads.

"Socrates was Plato's teacher, not his student," Moshe Chayit Lohoysker corrected.

"How do you know that Socrates was Plato's teacher and not his student?" Reb Duber asked, still not looking at him.

"What do you mean, how do I know? Who doesn't know that?

Every book says so in black and white," Lohoysker yelled, waiting for the students who sat there like clay statues to come into the battle.

"Well, then, your books are wrong," Reb Duber answered calmly.

"The mistake is yours, not the books'! Socrates was Plato's teacher, not his pupil. His teacher! His teacher!" Lohoysker clutched his head as though the veins in his temples would burst.

"He's right. Socrates was Plato's teacher, not his student," Zundl Konotoper looked apprehensively at the group leader who was getting into an argument with the heretic over a bit of foolishness.

Reb Duber saw by the faces of the yeshiva boys that he was wrong this time. He hunched his shoulders and said in a soft, deferential tone, "Now I recall that Socrates was Plato's teacher, not vice versa. Actually, it's nothing new that a wise man among the learned gentiles says the same thing as Musar. Musar doesn't put any stock in saying new things. It isn't a new way in Judaism at all. But it is a way to teach man through reminding him of duties that he knows but forgets, as we have previously mentioned. Here too we see the difference between worldly writers and the men of the Torah. In the introduction to their books the early gaonim wrote that they hadn't come to say anything new—while today every modern scribbler is absolutely convinced that he's discovered a new star. But vast as the distance between the stars and the globe is the distance between what man knows and what he fulfills. Is there anyone greater than Aristotle, the third after Socrates and Plato? A holy book tells us that when he was once found in a prostitute's house and was asked why he was there, he replied, 'Now I am not the philosopher Aristotle!' "

"That story is a lie, and a stupid lie besides." Moshe Chayit took off his glasses and rubbed the bridge of his nose with two fingers. "Aristotle may have had dealings with many promiscuous women, not just the one prostitute. But none of the writers of those asinine little books was there."

"We have faith in our holy sages." Reb Duber smiled pleasantly, and everyone around the table apparently agreed.

Lohoysker, even more infuriated now, began casting words like stones. "Musarniks are comfortable in their ignorance, like a worm in horseradish. They've convinced themselves that they know the world. The truth is that the only thing they know is how to scratch themselves. Chaikl Vilner is right. Man himself precedes his path in life.

That holds true for the individual as well as for the multitude. When an individual dies, God, who is nothing more than his character traits and feelings, dies with him. When a people perishes, its folk character, its way of life, and its vicissitudes in history go with it. There is no truth outside of man. Man decides whether things are true or false, and the same truth doesn't pertain to every person—my truth is different from yours, as Vilner correctly said . . ."

Chaikl sprang up. "I didn't say that!"

"Because you don't have the guts to say what's on your mind—but that's what you meant," Lohoysker said, laughing, and he went on reviling the Musarniks. "You Musarniks cause people terrible harm by persuading them that human beings can reshape themselves. You admit that the struggle with one's own *yetzer ha-ra* is the most difficult of battles, but you despise everyone who succumbs in this struggle. You convince yourselves that you are the only honest people in a world that is totally wicked and sinful. You console yourselves that the worldly man doesn't enjoy life because he can't get everything he wants. At the same time, you say that the punishment for the sin is in proportion to the pleasure derived. The logical conclusion, then, is that hell is always empty because, according to you, the sensualist has no pleasure in this world. Nevertheless, you put the whole world into that hell, except the Navaredker yeshiva students. You're doing this out of envy for the secularists. In the same way, you speak of compassion, yet you're the most cruel. What can be more cruel than demanding of a man that he renounce the benefit of having done a good deed?"

"We're heartless and you're the compassionate one?" Duber Lifschitz shrugged. And Zundl Konotoper roared, "We're jealous of *you?*"

"Yes, you're jealous of me because I'm not afraid of saying what you're even afraid to think. And I'm also more compassionate than you. I don't ask anyone to sacrifice himself," Lohoysker shrieked, his anger increasing as he went on. "Musarniks always like to base their arguments on a rabbinic quotation, so I'll expound on a remark of the sages too. The Talmud states that sometime in the future, the Holy One Blessed Be He will bind the *yetzer ha-ra* and slay him. The saints and the wicked will watch and weep. The wicked will cry because they were unable to overcome the *yetzer ha-ra*, which is as weak and thin as thread; the saints will weep because they were able to overcome the *yetzer ha-ra*, which is as large as a mountain. God himself, the Talmud states, will weep too. The weeping of the wicked is understandable. To them the slain *yetzer ha-ra* appeared to be as thin as thread, so they cry over their past inability to overcome such a weak *yetzer ha-ra* and over their lost rewards of the world to come. But why do the saints think that this slain *yetzer ha-ra* is as big as a mountain, and why do they weep? Why should they weep? The answer is that every unfulfilled desire seems to be as big as a mountain. And the yearning for his unattained desire always causes man to weep. Even the saints who are resurrected and see the wicked weeping with regret at having submitted to the *yetzer ha-ra* and now being subjected to everlasting suffering and everlasting shame—even the saints cry because they left the world with their lusts unsatiated. Unsatisfied lust after imagined but unattained pleasure seems as large as a mountain. Even if man believes with perfect faith in all the joys of the world to come and in the future perfect Sabbath, this cannot compensate or console him in his sorrow and shame at having had to renounce what he longed for and expected for years. He who truly suffers the anguish of being a recluse knows that man cannot rid himself of the *yetzer ha-ra*. Only the Navaredker windbags assume that man is free to do what he wishes."

"But there's no bigger windbag than you! The saints weep with joy at not having submitted to the *yetzer ha-ra!*" said Duber Lifschitz.

By now boisterous Yankl Poltaver and Pultusker the Hasid were roaring with laughter. The more restrained students smiled and were silent. Since everyone was exhausted from the long late-night discussion, the excitement with the heretic was a welcome respite for all. The mood was livening up, as in a classroom before recess.

Tsemakh Atlas alone was sinking deeper into apathy and gloom. In addition to his guilty self-torments over the dead fiancée in Amdur, he had recently been yearning for a married woman. The harder he tried to tear Ronya out of his mind, the more frequently she appeared before him. Was it possible, he asked himself in fright, that he regretted not having submitted to his lust for her in Valkenik? Hence, Lohoysker's words rang like an echo of his own thoughts.

"A heretic and sensualist can't imagine that there exist saintly people who don't regret resisting the impulses of the *yetzer ha-ra*," Reb Duber Lifschitz said, his beard pointing up to the ceiling.

"He's not even on the same level with the wicked, who at least regret their deeds later on!" Konotoper was shouting to Yankl Poltaver as if the two had never quarreled.

"The rabbi of Lohoysk," Yankl replied, "sent his beloved son to our yeshiva so he wouldn't grow up to be a Bolshevik and a commissar in Russia. But he's drawn to filth like a dog returning to its vomit."

Poltaver now turned to Lohoysker and teased him, "There! We've refuted your argument. You're completely discredited."

Pultusker was gayest of all. "In our shul they'd wallop his behind until it swelled up like a mountain," the Hasid shouted, glancing around the study room quickly as if looking for a twisted towel to beat the heretic.

"Savages! Lunatics!" Lohoysker jumped up, searing Tsemakh with fiery eyes. "And what do you say, you penitent? Are you laughing at me too? Aha! You're silent. You know I'm right, damn you, you lice-ridden loafers!"

Lohoysker ran out of the room and slammed the door. The bulb hanging over the table began to swing and the shadows on the wall swayed along, as if astounded that such a frightful renegade was allowed to stay in the yeshiva.

14

YEARS AGO a youth from Krasne named Asher-Leml had been among the Musar seekers. At that time Tsemakh Lomzher had not thought highly of him. He seemed to be sleepy, dull-witted, not a thinker. After remaining silent all evening in the presence of his friends, as if thinking about God only knew what, he was quite capable of declaring: "Tomorrow is the Tenth of Teves, a fast day," like an assistant beadle announcing an upcoming festival to the congregation from the pulpit.

But when Tsemakh Atlas returned to the yeshiva, Asher-Leml Krasner had acquired a reputation as a saint. He came from a wealthy home, and he had fine clothes and a good room. Nevertheless, he often stayed at the beth medresh to sleep on a hard bench. Students arriving in Nareva at night usually came straight to the yeshiva from the train. Sometimes it was a new student arriving, and sometimes it was a student who didn't want to wake his landlord. Krasner had a key to the place where he lodged and would lead the visitor to his own room. To keep the newcomer from grieving that he had taken his bed, Asher-Leml would say that he was studying all night at the beth medresh. If another student came on a later train, Asher-Leml would then give him his place on the bench. If the latter refused to accept, Krasner would be silent for a long time and then say, "If you'll sleep on my bench, I'll bed down on another bench; otherwise, both of us will sit here till morning." The visitor would have no choice but to obey. Sometimes Asher-Leml would doze in a corner of the beth medresh to make it more pleasant for a youngster who was afraid of the dark but wanted to stay up all night to study, holding a candle over his Talmud. Asher-Leml's clothes went from hand to hand until they were returned to him. But he either didn't remember, or pretended not to, that the returned coat, for instance, was his—to keep the borrower from apologizing for having the garment so long.

When the time came for private exhortations, two youngsters would flank Asher-Leml, ready for his sermon. But he would quickly step aside, place one of the lads in the middle, and ask him to speak. The boy wouldn't wait to be asked again and would begin to gesticulate with his little hands and would offer his own commentary. Krasner would beam with joy. Although such conduct was against the yeshiva's policy, everyone realized that Asher-Leml intended to boost the youngster's self-confidence, which in turn would give him a sense of responsibility toward others too. Asher-Leml wasn't a part of any one group. Sometimes he joined one, sometimes another. Students would sit and argue into the night—but he would remain silent, hunched over, his lids lowered as if dozing. No one could see what he was thinking because the hair on his face grew up to his eyes and a black beard hid his cheeks, chin, and the corners of his mouth. But everyone knew that he turned other people's beautiful words into beautiful deeds. And despite his friends' heated arguments, Krasner's overpowering silence made itself felt. They watched his gestures to guess his thoughts.

Once, at a Talmud and Musar session, Krasner was asked, "Reb Asher-Leml, why are you silent? Tell us the truth! Are you jealous of anyone?"

"Of course I'm jealous." Krasner was amazed at the strange question. "I envy everyone who has a good head."

When Daniel Homler's close friends stopped looking after him, it was discovered that Krasner had been visiting the sick boy. No one knew how often he visited him or how they got along. But the morning after the group session (ultimately no decisions had been made there because of Lohoysker), when word spread in the yeshiva that Daniel Homler had been left without care, Asher-Leml Krasner made an announcement. "Don't worry about the patient," he said, "I've been visiting him for a long time."

That Krasner should have done this without anyone's knowledge befitted his character and behavior.

"Doesn't Homler yell at you," the students asked, "the way he yelled at his other friends? Doesn't he say, 'Your hands are trembling as if you want to choke me'?" As usual, Asher-Leml was still for a long while, and then a smile slowly appeared from under his hairy cheeks.

"Daniel Homler has even agreed to move in with Henekh Malariter. Henekh and I visit the hospital on alternate days, and his landlady is willing to take Daniel Homler in."

People said of Henekh Malariter that he studied with the same ease and grace that he danced on Simkhas Torah, his long legs like a professional dancer's. Next to his open Talmud he kept a volume of Maimonides and some of the later rabbinic authorities. He turned pages, looked here, perused there, frowned—and immediately comprehended the matter and began on another problem. His method of studying Musar was also unique. One student would bury his head in his hands and hum from the depths of his soul. Another would pound his fists on the prayer stand. A third would run around the beth medresh, shouting. Henekh would prop one foot up on the bench, hold his chin with the palm of his hand, and look into *The Path of the Upright* on the window sill. As a youngster he too had belonged to Tsemakh Lomzher's group of seekers, but now he rarely attended the Musar talks because the discussions lasted till dawn, and no one had enough sleep. In contrast to the tattered Navaredkers, Henekh was always neatly dressed. No one had ever seen him angry or excited, but at the same time no one had ever seen him do anything for a friend.

Tsemakh Atlas, who had once held Asher-Leml Krasner in low esteem because he lacked ability, had thought even less of Henekh Malariter because he had too much ability. "Man is born to toil," as the Book of Job asserts: every seeker anguished on his path toward higher spirituality, but to Malariter everything came easily. He quarreled with no one, and lived at peace with himself as well. He understood the most difficult Talmudic topic at first glance and counted off recently resolved problems as though counting a bundle of shirts from the laundry and as he would someday count the hundred-zloty bills of his large dowry after the wedding. That had been Tsemakh's view years ago. But when he returned from the outside world to the yeshiva, he had realized that he had failed to appreciate Henekh Malariter properly.

Henekh knew that he had a weak heart, but he told no one—then one day he had a heart attack. Now everyone understood why he was so solicitous of himself, and he was surrounded with love and concern. Nevertheless, some people decided that Malariter had said nothing about his illness for fear it would hurt his chances for a match. Later it was learned that when a match was proposed, he himself would admit that he had a bad heart—and this would put a swift end to the discussions, even though Malariter was attractive to potential in-laws. He had grown tall and slim, and he still dressed well. In fact, at first glance it was hard to tell he was a ben Torah except for his yeshiva boy's habit of wearing his hat pushed back so that he could rub his forehead while he studied Talmud. The yeshiva principal was proud of him and called him by his first name.

"Henekh is one of our best students. He interrupts the lectures not to show off his acumen, but to make the problem clearer for those who don't understand it. In addition to his intellectual gifts, he also has a noble character. If only he didn't have a problem with his health! Oh, his health! Thank God he's been blessed with the sense to take care of himself."

Henekh was often seen standing behind the pulpit surrounded by a group of youngsters, deep in a Talmudic argument. One arm rested on the pulpit railing and the other continually moved the hat back and forth on his head. The greater the yeshiva boys' excitement and the more they displayed their analytic skills, the more his face beamed with pleasure. Occasionally he would interject a remark to bring the contenders back to the main point and then would proudly watch them gesticulating with their thumbs and arguing with chanting voices.

Of late Henekh had been spending even more time with the youngsters. Friends noticed that the wrinkles on his face had vanished; his cheeks had become full; he looked more rested—but his smile shone with a refinement of sadness. The beth medresh discovered that Malariter had become engaged in an unusual and depressing fashion.

He had moved into the home of a poor family, where he was treated like a son. At first he was oblivious to this; later he was astounded. When he realized why they were doing this, he mutely consented. His widowed landlady had a houseful of daughters and felt that she was worthy in the eyes of God of having a yeshiva scholar as a son-in-law. She knew that for wealthy prospective in-laws, her lodger was choice but defective merchandise. But she thought differently. Upon receiving the yeshiva's monthly payment for Malariter's room, she told Reb Simkha Feinerman's wife, "Who knows? We're all in God's hands." The landlady, wanting the yeshiva to know that she had her eye on the lodger, continually praised him before others and said that her daughters were obviously in love with him.

Henekh's friends understood that he had agreed to the poor and rather low-class match because he expected nothing better. Pretending that they were overjoyed at his good fortune or that they knew nothing about the reasons for the match would have been equally hypocritical. Consequently, his friends behaved as though they had wished him *mazel tov* long ago and had long since clinked glasses at his engagement ceremony. They knew the details and had nothing else to ask him.

Therefore, no one in the yeshiva wondered how Malariter had been able to persuade the landlady to take in the sick youth. To please their future son-in-law, the woman and her daughters would be kind to his friend. It was their ability to talk Daniel Homler into moving from the hospital to a private house that was amazing. He hadn't wanted to hear of this before and had shouted that people wanted to do away with him. Most amazing of all, however, was why Malariter had assumed the responsibility of bringing the sick, capricious, and perpetually malcontent Daniel into his home. Tsemakh Atlas pondered this problem more than anyone else: Why had Henekh Malariter grown up to be a fine, intelligent, patient, and benevolent young man, even though he hadn't toiled at character improvement and had never been considered one of the adherents of Musar?

15

IN THE DARKNESS women wearing kerchiefs proceeded mournfully along the Nareva lanes, as silent as a group of widows coming back from a cemetery. They plodded on for a long time, hunched over and chilled, until they came to Hannah-Hayke's beth medresh. The students turned their pale, bearded faces from their Talmuds and looked at the women surrounding Yankl Poltaver and pleading with him. Yankl sprang up terror stricken and disgusted, as though the women had ordered him to strip and crawl into a shroud.

A deathly silence fell over the beth medresh, and the yeshiva scholars at their prayer stands heard the women saying, "What do you care, rabbi? Go in good health and study Torah somewhere else, and let us live our lives in peace. Reb Zushe Sulkes didn't want to be the trustee any longer. But we threw ourselves at his feet, and the congregation appealed to him too, and he agreed to run the Free Loan Society again. But the trustee demanded that you not be allowed to set foot in the beth medresh any more. And if he doesn't have his way, he won't be the trustee, and we and our little children will have to resort to begging."

The besieged Yankl Poltaver barely managed to tear himself away to the wintry outdoors, where he paced around with no coat or hat, only his yarmulke, until the women dispersed.

The next morning the congregants warned the yeshiva students that if the young man who pulled wild stunts wouldn't leave, the poor peddlers would block the shul door and would not let the students in. Zundl Konotoper and the other responsible yeshiva people replied, "We can't make any decisions on our own. We have to wait for Reb Simkha Feinerman to return from the Vilna Yeshiva Council meeting. He'll be back soon."

Yankl Poltaver realized that he would have to make himself scarce in Nareva for a while. He didn't worry about where to go. He would be a welcome guest in whichever Navaredker Beth-Yosef center he chose. But he didn't like the ignominy of being the loser. That day his weekly turn to serve in the yeshiva kitchen began. Moshe Chayit Lohoysker sat at the table, frowning. His constant pretense to pride had vanished. He still had cramps in his abdomen from the laughter of the Musarniks who had recently driven him away from the group session with their mockery as if with sticks. And now, at the table, the same students expressed their silent hostility. Their thoughts could easily be read: How can we get rid of him? Yankl Poltaver would have thrown him out like a rotten herring into the garbage, but after the Sulkes incident, Yankl had become more careful. He knew that the yeshiva administration had its own reasons for not starting trouble with the heretic. Yankl therefore served the disgraced and humiliated student his portion, screwing up his face as if to say: Eat and choke on it!

Melechke Vilner sat in the kitchen too, a triumphant gleam in his eye. Although he was the youngest in the yeshiva, through Reb Tsemakh's intercession his pleas to stop eating daily meals in various homes and not to be in Reb Yankl's group had been granted. He was sitting at a table among the adults, and none other than his group leader was serving him.

Poltaver didn't care what the pipsqueak thought of him, but a boy like that had to be taught a lesson. While serving Melechke his bowl of soup with a piece of lung in it, he said loudly, "If a lad is so arrogant as to insist on eating in the kitchen and not at a congregant's house, we let him eat in the kitchen. And if that lad happens to be a glutton, we let him be a glutton."

Melechke's round cheeks flamed and his eyes grew damp, as they had three years ago in Valkenik when someone said something mean to him. But although he was as sensitive as ever and couldn't eat another bite, he now made a great effort not to say a word or let a tear drop. He sat quietly, head lowered, staring at the bowl. The older students around him either didn't notice or didn't care. Only Lohoysker looked on silently from the side.

This time the yeshiva students concluded the meal without discussing Torah matters. They said grace and made for the door as one. They couldn't bear spending an extra minute with Lohoysker, the yeshiva's deadly foe.

Moshe Chayit Lohoysker, the last to leave the kitchen, saw Melechke standing outside, wiping his eyes. Once out of the room, the boy could no longer keep back his tears. "You're crying." Moshe Chayit placed a hand on his shoulder. "And this won't be the only time they'll make you cry. And then you'll grow up and make others cry. That's the way of the Musarniks."

Navaredker yeshiva people were always very careful not to talk about a mature scholar who had gone astray in the presence of a younger one—to keep the latter from following in his path. Hence Melechke had no idea why Lohoysker no longer studied in the yeshiva, and he immediately trusted him.

"Did you cry too?"

A hoarse laugh tore its way out of Lohoysker's throat. He was so embittered that he forgot he was speaking to a little boy. "Oh, how the Navaredkers made me cry! The first few years I wept during prayers and Musar study because I wasn't pious enough. Later on the Musar scholars themselves made me cry."

"Why didn't you go to another yeshiva?" Melechke asked; then he admitted, "I wanted to go to another yeshiva, but my former principal at Valkenik, Reb Tsemakh, was able to get me out of eating days and out of Reb Yankl Poltaver's group."

"But even Reb Tsemakh couldn't persuade Reb Yankl not to make you cry." Moshe Chayit was careful not to utter a superfluous word. "Come to my room and I'll give you something to eat—you didn't eat a thing in the kitchen. When we get there, I'll tell you why I didn't go to another yeshiva."

Moshe Chayit offered Melechke bread, hard cheese, an apple, and a pitcher of cold water. He watched the boy pressing his eyes shut as he said grace. When he had finished, Melechke groaned, "I'm sorry I missed the afternoon study session."

At this his host sighed too. "When I was your age I didn't have enough sense to study hard. Like the other Navaredker seekers, I tore the hair from my head, toiling away at perfecting my character, until I ended up an ignoramus. I can sermonize on a biblical verse or a Talmudic passage better than anyone else—but like the rest of them, I don't know even one Talmudic tractate thoroughly. I first realized my error when I was eighteen. By then I was ashamed to go to Radun and sit on the same bench with twelve- and thirteen-year-olds. Now do you know why I didn't go to another yeshiva?"

Melechke understood and confided, "Reb Tsemakh isn't a great scholar either. But I'm not sure about Reb Yankl."

"You know the Talmudic saying: 'If Rabbi Judah didn't say it, how could Rabbi Hiya know it?' " Moshe Chayit laughed. "Reb Tsemakh Atlas isn't a good scholar, so how could his pupil Yankl Poltaver be one? It's only logical, then, for Reb Yankl's student to know even less."

"For my age I'm a good Talmud scholar," Melechke interrupted angrily.

"No doubt about it," Moshe Chayit agreed. "Just *because* you're a good scholar for your age, you should flee Nareva—and the sooner the better. If you become a Musarnik like Yankl Poltaver, perhaps they'll let you keep on eating in the kitchen, though there's no guarantee. You were just recently Bar Mitzva, right? People begin to eat in the yeshiva kitchen only when they're seventeen or eighteen. But if you keep immersing yourself in Talmud and commentaries and don't study Musar a couple of hours a day; if you don't spend entire nights with a group; and if you don't go out onto the streets and do stunts to show that you don't give a damn about the outside world—they'll force you to have eating days again; they'll humiliate you and torment you until they break you. You'll become a Navaredker seeker, and you'll grow up to be an absolute ignoramus."

Melechke looked down at his little palms and fingers and asked Moshe Chayit, "Have you looked into *Man's Spiritual Attainment*, by the Old Man of Navaredok? Yankl says it's a treasure-house of Torah and wisdom."

"I know by heart those head-in-the-clouds musings that Reb Yosef-Yoizl Hurwitz scribbled down. You see, those are the books that I'm an expert on," Moshe Chayit said, forgetting again that he was speaking to a youngster.

"I don't find any greatness in the things I've heard quoted from *Man's Spiritual Attainment*. Nothing to get excited about," Melechke replied with the cool tranquillity of an old Torah scholar who doesn't go near secondary sources.

"If you want to improve your knowledge of Talmud and commentaries, leave Nareva and go to Radun or to another great yeshiva," Moshe Chayit said.

"But they're not studying the same tractate that we are in Nareva, so I won't understand the rosh yeshiva's lectures, and I'll have wasted a term." Melechke's fingers searched in vain for a hair on his chin.

"True," Moshe Chayit Lohoysker answered. "Dropping into Radun or any other yeshiva in mid-semester is no good. Why not go back home and study on your own in the Vilna Gaon's beth medresh? Then the next semester you can go to any yeshiva you choose."

"Or why shouldn't I study with the author of *The Vision of Avraham* in Vilna? We know each other from Valkenik. Chaikl Vilner is no longer his student. I'm sure Chaikl came here because Reb Avraham-Shaye chased him away, but that loafer isn't doing any studying here either." Melechke was angry with his fellow townsman who, without any trouble whatsoever, had joined the older students in a group and in the kitchen.

"I'm not sure it's such a good idea for you to stay in Vilna and study with Reb Avraham-Shaye Kosover." Moshe Chayit stared at the huge, dilapidated old wardrobe against the wall. The landlord had left it in his tomb of a room for lack of anywhere else to store it, just as he himself stayed at the yeshiva for lack of anywhere else to go. "If I were in your shoes—that is, if I were your age—I'd go study in the Tachkemoni *Gymnasium* in Bialystok or in Warsaw. At the Tachkemoni school they study Torah *and* secular subjects."

"You want me to be a modern-style Vilna rabbi?" Melechke asked nasally, barely moving his lips.

"Why not be like Maimonides? He was a gaon and a philosopher, and a doctor as well," Lohoysker said positively, realizing at once that in fear of a secular education, the little saint might give up the idea of leaving the yeshiva altogether. "But if you believe in Torah without a mixture of secular learning, then you should study with Chafetz Chaim in Radun, or indeed with Reb Avraham-Shaye in Vilna. The question is, how do you plan to leave here?"

"What do you mean, how? It's simple. I'll go to the people in charge and tell them I'm leaving."

Lohoysker jumped up and stretched to his full height until he resembled a long, thin pole. "Obviously you haven't the slightest conception of who you're dealing with." He ran his hand through his hair and began describing what would happen if the Musarniks got wind of Melechke's intentions: "First of all, they'll drag you off to a group session and torture you all night and all day, and then another night and another day, until they make you take an oath on your share of the world to come and swear on the health of your parents that you'll never, ever leave Navaredok. There isn't a single pupil from Russia from whom Tsemakh Atlas didn't exact such a promise—and then Reb Tsemakh himself was the first to leave Navaredok, thereby breaking his promise to 'dwell in the house of the Lord forever,' as the psalm puts it. It was only later that he returned and established a small yeshiva in Valkenik. Even after you give them your handshake and your oath, they'll watch you with a thousand eyes, and if they suspect you might leave, they'll take away your suitcase. They'll even take away your coat to prevent you from going outside. You say that it was thanks to Reb Tsemakh that you now eat in the kitchen because you threatened to leave? Well, you can be sure that they won't let you go home for Passover either!"

"So what will we do?" The youngster sat there frightened, his moist mouth open.

"That's the way to talk!" Lohoysker sat down on the chair and offered his plan. "Come here from the yeshiva tomorrow at twelve, while everyone is studying. We'll go to your room, and you'll tell the landlady that you're leaving for home because your father or mother is in the hospital. I'll wait outside and help carry your bundle to the train station. Do you have enough money for a ticket?"

"My mother sends me spending money," Melechke said. "I've saved more than enough for a ticket."

"Good; otherwise I would have sold my coat. The Navaredkers hate me because I regret the years I wasted with the Musar books and because I want to save talented youngsters and give them a chance to grow up to be truly great scholars."

Melechke left, consoled, and a wide smile, like first light on cobwebs covering a ruin, spread over Lohoysker's face.

The next day Moshe Chayit escorted Melechke to the station and spoke to him as if he were a grownup. "Like the Musarniks, I enjoy doing good deeds, but you won't curse me later for the ones I do."

From the station Lohoysker went directly to the yeshiva kitchen. This time he entered in high spirits and announced, "Melechke Vilner just said good-bye to me. He went home because his group leader, Yankl Poltaver, was picking on him. He's going to prepare in Vilna for the Bialystok Tachkemoni *Gymnasium*."

No one at the table responded. That heretic and gypsy, the yeshiva students thought, was about to burst because he was being ignored; now he wanted to upset everyone with a concocted tale. After all, Melechke had just spent the morning in the yeshiva.

But that night at Melechke's room, the landlady told the other students, "Your little friend from Vilna came in this afternoon and told me that his mother was sick and he had to go home at once. When I looked out the window, I saw an older student waiting for him. He helped him carry his suitcase. I thought it was strange that the older student didn't come into the house. To tell you the truth, the whole affair amazes me. Every day the postman gives me all the mail for the boys, and there was no letter for Melechke today. How did he find out that his mother was sick?"

The morning session at the yeshiva buzzed with the news that that blasted Lohoysker had talked a youngster into leaving and had helped him run away. Reb Simkha Feinerman returned from the Vilna meeting that same morning. As soon as he entered the beth medresh—before he could even take off his fur coat—his frost-burned cheeks turned even redder with rage. The yeshiva leaders immediately told him about Yankl Poltaver's fight with Zushe Sulkes and the condition that the congregation had imposed: either Poltaver left Nareva or the entire yeshiva had to move out of Hannah-Hayke's beth medresh. Reb Duber Lifschitz reported about Lohoysker's crashing the seekers' late-night discussion; and Zundl Konotoper told Reb Simkha that Lohoysker had persuaded young Melechke Vilner to flee the yeshiva.

"Is that how you looked after the beth medresh?" Reb Simkha bristled, but he realized at once that he must not antagonize his associates. He let his blazing light blue eyes rove back and forth until his wrath abated; then he told Zundl Konotoper, "Find Poltaver."

When Zundl had gone, Reb Simkha thought the matter over. Driving Poltaver away would hurt the yeshiva, because he was good at getting things done. And besides, it would raise a storm among the Musarniks: they would say that Nareva was no longer a Navaredker yeshiva if congregants' threats could intimidate them. Therefore, the hothead should merely be sent away until the trouble died down.

Yankl Poltaver approached, pale but straight-backed, stiffly erect.

"Poltaver, you're to leave right now and seek out a village where you'll establish a small yeshiva for Reb Duber Lifschitz," Reb Simkha said, gesturing toward Reb Duber. That gesture bespoke all his contempt for the Narevke principal who had squabbled with congregants and, moreover, couldn't conduct a peaceful group discussion with mature yeshiva students.

Delighted that he had emerged relatively unscathed, Yankl Poltaver whinnied with joy and said, "I'll go!" He wanted to say more, but Reb Simkha turned quickly and, accompanied by his entourage, went to Reb Tsemakh Atlas. Although the Morning Service had ended long ago, the penitent was still wearing his tallis and tefillin.

"You're defending Lohoysker while he's destroying the yeshiva!" Reb Simkha cried.

Tsemakh was silent; he stared into space with glazed eyes, as if the tears had fallen back into him, as drops of water on the damp stones of an unused well fall back into the thick slime. He had hoped that Melechke Vilner would grow up to be a decent man, but Lohoysker had begrudged him his joy in his pupil. Then Tsemakh felt a muteness around him, as if everyone had slipped out of the beth medresh and left him alone. He looked up and saw Reb Simkha and everyone else gaping at the doorway. There stood Moshe Chayit Lohoysker.

His mouth twisted into a spiteful grimace, Lohoysker stared at Reb Simkha and his group, who stood dumbstruck by his impudence. Since the rosh yeshiva and the older scholars were silent, the angry younger students didn't dare say a word. So Lohoysker, even more brazen-faced, sauntered to the middle of the room, his head craned toward Tsemakh Atlas, who approached in his tallis and tefillin. Moshe Chayit's long face became even longer with fear, but he snickered triumphantly into Reb Tsemakh's face.

At that Tsemakh grabbed him by the shoulders and threw him toward the door. Lohoysker rolled over several times and lost his glasses. Although hurt by the edges of the benches and the corner of the pulpit, he didn't cry out. Instead, he began to crawl around on the dusty floor, looking for his glasses. When he finally found them, he put them on and slowly stood up to leave the beth medresh. But Tsemakh Atlas was standing in front of him again, apparently unwilling to have Lohoysker leave of his own accord. He seized the beaten youth by the front of his coat and with all his might pushed him out the door.

Tsemakh Atlas stood still and gazed down at the threshold as if it were a tombstone over a grave. At that moment he summed up his entire life: he had succeeded at nothing. He was one of those whose repentance would be rejected by a heavenly voice. He wouldn't have been surprised if someone had now thrown him out of the beth medresh, with people hooting after him: Everything lurking inside you has now broken out like boils on your students.

At the Vilna meeting of the Yeshiva Council, Reb Simkha Feinerman had not succeeded in getting a larger allocation of money for Nareva. Other yeshiva principals were displeased with their allotments too. Hence, everyone had decided to ask Reb Avraham-Shaye to be the arbiter. A special emissary was dispatched to his house on Zaretche Hill across from the Vilinke Bridge.

A fair was going on in the suburb of Zaretche. The market place seethed with buyers and sellers; villagers inundated the shops. The rebbetsin Yudis eagerly awaited customers but thought morosely: My selection of cloth isn't very large, and the store is quite far from the market; that's why customers don't come in. But my old man, long life to him, says it makes no difference whether my shop is near or far from the Zaretche market—no man enters a shop God hasn't sent him to. Wait! Here comes a customer!

The Yeshiva Council emissary entered. "May I see the rabbi?" the bearded young man asked.

"My husband isn't a rabbi," the rebbetsin replied in a hostile voice, adjusting the heavy wig on her forehead; she pointed to the door of the other room.

Reb Avraham-Shaye was pacing in the long, narrow room. Hands folded on his chest, head back and frowning, he was, as usual, deep in Torah thoughts. The visitor, a young rabbi still living with his in-laws, looked about in amazement, embarrassed at living in a bigger and more elegant house with new furniture and four times as many books. The young man reported who had sent him, happily enumerating the rosh yeshivas and leaders who had assembled for the meeting. But the brighter his tone—as festive as a cantor's on Simkhas Torah—the more gloomy and apprehensive Reb Avraham-Shaye became. He paced silently for a while, then put on his winter overcoat with its frayed fur collar and picked up his cane.

"It's no use. If so many Torah scholars summon me, I can't refuse. I must go." He sighed and opened the door to his wife's dry goods shop.

The rebbetsin Yudis looked at her husband from behind the counter and, noting his dejected appearance, knew at once that he was again being dragged off somewhere against his will. She therefore poured out all her bitterness on the bearded young emissary.

"Another communal busybody? Aren't there enough religious functionaries in Vilna? Why does everyone have to torment my old man?" she said, her tongue milling away behind her thick lips. "If he had the strength to be a rabbi and a public servant, I wouldn't have to sit in a shop without customers. Where are you going?" She waved her hands like a caged bird timorously flapping its molting wings. Reb Avraham-Shaye said nothing and quickly went out, accompanied by the bewildered emissary.

"There's no one more outspoken than one's own rebbetsin." Reb Avraham-Shaye forced a laugh, as if to placate the young man who had been insulted. He strode quickly so as not to keep the assembled scholars waiting. But the closer he came to the site of the meeting, the more often he stopped, until his face was burning with shame and anguish at his own weakness.

"Tell the yeshiva principals and leaders that I had to turn back midway. I can't be an arbiter for the distribution of money to Torah scholars. How can I say which yeshiva should get less?"

The great Torah scholars were angry and astonished at Reb Avraham-Shaye Kosover's response. Reb Simkha Feinerman was especially annoyed with him. Since the author of *The Vision of Avraham* had sent his pupil Chaikl Vilner to Nareva, he really ought not let Nareva be treated as a stepchild in comparison to Radun and Mir. Finally, he hadn't even deigned to come to the meeting. So why should Nareva keep that spoiled brat? Reb Simkha was about to leave for home when the innkeeper came to tell him that someone he didn't know was asking to see him. In the corridor Reb Avraham-Shaye stood waiting.

Certain that the visitor had come to justify his refusal to be an arbiter, the Nareva principal began elaborately, with a liberal sprinkling of Talmudic quotations, "Nowadays we're living at a time when we must do God's work. A Talmud scholar, then, ought not enclose himself in the seclusion of Torah study."

As usual, Reb Avraham-Shaye listened in silence, his chin resting on his stick. This encouraged Reb Simkha Feinerman to continue; he peppered his remarks with neatly rounded Musar interpretations while his long, sensitive fingers swiftly played with his long and narrow red-gold beard. When his visitor remained silent, however, Reb Simkha finally fell silent too. Only then did Reb Avraham-Shaye calmly say, "You're right. Something should be done, but I'm not a doer. I've come to find out whether Chaikl Vilner is studying diligently."

"It's hard to say, but at any rate he's more interested in discussions with the students than in sitting and learning," Reb Simkha replied coldly. Then, feigning innocence, he asked, "Is he really your student?"

Reb Avraham-Shaye understood the jibe: he wasn't doing anything special to spread Torah learning, and when he finally chose a pupil, he wasn't one of the elite.

"Chaikl has a good head for thinking and for making judgments, and his feelings are those of a truly great man." The corners of Reb Avraham-Shaye's mouth twitched with an angry smile, as always when he felt that his reverence for Torah was being impugned. "To my great regret, Talmud study alone can't hold him. That's why I persuaded him to spend a winter in Nareva."

Reb Avraham-Shaye's answer clearly implied that Reb Simkha Feinerman, who was rosh yeshiva of hundreds of students, didn't properly appreciate his new pupil. Reb Simkha turned red but, not wanting to quarrel with Reb Avraham-Shaye, began to smooth over the difficulty by saying mildly, "No doubt Nareva will be a good influence on Vilner. His former Valkenik principal, Reb Tsemakh Atlas, is now in the yeshiva—he's come back to Nareva after years of wandering. And Reb Tsemakh is close to Vilner."

"Reb Tsemakh Atlas still hasn't returned to his wife in Lomzhe?"

Reb Avraham-Shaye asked with an anguished laugh. "He hasn't changed at all."

It was known in Nareva that Reb Avraham-Shaye had ordered Tsemakh Atlas expelled from Valkenik. Reb Simkha Feinerman said, "There was a time when I was displeased, quite displeased, with Tsemakh Lomzher's conduct. But now he's repented. Will you please explain why you think he's behaving badly now?"

Expecting a long discussion, Reb Simkha got up to help his visitor take off his coat. But Reb Avraham-Shaye rose too, ready to leave.

"Reb Tsemakh Atlas' behavior isn't good," he replied, "because, after all his experiences in Valkenik and in Amdur, he should have returned to his wife in Lomzhe."

"She's from a nonreligious family, and he married her while he was estranged from Torah life. Now he wants to divorce her, but she doesn't want a divorce," Reb Simkha said, bewildered at Reb Avraham-Shaye's agitation. "Besides the fact that they're not suited for each other, Reb Tsemakh once explained that he can't live with his wife because he feels that his late fiancée is standing between them."

"And a man like that is considered a penitent? Does a penitent leave a young wife to suffer anguish and humiliation? And from which ancient holy book did he learn that one may shame a living wife for a dead fiancée?" Reb Avraham-Shaye inquired even more heatedly. He paused for a moment, eyes shut so as to see the matter more clearly. "And moreover, I'm not at all sure that his wife is not suitable for him. If she doesn't want a divorce, it's a sign that he can persuade her to change her ways."

16

ON THE RETURN TRIP to Nareva, Reb Simkha Feinerman deliberated with himself, weighing both sides of the issue as the train swayed to and fro, and at last decided not to intervene. First of all, he wasn't entirely sure that Reb Avraham-Shaye Kosover was right. Second, he didn't want to be accused of having sent away the Lomzhe penitent who had previously done so much for the yeshiva. And finally, he had more important things to think of. He had the responsibility for the big yeshiva at Nareva and for the surrounding small yeshivas—may their number increase. But he was surprised at Reb Avraham-Shaye. He had declined to be an arbiter among Torah scholars who pleaded with him to find a solution. Yet he wanted to intervene in a matter between husband and wife, even though neither of them had sought his advice or decision on their relationship.

When Reb Simkha Feinerman was back in Nareva and dealing with Yankl Poltaver's fight with Sulkes and the terrible scandal over Lohoysker, he put Reb Tsemakh's family troubles out of his mind altogether. But he did want to talk with Chaikl Vilner, and when the tumult in the yeshiva had died down, he summoned Chaikl.

"In Vilna, Reb Avraham-Shaye came to our inn to inquire about you," said Reb Simkha, swaying with his prayer stand. "Your teacher is a great gaon and is fond of you. But we didn't know what to say about your conduct."

At first Chaikl felt a hot surge of elation sweeping over him: the rabbi had asked after him. But he soon turned despondent: Reb Avraham-Shaye had, after all, told him to spend the winter in Nareva and was able to get along quite well without him.

Noting Vilner's gloomy silence, the rosh yeshiva asked, "Do you have a good room?"

"Yes, it's good."

"And are you satisfied with the food?"

"Yes, I'm satisfied," Chaikl again replied curtly.

Reb Simkha straightened his prayer stand and, standing erect, began shifting his weight from one leg to another.

"It's our custom to either talk or listen to others. We hear that you made some remarks at the seekers' group discussion that did not befit a pupil of Reb Avraham-Shaye. You declared that man is a small part of creation and that we must stand in awe of all of creation. Indeed, it's true that we should stand in awe of all creation aside from man, if we see in everything the wonders of the Creator—as the Psalmist says, 'Bless the Lord, O my soul.' But if we forget for a moment that He created everything, then our awe of nature is mere idolatry, as if we'd bowed down to stars and constellations, God forbid."

Reb Simkha Feinerman considered it beneath his dignity to speak at length to a younger student, especially in the presence of a crowd. He nodded, signaling an end to the conversation. But after the talk, Reb Simkha still didn't understand why Reb Avraham-Shaye had described Chaikl Vilner as a young man of profound feelings.

Since Reb Tsemakh had thrown Lohoysker out of the beth medresh, it was assumed that the brazen youth would no longer show his face in the kitchen. But instead of being delighted at getting rid of him, everyone felt a gnawing at his heart. The yeshiva students were nagged by a deep resentment toward the penitent for physically mistreating his former pupil. Men of refined feelings, especially Torah scholars, didn't display such cruelty. Everyone realized that since Reb Tsemakh had so often defended Lohoysker when he was threatened with expulsion, his bitterness was all the greater against him now. But still the question remained: How could a penitent have so much murderous fury in him? Everyone was dismayed at this, and some of the older students began to suspect that all his troubles and his years of wandering had not changed Tsemakh Lomzher.

The rosh yeshiva's associates had complaints too. Zundl Konotoper studied Musar for hours at a time with an angry, rasping voice—he felt as if he were hacking off pieces of himself with a blunt knife—but he still couldn't tear the anger out. "Is that how you looked after the beth medresh?" Reb Simkha Feinerman had shouted. And Zundl had wanted to shout back: Is that your gratitude for my having remained a bachelor to help you run the beth medresh?

Reb Duber Lifschitz, for his part, couldn't forgive Reb Simkha for throwing that long-sought crumb of a favor—having Yankl Poltaver go out and find a village for him—at him with the same contempt that one throws away challa crumbs on the Passover Eve when the leaven is burned, or shakes crumbs out of one's pockets on Rosh Hashana for the Tashlikh ceremony.

Only Yankl Poltaver was happy. He had realized for the first time what a power he was in the yeshiva. Despite all the slanders against him, the rosh yeshiva hadn't said one sharp word to him. Reb Simkha had merely asked him to go out and find a place for Reb Duber and stay out of Sulkes' sight for a while.

Yankl made a secret plan which he didn't dare tell anyone about. He stopped beside Chaikl and asked, "Which street does Melechke live on? Who are his parents, and what do they do?"

Chaikl gave him all the details and asked, "Why do you want to know?"

"No special reason," Yankl replied, thinking: We'll see who wins, Lohoysker or me! Then he contemplated his friends studying at their prayer stands and tried to recall who had a good suit, a new coat, a pair of brown shoes, shirts, and ties. His friends would grumble, but they would have to lend him their best clothes again, for he was going out to establish a new place for Torah learning.

PART IV

1

Beyla Gutgeshtalt, Chaikl Vilner's landlady, was a tall woman in her thirties with a high, singsong voice and a large, yeasty body. The skin beneath her big blue eyes was flecked with brown. She wore neither marriage wig nor kerchief. She covered her hair only when her lodgers were at home and when she lit the Sabbath candles on Friday night. Nevertheless, she was more refined and more pious than her pockmarked, cross-eyed husband Shloimele, who would good-naturedly slap Chaikl's back and tell him vulgar jokes. Then the landlady would yell, "Stop it, schnorrer!" and he would fall silent, his eyes still flashing slyly.

To get away from the incessant uproar of the yeshiva students in the beth medresh, Chaikl would occasionally go back to his room early. Once his landlady came in and sat down to talk. His ears were still ringing with the Talmud melody, but his eyes saw a warm, womanly body in a loose house robe. He sat on the edge of the bed with languid, half-open lips, listening.

"A year ago during the Days of Awe you looked much happier. Are you sad because you miss your home?" the landlady asked in her singsong, smiling with satisfaction because the yeshiva student was devouring her with his eyes.

Then Beyla Gutgeshtalt began slandering her husband. "I really don't know what I saw in him when I was young. I worked two knitting machines and sold what I made. Every young woman in town wore one of my knitted jackets. But instead of marrying a merchant, I accepted a schnorrer. Now he either plays cards till all hours or gets drunk with a bunch of roughnecks. Then during the day he says to me: 'What did I do! What did I do! I had a girl like gold, and I took you instead! And now misery is taking me!' And I say to him, 'I wish I'd never met you. Your former mistress, Tsipke, is skin and bones, a scrawny, shriveled thing to chew up and spit out.' And he says to me, 'Who's something to chew up and spit out? My Tsipke? Everyone carries on over her, but she says, "Oh, no! I love Shloimele and I won't marry anyone else, never ever!" And look who I got in exchange! Tsipke is a tight steel spring, and you're a hunk of flesh!' That's the way that schnorrer husband of mine talks to me. And to his buddies he complains, 'Better to rot in the ground than have a wife like that!' Then he comes home and tells me word for word what he told his pals. Should a man like that go on living?" asked Beyla Gutgeshtalt. She crossed her legs, and Chaikl saw under her loose robe a pair of naked white legs, too thin for such a heavy body.

By the smile on the landlady's broad, mealy face, Chaikl realized that she was aware of the turmoil going on inside him and was just waiting for him to touch her, whereupon she would thrust him aside with a laugh. Later she would tell her pockmarked, cross-eyed husband, and perhaps his own roommates too, that Vilner was snuggling up to her. All he needed was to have the yeshiva gossiping that he was fooling around with a married woman. Chaikl rose stiffly, as if disgusted by her boorish remarks and disheveled appearance. Beyla played along and clapped her hands.

"I've talked too much. But for the love of God, don't tell your friends what I told you about my husband. If they ever found out what kind of goods he is, they'd move right out." Then Beyla Gutgeshtalt began praising her lodgers: "They're saints! They'll never say they lack anything. I'm always afraid they're dissatisfied with something, and I'm always worried about my husband's trying to tell them his nasty jokes. Don't say a word to your friends, God forbid. After all, you're not like them." The landlady smiled again. She stretched, yawned, brought her hands up to her neck; the broad sleeves of her robe fell back, revealing a pair of robust, meaty arms. She shuffled away to her bedroom, lazy as a cat, leaving behind the warm, dry fragrance that confused and intoxicated him.

The next morning Chaikl left the house before the landlord and his fellow lodgers awoke, to avoid looking them in the eye. During the day the odor of his landlady's body slowly disappeared from his nostrils, leaving only the odor of her vulgar way of speaking, which reminded him of raw meat on a butcher block. He was irritated by her remark that he wasn't like his friends. Henceforth, his conduct would be such that she would no longer dare come to him loosely dressed and speak like a fishwife. Yet toward evening he again left for his lodging, earlier than the previous day.

The house was unlocked, and Chaikl went into the students' bedroom. He saw a strip of light coming from a door half open on the narrow corridor. Behind the door was a little room that contained a bathtub, a small wood stove, and a water pipe. Water was streaming from the faucet, and a big body was splashing in the tight confines of a brimful tub. White patches of steam, striped with the reflection of the wood burning in the little stove, floated into the corridor. The faucet stopped, and Chaikl heard gasping, the sound of soap on a moist, slippery body, and then a splash in the water again, as if a great white-bellied fish had dived down into the depths. Chaikl sat on his bed and felt his shame. The landlady knew he was there; she had known beforehand that he would come. She hadn't locked the outside door and had left the door to her bathroom half open to tease him all the more.

He heard her come out of the water, sighing with pleasure. She took a long time drying off, rubbing herself with a towel and humming. Chaikl imagined her standing naked before the mirror, laughing to herself about the yeshiva boy yearning for her. A few minutes later she emerged from the bathroom and passed the open door of the lodgers' room. Her bathrobe was wrapped tightly around her, which made her full belly, broad hips, and big buttocks even more prominent. Her cheeks were flushed from the heat. Her damp, shiny hair, twisted up into a knot at the top of her head, left her neck bare—a chunk of white marble. She stopped at the doorway for a moment.

"Are you back already? When that little oven is going full blast, the heat is just impossible to bear, and the bathroom door has to be left open," she explained, and shuffled back to her bedroom. But there too she left the door open, and her heavy body could be heard bouncing gently on the mattress springs. The landlady turned, rolled, and stretched out, luxuriating on the soft bed, while at the other end of the corridor, Chaikl lay in his room, curled up on his hard cot, thinking of her freshly washed limbs and despising himself. He saw that neither his years with Reb Avraham-Shaye nor the Musar environment had helped him overcome his *yetzer ha-ra*. He was so wild with lust for that crude married woman that he was undaunted by the sin and no longer afraid of her husband. The only thing that kept him from running into her bedroom was the fear that she might laugh in his face and chase him away.

The following day Chaikl stayed late at Hannah-Hayke's beth medresh and afterward went directly to the Musar meditation room on Seraza Street. Some yeshiva students sat in shadow-draped corners, humming a gloomy melody. Others swayed silently over Musar books or paced back and forth lost in thought. The Musar room was dimly lighted. Here and there a candle flickered, and above the pulpit a red eye burned numbly—a small electric bulb. In the half-light Chaikl identified his fellow students by their voices and movements. He tried to guess who else was suffering from fleshly lust. Modest Torah scholars never discussed this among themselves, not even in secret with an intimate friend. Nevertheless, Chaikl often noticed the hot stare an overpious youth would give a passing woman. An amazed look, a hidden fear, would come over the student's hairy face, or he would blush furiously as if caught stealing. Chaikl knew from his own experience that no matter how often he dragged his *yetzer ha-ra* off to the beth medresh, it grew no weaker, despite the Talmudic counsel: If you encounter that villain, drag him off to the beth medresh.

Shimshl Kupishker, the mindless fanatic as he was called in the yeshiva, sat reading in a corner. A candle was set on the headrest of the bench, and the yellowish light shining on his cheek made his face look as waxen as that of a corpse. He swayed and murmured ceaselessly from his little Kabbala books—sermons by wrathful itinerant preachers and ethical wills written by God-fearing old men for their grandchildren. Chaikl strolled by him several times, then finally stopped. He wanted to know if Kupishker too was struggling with his *yetzer ha-ra*.

"Reb Shimshl, let's hear some Musar commentary from you," Chaikl began in the Navaredker manner.

The shrunken youth looked at him with eyes from an abyss and began muttering with deathlike lips, "The Midrash says that before a man prays for Torah words to penetrate his body, he should first pray that no fine foods enter into him, so that he will have no pleasure eating. I read in an old holy book that if someone breaks off in the middle of a meal to deny himself the pleasure of his food, it is as though he had offered a sacrifice. But there is one food that indeed one may enjoy, and that is the bitter herbs we eat at the Passover Seder. We must eat at least an olive-sized portion and praised is he who eats more. The great Reb Aharon-Leybele of blessed memory once saw Elijah the Prophet in a dream. The great Reb Aharon-Leybele gave him a bowl of food and spoke to Elijah in the language of man: 'Rabbi, make a blessing and eat.' At which Elijah the Prophet retorted angrily, 'You putrid drop! Do you think I would mention God's holy name over a bowl of food?' It's obvious from this that we must refrain from eating altogether. A man must remember that he dies not only once but every hour, every minute—therefore, he must clothe himself all the more in Torah and mitzvas. Wearing modern short jackets or gentile fashions is as much a sin as wearing cloth with the forbidden weaves of linen and wool, God save us. We must not trust the tailors, even the most pious among them. As everyone knows, pride is the ultimate basis of impurity. That's why we must not smoke cigars or cigarettes—because blowing smoke through your mouth is a sign of pride and arrogance. It's true that there are saints who smoke cigars or even pipes, but when saints do it, it's as if they're smoking the holy incense on the sacrificial altar. Everyone knows that holy sparks are hidden in every impure thing. Among these tiny sparks are infinitesimal ones. Therefore, the only way a saint of our generation can extricate these sparks from their impure surroundings and lift them to sanctity is through smoking. But other mortals must not blow smoke because it is arrogance. God have mercy on us. Oh, woe; oh, woe! If a father sends his son to the market to buy merchandise, and he gambles away the money or spends it getting drunk, the father will demolish him. And man squanders all his time and his soul on vain, nonsensical things, on obscenities and foolishness, instead of storing up mitzvas for the world to come.

Ay-ay, for the disgrace! Vilner, I hear people saying that you study the Bible and also write poetry. Is that really true?" Shimshl Kupishker whispered, his eyes watering with fear of dybbuks, imps, and malicious spirits.

"Who says that?" Chaikl asked, amazed. He knew nothing of what people in the beth medresh were saying about him. "And what's wrong with studying the Bible and writing poetry?"

"Studying the Bible with its holy commentaries is no sin," Kupishker answered. "But may the Holy One above save us from the interpretation that the Song of Songs is about a pair of young lovers and not about the Holy One Blessed Be He and the people of Israel. You can use your poetic talent to write an inscription on a saint's tombstone, but only if you intend it for the sake of heaven and not to show off your talents. And woe unto you if you write wedding jests or songs. For wedding jesters are clowns, and clowns aren't worthy of receiving the emanations of the Divine Presence. If you don't want to wither away in hell, stay away from those little ditties as from a pit full of snakes. Also, one mustn't laugh when one hears a witticism, a clever joke, even though one may be considered a fool with no sense of humor. Our holy sages tell us that it's better to be considered a fool all one's life than to be a wicked person for an hour before the Holy One Blessed Be He, God have mercy on us."

"And what kind of remedy do you have against sinful thoughts?"

"Gadashnael!" Kupishker replied quickly. "You must write the holy name Gadashnael on a kosher piece of parchment and wear it around your neck. Then, when you think of a woman, you must spit three times and touch the parchment containing the holy name, and you will he helped immediately. If *that* doesn't help, and your eyes continue seducing you into looking at women, you must think: What do I gain by looking? Looking at them doesn't make them mine. As the Talmud says, 'Looking isn't acquisition,'" Kupishker whined. Eyes burning, he went on in a whisper, "If you happen to have a nocturnal emission, you must fast and go to the ritual bath. Even in the worst weather, you mustn't be too lazy to go to the mikva. You must also recite the confession and Psalms Seventeen and Thirty-two. Finally, you must recite the last psalm of the Sunday unit and the first of the Monday unit. And besides that, you mustn't touch any despicable thing—a frog or a secular book. You mustn't listen to a mean remark, and no foul odor must enter your nostrils. I forget which holy book I read it in, but I remember seeing in black and white that it is absolutely forbidden to go around in your underwear at home. This can make you succumb to the worst sins, God have mercy on us. Ay-ay! Woe, woe! Every living creature has lips, teeth, a tongue; but only man can speak. So what does he do with the treasure that is his tongue? He talks vain and nonsensical things. That's why we must keep a lock on our mouths except when we speak of Torah. It is said in the name of the holy Rabbi Isaac Luria that he who remains silent forty days in a row can achieve the level of divine inspiration. But in the yeshiva it's hard to carry this out because people speak to you and you have to answer."

"With all your books, you only look in them for what's forbidden," Chaikl said, ready to leave.

Kupishker suddenly screamed, "You search in the Torah for things that are permitted, and I search there for things that are forbidden!"—and his fingers with their overgrown nails fastened themselves into Vilner's arm as though to drag him off to hell. Chaikl felt a pain deep in his muscle and barely managed to tear himself away. He couldn't understand what he had done to infuriate the mindless fanatic.

2

ON THE EVE of the month of Shvat, observed by the Musarists as a minor Yom Kippur, the whole school gathered in the Musar room at noon to hear the rosh yeshiva's sermon. After the talk and prayers, Zundl Konotoper went up to the lectern, a coat instead of a tallis draped over his shoulders. He swayed back and forth several times, then roared the opening line of the *Ovinu Malkenu* prayer, "Our Father, our King, we have sinned before You!"

The students, standing in tightly packed rows along the benches, twisted and turned; they clapped their hands and repeated each line after the *baal tefilla*. With every line of the prayer Zundl soared higher, and the Musarniks pounded their fists on the prayer stands and raised their hands toward heaven to break open the locked gates of mercy. During an ordinary weekday the beth medresh stormed with the ecstasy of Yom Kippur. The tranquil light of a bright snowy day streamed in through the windows, but in the holy place darkness hung in the air among the shrieks and shouts. Konotoper stood at the lectern, in the middle of *Ovinu Malkenu*, and the assembly swam along as if in a powerful river current.

Suddenly a scream was heard. "Help! help!"

The deafening cry came from the library, which had a spiral staircase leading up to an attic. Several students ran up the stairs while everyone else waited in tense silence. Soon the students emerged from the library carrying Kupishker, his face yellow and his head thrown back. A moment later the crowd surrounded the youth and watched as he was revived from his faint. The rosh yeshiva and the older scholars were neither excited nor astonished. They avoided one another's eyes as if the incident were part of a stain on a family's honor that everyone knew about and was ashamed of. The only one who spoke was the assistant beadle, a simple man whose beardless face was large and rosy.

"Every day I find something else missing from the attic where I sleep. First I thought it was the stragglers who come into the beth medresh to warm up who were doing the stealing. I didn't suspect the yeshiva students, God forbid. But a few minutes ago, during *Ovinu Malkenu*, I discovered a student sidling toward the library on his tiptoes looking very wary, and it dawned on me: maybe he's the thief. I followed him through the library and up the steps to the attic room. Then I noticed him tying one towel to another and making a noose. He threw the noose over his neck, stepped up on a bench, and looked for a hook on the ceiling. Then I pulled him down from the bench and yelled for help."

"Don't tell anyone about this, or you'll be fired from your job," the Musarniks grumbled at the assistant beadle, who said nothing in reply. He was more shaken by their irate faces than by their threat.

Chaikl Vilner was stunned. He felt as if he had suddenly seen that the faces of old acquaintances were masks and something had happened that made them remove the disguise. He found it incredible that Kupishker would want to hang himself. And the behavior of the older yeshiva scholars was just as bizarre. Obviously this wasn't news to them.

Now they could no longer hide from the newcomers and the younger students the fact that Kupishker had tried to commit suicide twice before. Last summer the students had been vacationing in the forest near Nareva, where Kupishker went for private meditation. Once he had come running to the students in the forest with the cry that he wanted to hang himself. Everyone knew that the mindless fanatic was afraid of a joke because he felt that one must not associate with clowns. He wouldn't have concocted that story for the sake of playing the fool. Taking him seriously, his friends had decided to guard him—and had actually saved him the next time he tried to hang himself. He was brought back to Nareva, and the rosh yeshiva gave the order that neither the townspeople nor the younger yeshiva students were to know of the incident. From that time he was never left alone in his room or in the beth medresh. Even when he went to the toilet, someone followed and watched through a crack in the latrine door. The one most devoted to Shimshl Kupishker was Asher-Leml Krasner, the benevolent soul who was the saint of the yeshiva. But because several months had passed and Kupishker had not renewed his attempts, the watch around him had gradually weakened. During the recitation of *Ovinu Malkenu*, even Asher-Leml had forgotten about Shimshl. So he had taken advantage of the moment and tried for the third time to do away with himself.

Everyone said a silent prayer of thanks that Kupishker had been saved, and an increased guard was placed around him. At first Reb Simkha Feinerman had feared that Nareva might find out and claim that the Musarniks had driven the youth insane; now he was afraid they might take the opposite stance and say that a student had lost his mind and that the Musarniks weren't giving him medical attention. Reb Simkha felt himself becoming old and gray. He had never had a term with so many worries, and it was no coincidence that so many troubles had come upon Reb Tsemakh Lomzher's pupils since his return to the yeshiva. His repentance, then, was apparently not a lofty one if so much sorrow could ensue because of him. The Talmud taught that virtue stems from virtuous men, while bad men prompt bad deeds.

In the beth medresh, in the kitchen, and in their rooms, Shimshl's friends whispered again, "How is it possible for such a God-fearing youth to want to harm himself and lose his share in the world to come? Too much self-mortification evidently made Shimshl go out of his mind."

Chaikl Vilner, however, had a different explanation for the problem, and since he didn't want to discuss it with anyone except Moshe Chayit Lohoysker, he went to see him.

Since Reb Tsemakh had thrown Lohoysker out of the beth medresh, he hadn't even shown his face in the yeshiva kitchen. Consequently, Chaikl was surprised to hear that he knew every detail of the Kupishker incident. Moshe Chayit looked gaunt, disheveled, and neglected, as if he had become even more of a ragged yeshiva student after being driven from the yeshiva.

"Vilner, I knew you'd come to me sooner or later. Whether you want to admit it or not, I'm closer to you than anyone else in Nareva. Other Musarniks also slip in to see me without anyone's knowing. As long as I ate in the kitchen, they were afraid to trust me with their secrets and doubts, but now they come and plead with me to explain why that crazy Kupishker wanted to hang himself."

"Out of despair! He saw that all those self-imposed torments to get rid of his *yetzer ha-ra* were to no avail. He wanted to hang himself because he was in the depths of despair," Chaikl said quickly, impatient to offer his opinion. "Still, it's puzzling. In Vilna I often heard despondent beggars telling me that they didn't try to kill themselves because they feared God. Why wasn't Kupishker afraid of the great sin of committing suicide?"

"No comparison!" Lohoysker answered, his eyes burning with hate, as was usual when he spoke about the Musarists. "The despondent beggars in Vilna and Nareva love life. Even in a moment of despair, they remember that God ordered man to hold life precious and hope for better times. But Shimshl Kupishker doesn't love this world. His only existence is the world to come, which he prepares himself for by mortifying his body. But the more he torments himself, the more intensely the *yetzer ha-ra* burns in his thin bones. Let's say that his enormous lust for a woman may have made him have a nocturnal emission. Or very possibly he masturbated. But afterwards, or perhaps even while doing it, he knew he was committing a terrible sin—he was spilling seed in vain. So he began to consider what kind of punishment he must administer to redeem himself from that sin. Fasting and rolling in the snow is nothing to him. To be eternally cut off from the people of Israel, as Er and Onan, the sons of Judah, were—that too means nothing to him. Even the fires of Gehenna aren't hot enough to burn out the sin he had committed. So that onanist plucked at his body with his dirty fingernails until he came up with the proper punishment and revenge on himself: he would deprive himself of his most precious possession. He would commit suicide and thereby lose the world to come, just as he refused to have this world of here and now. Saints renounce the world to come in order to earn a mitzva, and he would renounce the world to come in order to punish himself for that transgression.

"Desire torments me," Lohoysker continued, "even more than Kupishker. And you, Vilner—desire is driving you to the grave. But, at the same time, you're swimming in misty fantasies, as I once told you." Lohoysker laughed, and his thin, pointed knees trembled and twitched. The trembling of those frail, bony knees disgusted Chaikl. He could have sworn that Lohoysker was doing what he suspected Kupishker of—spilling seed in vain. Now, as after their talk on Yom Kippur night, Vilner left Lohoysker enraged at him for undermining his faith in Navaredok.

Chaikl learned from the yeshiva students that Shimshl Kupishker's roommates, Asher-Leml Krasner and Reuven Ratner, wouldn't let him leave the house. They gave no reasons for keeping him locked up. Perhaps the rosh yeshiva had ordained silence. Chaikl knew now that the expelled heretic would know more about Shimshl than anyone in the yeshiva. He visited Lohoysker again, and indeed the latter knew.

"That maniac is now demanding candy, sugar, and chocolate," Moshe Chayit said, laughing, and he related the bizarre story. "For a few days in a row Kupishker lay in bed without moving. Then one bright morning he suddenly sat up and asked for hot tea and lots of sugar. His two guards were delighted—it was as if he had come back from the dead. They gave him what he asked for. He poured the steaming tea into himself and asked for other kinds of sweets: biscuits, honey cakes, strudel, chocolate. Since Asher-Leml and Reuven didn't have such delicacies, they could only give him sugar and sugar lumps. Shimshl Kupishker sat there and gnawed away at the sugar lumps; he kept crunching until the two youths were horrified. Then he lay down again like a golem and didn't say a word the rest of the evening and the whole night. The next morning he crawled out of bed and demanded hair clippers. Reuven Ratner gave him a pair, and Kupishker stood before the mirror and trimmed his beard to the roots. Most students with beards trim them occasionally, but Shimshl had never done it before. His remark that he wanted to go to the beth medresh to pray frightened his friends even more. They realized that Kupishker's appearance in the yeshiva without a beard would cause a turmoil. While Asher-Leml Krasner remained to guard him, Reuven Ratner ran to Reb Simkha to ask for advice. Reb Simkha clapped his hand to his head in astonishment and ordered the maniac kept in the house. But Kupishker ranted that he wanted to be among people. Finally, after much difficulty, they calmed him down and let him munch on sugar to his heart's content."

"Sugar?" Chaikl stammered. He felt now as he had as a boy when a rascal quicker than he would trip him, much to the glee of other pranksters. "Why is he asking for sugar, of all things?"

Moshe Chayit shrugged. "I don't know. Why did Daniel Homler ask that nurses, and not his friends, dress and undress him after his operation? It seems there's a connection between Daniel Homler's wanting the hospital women to see his skinny body and Shimshl Kupishker's lust for sugar after his unsuccessful struggle with the *yetzer ha-ra*."

A thought tormented Chaikl like a smarting eye: In the yeshiva the students knew nothing about what was happening to Kupishker. Lohoysker could have heard these reports only from Kupishker's roommates. It certainly wasn't Asher-Leml Krasner, who didn't speak to the heretic. This meant it was the other roommate.

"Now I know who's bringing you all the news. It's Reuven Ratner. He's been visiting you." Lohoysker didn't deny it, and a heavy stone lay on Chaikl's heart. He was sorry he had guessed correctly. Just a year ago, Reuven Ratner, like the other students, had been a fiery Musarnik. When had his enthusiasm cooled? Perhaps, Chaikl thought, he himself hadn't really known the students a year ago because he had merely been a guest in Nareva for the High Holy

Days. In that case his envy of the Navaredker seekers had been in vain and his urge to go to the yeshiva misdirected.

"Tsemakh Atlas shoved me out of the beth medresh with his big paws, so that everyone who looked on would participate in my humiliation. But it had just the opposite effect. Now his pupils come to see me," Moshe Chayit crowed triumphantly, and he went on to describe Reuven Ratner's first visit. "This is the song he sang: 'Everything they say about you is a big lie! I'm sure you put on tefillin every day, and you don't desecrate the Sabbath!' Reuven Ratner had to convince himself of this so that he could come more often and slap his forehead in astonishment—at the same spot where he puts on tefillin—and declare: 'I don't understand! I just don't understand what made Reb Tsemakh Lomzher so popular with prospective brides when he was young.' "

After this conversation with the heretic, Chaikl avoided Ratner. He felt like someone who comes into a neighbor's house, is an unwilling witness to a family scene, and later is ashamed to look the neighbor in the eye. Reuven Ratner began coming to the yeshiva again, but his roommate Asher-Leml didn't show up at all. The curious students sniffed and searched until they finally discovered the latest developments. Shimshl Kupishker did not want to go to a doctor and wouldn't let one come to him. "I'm not crazy," he raged, and he added the threat: "If you don't let me out, I won't eat or drink till I die."

Finally Reb Simkha himself came to Shimshl and spent hours trying to persuade him not to stay in Nareva. "Everyone in town knows you wanted to commit suicide. You won't be able to study Torah in peace any more, and you won't be able to make a good match here. You must go to a yeshiva where no one knows you and conduct yourself like all other Torah scholars until you marry. You should return to Nareva only after that."

At last Shimshl Kupishker had agreed to go to a little Navaredker yeshiva in a far-off village in Volhyn, and Asher-Leml Krasner had escorted him there.

3

A TELEGRAM CAME from Yankl Poltaver: "Have established a yeshiva in Amdur near Grodno. Reb Duber Lifschitz come immediately." Everyone in the beth medresh understood that Poltaver had chosen Amdur to demonstrate his success in a place where his former group leader, Reb Tsemakh, had failed. Instead of being delighted, Reb Duber Lifschitz wove his fingers into his stiff little beard and said, "If Reb Tsemakh couldn't accomplish anything there years ago, I don't think Amdur is the proper place for a little yeshiva. But on the other hand, the situation in town may have changed for the better, with new leaders in the community. In any case, I'll go. I've spent more than enough time in Nareva doing nothing, and my family has suffered more than enough in Narevke."

After Reb Duber's departure, Reb Simkha waited for Yankl Poltaver to come home. But days passed with no word from him. Reb Simkha Feinerman became anxious. Perhaps Poltaver didn't want to return because he had been ordered to leave the yeshiva for a while to avoid Sulkes. And besides, Amdur was a place ripe for trouble—Tsemakh Lomzher had gone astray there. Perhaps Poltaver, imitating his group leader again, had arranged a marriage there and had also gone astray. Reb Simkha now regretted having sent Yankl. Losing such a dedicated worker was a great loss, even though he was wild. The rosh yeshiva addressed a letter to Reb Duber Lifschitz in care of the Amdur rabbi, telling him to send Poltaver back immediately because he was urgently needed in Nareva.

A letter came back from Reb Duber Lifschitz:

Yankl Poltaver left Amdur even before I arrived. He is

indeed irresponsible. Yankl got the consent of only a few townsmen. The others are still opposed to a yeshiva, as they were in Reb Tsemakh's time. If assistants aren't sent to me who will work for a yeshiva, I'll have no choice but to return to Nareva.

Reb Simkha Feinerman was furious. Reb Duber had always leaned more toward the Navaredker yeshivas of Mezeritch and Warsaw than to the Nareva center. Why had he attached himself to Nareva? And where had Yankl Poltaver disappeared to?

Yankl had felt that having to uproot himself from Nareva because of the fight with Sulkes was destroying his group's respect for him. Consequently, he had to be successful where even the great eagle, Reb Tsemakh Lomzher, had failed, even if the world came to an end. The Amdur rabbi had told him that since Reb Tsemakh Atlas had rolled in the mud before old Namiot's door, the village had begun to believe that it was indeed the Musarnik's fault that Dvorele Namiot had died. That was why Amdur would not support a Musarnik yeshiva. But Yankl Poltaver tried to use this notion to create an opposite opinion. "Many fiancés break off their engagements. Nevertheless, no one comes and rolls in the mud to obtain forgiveness. That's why the village will have great respect for Navaredok for having trained and brought up a Reb Tsemakh Atlas."

Poltaver spoke in the same vein to a minyan of congregants, and they nodded in agreement. He then telegraphed Nareva for Reb Duber Lifschitz to come. Meanwhile, he himself would go to Vilna to bring Melechke back—so that Moshe Chayit Lohoysker would have a fit.

Instead of the deliriously happy welcome that Melechke had expected, Zelda and her three daughters pinched their round red faces in despair because he had returned home in the middle of the term. When he complained that a yeshiva scholar named Yankl Poltaver had been picking on him, the women replied, "You crybaby! Why didn't you make *him* run away from the yeshiva?"

Melechke bit his lips and thought that his mother and sisters really did deserve the nickname Sennacheribs because of their big mouths.

Nevertheless, he tried to explain the kind of yeshiva he was studying in. "But for the new term I'm going to go to a yeshiva that's called Tachkemoni, where they study Torah and secular subjects."

"If that's the case," his mother shrieked, "you'll become a rabbi, a gaon, and a saint like I'm the Vilna rebbetsin."

His three sisters stood before him again, arms akimbo. The oldest one laughed. "A businessman doesn't change his mind. The wholesalers would be in a pretty fix if all the peddlers returned their merchandise. All sales are final."

The middle sister mimicked him. "So you want Talmud and secular education both, huh? Make your choice. Be either a rabbi or a priest!"

"You once used to go around with your ritual fringes hanging out," the youngest sister reminded him. "You had long earlocks, and you drove everyone in the house crazy with your piety."

The only one who rubbed his hands in pleasure at Melechke's return was his father Kasrielke. He still said the same thing again and again: "If the father's a tinsmith, the son must be a tinsmith too."

But his wife and daughters snapped back, shouting in his face, "And if you're a loafer, a drunkard, and a braggart, does Melechke have to be a loafer, a drunkard, and a braggart too?"

Every time Melechke had come home for an end-of-term vacation, he had been caressed and pampered. His mother and sisters would stop abusing the customers who bargained with them, and on Friday afternoon they would close their fruit store before sunset. But now the family squabble intensified, and everyone poured out his anger on Melechke. "For years now," they reprimanded him, "we've sent you packages full of marzipan to Valkenik and this past winter to Nareva. And all for nothing!" But most of all, Melechke was cut to the quick by one remark from his woman-dominated family: "Now Vella, our competitor across the way, will live to have her revenge, because Chaikl didn't run away from the yeshiva in the middle of the term."

To keep the street from finding out and laughing at the Sennacheribs who couldn't raise a Torah scholar successfully, Zelda spread the word that the doctor had ordered her only son to come home and recoup his strength because he had grown weak from too much Torah study. Melechke sat dejectedly over the Talmud in Reb Shaulke's beth medresh while the women sat dejectedly in their shop next to their boxes of smoked fish, barrels of schmaltz herring, and baskets of various fruits. They couldn't lift their hands to weigh and measure, they couldn't open their mouths to call out for customers, and their eyes stared dully, like those of people squatting on chunks of charred wood before a burned house.

Zelda and her daughters had considered the baby of the family their jewel. Even when they ranted that he was driving everyone crazy with his extreme piety, deep down they had been proud of him. But now everything had dribbled away into nothingness. Now his drunken father would be proved right. The son would become a tinsmith like the father, and, like the father, he would guzzle whisky by the quart at the tavern.

While they were in the midst of such gloomy thoughts, Melechke dashed into the store with good news. "A special emissary from Nareva has come to see me in Reb Shaulke's beth medresh to take me back to the yeshiva. And this special emissary is the very one who was tormenting me in Nareva, trying to make me into a Musarnik."

Neatly dressed in the clothes he had collected from friends before his departure, Yankl Poltaver stood in the large fruit store, and Zelda's overgrown daughters woke as if from a bad dream. In their felt boots, kerchiefs, and big aprons, they wiped the perspiration from their faces with the palms of their hands and stared open-mouthed at the handsome young man. Had such a gentle youth tormented their Melechke? Impossible! Yankl spoke very gently, but, at the same time, he burned Zelda's daughters with his dark brown eyes until their reddish-blue frozen cheeks began to steam, melting like kosher wax. They felt hotter from the scholar's gaze than from the fire pots beneath their market stools.

"It was a heretic, a wicked student, who persuaded Melechke to run away," Yankl Poltaver said. "We tried to bear with this heathen because he was from Russia and had nowhere to go. We kept him on out of pity. But now we've expelled this corrupter, and the entire yeshiva is longing for Melechke."

A pious look came over Zelda's face as she listened to Yankl, and her three daughters wore honeyed smiles. To avoid giving the impression that Melechke wasn't wanted at home, Zelda purposely postponed giving her consent. The girls simply wanted the handsome scholar to pay them another visit. Later, Zelda and her daughters told customers, "The yeshiva sent a special messenger from Nareva to get Melechke. Even though the rosh yeshiva at Nareva has hundreds of students, he considers Melechke the apple of his eye."

When Melechke was aboard the train, however, his face was wrinkled like a winter apple. He felt ashamed before his yeshiva friends; he was also enraged to the point of tears by his mother's farewell. He understood from her remarks that since he had just been at home, there was no need for him to return for Passover. They'd get along without him for the Seder. He began enumerating a list of complaints and told Poltaver frankly, "It's more your fault than Lohoysker's that I ran away. You dragged me into the fight against Sulkes and then made me go to him for my Sabbath meals. He grabbed me by the collar and threw me out of the house. You wouldn't have gone to him because you were afraid you might be kicked out."

A twitch ran through Poltaver's body. A mere stripling had the nerve to tell *him* that he was intimidated by the outside world? But since he first wanted to bring Melechke back to the yeshiva, Yankl merely answered, "We'll see who's prepared to sacrifice himself for Torah!" and added, "Once and for all, if one *can't* overcome—one *must* overcome!"

4

FROM THE WAY he stormed into the yeshiva, all the students knew at once that it was Yankl Poltaver—even before he emerged from the whirlwind of snow he had brought with him. From under his armpit—like the head of a kitten—peeped Melechke Vilner. The students leaped up and stood on tiptoe. The young yeshiva leaders blinked in disbelief and tugged at their beards to see if they were dreaming. Astonished and happy, Reb Simkha Feinerman turned beet-red to the ears. He even forgot for a moment that he was a rosh yeshiva and tweaked Yankl's ear like a prankster, then burst out laughing. "You devil!"

Everyone greeted Melechke and was delighted at the defeat of that troublemaker Lohoysker who had persuaded Melechke to run away. But Melechke already looked gaunt and depressed, like a sick man just out of bed, and Yankl Poltaver's joy at his triumph didn't last long either. Since in Navaredok the period before Purim was considered one for doing bold, courageous deeds, Reb Yankl urged his students, "You have to go out and show that the world doesn't intimidate you, just as the saintly Mordecai wasn't fazed by the wicked Haman and didn't bow down to him." But he was too late; the next day was the Fast of Esther. Nevertheless, all was not lost. He would show them a deed of courage that would astound all of Navaredok. Melechke Vilner would no longer have the nerve to say that Reb Yankl demanded more self-sacrifice in the name of Torah than he himself displayed.

Next to Simkhas Torah, Purim was the liveliest holiday in the yeshiva. The whole school spent the day of Purim singing and dancing. Only Yankl Poltaver roamed around in a workaday mood and didn't even glace at the pupils who submissively pressed close to him and gazed trustingly into his eyes. Toward evening everyone dispersed and went to the Purim feast: the older scholars to Reb Simkha's house; the youths to the kitchen; the boys to various congregants' homes. Poltaver ordered his pupils to finish eating quickly and meet him in the kitchen. Melechke, however, didn't go to a congregant's house. He invoked his right, granted before he had fled, to eat in the kitchen with his townsman Chaikl Vilner.

At the Purim feast, Yankl Poltaver was as merry as the other scholars, but he ate little and didn't drink a drop of whisky. Even his laughter and his Purim parodies on Talmud learning were solely for appearance' sake to avoid arousing suspicion. After saying grace, he left the kitchen with everyone else and went to the beth medresh, ostensibly for a good time. But he purposely lagged behind the other students and soon returned with Melechke to the empty kitchen. The boys who had eaten in the congregants' homes assembled quickly; they had rushed through the meal on the pretext that they had to be at the yeshiva early. Reb Yankl's grim silence was a hint that something would happen. They gazed at him with sparkling eyes, like young wolves at their sire. The group leader counted his pupils with a glance to see if anyone was missing and barked. "Let's go!"

The boys noticed that Reb Yankl had taken a huge broom from the kitchen corridor. Nevertheless, no one asked why, or where they were going. Reb Yankl had taught them that a seeker had to have a Musar scholar's faith in his group leader and ask no questions. The young seekers marched after him with lips pressed together, swinging their arms and panting. Reb Yankl walked so quickly that they could scarcely keep up with him. He held the broom under his left arm and led Melechke with his right, as if afraid he might run away again.

The narrow lanes were frostily silent and desolate. The small houses huddled in groups as if afraid that whichever one strayed away from the wooden flock of snow-covered cottages would wander off and not know the way back in the dark. Despite his warm coat, a chill of fear went through Melechke's body, and he soon realized that there was good cause for alarm. Reb Yankl stopped in front of Reb Zushe Sulkes' stone house. A ray of light seeped out of the shuttered windows; from within came sounds of voices and joyous chatter. At the trustee's home, the Purim feast was still going on.

"Now's the time for a deed of courage against the Haman of Nareva, like the saintly Mordecai's deed of courage against the Haman of ancient Shushan. Remember, Mordecai wasn't intimidated at all!" And Yankl reminded his pupils, "Because of Sulkes, I had to uproot myself from Nareva. And because I wasn't here, no one in this group was working at not being fazed by the world. So now we must do something to surprise all Nareva, and to bring triumph and rapture to Navaredker seekers all over the world."

The lads still didn't know their group leader's plans, but they were prepared for anything. Only Melechke stood rooted in place, his hands and feet paralyzed. He remembered the trustee's kick when he had come for his Sabbath meal.

"Take the broom and stop trembling!" Reb Yankl roared, and Melechke seized the broom with both hands, as a pious Jew seizes the lulav. Yankl pushed him into the hallway with the rest of the group and then, with a leap, quickly and boldly opened the door.

Reb Zushe Sulkes sat at the head of the table in the large dining room, flanked by his family—children, grandchildren, daughters- and sons-in-law—and by some prominent townsmen who had come to visit after their own Purim feasts. The table was heaped with leftovers: plates full of half-gnawed chicken bones, saucers containing the cracked pits from the fruit compote, half-filled glasses of seltzer water, pieces and crumbs of challa, Purim loaves, and the burned corners of *homentashen*. The electric chandelier hanging from the ceiling and the burned-down candles in the candelabra glinted in the empty wineglasses and in everyone's moist, drunken eyes. His yarmulke on his perspiring head and a napkin tucked around his neck, Sulkes turned to the doorway—and his jaw dropped. The rest of the family stared at the young man and his group. Everyone knew that this yeshiva student was Reb Zushe's deadly foe.

"Happy Purim! Happy holiday!" Poltaver called joyfully, and the lads chorused, "Happy holiday! Happy holiday!"

"Happy holiday!" Reb Zushe stood up slowly, eying them with suspicion. He hadn't known till then that the exiled Musarnik had returned to Nareva. He had no intention of reconciling with his blood enemy. But since the latter had come to his home with his troublemakers, that pack of Bolsheviks, it wasn't fitting for him to kick them out.

"My students and I have brought you Purim sweets," the Musarnik called out even more joyously.

"Purim sweets indeed! Then why are you standing by the door? Come in! You're welcome guests! Purim sweets indeed!" Sulkes' astonishment grew from minute to minute.

"Yes, Purim sweets! And as our representative, we've chosen the Vilna ben Torah who used to eat Sabbath meals at your house until you kicked him out and hurt him, just as you kicked the other yeshiva students out of your store and bloodied them up because they stood up for widows and orphans."

Yankl Poltaver nudged Melechke, who held the broom with both hands, to step forward. But seeing Melechke standing there like a golem, Yankl took the broom from his hands and gave it to the bewildered trustee.

"Here; this is our platter of Purim sweets! Sweep your licentious daughters and daughters-in-law away from your home. Sweep away theft and robbery from your shop. Clean up the refuse can of your rotten heart." And then, in the spirit of the merry festival of Purim, Yankl concluded with a merry rhyme, "You're mean, hard-hearted, cold, and rough; all your life you've thieved enough."

The entire family was stunned. The visitors couldn't believe their eyes and ears. For a moment the sputtering of the melted-down candles was heard in the dead silence. Then some of the people at the table moved, and someone said with a frightened laugh, as if to smooth matters over, "Oh, Purim players!"

Only then did Sulkes recover somewhat, although he still couldn't say a word. He raised his hand and gave the Musarnik a resounding slap. Faces pale and eyes smoldering, the yeshiva boys lunged at the trustee, prepared to tear him to pieces and be martyred for the holy cause. But Reb Yankl blocked their path. His face beamed with joy at the blow, as if it were a found treasure. It was obvious that he could have crushed the trustee with his iron hands—juice would run from Sulkes as from a lemon. But instead of raising his hand he courteously bowed before Sulkes.

"Thank you. My heartfelt gratitude to you for the Purim sweets you've given back to me," he said, and swiftly left the house with his group.

Melechke Vilner realized that his group leader had shown that he could display even more courage than he demanded of his pupils.

Once outside, Melechke rushed up to him. "Rabbi, forgive me!"

"I forgive you with all my heart!" Reb Yankl replied generously, and then said to his band, "Don't tell anyone in the beth medresh what happened tonight. People might be afraid of the trustee's revenge, and that would spoil the holiday mood."

The boys vowed silence. If their group leader had been able to control himself and not strike back at that wicked Sulkes, they too could keep themselves from reporting Yankl Poltaver's heroic deed. Melechke Vilner went further: he swore in his heart that henceforth he would become a seeker and stay with Navaredok forever and ever.

Poltaver strode along silently, thinking of his friends in the beth medresh who were probably so drunk by now that, as tradition had it, they no longer knew the difference between blessed is Mordecai and cursed is Haman. But soon he would outstrip them in drinking whisky and making merry. No doubt the war against the trustee would flare again and things would get lively, Yankl thought. The struggle for Torah and Musar would keep his spirits up and keep him from falling from the heights he had achieved. His passion would not cool, unlike that of members of Reb Tsemakh Lomzher's group of seekers. True, the older scholars, and perhaps Reb Simkha Feinerman, would call him a wild ass. They would rant that because of him, the townsmen would stop supporting the yeshiva. Never mind, let them rant. Navaredok was great indeed when it waged war. Navaredok was great indeed when it went hungry.

5

THE MORNING AFTER PURIM, the huge black wing of the Angel of Death fluttered over the yeshiva. Henekh Malariter's landlady, who had taken in the ailing Daniel Homler, rushed into the beth medresh with the cry, "He's gone!" People gathered from all sides and shouted, "What happened to Daniel Homler?"

"It's not Homler. Not the sick boy. It's Henekh Malariter," she gasped. "He died of a heart attack"—and the landlady fainted.

The tragedy was discussed everywhere—in the shuls, the shops, the houses. A mass of people attended the funeral, including all the Nareva rabbis, who expected the honor of delivering a eulogy. But the yeshiva crowd didn't deign even to glance at these worthies; they pressed close to the coffin and split the heavens with their wailing. The little alleys around Hannah-Hayke's beth medresh billowed with the crush of mourners. Over the heads of the crowd outstretched hands passed the coffin, which floated like a low, ominous cloud over treetops until it was brought to the yeshiva and placed on the pulpit table. Reb Simkha Feinerman went up the steps of the Holy Ark. His appearance frightened everyone. Within a day he had become old and stooped. His face was as gray as cold ashes, and his long, narrow beard hung from his chin as if from a scaffold. He gestured and moved his lips, but couldn't utter a sound. The rosh yeshiva stepped down, followed by a series of Navaredker scholars who were famed as fiery preachers. But they too were unable to speak; they merely made rattling sounds and wept bitterly. The dead youth was carried from the beth medresh, and someone wailed, "The Holy Ark is lifted up . . ."—and everyone burst into tears again. In the fog of heat, perspiration, and tears, the electric lights wavered to and fro—the blood-red ox eyes of the lighted bulbs. The walls of the beth medresh seemed to bend and join in the weeping.

A shudder ran through the heart of the town as the funeral procession made its way to the cemetery. When it came to one street, the merchants on the next street rushed to close their stores, as on Yom Kippur Eve before Kol Nidrei. Artisans cast aside their work in their shops to join the funeral of "the saintly yeshiva scholar." Women abandoned their houses and their small children; they piously donned kerchiefs and followed the funeral, wringing their hands. Even the nonreligious youths, who usually mocked the yeshiva students and their tattered appearance, stopped on the street corners and watched, grief-stricken. Along the entire route the students took turns carrying the coffin, heads bowed and in complete silence. But Henekh's landlady and her daughters tore their hair and deafened the town with their shrieks. From the honor being bestowed on the dead scholar, the family realized what a distinguished fiancé had been denied them, so they screamed and wailed as though Malariter had been the head of the family and its sole provider for years.

At the cemetery, housewives surrounded the landlady and pleaded with her. "It could have been worse. The fiancé, may he rest in peace, could have married your daughter and died of a heart attack the morning after the wedding."

The woman wept more softly, while her oldest daughter said nothing. Her glum silence seemed to reply to the would-be consolers: A spinster is no happier than a young widow. Congregants and the Nareva rabbis with no links to the yeshiva stood in a circle and complained, "Even at a time of tragedy, God forbid, we see the Musarniks' contempt for the town. They didn't ask one Nareva rabbi to deliver a eulogy." The yeshiva people indeed held themselves aloof from the local townsmen. They surrounded Reb Simkha Feinerman, their bearded faces pale, and the tears froze on their cheeks like frozen dew on tombstones.

After the body had been washed in the purification chamber, Reb Simkha Feinerman again attempted a eulogy, but he could only say, "Torah, Torah, garb yourself in sackcloth," and then a wave of dizziness engulfed him. The students rushed to his side and kept him from falling.

Seeing that none of the Musarniks would be able to eulogize Henekh Malariter, one of the local scholars, a man with a short blond beard and gold-rimmed glasses, stepped forward. He coughed awhile, then began in a sweetly melancholy voice: "Teachers and friends!"

The women were already wiping their eyes, and the congregants were sighing. But the Musarniks' faces were stony and morose; their silence expressed their hatred of the householders' world. The trim young man in the gold-rimmed glasses went on with an appropriate Bible verse: "The dead youth was called Henekh—Enoch—and we learn in the Torah, in the Book of Genesis, 'And Enoch walked with God, and he was no more, because God had taken him.' "

Suddenly dozens of Musarniks raised their heads and shouted, "No sermonizing!"

The befuddled eulogist stepped away from the coffin, and the people of Nareva exchanged glances as if to say: Well, does this town have to support them? Now the Musarniks had revealed their true colors—their hatred of the Nareva congregants and rabbis. But everyone's grief was too great for any of the townspeople to make an issue of it at this time. The students lifted the coffin and proceeded up the hill to the prepared grave. From among the snow-covered mounds of earth came a gust of wind, moaning as it passed the pallbearers and the mourners behind them. The Torah students continued climbing among the crooked and scattered tombstones. The psalms that had been tearfully chanted fluttered like huge blackbirds over the white-wrapped corpse. The wind howled even more despairingly, as if reincarnations of sinners were demanding that the yeshiva scholars redeem them. And down at the foot of the hill by the purification chamber, the Nareva townspeople looked up at the Musarniks carrying their friend higher and higher toward heaven.

The Nareva congregants stood in silence. Old heads shook and white beards trembled like the snow-covered trees nearby. The local people now pitied the students. Yes, they're rather wild, they thought, but on the other hand they're exceptional youths. They live in poverty far from home so as to study Torah, and they're devoted to one another heart and soul. The dead youth, for example, had a heart defect, yet he took on the responsibility of caring for a sick friend. Then he himself fell victim and not the sick youth. How can one question God? The Jews stood there, frozen, chilled to the bone in the snowy, grayish light that was neither day nor night.

The wintry twilight at the cemetery was reflected on people's faces and remained in the hearts of the students for many weeks. At other times, the older scholars would spend the first part of the day studying privately in some other beth medresh. No matter how often Reb Simkha said that everyone must be present in the yeshiva for both sessions, it had no effect, because studying alone in the morning in some far-off little beth medresh was a sign that the scholar was an independent Musar thinker, one who sought his own way in learning. Now, however, everyone stayed in the yeshiva from morning till late at night, like a big family mourning together.

Two youths studying would suddenly stop debating for no reason, one sitting immobile while the other swayed over the Talmud even more quickly, but with no sound coming from his throat, as if it were a distant abyss. The students no longer ran about clapping their hands when they studied Musar; they sat over their books, brows bunched, teeth clenched. At prayers the worshipers swayed more gently; they stood in melancholy silence, rooted in place. If a younger student suddenly sobbed, like a beaten child in his sleep, an older scholar wearing the large head tefillin would turn and burn him with a look until the sobbing stopped. Reb Israel Salanter had once said that Hasidism made even whisky kosher but that Musar considered even tears unkosher—for weeping was also a kind of lust.

The immediate impact of the tragedy faded gradually, and people began thinking of Malariter's conduct during the last weeks of his life. Everyone was tormented by the notion that perhaps the talented youth could have been saved from the Angel of Death.

After Henekh Malariter took Daniel Homler into his room, he had spent half his days at home looking after the patient. Henekh couldn't leave for the yeshiva until three in the afternoon, when the landlady returned from her shop—business was usually slow by then—or sent one of her daughters home. Everyone regretted that such a pious student was losing precious Torah study time; he was especially missed by the youngsters who had reviewed the rosh yeshiva's lecture with him. Reb Simkha Feinerman had said that to relieve Malariter of his nursing burden the yeshiva was prepared to strain its resources and send Homler to a hospital again.

But Henekh had answered, "Daniel Homler would regard returning to a hospital where hired nurses would tend him as a terrible sentence. And I would view it the same way. I've grown very fond of him."

Everyone had remembered Daniel Homler's demand that nurses and not his friends take care of him; his attachment to Henekh Malariter had astonished them. But more astonishing had been Malariter's selfless devotion to Daniel. The landlady had spread the word that Henekh had promised to marry her daughter because she had treated his friend so well.

Once, at an Evening Service two days before Purim, Malariter had stood in Silent Devotion for a long time, weeping aloud. The students had exchanged glances and wondered: When the month of Adar begins, joy abounds—yet he was weeping. Perhaps he prayed for the recovery of his sick friend. Possibly he was upset because the patient was causing him to lose so much time from his Torah studies. And perhaps he was crying because he had agreed to the match with his landlady's daughter. His fiancée was neither young nor pretty, and she came from a family with neither money nor lineage. But no one had dared ask what was bothering him. Everyone had felt guilty that the exemplary youth had singlehandedly assumed the responsibility for a sick friend.

After the Purim feast, Henekh had joined everyone and had danced with a hitherto-undisplayed enthusiasm. Long after the seven-day and thirty-day periods of mourning for him, the students were still puzzled: Were we so drunk with wine and song on Purim night that we didn't see what was happening before our eyes? The youths had surrounded the tall, straight Malariter, who was an extraordinary dancer. They had watched in awe as he performed the Cossack dance, squatting down, then leaping high in the air, kicking to all sides while swiftly turning. The rosh yeshiva's eyes had been masked that evening. Noticing that Yankl Poltaver and his group were missing, he had become ill at ease: Who could guess what that wild ass was doing in honor of Purim? Finally Yankl and his group had appeared and said that they had been busy with Musar somewhere to sanctify the Purim festivities. Then Yankl had gulped down a pint of whisky. He had let his pupils drink too and had begun to dance with them as Reb Simkha Feinerman stood watching, clapping his hands. That was why Reb Simkha hadn't known that in another part of the tumultuous beth medresh, Henekh Malariter was dancing with such wild abandon that he danced his soul away.

6

THE YOUNG SCHOLAR'S DEATH slowed down the relentless war that the trustee's family and friends had sworn to wage until they smoked out Yankl Poltaver and the other Musarniks like wasps and drove them away. After Malariter's death a friend advised Sulkes, "Best keep it quiet. Everyone sympathizes with the yeshiva students now, and they'll side with them." Another man argued, "People say that the dead youth was a saint. Chances are, then, that there are others like him in the yeshiva. It wouldn't be Jewish for the innocent to suffer along with the guilty." A third warned Sulkes, "Don't start trouble with people whose hearts are bitter." Finally the trustee's children said, "Father, that young man looks like a maniac, and nobody can win a fight with a madman." Reb Zushe Sulkes spat, "Let him go to hell"—and satisfied himself by pouring out his heart to the rosh yeshiva.

"The Talmud states that a man who shames his friend is like a murderer, and he loses his share in the world to come. So how could a yeshiva student and his gang of fresh brats have the nerve to charge into my house during the Purim feast and give me a broom for a Purim gift in the presence of a house full of guests and tell me to sweep the sin out of my house?" Sulkes reckoned up all the humiliation that he had suffered from Poltaver and concluded, "If it weren't for the tragedy of the student's death, which has saddened everyone's heart, the yeshiva would be suffering terribly right now."

"For God's sake, please see to it that the yeshiva doesn't suffer." Reb Simkha Feinerman groaned like a man in great pain, and with the same anguished demeanor, he spoke to Yankl Poltaver while the older leaders of the yeshiva looked on.

"Occasionally you do the yeshiva some good, but the harm you cause it is greater. We were right to worry about where you were during the Purim night festivities. Later you came and told us that you and your group were busy with Musar. But in fact you acted against Musar and decency. You humiliated a man and almost brought new grief upon the yeshiva." Reb Simkha added bitterly, "While I was looking at the door, wondering why you and your pupils weren't there, I didn't exercise my usual caution to see that Henekh Malariter didn't overexert himself at the festivities."

The rosh yeshiva's soft-spoken rebuke and the older scholars' disheartened silence hurt Poltaver more than loud abuse. Indeed, the iron youth whom no one could intimidate had been more affected by Henekh's funeral than anyone else. Terrified of corpses, Yankl didn't dare go near the purification chamber. While everyone else was grieving, he was living in fear that his friend would appear to him in a dream. Reb Simkha's relief that he had avoided a fight with Sulkes thoroughly bewildered Poltaver. He realized that the older Navaredkers had become submissive and wanted to live in peace with the world. And his friends too, who had once been seekers, were now downright expedient, seeking good marriages and rabbinic positions. He felt suffocated in their company.

The other yeshiva students began to struggle with the age-old question of why the righteous suffered. The extremely pious among them had their ready answer from the Talmud: " 'The righteous are held responsible for the sins of their generation.' Malariter died because of the sins of others."

But that easy answer couldn't satisfy those who were less perfect in their faith. Some had complaints against Divine Providence, and others looked for someone closer to blame. As a dried river bed reveals sharp, crooked stones, so the yeshiva students revealed their hatred of Daniel Homler after pouring out all their tears over the dead Henekh. Homler was the one to blame!

They recalled that Daniel the greatly beloved, as Reb Simkha had called him, had become a miser and a grouch even before his operation. In the hospital after the operation he had been unbearably irritable. To compare him with Henekh Malariter was impossible. They had *nothing* in common. Homler wasn't talented, he wasn't a diligent student, he wasn't truly pious, and he certainly didn't have fine character traits. Homler was an absolute nonentity. And for the likes of him Henekh Malariter had to sacrifice his life!

The yeshiva people didn't spare themselves either. How could old friends who had studied the whole Talmud with Henekh have let him promise his landlady to marry her daughter? There was no doubt that he had suffered immensely because of that promise. That was why he had wept so bitterly during the Silent Devotion two days before Purim, and why he had danced so exuberantly at the Purim festivities—to make himself forget. "A prince of Torah and we abandoned him!" the youths rebuked themselves, but they criticized Daniel Homler even more bitterly.

"Someone like him isn't capable of loving anyone, even if he were dying to express his love. The object of someone's selfless love has to be admired. But an insignificant person who has achieved nothing can neither admire nor love another. With Homler it's even worse. If he had at least realized he was a midget, he might have been able to seem taller by standing on his tiptoes; but he doesn't even realize that he's a minuscule person, a nothing!" The students measured off with their fingers how small Homler was, and they didn't care that they were speaking slander. It seemed to them that Homler had fooled all of them, and not only them, but the Angel of Death too. The Angel with a thousand eyes had apparently not noticed him and had taken Henekh in his place.

Reb Simkha Feinerman asked the group to visit the sick youth and find out how he was faring, but the students washed their hands of the matter like someone beset by ants after a dirty rain. Soon the landlady herself came to the rosh yeshiva, crying, "Take Homler out of my house. My daughters and I can't stand looking at him any more. We thought he wouldn't be able to bear his friend's death, but now he's more concerned for his own life than ever, and he's become even more grouchy and unfriendly."

The rebbetsin and Reb Simkha talked at length with the woman and persuaded her to keep Homler with her, at least temporarily.

"All right," the woman finally agreed, "but on condition that neither I nor my daughters have to take care of him. He really hasn't been as sick all along as he's pretended to be. And since he doesn't have anyone to boss around, he takes care of himself very nicely."

Later on, reports reached the yeshiva that the landlady and her daughters had become somewhat fonder of Homler. Even students who were naïve about the ways of the world immediately realized the landlady's intentions: instead of Henekh Malariter, Daniel Homler would become her son-in-law. For the woman it was an even better match. After all, Henekh had had a heart defect, and her daughter would have had constant anxiety for his life; Daniel Homler, however, was basically healthy. The only thing wrong with him was the long illness after his appendectomy. Now he was getting stronger every day, and a wife would live out her years with him in peace.

The spring thaw melted the snows; holes appeared in the snowbanks, and they began to collapse. Thin, grayish clouds hung low and dripped like laundry on a line. Patches of milk-white and bluish fog hovered among the houses. Smoke rose slowly from the chimneys. The outdoors tried to shake off the sleep of winter, but couldn't quite get rid of its spell. In the yeshiva the floor was wet and muddy from the snow tramped in by the students' boots. The damp, rumpled towel above the hand basin spread a sour smell, like a barrel of sauerkraut gone bad. Nostrils twitched with the sweaty odor of sweltering bodies, reminiscent of the bathhouse dressing room. The side room in the beth medresh, used as a library, reeked of old, unaired books. The grayish daylight blended with the cigarette smoke, and the blurry faces looked even paler than usual.

On the eve of the first of the month of Nissan, most of the yeshiva students were preparing to go home for Passover, but since a good many of the Nareva Torah students couldn't go home because their families were on the other side of the Russian border, these students turned gloomy. All they could do was quietly console themselves with the hope that, with the help of God, they would marry into a fine family and get a bride who would appreciate a scholar husband's learning and his gentle ways. Consequently, the news of the match between Homler and the landlady's daughter brought the students out from behind their prayer stands to gather behind the pulpit and discuss the matter.

"It's clear why Homler has accepted. Why shouldn't the match appeal to him? He's never dreamed of anything better than becoming a businessman, a little shopkeeper. The question is about the girl. Can't she tell the difference between a Henekh Malariter and a Daniel Homler? The answer to the problem is that there was no problem in the first place, because the girl didn't understand the difference—the main thing for her was that she had a fiancé," the youths concluded sadly, and returned to their Talmuds, heartbroken all over again at the death of their friend. Henekh had been a brilliant scholar with a pure soul, but he hadn't known how to limit his goodness and hadn't remembered that under no circumstances should one become intimate with a family that didn't properly appreciate one's fine character traits.

The yeshiva students assembled behind the pulpit again to greet Asher-Leml Krasner when he returned from the Navaredok yeshiva in Volhyn to which he had taken Shimshl Kupishker. Asher-Leml had heard about Malariter's death in the Volhyn village, and his friends in Nareva greeted him with reawakened grief, like a mourning family greeting a brother who arrives after the funeral. The students recalled how afraid they had been that the fanatic Kupishker might commit suicide, God forbid, but they had never dreamed that danger lurked for the wonderful Henekh Malariter.

"How is Kupishker? Is he still nibbling his sugar?" the yeshiva students asked.

The kind and sedate Asher-Leml thought it odd that Torah scholars were so sarcastic about a friend who had fallen into a state of depression because he had overexerted himself in the service of God. But Asher-Leml said nothing; his beard seemed to grow closer to his eyes and more modestly around his mouth, as if to keep him from talking too much.

After thinking awhile, he finally replied, "Shimshl Kupishker has fully recovered, thank God."

"Hallelujah! We were afraid he'd try to hang himself again," someone said, and the others smiled bitterly.

7

WELL, this is my consolation! Tsemakh Atlas had thought, seeing Henekh Malariter maturing into an exceptional young man. Henekh has gone his own way; still, because he was once in my group, his progress consoles me. When the tragedy occurred, Tsemakh felt that his student's death and that of his first fiancée were linked. He had not properly appreciated either of them. Perhaps it was because he had not sufficiently mourned for Dvorele Namiot that heaven had ordained another mourning.

Tsemakh didn't weep at Malariter's funeral, and he never discussed his loss with anyone. His way of walking became stiffer and more erect, as if his spine had turned into a dry autumnal stalk after all its blossoms have withered. At night in bed he felt his hands and feet shriveling. He was alert, as always, and had a normal heartbeat—only one thing was wrong: his hands and feet were shrinking. Tsemakh recalled walking around all day; yet he had the impression that he'd been lying in his bed for years. He felt as if his legs had become scrawny, like a chicken's, and they could not support his big, lumbering body. His short, tiny hands could not hold onto anything.

The next morning he paced around his room, on the street, in the beth medresh, as if nothing was wrong—that night he experienced the same terror. "But it wasn't I who caused Henekh Malariter's death," he groaned, tossing and turning and cursing the Musarnik in him that sought to find fault with himself. "Oh, Henekh, Henekh, would that I had died instead of you!" Tsemakh had become so sick of life that he would gladly have told the Angel of Death, "Come; take me instead of Malariter!"

Even during the day, in the yeshiva, Henekh floated toward Tsemakh from every corner: tall, head up, hat back, hands behind him, a radiant smile on his pale face. He walked between the benches, his brow glowing with the Talmudic passage he was contemplating. Then he stopped near the pulpit where the younger students gathered around him to discuss the rosh yeshiva's lecture. . . . Tsemakh felt a chill run down his back, a shiver through his body. Suddenly he asked himself why he'd never gone to visit Homler in the hospital or, later, in his room. Probably because Daniel Homler, like Moshe Chayit Lohoysker, might hate him for taking him away from his parents in White Russia when he was a boy. But why had Malariter and Homler become so attached? He would have to discuss this with Homler, Tsemakh thought, no matter how difficult a visit to him might be.

Tsemakh went to see Homler in the afternoon, while the landlady and her daughters were in their shop. Spring overran the streets with warm breezes and rivulets of melted snow. But in the sick youth's spacious room, everything was brightly neat, cold, and angular. Shiny new oilcloth covered the table. The bed, painted light blue, was nicely made, with a white, puffed-up pillow. Next to one wall stood a dark brown varnished wardrobe, with a little key in its lock, and a small glass closet full of polished, sparkling dishes. The room looked as if it were the quarters of an irascible old bachelor who hated the turmoil of children and was too finicky to use the household dishes. Like the furnishings, Homler himself had a bright, angular face; he had a low forehead, dry, broad lips, a sharp little chin, and large, protruding ears. Indoors and during mild weather outdoors he wore a warm hat, fur-lined slippers, and a shaggy red dressing gown. His thin, bony hands and long, bony fingers with pointed nails stretched from beneath the broad sleeves. Even after his unexpected visitor arrived, Homler sat on the edge of his bed with his eyes downcast, as if drilling a hole in the floor with his penetrating glance. One could tell at once that Homler was constantly aware that he had been seriously ill, and that he still felt he had to be careful of himself.

"If you're wondering why I didn't come before now," Tsemakh began, and, uninvited, sat down on a chair next to the table, "it was because I heard you didn't want to see your friends. I assumed you didn't want to see me either."

"The yeshiva students came to save my soul when they should have saved my body—that's why I didn't want to see them," Daniel Homler muttered, still not looking at his guest.

"That's not true!" Tsemakh cried, feeling the same revulsion toward his student that the other scholars had felt. "The students were primarily concerned with your body and only then with your soul. And why shouldn't friends who're waiting on you want to discuss Torah and Musar?"

Daniel snorted and remained hostile. "The yeshiva students were concerned with my body in order to save my soul, just like the nuns who came to the hospital to visit the Christian patients. Nevertheless, it seems that a sick body doesn't disgust the nuns in black with the big crosses hanging from their necks, while the yeshiva students were disgusted at tending me. They came to see me in the hospital like Musarniks who go to the cemetery to learn a lesson about mortal man's ultimate fate—they came to learn a lesson from my sad state. They even demanded that my own body disgust me and that I look deeply into myself and think of repentance. One of them, while he was taking care of me, sighed and moaned. Another said openly, 'Look; look what can become of a man!' A third reminded me of a Musar sermon the rosh yeshiva delivered: 'If we don't provide a friend with the world to come, we provide him with nothing.' So I got rid of those supposedly devoted friends of mine.

"In the yeshiva," Homler went on, "they concocted a tale that I was gripped by an unhealthy lust to have women see me naked, and everyone laughed at me for not being ashamed of my scrawny body in front of the nurses. Everything they said about me was a lie. But I admit that I preferred hired women attendants who treated me like any other patient to the Musarniks who told me to think of a higher life when I was writhing in pain."

"And did Henekh Malariter treat you differently?" Tsemakh asked.

"Absolutely! Because he himself was ill. As soon he came to see me, I realized that he came to help me, not to save my soul. That's why I went to live in his house. He used to say that there was much wisdom in the saying that a healthy person can't fully understand a sick one. A man who knows that he's in constant danger because of an ailment is an entirely different sort of person. He's enmeshed in his body. He's in the grip of his limbs as if he were in chains. Even when he's with healthy people, he never forgets the abyss that separates them. A sick person who according to the doctors is miraculously alive thinks of himself as the reflected mirror image of a real person. That's what Henekh used to say."

"Henekh was a very lively youth, even though he was ill," Tsemakh murmured. He had never suspected Malariter of having such dark thoughts.

Daniel Homler's angular face twisted into a cold grimace which resembled a smile the way a stillborn child resembles a newborn baby.

"A sick person can be gayer and happier than a healthy one, but that's the joy that follows despair. The fact that Henekh had lost hope was obvious from his telling prospective in-laws about his heart defect and then laughing while he mimicked the horrified reactions of the marriage brokers and in-laws. When he discovered that his landlady wasn't put off by his bad heart, he promised to marry her daughter because he was overjoyed that she and her family had faith he would live."

"And I thought he did that because he was sacrificing himself for you," Tsemakh said with increasing rancor.

"How did he sacrifice himself for me? He took me into his room because he saw that we understood each other," Homler replied with the dry cough and cold rage of an unsuccessful man who is supported by relatives but doesn't feel that he owes them any gratitude.

Why was Homler sitting with downcast eyes all this time? Tsemakh asked himself. Then he thought: It's because he's certain that he has seen everything, that only he is right, and that no one should be trusted—that's why he keeps his eyes down. There was a little key in the lock of the wardrobe. Was Homler afraid the landlady or her daughter, his bride-to-be, would rob him? Homler was beneath contempt, Tsemakh screamed in his thoughts—and he spoke to the youth as sharply as when he had been Homler's group leader.

"Your friends weren't overgenerous with affection because you aren't a good friend either. You were always concerned with yourself; only with yourself."

"What's wrong with being concerned with myself?" Daniel looked down at his thin hands. He spoke slowly, deliberately, but his attempt at restraint brought out the blue vein on his right temple.

"When I first came to the yeshiva, I was an altruist. I gave away my meat portion; I lent my coat while I froze. If I got angry at those who took everything from my trunk without my knowledge, they reminded me that the *Ethics of the Fathers* states that he who says 'What's mine is mine and what's yours is yours' doesn't have a decent character. Then when I pleaded with them, 'Take it!' they chided me again, saying that my 'Take it!' was too hasty, too loud, as if I were forcing myself to do it. Nevertheless, I still couldn't overcome my *yetzer ha-ra* for a clean towel, and I still couldn't stand it when someone stretched out on my bed in his shoes or when Yankl Poltaver brought my hat back battered and wrinkled. The yeshiva students go around with overgrown hair and are infested with vermin. They're too lazy to wash with cold water in the winter, and the backs of their hands are caked with dirt. They drink from dirty glasses which I get nauseous just looking at. And why can't I get away from my group once in a while to lie down in my room or sew on a button or write a letter? Why do my roommates have to come from the Musar room at two in the morning and make me get out of bed barefoot to open the door for them? The constant noise in the beth medresh, the Musar room, the kitchen, the rooms we sleep in can drive you crazy. People even yell in the middle of the Silent Devotion. They even go to the forest for private meditation in groups of ten and twenty. That's why I wanted a little corner all for myself where I could quietly drink a glass of tea and where people wouldn't swarm around me like ants over a tree trunk, or make a garbage dump out of my bed. And what did I get for that? They scorned me, they despised me, and when I got sick, they became even more antagonistic. My friends took care of me, but with angry faces and trembling hands, as if they wanted to choke me. Of course they couldn't tell me they hated me, so they said, 'Think of spiritual things; the body is just dust and ashes.' Only Asher-Leml Krasner didn't forget Reb Israel Salanter's saying, 'Think about your fellow man's body and your own soul, and not the reverse.' But Henekh Malariter understood this best of all."

Daniel Homler stopped for a moment, then continued, "And you too, Reb Tsemakh, once longed for a little corner all your own, and you suddenly got engaged, even though you had left Nareva on a holy mission for the good of the yeshiva. Why can't I have my own little corner and guard my things?"

"You can. Of course you can. Before I brought you from your native Homel into Poland, your parents told me that you were always neat and careful even as a child, and that you were possessive about your toys even when you were still crawling on all fours. Well, your middle-class merchant's heritage came out in you. But there isn't a word of truth in your statement that Henekh Malariter took you in because he saw that you were like him. He took you in and watched over you because he was your exact opposite. Good day!"

Two women stood in the hallway—the landlady and one of her daughters, a girl with an old face. Her straight black hair was parted in the middle over a high, protruding forehead. She had a tray of food in her hands and apparently had been undecided whether to enter the lodger's room while he had a guest. Probably Homler's fiancée, Tsemakh thought, as he shook his head and left. Instead of sympathizing with his former pupil, he pitied the fiancée who stood in the corridor holding the tray—sad, weary, and bent, as if she'd been standing outside in a downpour. Tsemakh hadn't gone ten steps down the street when he sensed the landlady running after him.

The woman had narrow eye slits set in a web of wrinkles; her gray hair was disheveled under her kerchief. She looked around to see if her lodger was watching and began complaining, "I'm a poor widow with a houseful of unmarried daughters. Daniel has promised to marry my oldest daughter, but I'm afraid the rosh yeshiva will soon stop paying for his room and board."

"As long as Daniel isn't well," Tsemakh calmed her, "and hasn't become formally engaged to her, the yeshiva will continue to pay for him."

The woman looked around again and, ill at ease, continued in a confidential tone, "None of the yeshiva students come to visit him. As I understand it, you're an older friend of his, or a teacher. So tell me the truth, rabbi; do you think he really intends to marry my daughter? I wouldn't have asked about Henekh Malariter. He was an entirely different sort, may he rest in peace. But this one—has he said anything to you? It's forbidden to fool a poor widow."

"He said nothing to me," Tsemakh answered, amazed that he hadn't thought of that himself. "Believe me, I don't know what to tell you. Your lodger and I spoke of other matters."

The landlady's eye slits broadened and her pupils became large and sad, like the eyes of her harried daughter with the bent shoulders and parted black hair. The woman was apparently afraid to probe further because she didn't want to know more than necessary. She merely sighed again, bemoaning her poor widow's luck, and shuffled back through the melted snow to her house.

Would Homler fool his fiancée as Yosef Varshever had fooled the young cook who worked in the Valkenik yeshiva kitchen, or would Homler indeed marry the landlady's daughter? Tsemakh didn't know; even if Homler kept his promise, he was still a worthless good-for-nothing. He had persuaded himself that Henekh Malariter had taken him in for Henekh's own benefit and not to help save him; and that Henekh had his own advantage in mind, and not the ailing Homler's, when he became engaged to the landlady's daughter. Homler's grief for the dead Malariter was less profound than that of the other yeshiva students. Perhaps he feared that an evil eye might be cast upon him for having remained alive. Perhaps he also envied the dead student all the praises showered on him. Daniel Homler knew that he wouldn't have been mourned and wept over that much.

Moshe Chayit Lohoysker too had complaints against Navaredok, Tsemakh thought, but at least he was stumbling and searching. What was he doing now, and how was he supporting himself? He had no nonreligious friends, and the yeshiva students weren't friendly with him. The very least he could do, Tsemakh said to himself, was to find out if Moshe Chayit was starving. Instead of taking the paved main street to the yeshiva, Tsemakh walked through the snow-covered side streets toward Lohoysker's.

Tsemakh made his way to the end of the narrow, twisting corridor where during Yom Kippur night he had groped in the dark and found the little room. When he found it again, from behind the closed door he clearly recognized the voices of students who as youngsters had sat in his seekers' group.

"Since the Socialists don't believe in a divinely revealed Torah and don't believe that wealth and poverty come from Divine Providence, from their point of view they're not wrong in wanting to make over the world," Yankl Poltaver was saying angrily.

Lohoysker contradicted him. "Yankl is still a Musarnik. First he believed that a man must start by making himself over, and now he believes that man can't make himself over if he doesn't change the entire world order. But he's still a Musarnik and a do-gooder. I don't want to do good for anyone—I want to enjoy life."

"If the distribution of poverty and wealth is basically unjust, it's impossible that this is God's will." Tsemakh heard Chaikl Vilner's voice.

"Yankl Poltaver wants to wage war. And because he's become convinced that the Musarniks don't want to stand up and fight for poor women peddlers, not even against that trustee Sulkes, Yankl is being drawn to the union workers." Lohoysker laughed.

"I've fallen into a den of clowns," someone sighed, and added something so softly that Tsemakh couldn't hear. He couldn't guess whose voice it was. Lohoysker once again interrupted loudly and gaily, as if he were aware that Tsemakh Atlas was outside the door and took pleasure in naming those in the conversation.

"Reuven Ratner wants to persuade me that I put on tefillin daily so that it's kosher for him to visit me. But even the Nareva congregants whose children I tutor in Bible and Hebrew know I don't wear tefillin."

"The yeshiva is in mourning for Henekh Malariter, and we're sitting here as if in a den of thieves, discussing everything under the sun." Reuven Ratner sighed again.

But Lohoysker replied even more arrogantly, "Doubts were gnawing even at Malariter. 'How can we tell someone that he'll die soon?' Henekh would ask. 'Even when the sick man himself says that he feels the end is near, the people around him should not concur, because the patient wants them to contradict him. And what value is there to the confession of a broken, doomed man? Why does the Master of the Universe need such a confession?' I noticed that Henekh Malariter couldn't forgive the Talmud for the heartless dictum that a dying man has to recite confession, just as he couldn't forgive our former group leader for tormenting us to break our wills. Tsemakh Lomzher's students have certainly made a mess of themselves, haven't they? What successes he's had! He won't be masquerading as a penitent in Nareva much longer. It won't be long now before he has a new pack of troubles."

The students urged Lohoysker to explain, but he merely said, "Meantime, it's a secret."

Tsemakh slowly made his way to the outside door. He walked through town with half-closed eyes, didn't remember crossing the streets, and was amazed that he found his way home.

When he entered the house and went to his room, his landlady approached him happily and said, "A woman has been here looking for you. A young and pretty one. She's from Lomzhe, and she says she's your wife."

8

THE COUPLE sat facing each other in a room in a little hotel in Nareva, as they had done once before in the Valkenik inn. Slava gazed at the man with the pinched cheeks behind his full beard. In the old days, when Tsemakh was silent, one could see his strength even in his tight-shut lips; now, through his half-open mouth only bad teeth were visible. His rumpled jacket was frayed at the elbows. The lapels were greasy. Instead of a shirt, he wore a set of ritual fringes that came up to his neck. Slava looked into the little wall mirror and felt that she too had changed. Tiny wrinkles were etched into the corners of her mouth; the skin under her eyelids was webbed with blue veins. Her neck had lost its youthful firmness and had become too thick. Her hair, still blond, looked thinner and not as soft. Shingled in the back, it was cut in bangs over her forehead. Such a hairdo surely didn't suit a yeshiva scholar's wife. To offset this, Slava had pinned a golden brooch with three tassels to the front of her striped black-and-brown silk blouse. But Tsemakh hadn't even noticed this old-fashioned jewelry. Head bent, Slava looked down at the brooch.

The tassels reminded her of gilded candelabra on a white-decked table in her father's house. Her brothers and sisters-in-law still celebrated the Sabbath and festivals with the traditional lighting of candles and Kiddush. When she met Tsemakh, his appearance and behavior had reminded her of the atmosphere in her father's house. Tsemakh had been Volodya's friend when they were children in cheder, so she had trusted him. But he had betrayed her trust, and for years she had had neither Sabbath nor festival. Because he detested her husband, Volodya no longer let yeshiva fund raisers cross his threshold. Volodya had grown fatter and lazier. He had given up tossing coins and playing with his pet cat. Naum had become entirely gray. He no longer ranted and raved and, because his own affairs were going badly, no longer meddled in community affairs.

"You know," said Slava, still gazing down at her tasseled brooch, "my brother's son Lolla is married and has a child. He settled down, became a merchant, and is in business with my brothers. Did you know that?" Tsemakh shook his head. It was obvious that he didn't regret not hearing this family news until now. In the mirror Slava saw his bent back and asked herself for perhaps the thousandth time in her life: Who is this man? She recalled the tall Tsemakh with the sharp, pale profile, lips pressed sternly together, and the black glow of eyes that pierced one's soul. The fantasy of the old Tsemakh, the man of their first half-year together, was still very much with her.

A moment ago Slava hadn't known what she would say to her husband, or whether she'd say anything at all. But before she could stop herself, she burst out in a hoarse, almost rasping voice, "Remember the fight you had with the family because Lolla didn't marry the maid he got pregnant? But the fact that he's married now and living a decent family life doesn't interest you. Lolla is also supporting the child he had with Stasya. She and her child live in a village among Jews. Even Stasya and her child don't interest you any more. Standing up for the maid was just an excuse for you to leave home . . ."

The more Slava talked, the surer Tsemakh was that she had come to discuss a divorce. She wouldn't have flung all his old sins in his face if she hadn't come to separate from him for good.

"Once I was changing clothes in midday," Slava reminded him, "to show you how nice I looked. But instead of saying a kind word about my dresses and my taste, you vulgarly asked me why I didn't have a baby. It's lucky I didn't have a child with you. You would have left me anyway, and the child would have had to grow up without a father. And when I pleaded with you not to break up our marriage over a serving maid who tumbled with our nephew, you snapped back, 'Were you any better?' And when you'd had enough of me and wanted to return to the Musarniks, you still wanted to be the saint, the one in the right, and you compared me with an immature, silly goose of a girl who let herself be thrown on a bed by the first man she met. And that's the most disgusting thing you did to me!

"Do you hear from Ronya? I can imagine you two regretting that you're both already married. Ronya didn't realize that you would have left her just as you left me. She's a woman who needs a man and nothing else. Indeed, she's miserable because her husband comes home only for the holidays—but you didn't come home even then. Furthermore, she has two little boys, so she can't be entirely unhappy."

Slava herself was embarrassed and frightened by her explosion of rage. She jumped up from the chair and stood before her husband, full-bodied, rather heavy, wearing a wool skirt that accentuated her hips. Slava gathered from Tsemakh's astonished look that he was asking himself if she was the same woman who had once seduced him, fluttered about him, and put him to sleep with her feline purring. She thought of saying that she looked shorter now because she was wearing low-heeled slippers. But his estranged, baffled look cooled the warm words on her lips.

"My brothers are right!" Her voice was more strident, her eyes blazed. "Since the time we took you into the store, everything's been going downhill. The customers you chased away with your abuse have never come back. We fired your three cousins, the Atlas brothers, because we don't need clerks. Speak up, Musarnik! Are you enjoying this lambasting?"

"The older a person gets, the more he resembles himself. The years make of a person what he is," Tsemakh replied.

"Really? Am I already old in your eyes? And what am I?" she asked in one breath.

"A contentious woman. Stubborn and contentious. That's why you married me and that's why you haven't accepted a divorce from me to this day," Tsemakh said, seemingly to himself, and shrugged his shoulders in amazement. "Why do you need me?"

Slava shrugged too. "Actually, I don't need you." She thought she'd burst out laughing. He, who fought with everyone, had called *her* contentious. She sat down in a deep armchair, nervously swung one crossed leg, and repeated, "Actually, I don't need you. If I could turn back the wheel of bygone years, I'd be much smarter next time.

But now it's rather hard for me to start all over again. What do you plan to do from now on?" she asked in a mocking voice.

"I myself do plan to start all over again. I'm going to establish another yeshiva. But I'll have a different attitude toward the congregants and the students. Nowadays one can't be a fiery zealot. I'll be more easygoing, more flexible . . ."

Tsemakh didn't finish. He could no longer outshout his own incredulity at his plan to start all over again. His ears still rang with the words and laughter he had heard on the other side of Lohoysker's door. The expelled yeshiva youth had told his friends that Tsemakh Lomzher wouldn't be masquerading as a penitent in Nareva much longer, but Lohoysker had not explained his remark. Slava too had just asked him sarcastically what his future plans were, as if knowing that he couldn't remain in Nareva much longer.

Tsemakh stood up and gave his wife a searing glance. "Why did you come here all of a sudden?"

"All of a sudden? Isn't it time?" She swung her right leg over her left knee and continued, apparently in a better mood, "I got a letter from one of your students signed Moshe Chayit Lohoysker. He tells me that you and he are at war with each other and that I should come and take you home or get a divorce from you, because you won't be able to remain in the yeshiva much longer. He says that all the students you tore away from their parents in Russia and brought to Poland have grown up and have become your opponents. He wrote that you'll soon have to flee Nareva in shame, as you fled Valkenik before. When I read his letter, I was frightened. You might indeed disappear, and I'd be left an agunah. Who knows? You might even go off to London and become a Christian missionary." Slava laughed and chattered on. "I've already met the youth who wrote the letter. No, he's not the schemer I thought he'd be. A schemer wouldn't have told me that I could tell my husband who had written me to come to Nareva.

"Your student explained that your former pupils are now against you because you taught them to hate the world—and then you yourself ran away into the world. And now you say that you're planning to start all over again with different attitudes. But you just told me that the older a person gets, the more he resembles himself—that the years make of a person what he is. If that's true, you won't be able to have different attitudes toward your new students, and the congregants who would have to support the yeshiva. Perhaps it would be better for you to come back home."

"I've often thought of going home," Tsemakh answered, "and setting our broken marriage aright. But as soon as I see you, I realize that we wouldn't be able to live under the same roof . . ."

"Is it because I'm contentious or because seeing me reminds you of your first fiancée?" Slava interrupted.

"Your character and conduct don't make me think of her. Each time we meet I become more persuaded that we're not compatible," Tsemakh concluded, and left the room as quietly as a shadow that glides out of a lighted window into the dark outside.

Slava's first reaction was to run after him, crying that he was a monster. A decent person doesn't leave without saying good-bye. She was his wife, and he hadn't seen her for two years! But instead of giving chase and shouting after him, she glanced wistfully at the wall mirror, as if ashamed of her husband's conduct before the woman in the glass. Her brow furrowed, and memories quivered in the little net of wrinkles.

After Tsemakh's second departure from Lomzhe, Slava's group of admirers had gradually dispersed. The oft-repeated stories of the flour merchant Feivl Sokolovsky—a man with a low, hairy forehead and hands as broad as shovels—about how clever and sly he was at business, made her sick. She openly laughed at him so often that he realized she considered him a fool and stopped coming to see her. She found it pleasant to sit in silence with the teacher Halperin, who taught Hebrew in evening courses; she liked his sad, clever smile. If it weren't for his scrawny neck, protruding Adam's apple, and weak, shiny-blue chin with its loose, rough skin, she might even have kissed him. Halperin too gradually realized that he could expect nothing and stopped coming. There remained only the actor Herman Yoffe, who—like Slava—hated monotony. Longing for a caress and a tender word, Slava sat close to him and looked into his kindly, aging face, or tugged at his thick shock of gray hair. "I'm twice your age," he would say, explaining why he never attempted more than a kiss. But she didn't care how old he was or that behind his laughter and jokes there was a man of no substance. She didn't mind either that he considered her merely a very nice and frivolous young woman. But lately the amateurs of the Lomzhe Theatrical Society had quarreled and Herman Yoffe, their director, had gone away.

Slava's days became as monotonous and slow as a thin autumnal rain. She reached the point where she would have been satisfied with any man. But the young men of Lomzhe still saw her as a pampered rich girl who had chosen a husband from a strange background just to be different. Slava didn't want to tell her acquaintances that she regretted marrying Tsemakh and that she wasn't as frivolous and stupid as people assumed—since she had once loved Tsemakh, she could not divorce him. Moreover, there was no fine, down-to-earth man who could inspire her to start all over again. So she became lazy; she neglected herself. She spent half her days lolling about on the sofa, browsing through magazines or reading old letters, and shuffling around in her slippers until evening. Her brothers urged her to take a trip to Bialystok, Vilna, or Warsaw. Chances for a suitable match were better in a large city, and she'd be free of her Musarnik. She wanted this too. But whenever she thought of a trip, her anger against her husband flared anew. Indeed, her rage against Tsemakh bound her with fetters—it kept her from tearing herself away from her voluntary prison. Oh, if she had known that he yearned for her from afar, she would have taken anyone for a lover and enjoyed deceiving that bearded Musarnik! But because she knew he didn't miss her, she didn't have the strength to betray him or to tear herself away from provincial Lomzhe. Moshe Chayit Lohoysker's letter had finally spurred her, but now Tsemakh had given her an even colder reception than in Valkenik. He considered her an old woman. All the same, he won't get off that easily, she thought. She'd put on such a show for him here that he would no longer think of her as old. The impression she had made on Tsemakh's former student, Moshe Chayit Lohoysker, had not escaped her notice.

9

SLAVA WALKED with Lohoysker and Chaikl Vilner along the road that led to the forest. The fur collar of her light gray coat was wrapped around her neck like a cat, and her broad-brimmed fur hat was tilted over her left temple. Swinging her handbag, she proceeded deliberately in her carriage boots. Occasionally she stopped and looked around as if she'd never seen such a beautiful landscape. Lohoysker too would stop and inspect the scenery. He was poorly dressed and had all the earmarks of a forlorn bench warmer. Still, his face shone with joy and triumph; he was hoping that some of the Nareva congregants and yeshiva students would see him with the penitent's wife.

Chaikl Vilner, however, felt the perspiration freezing on his brow. He was afraid to raise his head and meet the glances of passers-by. In full noon, before the eyes of all Nareva, he was strolling with a married woman.

It had happened by accident. Chaikl had dropped in on Lohoysker, and in that cramped, messy, moldy den he had found the beautiful rebbetsin. She gave him a friendly, inquisitive glance, and he said, "I remember you. We met in Valkenik." He must have sounded in high spirits, because she too said blithely, "Yes; yes. I remember." The rebbetsin shook hands with him and asked, "Do you want to go for a walk in the woods? Coming into Nareva I saw that they're still full of snow, and I love snow-covered trees." She laughed as she spoke, as if realizing that he wouldn't dare be seen on the street with a woman. Lohoysker obviously didn't want Chaikl along, but since Slava asked, "Are you ashamed? Are you afraid?" Chaikl had to go with them so she wouldn't consider him a bench warmer—a fanatic.

The snow along the road was yellowish and trodden by wagons and strollers, but in the forest it gleamed white and fresh. Slava looked at the white-garbed pines with amazement and yearning, as if she had spent the summers of her youth among them. She turned to Chaikl, "Do you remember? There was also a big, dense forest near Valkenik, and I was there in the winter, too. You know, you've changed a lot in the past two years. In Valkenik you still looked like a youngster."

Slava's warm glance and pouting upper lip prompted Chaikl to muse: If it weren't for Lohoysker, she might have said something entirely different. She might have confided a secret. Instantly he forgot his fear of what the yeshiva would say and looked at the forest clear-eyed. The topmost branches of the pines sparkled like silver chandeliers; on the lower branches, bare of snow, damp green needles glistened. The thick, notched trunks of tall maples crept out of the forest depths in mossy boots. Here and there ancient oaks revealed swollen roots that looked like bare feet with spread, steamy toes. Icicles dripped in the sunshine like wax candles; frozen bushes melted under the sun's rays. A flat piece of wind-swept ground revealed last year's yellowish grass and rust-red carpets of moss, but the rest of the forest was still in the wintry grip of ice and silence.

"It looks like a big temple with thousands of crystal chandeliers," Chaikl said. "A mysterious temple that one can enter but not leave. And the farther in you go, the surer you are that somewhere in it there's a clearing where a golden altar stands and on which the sun rests like a fiery lion."

"Chaikl read about this fiery lion on an altar in his sacred books. As for the temple, he either read about it or saw a picture of it in some secular book. Or he may even have concocted it himself." Lohoysker's laugh made his long face even longer. "In the Nareva yeshiva of the Navaredker Musarniks you can see greasy gaberdines, discolored ritual fringes, and beards and earlocks flying in all directions. But no crystal chandeliers; no golden altar."

The beautiful rebbetsin graced Lohoysker with a rapturous look for his cleverness and offered Chaikl a broad, sparkling smile. "Can you still throw snowballs?" she asked the students, and before they had a chance to reply, she jumped forward to begin the game. Her two escorts stopped and stared down at their pathetic yeshiva students' garb.

"Are you sure they're going to divorce?" Chaikl whispered, and that instant a snowball spattered his face.

"What difference does it make to you?" Lohoysker grumbled—and a snowball struck his face too.

Delighted that she could still take aim and hit her target, Slava laughed and bent down to make a new snowball. She either became entangled in her broad coat or purposely fell down. "Help me up," she shrieked to the two students who stood there like rooted poles.

Chaikl was the first to move, and Lohoysker followed immediately. As both helped Slava up, she commanded, "Brush the snow off my coat." She handed Chaikl her handbag and bent down to adjust her slightly wrinkled stockings. The rebbetsin turned her shapely foot and complained, "Oh, now the snow's in my boots." She stretched out her right foot for Lohoysker to pull off the boot and shake it out. To support herself, Slava held on to Chaikl's arm, and he eyed her gloved fingers hungrily, as if he were of a mind to gobble them up. Lohoysker huffed and puffed until he finished his task. Chaikl had the privilege of shaking the snow out of Slava's left boot, and this time she leaned on Lohoysker, who stood like a post, afraid even to breathe. Chaikl fussed clumsily until he got the snow out and put the boot back on her foot. "You're quite good at this," she consoled him, "as if you've had lots of practice."

Slava buttoned her coat and made her way back to town with her escorts. She soon tired of walking and paused, turning an unsmiling face to Chaikl, "Your friend hates my husband with a passion. What do you say? You studied with him in Valkenik, so you must know him."

Her high forehead pale, her eyes misty and sad, Slava waited for an answer. But Chaikl had no desire to backbite his teacher. "Reb Tsemakh is an honest man," he said. "On the one hand it's a drawback, because telling everyone what you think of him leads to arguments. On the other hand, it's a great attribute when a man is prepared to do anything for the truth."

Moshe Chayit too realized that it wasn't nice to talk badly about Reb Tsemakh to his wife, even if she had come to divorce him. Nevertheless, Moshe Chayit couldn't overcome his hatred for his former group leader and said crossly, "Vilner is a dreamer. He sticks his head into the sand like an ostrich to keep from seeing how things really are. Everything Tsemakh Atlas has done—from taking children away from their parents in Russia, to his plan to burn the books of the

Valkenik library, to his rolling in the mud in Amdur so as to eke out a pardon from a bedraggled provincial Jew—all shows that he's an adventure seeker, a man who loves adventures and lives only for adventures."

"A person who loves adventures is irresponsible, but Reb Tsemakh has a great sense of responsibility. Even Reb Avraham-Shaye, who ordered him sent away from the Valkenik yeshiva, told me that Reb Tsemakh is a great man," Chaikl said heatedly, and he went on to tell Slava about Reb Avraham-Shaye.

Slava listened with warm, parted lips and tender glances, looking ready to embrace and kiss Chaikl for his remarks. Chaikl felt a tug at his heart. Yet it annoyed him that the beautiful rebbetsin beamed at hearing complimentary remarks about her husband.

At the edge of town, Slava thanked her escorts for the walk and bade them farewell. "Come to see me," she said, smiling at Chaikl. "And you too." She nodded to Lohoysker. No longer fatigued, she walked away with the light, agile step of a young girl, swinging her handbag and her shoulders as the two yeshiva youths watched her open-mouthed. When she turned into a side street, Chaikl said what was on his mind.

"She doesn't seem to be at the point of divorcing her husband."

"Whether she divorces him or not, you'll get nothing out of it anyway." Lohoysker looked down, digging the sole of his shoe into the yeasty spring mud. "Apparently you'll be going to see her. Go right ahead. I don't know yet whether I will."

In his rumpled, spattered coat, with head hunched forward, Lohoysker walked off lazily to his cramped, stale nook in the cold, winding corridor of the deaf old couple's house. Chaikl watched him go; he too felt joyless and was ashamed to return to the beth medresh or appear in the kitchen. He didn't even know how he would face his friends in his room.

10

Wearing a sleeveless jacket with a wide collar, Slava sat at the table, her chin on her round, bare arms. She bit her firm flesh and stared at the tall, narrow vase of flowers which the innkeeper had put in her room as a mark of deference. Slava was waiting for Chaikl. He always came in the afternoon, Lohoysker in the evening. She expected both youths daily so as to prove to herself that she was still a woman. It pleased her that the two students, both younger than she, were in competition over her. But the fact that her conduct embarrassed her husband pleased her even more. She wanted to shame him and make him create a scandal—that was the only way to force him to come home.

When Chaikl arrived, Slava looked him over more carefully than on other days. She saw that his broad shoulders and stocky body were out of proportion to his small hands and lips. His voice was loud and impassioned and he seemed to have an overabundance of manly strength—but his eyes shone blue and dreamy. Slava gazed at his piously bearded cheeks, soft blond mustache, and strong white teeth. She realized that he was vexed with himself for coming to see her. "You look more than twenty, but I often think of you as only a boy." She caressed him with her big luminous eyes. "Your friend Lohoysker is clever, isn't he?"

"Cleverness is like salt. Good and necessary as a seasoning, but no good by itself," Chaikl answered, infuriated at her constant talk of Lohoysker.

Slava liked his sharp, candid replies. He speaks like a young Tsemakh, she thought—although apparently Tsemakh himself was never young. Slava rose and, without thinking, caressed Chaikl's face. Her bare arms with their firm muscles flashed before his eyes. For a moment he gazed at her full breasts under the brief jacket, then seized her with both arms as if with pincers. He pressed close to her with his knees and chest. His breath singed her face; his teeth were clenched like a vise. A rasping sound tore out of his throat, but when the seductive rebbetsin pushed him away from her, he did not resist.

Slava felt her knees and elbows trembling. Her face glowed dimly, like flames smothered under coals. She stood with eyes lowered and touched her high forehead as waves of shivers ran through her. When she pulled herself out of the sweet intoxication, a secret gloom oppressed her heart at the lost years without love and fulfilled desire. But looking at Chaikl, she smiled at his pathetic appearance. He stood there dispiritedly, terrified that she might chase him away. "Take off your coat and sit down," she said. As he obeyed, she continued smiling and shook a warning finger at him. So that they could face each other unashamed, she sought to make his conduct seem like friendly fun between brother and older sister. "Just sit still and tell me about your home—or talk about the woods as beautifully as you did before. Moshe Chayit Lohoysker says you're a poet, and indeed you are. Would you like to read me some of your poems? Do you write about women too? Will you write about me?"

Lohoysker came in the evening. Slava had arranged her room at the inn as comfortably as her Lomzhe home. On the table stood a shaded lamp that illuminated only one's face while everything else sank into darkness; at one's feet shadows lay like a warm blanket. Slava wore a dark blue dress, and her short hair glistened as if she had just come in from a springtime shower. Occasionally she still felt the storm that Chaikl had stirred in her during the day. But her evening visitor was a different sort of youth; his attempts at sophistication seemed pitiful and ridiculous.

Entering the room, Lohoysker removed his hat but didn't let go of it until Slava showed him where to put it. She asked him repeatedly to take off his coat, but he didn't—as if he had just dropped in for a few minutes. His face was bristly and nicked; he had apparently shaved in a hurry or hadn't yet mastered the use of a razor, forbidden by Jewish law. He reviled the Musar books without stopping. His hatred of books—they seemed to be living enemies to him—shocked Slava.

"I'm sure you've heard of Bachya ibn Pakuda's *The Duties of the Heart*

. . . You haven't? I'm surprised your husband hasn't told you about it. The Ten Gates, as the author calls them, that lead men to God are considered holy by the Musarniks, almost as holy as the Ten Commandments. And this is what *The Duties of the Heart* asserts: 'Brother, kinsman mine, first of all renounce everything that is forbidden. Your neighbor's wife, for instance, should revolt you like insects and worms. As you would not eat mice, so should you have no desire to touch another woman. Thereafter, renounce those things which are permitted by law. If it is not necessary for the maintenance of your life, renounce it, brother, kinsman mine. And finally, brother, kinsman mine, accustom yourself to fasting at least once a week.' "

"But religious Jews have wives and children too," said the beautiful rebbetsin. "One is permitted to be with one's own wife."

"Yes, one may. But woe unto him who does so for his own pleasure." Moshe Chayit laughed with a queer, vengeful joy. "The holy books state that when a Jew approaches his wife, his purpose should not be his own bodily pleasures, God forbid; his purpose should be the mitzva of being fruitful and multiplying—so that the baby is born hale and hearty. But if despite this he cannot direct his thoughts to heaven and still desires his wife, he must remind himself that he is but a putrid drop, that he will return to the earth which swarms with worms, and that his soul will have to stand in judgment before the King of Kings, the Holy One Blessed Be He. If he sees, however, that even this is to no avail, then he must recall what Solomon—the wisest of men, the king who had a thousand wives—once wrote in Proverbs: 'Give not your strength to women.' But what happens if even then he cannot subdue that filthy, unkosher *yetzer ha-ra* for his own kosher wife? Then he must recall what the Talmud says, what doctors say, what all good and pious people say. Too much sexual intercourse, they say, makes a man prematurely old. His eyes drip, his eyelashes and eyebrows fall out, he goes bald and loses his teeth. A man should ponder all this when he lusts for his own wife and it is not for the sake of a mitzva. But nevertheless, if none of these warnings works, if he finds his bones breaking from the base of his spine and lower down, and if he still has unclean thoughts no matter how much he distracts himself—well, then, there's nothing to be done; there's no way out; it's better to lust for his own wife than for another man's. There is even a smattering of mitzva in this. He is permitted to. Is it any wonder there are so many maniacs and melancholiacs among the Musarniks?"

"It's true that a Musarnik is a melancholiac. No matter how loudly he laughs, he laughs only with his voice, not with his heart or with his eyes!" Slava cried out, as if an old riddle had suddenly been solved for her. "It seems to me that one can be a Musarnik and yet not be pious; right?"

"One can even be a Musarnik and a heretic." Moshe Chayit sighed deeply. "A Musarnik is a man who considers himself sinful—hence he can't enjoy life."

"Your friend Chaikl doesn't talk about books, but he talks beautifully about nature. I think he *can* enjoy life and not feel sinful, even though he is a Musarnik."

"Chaikl Vilner a Musarnik? So far he's still a butchernik, a boy who grew up among the Vilna butcher shops. He's a fleshy sensualist. But since it's beneath his dignity to admit that, he talks about the forest and the birds, that poet! But the Navaredker scholars have planted in him their seed, so thorns will grow there indeed . . . You see, I too can talk in rhyme. I'm a poet too." Lohoysker laughed and added, "I've learned to speak in rhyme from the Musar books."

Slava felt a dull pain in her temple. Her eyes were veiled, like those of someone with insufficient sleep. She wanted to say something, but Lohoysker began talking again. He shook himself and chanted dolefully from another Musar book:

" 'My soul is a princess kidnaped from worlds supernal—and yet her celestial habitat she cannot forget; a tender princess she, who must languish in physicality, while recalling her nobility, sweet angels' lineage. She weeps, she wails, like forlorn widows in black veils. Alas and dole, how low she has fallen, my tender soul!' . . . That's the kind of ornate, flowery Hebrew on which your husband forced me to waste my childhood. I don't know whether Tsemakh Lomzher himself believed in the existence of the soul at that time or whether he believes in it today. But he demanded that I amuse myself with those broken verses of that mindless booklet, suitable for Sabbath-afternoon browsing after cholent—and with rhymes and fairy-tale imagery . . ."

"Stop it!" Slava cried weakly. "Why can't you forget that? After all, you've left the yeshiva and the Musar books!"

"I still haven't left. I wasted too much of my youth on the Musar books to be able to forget them. I burrow into them more than ever," Lohoysker mumbled, and in the lamplight patches of green, brown, and yellow flickered on his face. "And aside from the fact that Tsemakh dragged me away from home as a lad and tormented me here for many years, he recently pushed me in the presence of a crowd of people and kicked me out of the yeshiva because I wanted to save a boy from growing up to be a crippled Musarnik. I wrote and asked you to come here so that your husband would have no rest. But since we've met a few times, I've also begun to think about you, not just about myself and my quarrel with your husband. That's why I'm telling you how the Musar books poison the ones who read them, and that whoever is a Musarnik once is a Musarnik forever."

He gesticulated so much that his coat flew open, and Slava noticed that his trousers were frayed at the knees and patched in another spot. Now she understood why he always kept his coat on: he was ashamed of his tattered clothing. Perhaps he hated Tsemakh more for his frayed trousers than for the Musar books. To keep her visitor from discovering that she had noticed something amiss, Slava turned and faced the window. He gathered from her silence that his remarks no longer interested her.

Moshe Chayit rose unwillingly and buttoned his coat. "When I told you my opinion of your husband's fiery temperament"—Moshe Chayit didn't want to repeat his accusation that Tsemakh was an adventure seeker—"I was still under the impression that you came here to divorce him. Now I'm sorry I said that."

Pleased that he was leaving, Slava consoled him, "Don't regret speaking your mind about my husband. The Musarniks are strange people. They're always regretting something. They're always ashamed of something. Except Chaikl. He's not shy. He's not ashamed of anything . . ." Slava broke off because Lohoysker burst out laughing.

"Chaikl Vilner not shy? Why, he's ashamed to go into the yeshiva kitchen because he took a walk with you and because everybody knows he comes here often. I see you're distressed. Don't be distressed for his sake. He told me he still has a little bit of money saved up from Vilna, so he buys himself food. And anyway, he'll soon be going home for Passover. But I have nowhere to go—and what's more, today I lost my job tutoring Hebrew."

Standing in the doorway, Lohoysker continued, "Until today, my quarrel with the yeshiva was of no conern to my few employers. In fact, they even regarded it favorably because they're maskilim and opponents of the Musarniks. But now they've found out that I urged a woman to come here whose husband, a rabbi, had run away from her, and that I am seeing this woman. Now these congregants don't want me to teach their children any longer." Moshe Chayit Lohoysker said an abrupt "Good night" and left before the dumfounded Slava could utter a word.

11

ON THE WAY BACK from prayers, Tsemakh went to see his wife at the inn. He stood in the middle of the room holding his tallis bag under his arm and reproved her as if he were her father. "Make up your mind! It's either or! If you want a divorce, then at least wait until you're free. And if you don't, then you surely shouldn't behave licentiously." Unable to remain calm, Tsemakh waved his fists. "You she-devil! If you're not ashamed before God or man in Nareva, I can imagine how you behave in Lomzhe! I know what Moshe Chayit Lohoysker is up to! He wants to drive me out of Nareva. But what are *you* up to? What do *you* want of me? Tell me!"

I want you to go back home with me, she wanted to reply. But if she said this, he would leap back and perhaps even grimace in disgust. At the thought that he might look at her with disgust, Slava wanted to spit into his face. But she held back because that might please him, that

Musarnik. Slava sat down in a rocking chair, tucked her feet under her, and slowly rocked back and forth.

"Are you sure I behave even worse in Lomzhe? You can really take pride in your students if I can lead them astray just like that." She snapped her fingers lightly. When she had tucked her feet up, Slava's dress had flown above her knees, and now she looked at it and laughed, as if to show Tsemakh that she was more promiscuous than he thought. Suddenly she sprang to her feet and screamed so furiously that she could have been heard in the farthest room on the corridor. "If you could debase me by rolling in the Amdur mud at your first fiancée's door, I can do what I please in Lomzhe, and I can amuse myself with your students in Nareva as I see fit!"

Tsemakh could not comprehend why she considered his having begged Dvorele Namiot's father for forgiveness a humiliation and what connection it had with her present conduct. And look at how she described it: amusing herself with his students! Tsemakh strode out of her room, not even responding to her parting shout, "You're afraid I might tell you something even worse about my conduct. That's why you're running away, you coward!"

Other yeshiva scholars wanted to look at Reb Tsemakh's rebbetsin too. On their way to the kitchen or on their way back they would stop in front of the inn. Occasionally Slava saw a group of yeshiva youths gaping at her as she went out. She would smile amiably at them, and they would walk away quickly. Later the yeshiva boys discussed her and concluded, "She's no different from other women, absolutely no different." Nevertheless, Slava invaded their thoughts like the bird that invades another bird's nest. "What does Chaikl Vilner expect to gain by going to see her?" they asked one another. "Reb Tsemakh still hasn't divorced her, so she's still a married woman."

But Yankl Poltaver replied, "That's clear enough. Chaikl Vilner has desires even for a married woman." It was beneath Yankl's dignity to wander around outside the inn like his naïve friends. Entering Sulkes' home on Purim and presenting him with a broom instead of Purim sweets hadn't frightened him—would he now stand in awe of a Lomzhe woman? Yankl frowned and had an idea: He would go to see Reb Tsemakh's wife on the pretext of looking for someone in the inn—but meantime he'd have a look at her. And so he did, striding through the inn corridor as quickly as he strode through a train when he was traveling without a ticket and didn't want to meet the conductor. At noontime the guests were out in Nareva, and the inn was nearly empty. Yankl tried one door—locked; a second door—open, but the room was empty; a third door—on the mark! Chaikl was sitting in an easy chair talking to a woman facing the door.

"Vilner, the whole yeshiva's looking for you. You have a message from home."

The thought immediately flashed: Something's happened to my mother. Chaikl stood up, pale, hands trembling. Slava too looked anxiously at the newcomer. "What happened?" Chaikl finally managed to say.

Yankl didn't answer at once. He gazed impudently at Reb Tsemakh's wife and finally said, "Come into the hall and I'll tell you." There he whinnied into Chaikl's face, "Nothing's happened. I just wanted to have a look at your beauty. I see you're quite chummy with her." And before Chaikl could lunge at him with his fists up, Yankl Poltaver was already outside, leaving behind only his whinnying laughter, which swirled in the empty space like smoke from a locomotive.

When he looked at Reb Tsemakh's wife, Yankl's eyes had been as dazzled as a window reflecting a distant, hidden flash of sunlight. Yankl knew that he was handsome and that when he turned his burning, ardent eyes upon the rich girls in town, they were so flustered that they dropped whatever they had in their hands. Consequently, he had no doubt at all that he could have impressed the Lomzhe beauty if that Vilner ox hadn't been there. "I wouldn't say she's a run-of-the-mill woman. But if I went out into the world, I could get myself an even more stunning beauty," Yankl assured his friends.

At that time yeshiva youths who hadn't previously visited Lohoysker began to come to his room. The boys hoped to meet the beautiful rebbetsin there, or at least hear interesting things about her. This turn of events was helped by the end-of-term mood, in which the regular order of study in the yeshiva began crumbling. The deep mourning for Malariter had also undermined the desire to study, but thinking and whispering about the woman tore the youths away from their grief for the dead scholar, as a spring freshet tears itself away from the iron grip of the ice.

The pious Torah scholars were outraged at the yeshiva administration for permitting such a state of affairs. Reb Simkha Feinerman took advantage of the fact that he never gave Talmud lectures at the end of the term. He stayed at home and merely waited for the yeshiva youths to leave for their holiday. Zundl Konotoper, however, felt that the danger would not pass of its own accord. And Zundl, his small eyes glowing, found a partner, Asher-Leml Krasner, to help him save the yeshiva.

Asher-Leml Krasner, the kind, quiet youth with the untrimmed black beard, the saint of the yeshiva, had showed that he could also be talkative and mean. It was he who had gone to Lohoysker's employers and shouted in an otherworldly voice, "Your children's Hebrew teacher is going around with a married woman. Her husband is the penitent, Reb Tsemakh Atlas, who barely managed to get away from her. And that heretic Lohoysker brought this licentious woman here to make trouble for her husband and humiliate the yeshiva. If you don't fire the teacher, your children will grow up as lawless as he. You're helping to destroy the whole yeshiva, and you won't be forgiven for this to the end of time."

When the congregants dismissed Lohoysker, Asher-Leml Krasner and Zundl Konotoper had gone to the yeshiva principal's house and demanded, "Get the police to put Lohoysker out of Nareva."

"Are you mad?" Reb Simkha looked at his associates in fear, as though they had guessed the very thought that had long tormented him. "We brought Lohoysker from Russia, and he has no Polish passport. Do you want to hand him over to the gentiles? Is that permissible?"

But Asher-Leml Krasner, who had always been self-effacing, even in the presence of a precocious boy, now told the rosh yeshiva, "Not only is it permissible, but you *must* do it. If Lohoysker remains in Nareva, he'll lead others astray, as he's led Chaikl Vilner."

"It's all Reb Tsemakh Atlas' fault!" Zundl Konotoper roared. "If he hadn't settled down in Nareva, then his wife wouldn't have come here. He too should be told to leave Nareva at once."

Reb Simkha's blue eyes turned even bluer in cold rage at the scholars who were demanding that he fight with everyone. But since he wanted to think the matter over carefully before replying, he went to consult his wife.

The rebbetsin, a rather chubby woman with a large, puffy face and a heavy marriage wig over her own blond hair, lay in the bedroom, fully dressed, groaning. The damp weather just before Passover was aggravating her painful gout. Even during dry weather, when her gout was better, she went about grieving and angry because the Navaredker yeshiva in Nareva received a smaller subsistence than the yeshiva in Mir. "The Mir yeshiva has only one motto: *Git Mir.* Give me," the rebbetsin punned in Yiddish. She could outdo a dozen Navaredkers at acerbic remarks. Other rebbetsins feared her sharp tongue, and rabbis as well as her husband's pupils stood in awe of her. It was rumored that Nareva yeshiva politics were entirely in her hands. If a visitor saw that the Nareva rebbetsin was lukewarm toward him, he realized that the decree had been handed down and he was finished. The Nareva rosh yeshiva would have no time for him, no heart, no ear. Besides her husband, others too respected her "masculine mind" and her complete devotion to Torah. Ten youngsters always ate at her table, and she herself cooked for them all. She often slept in the same bed with her daughters because her house was full of guests. Nevertheless, she never complained that her home was a hotel; that she had no money for Sabbath provisions until Friday afternoon; or that she couldn't afford to go to the hot baths for the cure, while healthy rebbetsins spent whole summers on vacation. Reb Simkha therefore had great esteem for his wife and spoke to her as an equal, sometimes with a rabbinic quotation, and always cryptically. Now too he was brief.

"What's her strength? And what does she hope to accomplish?"

The rebbetsin understood that her husband was asking what sort of power the Lomzher's wife had that yeshiva students were losing their heads over her, and why she had dragged Vilner and Lohoysker into her net. Did she intend to divorce her husband and marry one of those two recalcitrant youths? The rebbetsin answered Reb Simkha's first question with an interpretation from the Balak portion of the Pentateuch:

"The great God-fearing generation that made the Exodus from Egypt, crossed the Red Sea, and was present at the Revelation at Mount Sinai was nevertheless unable to withstand the temptation of Moab's daughters." And she replied to Reb Simkha's second question by saying, "The Lomzhe woman no more intends to take Vilner or Lohoysker as a husband than you intend to take them as sons-in-law. It looks as if Reb Tsemakh's wife is just doing this as a way of forcing her husband to return home."

"But is that the way to go about it?" Reb Simkha wondered.

Reb Simkha's rebbetsin had disliked Tsemakh since the time he was a group leader in Nareva and hadn't kowtowed to her husband. In addition, the rebbetsin, who was so independent that she wore her own hair under her heavy marriage wig, was by nature a happy woman and sided with women. But the gout pains kept her from speaking at length.

"From what I've heard about Lomzher's wife, I understand that she's a clever woman. For reasons I don't know, she doesn't want to separate from him. She's not a saint, and since she has no other way of persuading him to come home, she's enticing the two youths." The rebbetsin sat up and adjusted her wig as if preparing to light Sabbath candles. "Her remaining in Nareva is more dangerous to your daughters than to your students. Your daughters like the fact that Lomzher's wife doesn't care what anybody thinks of her, and they're whispering about her in their little room."

Reb Simkha retreated to the door and stared silently at his wife. Then he returned to the library where Konotoper and Krasner were waiting for him. "Tell Reb Tsemakh to come to see me immediately," he told them.

12

"YOU MUST LEAVE Nareva as soon as possible," Reb Simkha said, approaching the penitent as he entered.

"I know. The question is where I ought to go."

"My rebbetsin, may she live and be well, understands the ways of the world very well," Reb Simkha said quickly, not looking at

Tsemakh. "She feels that your wife means no harm, that she is free of sin. My rebbetsin thinks this is her way of forcing you to go back home."

Tsemakh listened, looking down at his hands as if he didn't recognize them. "If she means no harm, then the injustice is all the greater. Another woman would have summoned her husband to a rabbi or to arbitration and not behaved in such a fashion."

The rosh yeshiva wanted to shout out: But you wanted a worldly woman! To contain his outburst, Reb Simkha looked at a bookshelf for a moment and then paced back and forth in the room, hands behind his back as if to bind his rage.

"I never interfere in marital matters. That's why I haven't offered my opinion about your quarrel with your wife. Nor do I think it's fitting to repeat what others are saying. But since things have come this far, I must say that last winter, when I was in Vilna for the Yeshiva Council meeting, Reb Avraham-Shaye Kosover visited me. He came to inquire about Chaikl Vilner—Vilner is certainly cut out to be a pupil of the author of *The Vision of Avraham*! . . . Well, we began talking, and we also spoke about you. Reb Avraham-Shaye leaped up and said he had never heard of a man abandoning a living wife because of a dead fiancée, and what's more, considering that the proper way to repent."

Reb Simkha saw that Reb Tsemakh was sitting with his head lowered; he bent over him and said quietly, "Please forgive me. I don't want to cause you anguish. But in any case, it's no coincidence that since you've returned to Nareva, we have had more trouble—especially with your former students—than we've ever had before. That seems to be hinting at something."

"I've understood that hint for a long time." Tsemakh raised his head. "And, as if I haven't had enough punishment already, I see in my pupils, as if in a mirror, that my path in life was crooked. But my marriage too is a part of this false and crooked way. My wife and I are incompatible."

"Well, you know best, Reb Tsemakh. I've only reported what Reb Avraham-Shaye said. I can't decide what you ought to do. And especially now I can't put my mind to it because of the trouble Lohoysker is giving us. There are fine and upright youths in the yeshiva who feel that we should tell the police that Lohoysker is a

Russian without a Polish passport and that the yeshiva has no responsibility for him because he's become a Communist. But I won't permit this because I fear a desecration of God's name and because, in spite of everything, I feel sorry for him. Reb Tsemakh, help us get rid of him. You brought him from Russia, and his main contention is with you. Try to persuade him to leave Nareva peaceably. Even though we're short of money, we'll give him as much as he asks—as long as he leaves."

Reb Simkha's plea was so heart-rending that Tsemakh wanted to tear his lapel in mourning at the miserable luck that always wrought havoc upon himself and those around him.

At night in bed, between sleep and wakefulness, Tsemakh thought: If I don't go home, where shall I go? Could I start another small yeshiva? Even if I wanted to, the Nareva rosh yeshiva wouldn't give me an assistant. Tsemakh dozed off for a while—and saw himself sitting in the women's gallery of the Cold Shul in Valkenik. He was swaying in a corner over a holy text, thinking of Reb Avraham-Shaye's statement that he must not deliver Musar talks to the students because belief in God didn't emanate from his words. Tsemakh knew he was in a bed in Nareva, yet he saw himself in the Valkenik women's gallery, glancing up from his book at his prayer stand and looking through the grating into the men's shul. He knew that the Thirteen Articles of Faith were hanging on a cardboard poster on a pillar by the pulpit. Suddenly he saw Henekh Malariter in the men's shul. Wearing a shroud, hands clinging to the grating of the little window, he screamed open-mouthed, as if he had raised his head out of water, but his screams were inaudible. Tsemakh too wanted to scream but could not. He sensed that the dead man was asking to be dug out of his grave because he had been buried alive. Soon Malariter would ask if his friend Daniel Homler was going to marry the landlady's daughter in his place. Suddenly the dead man burst into laughter and made strange faces, like a deaf mute trying to speak. "When I was in your group, you used to torment me, asking how I stood in the service of God. Now I ask you: Do you believe in a Creator of the Universe?" Then he plunged down the other side of the grating as if into an abyss.

Tsemakh awoke with a choked cry. He lay there without moving, feeling his heart within him numb as ice, like a full moon at midnight in a cloudless, cold, and distant sky. From one side of his forehead to the other swung the pendulum of a clock—a grandfather clock with Hebrew letters for numerals that had hung in his dead Aunt Tsertele's house. The pendulum swung to and fro, and before Tsemakh's eyes swam the beth medreshes of Krinik, Sokolke, Ostrolenke—villages he had wandered to before he returned to Nareva. Eyes closed, he saw cold shuls and study houses with rows of prayer stands lined up in front of empty benches—like wooden tombstones erected for dead worshipers; and in every holy place, he saw himself pressed into a corner studying a text. In every village there were a few men and elderly women who provided him with a bed and food. He was always alone in the beth medresh, and his silence encompassed him like a cloud that kept others away.

But the local rabbis and yeshiva people knew who he was, and gradually the congregants too would discover that the recluse was a Navaredker Musarnik who had become a penitent. Then he would leave for another village, fearing that his repentance would be less efficacious if people knew why he had come. He grew accustomed to pacing around in an empty beth medresh, feverishly recalling how he had rolled in the Amdur mud and wept over Dvorele Namiot's grave, and how her father had stepped over him. Finally he realized that he was enjoying these somber memories, deriving a sickly pleasure from his self-torment. So he had put down his wanderer's staff and returned to Nareva to try to find some satisfaction in his former pupils, by now grown up.

The pendulum between Tsemakh's temples swung again and brought a market place with stalls and peasant carters before his closed eyes. A bearded Jew in a long gaberdine was putting a purse into his rear pocket and smiling with pleasure. Tsemakh remembered passing the Ostrolenke market place and seeing this unknown Jew, who was delighted because he had managed to make a profit. Tsemakh was delighted too. Then he stopped, amazed at himself. After all, he had always treated people who sought the pleasures of this world with contempt; he had mocked little merchants who chased after profits. For the first time, he had enjoyed a businessman's success, and he thought that this was more in line with Reb Avraham-Shaye Kosover's way of thinking . . .

Tsemakh quickly sat up in bed, and the pendulum in his temples stopped swaying. This was the second time Reb Avraham-Shaye had intervened in his life. When Tsemakh had to leave Valkenik, Reb Avraham-Shaye had castigated him for breaking his first engagement in Amdur. Now that he had to leave Nareva, the rosh yeshiva had informed him that the author of *The Vision of Avraham* was once again angry with him, this time for abandoning his wife. Tsemakh felt tears rolling down his face and hanging on his mustache at the corners of his mouth. His former teacher Reb Yosef-Yoizl Hurwitz of Navaredok had been right. The worst sentence a man could receive was that he could not make himself over. All his life he had persuaded himself and others that a man can change and must change. But in fact he had hardly changed at all. As far back as he could remember, he had been the same, always the same. . . .

The next morning Slava sat in Tsemakh's room, worried. Tsemakh lay in bed ill. He felt no pain and had no fever, but could not get up. He had sent the landlady to summon his wife. His pale, haggard face with its silvering black beard and its sheen of gentle sadness looked like a black-and-white-striped tallis.

"When I returned to Lomzhe from Valkenik, I think I told you that my biggest opponent in Valkenik was Reb Avraham-Shaye Kosover, a saintly gaon who spends his summers there. He is also known as the author of *The Vision of Avraham*. He was the man who ordered me sent away from the Valkenik yeshiva. Now I admit that he was right. So with God's help, as soon as I'm better, I'll go to see him in Vilna—and if he advises me to return to you in Lomzhe, I will do that. Meanwhile, go back home. Leave as soon as you can. Go today if you can manage it."

"Doesn't your heart tell you what to do?" A tremulous smile flitted over Slava's face, from her eyes to her lips and back, like a bird with nowhere to light. "Must you consult someone else about whether you should return to your wife?"

"I won't ask him if I'm permitted to live with you, even though I should ask him that too," he murmured, an angry wrinkle forming between his heavy brows. Slava's tear-filled eyes immediately ignited with sparks of rage. But she restrained herself and let him continue. "I'll ask him if, after so many years of toiling for Torah, I should end up as a shopkeeper. In the meantime, go home."

"You can ask *me* if you're permitted to live with me—I know the answer better than your saintly gaon. But if he advises you to become a rabbi or a rosh yeshiva, I won't stand in your way. I will not become a rebbetsin. But I won't go back to Lomzhe now. I'm going with you to Vilna and to Lomzhe from there, either with you or with a divorce."

Slava spoke slowly, and Tsemakh, after lengthy deliberation, answered slowly too.

"Fine; come to Vilna with me if you wish. I can't leave this place until I persuade Lohoysker to leave too. He's destroying the yeshiva, and I'm responsible because I brought him here. The yeshiva is prepared to give him as much money as he needs if he'll only go."

"He'll do exactly the opposite of what you ask him to, but if I talk with him, I can persuade him," Slava said.

She saw Tsemakh gazing at her with a calm, searching glance. A flush came over her cheeks. She was not insulted that he had suspicions about her and his student; she was insulted that his suspicions didn't prompt envy or rage. He merely expressed a silent regret and pious anxiety about whether, according to Jewish law, he could continue to live with her. Why did she love him? She had once loved him for the very traits that had destroyed their marriage—his courage and intransigence. But why did she love him now? Perhaps because he could suffer so deeply and still be the same obstinate Musarnik. Who could tell? If he hadn't been so crazy, perhaps she would never have loved him, or would have divorced him long ago.

13

"WHAT DO YOU THINK, Chaikl?" the beautiful rebbetsin wanted to know. "Will your teacher in Vilna advise my husband to become a yeshiva principal again? Or will he tell him to return home?"

"If I know Reb Avraham-Shaye, he'll tell your husband to go home with you," Chaikl answered glumly.

Slava's eyes lit up; a feeling of well-being coursed through her. She pressed the infatuated youth to her and caressed and calmed him as if she were an older sister. "Don't be so downhearted. I'm much older than you. One day you'll love women and women will love you."

But Chaikl extricated himself from her embrace. "I'm not thinking of that. Not of that at all. Now Reb Avraham-Shaye will find out everything!" he cried as he fled from the hotel room.

After a while Slava guessed what the youth meant. He's a child, she thought, shrugging. A youngster. He had apparently thought she would stay here forever and that he would be near her. A spring breeze came through an open window, billowing the curtain, whispering tidings of hope for a renewed family life. But Slava was not happy. Even if Tsemakh no longer tried to make the world over, he wouldn't become a worldly man, and she would have to adjust to him.

In the evening Moshe Chayit Lohoysker came and opened the conversation with a sarcastic gibe: "I hear the Musarnik Reb Tsemakh Atlas is going advice hunting like a Hasid to a Vilna rabbi and that you're going with him." A tuft of wiry hair stood out on his wrinkled and perspiring brow. Behind his glasses his eyes stared as if from a dark cellar. Lohoysker's heart obviously trembled within him; nevertheless, he attempted to speak gaily and mockingly.

"Chaikl Vilner is beside himself at your leaving, so he's going to Vilna too. Running after you."

"He's not running after me. He's going home for Passover," Slava replied. "Chaikl is depressed because he's suddenly afraid—embarrassed—that his teacher in Vilna may find out that he has visited me here and talked with me."

"Is that why he's so befuddled? He wouldn't tell me the reason." Lohoysker laughed and felt a wave of real joy. "I'm glad you understand that Vilner doesn't really have any deep feelings for you. I didn't want to tell you this before you realized it yourself, so that you wouldn't think I'm jealous of him. He likes you the way he likes the forest and the birds—so that he can write poems about you. Perhaps he likes you as a woman too, but it's not love from the heart."

I shouldn't have played with him, Slava thought, looking at the overwrought Lohoysker. As she withdrew from him in her thoughts, her face too seemed to recede. The table lamp cast a gold-red orb of shimmering light between them; it deepened the stillness in the room and the earnestness of what she said. "It hurts me that my husband took you away from your parents in Russia and that you've been living in misery all these years. And it hurts me even more that because of me you lost your few lessons in Nareva. I'm prepared to help you get established wherever you choose to go."

Moshe Chayit shuddered, Slava saw, because he, like Chaikl, didn't want to leave her. "I have an idea! Come to Vilna too," she said, and immediately regretted her words. Her voice became dry. "I don't want to fool you. I love my husband. And if the rabbi whose opinion Tsemakh respects tells him to return to Lomzhe and he obeys, for my part I'll try to forget the wrongs Tsemakh has done me."

"And what—what if the rabbi in Vilna doesn't tell your husband to go back to Lomzhe with you?" Moshe Chayit stammered pathetically, eyes lowered. "What will happen if you don't make peace with your husband?"

Slava was ashamed that she had to be crafty and guess how her husband would act upon the advice of a strange Jew. But she didn't have the heart to hurt the youth by telling him that she wouldn't stay with him no matter what Tsemakh did. So she remained silent, and Moshe Chayit's hopes revived.

"I'm not so sure that your husband's adviser in Vilna will order him to return to Lomzhe with you." From her expression he realized that Slava was keeping something from him, and he immediately became suspicious. "Was it your husband who told you to talk me into leaving Nareva?"

"My husband didn't tell me to do anything. It was *I* who told *him* that I would talk with you. The yeshiva wants to give you as much money as you need to leave and settle down somewhere else. Is it sensible for you to stay in Nareva and suffer just to spite the yeshiva?"

Moshe Chayit had waited impatiently for her to say this. Now he flared up arrogantly. "I won't stay in this rotten town under any circumstances. I have nothing against my yeshiva friends. They too regret the years they've wasted."

Slava listened to Moshe Chayit fantasizing, but she didn't say a word. She wasn't deceiving him, she thought. All his love for her stemmed from his hatred for Tsemakh. The minute he settled down somewhere, his hatred for Tsemakh would vanish along with his imagined love for her.

A week before Passover, the rosh yeshiva's house was full of students come to bid him farewell. The youths were dressed in their Sabbath suits, with white collars and ties. They wore their hats tilted modishly to the side or pushed back as though to display the foreheads that had absorbed so much Torah study.

When one of these yeshiva students—perhaps one who had plowed through an entire Talmudic tractate that term—returned to his village for the holiday, the local rabbi would become alarmed: the scholar might initiate a Talmudic dispute with him and discover that the rabbi had forgotten all his Torah. Such a youth would wander about in the local beth medresh stiff-backed and not say a word to anyone. Occasionally he would glance at the wall clock and at his wrist watch to check the time and then stare out the window as if he had to be somewhere at a certain hour. Having nowhere to go, he would throw a contemptuous sidelong glance at a congregant studying a text. The old congregant would remember the young scholar not only from the time he was a little brat, but from the time he was crawling on all fours. Nevertheless, out of love for Torah and respect for Talmud scholars, the old man would stand up to honor the young ben Torah, as if in the presence of one of the shining lights of the generation.

In Nareva, however, among their friends in Reb Simkha Feinerman's house, the scholars were having a good time; they laughed temperately with the corners of their mouths and enjoyed their conversations as they waited for the rosh yeshiva to escort one student from his library and summon another. But now, when Reb Simkha left his study and entered the crowded waiting room, he noticed the subdued astonishment on their faces, and soon he saw the cause of it. Moshe Chayit Lohoysker approached from a corner of the room and spoke without the slightest trace of deference. "I've come to say good-bye too. I'm leaving Nareva." Lohoysker strode into the rosh yeshiva's study, and Reb Simkha followed him as if captive to his impertinence.

"I've heard you're prepared to give me as much money as I want, as long as I leave Nareva. So give me three hundred zlotys—all right, let's make it two hundred and fifty—to buy some clothes and support myself until I start earning money. But I want it now. I can't wait."

Moshe Chayit's effort to be so extremely impudent warned Reb Simkha to give in immediately; the heretic might still change his mind. The yeshiva principal asked him to wait and went into the kitchen to his rebbetsin. "Give me all the money I gave you for

Passover. We're getting rid of Lohoysker." The rebbetsin looked at her husband and liked the idea of jeopardizing the Passover in favor of saving the yeshiva. With the paper money in his hand, Reb Simkha went to his students in the waiting room.

"Friends, we're getting rid of Lohoysker. I've taken from the rebbetsin all the money she had for Passover. Now I want every one of you to give me a share of your travel money. If I can't repay you, then you'll spend the holiday in Nareva, and we'll all starve together."

None of the students hesitated. Everyone immediately took out his purse. Hands trembling, Reb Simkha asked the students to contribute enough to make the total two hundred and fifty zlotys and not a penny less.

In the library Moshe Chayit felt that the veins in his temple were swelling to the bursting point. Where can I go? I'm in a world full of strangers, he thought. How can I be sure that Slava will look at me even if she does divorce her husband? After all, she didn't promise me anything. Nothing at all.

Reb Simkha Feinerman returned holding the money, and Lohoysker burst out laughing even more brazenly. He greedily seized the handful of paper, counted it, and stuffed it into his pocket. "Two hundred and fifty zlotys for seven years down the drain," he rasped as he left the study.

Lohoysker knew he was behaving crudely and vulgarly. He wanted to return to Reb Simkha, give back the money, and burst into tears. But this would only prompt the rabbi to give vent to his hatred and contempt, so Lohoysker marched through the rooms with a resounding tread, gazing derisively at the students. The latter turned their heads, looking down at their fingers and at their shoes to see if they were properly shined in honor of the journey. The students were careful not to glance at him. The main thing was for him to leave, for them to be rid of him.

At the doorway Moshe Chayit bumped into Chaikl Vilner. "I'm going to Vilna too," Lohoysker sang out for the Musarniks to hear and remember that just as he hadn't left Vilner alone in Nareva, he wouldn't let up now until he had turned him into a spiteful corrupter like himself.

Although Lohoysker's announcement surprised Chaikl, he didn't have time to ponder it, because the yeshiva students turned away from him too. The chilly reception made his throat constrict. He knew that it would be proper to wait for the rosh yeshiva to summon him, but to avoid remaining in such hostile company, he knocked on the door of the rabbi's study and went in.

Reb Simkha Feinerman was standing at the window to see if Lohoysker had gone. When he turned and saw Vilner, he thought: New troubles! But Chaikl, looking guilty, mumbled politely, "I'm leaving, and I've come to say good-bye."

"And when are you returning?"

From Chaikl's amazed and happy expression Reb Simkha realized that he had asked the question automatically, as was his custom with every yeshiva student who came to say good-bye.

"I understand that you want to stay at home next term and study with Reb Avraham-Shaye again. I agree; that would be better."

Occasionally Reb Simkha Feinerman would tell even a younger student about his troubles in order to win him over. It was especially appropriate now, since Vilner saw Reb Avraham-Shaye often. All the more reason, then, to be extremely careful, Reb Simkha thought, and not let him leave Nareva in an angry mood. Reb Simkha began pouring out his sorrow and bitterness at Lohoysker. "He spent seven years here, God help us. How much suffering he has caused us! And now that he's leaving, he's still our blood enemy. And what about you, Vilner? Are you our enemy too? Have we done you any harm?"

"An enemy? I came here to express my gratitude," Chaikl stammered. He was so touched by the rosh yeshiva's confiding his anguish to him that he wanted to add that he begged Reb Simkha's pardon for having grieved the administration. But Reb Simkha didn't let Vilner say a word, lest he suddenly get the idea of asking permission to come back next term. His arm around Vilner's shoulders, the principal escorted him—to the astonishment of all the students—out of the study and through the dining room and entranceway to the door. There he shook hands with Chaikl and blessed him. "May it be the will of the Almighty that you not forget what you have learned here with us."

14

REB AVRAHAM-SHAYE KOSOVER and Reb Tsemakh Atlas talked for a long time in the side room of the Poplaver beth medresh. Tsemakh stood in the middle of the room, both hands on the pulpit table. Reb Avraham-Shaye sat opposite him on the bench by the eastern wall. "In which holy text is it written," he said, "that being a rabbi or a yeshiva principal is nobler than being a businessman? Why put the question in such a derisive manner as to say that after so many years of toiling for Torah, you'll end up being a shopkeeper? You're not ending your link with Torah, and it's not your end. The attitude that greatness and insignificance depends on the position one holds is a thoroughly false one. It's a completely worldly criterion, totally counter to the spirit of the Torah. Whoever is imbued with the Creator of the Universe also feels His presence when he is in the market place and in the shop. His thoughts are celestial, even though the people around aren't aware of this—and shouldn't be. After morning prayers he studies a chapter of the Mishna with fellow congregants and a page of the Talmud by himself. And if he has no more time, he closes the text without a moan and goes to attend to his business. He sends his children to cheder and sits down to breakfast. He stays in the store and gives honest measure and honest weight. When he has time, he returns to the beth medresh and to the Torah. People describe him as a quiet man, and he aspires to be no more than that. And if he happens to be a great man, his greatness is a secret between himself and the Master of the Universe. A true Torah scholar sighs at having to be a rabbi or a rosh yeshiva. Reb Akiva Eiger once asked a student of his, a village rabbi, to help him get a job as a children's teacher, for he no longer wished to be the Poyzner rabbi. Hence, if a man is destined to lead a quiet life in a secluded corner, he should thank God for the privilege."

Hands folded on his chest, Reb Avraham-Shaye paced back and forth in the beth medresh and said in an anguished voice, "Even if I knew that your request to be a rosh yeshiva once more stemmed from your concern for the Torah itself—and respect for Torah *is* diminishing of late—even if I knew that you would succeed as Reb Chaim Volozhiner and Chasam Sofer did, I'd still advise you to return home and become a shopkeeper. Those two scholars didn't have to leave their rebbetsins to become yeshiva principals and rabbis. What good can come of your studying Torah and Musar with others when, by doing that, you are ruining your wife's life? She must be a noble woman if she's suffered so long and still refuses to part from you."

"It's her stubbornness," Tsemakh said.

"I don't believe it." Reb Avraham-Shaye laughed curtly, as he did when he saw that commentators had constructed a mountain of pilpul on a Talmudic passage whose difficulty stemmed from a printer's error. "I just don't believe that an intelligent woman from a well-to-do home would really suffer just for the sake of prevailing. I'd sooner believe that she's suffering because she's so deeply committed—that itself is a sign of a noble woman. You maintain that she should accept a divorce. But if she did accept it, would this repair her broken life? And carrying the knowledge that you had destroyed her life, would you still hope to succeed with students?" Exhausted from his pacing, Reb Avraham-Shaye sat down, propped both his elbows on his prayer stand, and pressed his fingers to his temples.

"Of course I realize that being a recluse and having nothing at all to do with the world is easier than being a shopkeeper, a merchant, an artisan—and at the same time having to remain estranged from the world. But the way of the Torah is indeed the difficult one of participating with everyone in the affairs of the world while still remaining a recluse in your mind and heart."

"To do that one would have to stop telling everyone the truth." Tsemakh's eyes glittered like dying sparks in ashes.

"Of course you would!" Reb Avraham-Shaye shouted impatiently from the opposite bench. "Except for certain extraordinary instances when one must not look on and keep silent, we shouldn't tell another person anything about his character and behavior until he asks us and until we're certain that he has asked the question so as to improve his character and behavior. Even then, we shouldn't tell him anything beyond his understanding and his ability to change."

The beadle poked his head into the side room with the summons to the Afternoon Service. With the beginning of warm weather, the minyan prayed in the large beth medresh. The worshipers were fish dealers from the nearby market, several merchants, and a few artisans. The *baal tefilla* at the lectern rushed through the prayers, and at the end of the service, the worshipers left quickly, all in a holiday rush. Reb Avraham-Shaye remained alone in his corner by the eastern wall, immersed in the Silent Devotion, and Tsemakh, standing behind the pulpit, observed him and thought: He lives the kind of unobtrusive life that he advises others to live. He prays and studies among poor, plain Jews who may esteem his noble deportment but not his Torah scholarship.

The long row of windows in the beth medresh faced a huge field set among little hills that contained two round fish ponds. The sun's rays played on the water as in a pair of smiling, tear-filled eyes. On the other side of the valley stood a tall white church flanked by two taller towers. Hands behind his back, Tsemakh looked out the window and thought of Chaikl Vilner, who had probably lost much time from Torah studies because of those two ponds. Chaikl Vilner had an intense feeling for beauty. But Reb Avraham-Shaye apparently felt that even in this big empty beth medresh one could maintain discipline over a student by studying Talmud and commentaries with him. Similarly, he thought that by being a busy shopkeeper, a person could keep his inner being removed from the world.

Reb Avraham-Shaye came away from the eastern wall with a ruddy, refreshed face, as if the prayers had renewed his strength. He put on his coat, picked up his cane, and went to stand with Tsemakh behind the pulpit. "The Nareva principal wrote me about some new Torah interpretations and incidentally noted that Chaikl Vilner has been behaving improperly. What did he mean by 'improperly'? Hasn't he been studying?"

Tsemakh looked down at his beard for a long time before he replied. "Earlier, when we were talking about my students in Nareva, I told you about Lohoysker the rabbi's son who's gone astray. Chaikl Vilner made friends with him. Then something even worse occurred. When my wife came to Nareva, Chaikl took an immoderate fancy to her. Apparently he was ashamed of this before his friends; anyway, he stopped coming to the yeshiva. She made friends with Vilner and Lohoysker to force me to return to Lomzhe with her. If you hadn't had Reb Simkha's letter and asked me about it, I'd never have been able to bring myself to tell you this."

"Has Chaikl already left Nareva?" Reb Avraham-Shaye asked again after a long, portentous silence.

"He came back to Vilna with Lohoysker. The yeshiva gave Lohoysker money to leave." Tsemakh too fell silent for a while. "On second thought, perhaps it's better that you know everything. You said before that my wife is a noble woman. Now you'll be able to judge her better. To tell the truth, I must add that I have no reason to suspect more than I've told you—that by chatting in the hotel room and on the street with these two students, she was trying to make me go back to Lomzhe with her."

"Then don't mention it or even think of it," Reb Avraham-Shaye cut in sharply. With bent back, he approached the door, tapping his cane ahead of him, as if he had become old during these few minutes. Before descending the steps, he addressed the handle of his cane: "Chaikl has a great imagination, and every impossible thing can become real for him. I have to admit that in our dispute about Chaikl in Valkenik you were right, not I. He should have studied in a yeshiva. That's why I persuaded him to go to Nareva. But it turns out that I realized my mistake too late."

Outside, Reb Avraham-Shaye asked his visitor to come home with him, but his uneasiness grew from minute to minute. He wanted to say something, but restrained himself until they approached his house.

"My wife is in a bad mood today. Our cloth shop has been robbed," he said. And as if expecting the shock this would be to his escort, he added with an anguished smile, "Quite simple. During the night someone cut a hole in the wall of the courtyard and carried off all the merchandise. So don't be alarmed if my wife starts complaining."

All the gloom of a shop with neither merchandise nor customers was reflected in the rebbetsin's big black eyes. The few pieces of cloth wrapped around hard cardboard accentuated the emptiness of the bare shelves. Of late, Yudis had stopped admonishing her husband's guests not to exhaust him. Now she looked forward to guests so as to unburden her heart. Her present visitor pleased her because of his appearance and his height. Yudis liked a rabbi who cut a manly figure, not one who was stooped or had a wispy beard.

"Do you have something to eat?" Reb Avraham-Shaye asked softly.

"I do; I do," his wife grumbled, coming out from behind the counter. "I wish the wholesalers a Passover like mine!"

Reb Avraham-Shaye went quickly into the other room to avoid hearing her curses. He stepped into the little kitchen behind the large wardrobe and returned at once with washed hands. Sitting on the sofa, he muttered the blessing over a piece of dry white bread. The rebbetsin brought two soft-boiled eggs on a tray and once again looked at the newcomer.

"Why don't you introduce me to your guest? I'm human too, and people should also say how do you do to me," she said angrily.

Reb Avraham-Shaye choked as he swallowed and replied defensively, "You're right; you're absolutely right. I forgot. Our visitor is the former Valkenik rosh yeshiva and, most recently, a recluse in the Nareva yeshiva."

"If he's a recluse, his wife can't possibly have a good life with him." Yudis turned from the visitor and shouted at her husband, "Eat! Why aren't you eating?"

Reb Avraham-Shaye looked faint from her screams and pleaded with her, "But I am eating. I can't eat more than one egg. You eat the other one."

Yudis brought her husband a bowl of cold rice with milk and Reb Tsemakh an apple on a plate, which she put on the table with a bang. "Eat an apple. You won't eat my head off by doing it!" she ordered, and talked on in her loud, masculine voice. "I've had three kinds of slaughterers and skinners on my back—let them all go to hell! The first is the landlord who skinned me for the apartment. Do you call this an apartment? A chicken coop, that's what it is! And then the Polish government skinned me with taxes. The taxes are outrageous! But worst of all are the wholesalers. They suck the marrow from my bones. They made me a pauper with their high prices even before the robbery. And I had to shut up because, after all, they gave me the goods on credit—may God give them a new soul and throw the old one to the dogs! After the robbery, the textile merchants said they wanted to strike a bargain with me—may they be struck with a pain in the side. They said I should pay them a third less than I owe them for the stolen cloth and they'd call it quits. I told them, 'I don't want to put other people's money in my pockets. No deals, no bargains. Just give me new merchandise on credit, and little by little I'll also pay off my old debt.' But those wholesalers are a bunch of connivers, typical Vilna pickpockets. They think I'm like them; they think I want to fool them. 'After all, your husband is a rabbi,' they tell me. 'So first pay your old debts before you make new ones.' For the least trifle they mention my husband the rabbi—meaning that I have to be better than anyone else."

"She has complaints against everyone except the thieves," Reb Avraham-Shaye said, unable to restrain his laughter. This prompted an even greater outburst from his wife.

"It's your fault!" She placed her right finger on her left palm and began to enumerate: "You leave for shul in the morning while I'm still sleeping like the dead, exhausted by our troubles. The thieves took note of the time you leave and broke through the wall into the store. If you didn't go to shul so early, nothing would have happened." The rebbetsin turned to the visitor. "My husband tells me to close the shop to cut my losses. Suppose I do? What should I do then? Sit with my hands folded? My enemies the wholesalers won't live to see that day!"

The door opened, and a customer entered. Yudis dashed into the shop and slammed the glass-paneled door behind her so forcefully that the panes shook.

"When she's angry with the wholesalers, she slams the door," Reb Avraham-Shaye said, irritated, then shut his eyes and immersed himself in the Grace After Meals. Tsemakh looked at him and recalled that during their argument in Valkenik, Reb Avraham-Shaye had moaned in his presence, ". . . lifelong suffering . . . I'm still suffering—but I'm not sorry that I didn't humiliate a Jewish girl, and I don't regret marrying her." That was how a quiet man whose path in life was a quiet one lived and suffered.

Busy with her one customer, the rebbetsin paid no attention to her husband and his guest, who slipped through the store on their way out. After going down Zaretche Hill, Reb Avraham-Shaye stopped on the corner of Poplaver Street.

"The theft took place in the morning, even before I was out of bed, and I heard the footsteps in the store . . . You're amazed that I kept still. But if I'd cried out, the intruders would have broken into our room with their axes and killed us, or at the very least tied us up and taken our Sabbath candlesticks. So I kept silent."

And he keeps on being silent! Tsemakh thought, escorting Reb Avraham-Shaye back to the Poplaver beth medresh. At the entrance Reb Avraham-Shaye stopped again.

"At first I thought of inviting you and your wife to my house to bid you farewell before you return home. But after my wife's thunder and lightning today, I'm not sure she'd control herself even in your wife's presence. It won't set a good example if your wife sees how loudly a wife can shout at her husband," Reb Avraham-Shaye joked, his cheeks red with shame. "I'll come to your inn about noon tomorrow to say good-bye. Just tell me how to get there."

15

HUSBAND AND WIFE LIVED separately in the same hotel. Moshe Chayit Lohoysker was there in a tiny room. This astonished and upset Tsemakh, but Slava reminded him with a spiteful little smile, "This is the third inn in the third town since I've been chasing after you. Valkenik. Nareva. Vilna. And you're living here in your own private room as though you weren't my husband at all. Why shouldn't Lohoysker stay here? Too bad Chaikl Vilner isn't along—it would be much jollier. Why do you suppose Chaikl hasn't shown up? Is he hiding behind his mother's apron? Or is he afraid his teacher might give him a spanking?"

Every day Slava felt more confident that her wishes would prevail. And because she stopped worrying about her prospects for the future, she grew increasingly irritated at Tsemakh for consulting a stranger about how to behave toward his own wife. Therefore, she kept laughing and joking so as not to start hating him. But when he told her about his talk with Reb Avraham-Shaye, she sat stunned for a long time. "Is that what he said? And he doesn't think it's just stubbornness on my part? He said that I'm doing it because I'm deeply committed? Is that what he really said? In that case he's a better man than you, and smarter too."

"Then will you wear a kerchief when he comes?" Tsemakh asked.

"Yes, out of respect for him, not you. And I'll wear my long-sleeved black silk blouse and my brooch with the golden tassels," Slava replied.

But Tsemakh was upset again: My surroundings are so foreign to her that she doesn't even realize that a man like Reb Avraham-Shaye doesn't look at another woman's clothing.

Reb Avraham-Shaye came the following day at noon, as promised. He knocked on Tsemakh's room and then entered, carrying his cane and a large tome. A gentle smile hovered behind his mustache as he scrutinized Slava through his spectacles. Still in his coat and cane in hand, he sat down at the table and placed the volume on it.

"I've brought you a gift—my commentary on the *Code of Law*. When you have time, look into it." He addressed Tsemakh but didn't remove his quiet, penetrating glance from Slava. "There is a big yeshiva in Lomzhe. You used to study there, didn't you, Reb Tsemakh?"

"No," Tsemakh murmured. He looked embarrassed and surprised at himself. Reb Avraham-Shaye laughed—in his youth Reb Tsemakh Atlas, the founder of yeshivas, had not set foot in the yeshiva at Lomzhe, where he was born and had married.

"Such is man's nature." Reb Avraham-Shaye smiled at the woman as though in apology for her suffering. "A man leaves his house by the front door to search for what he lacks. He searches far and wide, to the farthest corners of the earth. Years later he returns home, to the back door, bent, begging to be let in, only to discover that what he sought for years in far-off places was waiting for him in his own home."

Slava's eyes became moist and her lips dry. A minute later she wanted to laugh at the way she was sitting with the pious expression of a young rebbetsin the first Friday night after her wedding. She cocked her head and in a tone that was somewhat too loud and daring said, "I'd like to ask a question."

Tsemakh looked at her terror stricken, assuming that Slava was going to punish him for his anxiety over her behavior. But she spoke reverently to the visitor. "What's your opinion, rabbi—was it necessary for my husband to come and ask for advice, or could he have relied on our own judgment?"

"He should indeed have come to seek advice," the rabbi answered at once, and Slava didn't know whether he meant it or said it just for the sake of domestic peace.

He sat in silence for a while and then got up to leave. "Please forgive me for this short visit, but I have to see a wine merchant and buy wine for the Seder." Reb Avraham-Shaye wanted to wish the woman well before he left, but he didn't quite know how to articulate it, and it wasn't his nature to bless people like a Hasidic rebbe. He blushed and merely wished her a happy holiday. Tsemakh escorted him out to the corridor, where Reb Avraham-Shaye removed his glasses and put them into a flat, hard case.

Moshe Chayit Lohoysker was standing at the door of his little room. Tsemakh spotted him down the hall and was overcome with anguish, knowing that he'd be ashamed the rest of his life at what the youth would probably do. But Lohoysker let them pass, and nearsighted Reb Avraham-Shaye didn't notice him. Outside, Reb Avraham-Shaye bade Reb Tsemakh farewell.

"Last night, Reb Tsemakh, we spoke about you. Today I'd like to tell you something about myself. It's been my habit never to intervene in any matter, but only to sit in my own little corner. Nevertheless, I don't always give in to this *yetzer ha-ra* of mine, and I do intervene when I think it necessary—in your case, for instance. Your *yetzer ha-ra*, on the other hand, continually drives you to say what's on your mind, no matter where you are. You must take the opposite course and be wary of looking for faults. And indeed, if someone has to be chastised for being unjust and untruthful, it must be done without anger. Otherwise we are left only with anger and not with justice or truth. And now you've escorted me far enough, well beyond the call of duty." Reb Avraham-Shaye was trying to joke, as if to drive away the sadness of saying farewell.

Returning, Tsemakh climbed the stairs slowly and with difficulty, as if Reb Avraham-Shaye had given him a bigger burden than he could bear. He had expected to meet Lohoysker at the door of his room, but the boy was no longer there. Tsemakh went into his room, and Slava bounded toward him, chattering gaily. "Aha! You told me he doesn't look at other women—but he looked at me. It's good that I dressed like a rebbetsin and wore the long-sleeved blouse and the tasseled brooch. What did he say about me?"

"I saw Lohoysker standing in front of his door. He looked like someone who wants to do away with himself. Go to his room and see how he is," Tsemakh gasped. He seemed so alarmed that Slava left at once without a word.

Moshe Chayit paced in his room and didn't stop when Slava entered. He threw a sidelong glance at her and screwed up his face. "Well, rebbetsin, when are you going home?" But when she retreated toward the door, insulted by his sarcasm, he began to plead, "Don't go! Don't be angry with me. I know that the man who came to see you is the author of *The Vision of Avraham*. He made peace between you and both of you are returning to Lomzhe. But what's going to become of me?"

Slava felt as if she were being forced to watch an execution. Lohoysker's despair and his disheveled, gaunt, unshaven face repelled her. Although he did not touch her, she imagined the bristly hair on his face piercing her skin. He probably has sweaty palms, she thought. His falling in love with her irritated her too. Had he really assumed that if her reconciliation failed, she would marry him, just because she had listened to him in Nareva? Otherwise he seemed to be a bright fellow, well-read, an adult—yet he was still a naïve Torah scholar. "Compose yourself. Sit down," she told him, while she herself remained standing.

"I'm composed. I'm entirely composed," he said. He sat down and said in a broken voice, "You've become my home. After so many years of roaming around in foreign places, I found a home in you. My dream in life is a little corner of my own with a clean pillow. The Bible tells how the Prophet Jonah predicted the destruction of Nineveh and then waited on the outskirts of the city for its destruction. He sat in the shade of a broad-leafed gourd tree, but God sent a warm wind that dried the tree, and it withered. The heat was so great that Jonah fainted and asked to die. Even a prophet can't live in the heat without shade, without a hut, without a little corner of his own." Lohoysker buried his face in his hands.

Touched, Slava approached him softly, one hand outstretched, not knowing whether she intended to caress him or to push him away if he tried to caress her.

"I love my husband, even though I've suffered so much at his hands. And perhaps I love him *because* I've suffered so much at his hands. Should I leave him now, when we've become reconciled and he's going home with me?"

Moshe Chayit stared wildly at her, and she hunched into herself. She thought he would either fall at her feet at once or grab her by the throat and choke her. Nevertheless, she stood beside him and went on. "You've convinced yourself that you love me. Your imagination has run away with you. As soon as you settle down and stop thinking about my husband, you'll forget me. And as soon as you stop hating him, you'll stop loving me. I'll see you again before we leave." She backed to the door and left quickly before he had a chance to shout, Stay!

Slava went to Tsemakh's room and saw him pacing back and forth as Lohoysker had done. She gestured to him to go to his crazy pupil. "It's all your fault; yours!" she muttered, and she opened her purse for Tsemakh to take as much money as he needed to help the mad Lohoysker get settled. "He won't take any money from me. He wants me to be his home, his pillow—and I haven't the slightest intention of becoming his pillow. Even if I agreed, he'd probably regret marrying me. After all, I know his teacher, his guide."

Moshe Chayit sat where Slava had left him, his head in his hands. Only when Tsemakh sat down at the other end of the table did Moshe Chayit look up, his eyes glittering with intense hatred.

"You've been play-acting all your life, and now you're acting out another hypocritical charade. You've had your fill of adventures, and you yearn for a quiet life. You made believe you wouldn't return to Lomzhe unless Reb Avraham-Shaye told you to. But since he's a clever man, he agreed to what you wanted. But even though this Reb Avraham-Shaye had once ordered you chased out of Valkenik because of your fanatical burning of the Valkenik library, he still doesn't know you. He doesn't know that even in Lomzhe, you won't be at ease until you start a new conflagration."

"You're mistaken. I'm returning to Lomzhe to become a shopkeeper, and I won't interfere anywhere," Tsemakh answered, sounding as numb as he looked.

"You a shopkeeper?" Lohoysker chuckled and made a face. "But of course—you have to change your role and your mask continually, because at bottom you're empty, like the rotten trunk of a tree. We'll see how long you last in the role of shopkeeper! And if you do get used to your new false repentance, and if you no longer look for anything else, then you'll become a little person, an insignificant man whose sparks have been extinguished. You always have to show off with heroic deeds, and without a constant tumult around you, you'll become shriveled and dull. I know you well. I know you better than your adviser, Reb Avraham-Shaye, and better than your wife."

"It's quite possible that I'll become an insignificant man whose sparks have been extinguished, a dull, shriveled little man. There's no doubt that this is the most difficult moment in my life. Nevertheless, I feel that I won't look for anything else. I'll see this through," Tsemakh answered, calm and sad once again. His despondent look and bearing cooled Lohoysker's rage, so that he spoke without malice or rancor.

"I told your wife that when God sent the worms to devour Jonah's gourd, Jonah begged God to let him die, because even a prophet can't live in the noonday heat without shade, without a little corner of his own. But you've always been successful. You ran off, leaving people behind, and everyone ran after you. So you can't understand or sympathize with the shlimazel who has never been able to achieve anything."

At first Lohoysker struggled to contain his tears; then, when he felt them rolling down his cheeks, he began sobbing aloud. Tsemakh at once forgot that he'd promised himself not to rage and admonish, to be a Navaredker Musarnik no longer. Now he was ready to pummel Lohoysker again.

"Aren't you ashamed of such self-pity? Have you ever set foot in the outside world? Don't you know that among the worldly, if you cry because a worm devoured Jonah's gourd, everyone will snicker at your tears? When I left the beth medresh, I left alone. I made no effort to lure anyone else away from piety, just as later I blamed no one for my troubles and failures. I even criticize myself more than you for your own unbelievable impudence and licentiousness. But you moved heaven and earth so that others would abandon the beth medresh too; and now, out of rage that you didn't achieve what you longed for so passionately, you're looking for words that will kill me like poisoned arrows. You're one of those embittered souls who are basically the most satisfied of men because they blame this, that, and the next person for their flaws and failures. Everyone else is sly and corrupt; everyone's a liar—they alone are honest and pure, the deceived innocents. Such self-proclaimed saints made life difficult for me, and I ran back to the beth medresh. And now I, the man you call successful, must go back to this kind of world, to that kind of person. I'm going back to a world where one rarely meets a true friend and a responsible man; where a man is imprisoned for stealing a bagel and nothing happens to one who lets his fellow man die of hunger. I'm going back to a world inundated with all kinds of swindlers—those who fool others and, even worse, those robbers of the mind who lie first to themselves and then to others. That's the sort of world I have to return to and teach myself to be a deaf mute, as the Talmud advises: 'What should be man's trade in this world? Let him be mute!' "

Tsemakh wanted to weep too, but he wouldn't let himself. He knitted his brows to keep the tears from falling. From his coat pocket he removed the paper money he had gotten from Slava and placed it on the table.

"I'm leaving you two hundred zlotys. You probably still have some money left from what the Nareva rosh yeshiva gave you. This should be enough for you until you get settled and begin to earn money on your own. If you find yourself in need, write to me, and I'll send you as much as I can."

Moshe Chayit, dejected and silent, ignored the money on the table. But as Tsemakh left the room, he felt a pair of eyes as sharp as knives piercing his back.

Tsemakh returned to his room with such a grieved look that Slava didn't dare say a word. He sat for a long time with his eyes closed, while a verse from Jonah's complaint to God tumbled into his mind: "Was not this my saying, when I was yet in my country?" When an orphaned housemaid was made pregnant by his brother-in-law's son, Slava had seen nothing wrong in her family's trying to send the unfortunate girl off to a village to have her baby among gentiles. Now too Slava didn't understand that one must not lead a person on and deceive him—as she had done with Lohoysker. First of all, Slava would say she had done no wrong. Second, she'd say that Lohoysker and her husband and the entire world were to blame, but not she. And finally she would say that even if she had done something wrong, it was nothing to get so upset about. Would he have to close an eye to all this to keep them from quarreling anew? Was such a life worthwhile?

But when Tsemakh opened his eyes, he saw that now too he had been hasty and wrong in his judgment. Slava stood bent over him with an abashed, tear-laden smile. In Tsemakh's mind a secret door opened and brought him into the dim Amdur shop where he had said good-bye to his first fiancée. Dvorele Namiot had realized that he would not return and had given him an abashed, tear-laden smile. He would have to be extremely careful not to repeat the same terrible mistake in his life, not to treat his wife as he had treated his first fiancée.

16

VELLA THE FRUIT PEDDLER had expected her son to return from the yeshiva with a beard, as befitted a Torah scholar. But he came back clean-shaven, like a village peasant, with no hint of a beard. Because of this she clutched at her high forehead and told him, "I'm wearing my Sabbath wig during the week now because the one I use on weekdays has completely fallen apart. I'm looking for a pious wigmaker who will sell me a Sabbath wig that's not too expensive."

Chaikl listened mutely, and his mother continued as if to distract him from his gloomy silence. "During the winter I made friends with your teacher's wife. Every time the rebbetsin Yudis walks down Shavle Street to the textile merchants', she drops in to ask for news of you. The rebbetsin doesn't snub the poor common people, even though her husband is a great scholar and a saint. She's a bit loud herself, but she hates other women who talk a lot. Her husband is apparently a very patient man . . . And you can't dismiss her lightly either . . ." Vella was still flustered. She wiped her mouth as if to wipe away the poison of slander and suddenly concluded, "I see you don't know that her store was robbed and all her merchandise stolen."

Afraid that Reb Tsemakh Atlas had told Reb Avraham-Shaye everything that had happened in Nareva, Chaikl didn't visit the rabbi even after he learned about the theft. In his thoughts he continually reviled Reb Tsemakh's wife, that woman who to his great shame had caused him to make such a fool of himself. Vella felt that her son was keeping something from her but was afraid to ask why he didn't go to see Reb Avraham-Shaye. Every day she would say to Chaikl, "It's strange; the rebbetsin has stopped coming in to see me. Do you know anything about it? Doesn't she go shopping here any more?"

Chaikl didn't know what to say. He tried to persuade himself that it was good to be home again. On Passover Eve he wandered around in the courtyard with its shabby little houses and peeling plaster just as he had as a youngster.

The neighbors, sleeves rolled up, were airing their pillows in their red casings and beating the bedding with woven straw beaters until the feathers flew. Housewives scraped benches and tables with kitchen knives and scoured pots with sandpaper. Girls shook the mothballs out of their summer dresses and packed away their winter clothes. Dirty little children frolicked by the full gutters and by the puddles around the pumps, where dry wooden tubs were soaking in water. A cooper was fastening new metal bands around an old barrel to keep its staves from falling out. From a smith's workshop women emerged with whitened copper frying pans. Two men in white aprons, carrying big mortars with which they would pound matza into fine meal, came into the courtyard and were immediately surrounded by women and skinny children. Still wearing her winter felt boots and with a woolen kerchief over her head, a squat, toil-worn woman was carrying a round glass bottle of Passover beet borscht. A porter, bent under a huge, heavy basketful of matzas, was followed by a happy official from the Free Matza Society. Everyone was rushing to prepare for the festival.

Vella was the first to make her home kosher for Passover. It was a big event. Her scholar was back from the yeshiva! The only mitzva she left for him was buying wine for the Seders, but she finally realized that if he weren't reminded, he would forget the traditional ceremony of *Bedikas Chometz*—searching for the leaven.

Two days before Passover, Vella told her son, "The rebbetsin Yudis dropped in to see me. The wholesalers didn't want to give her any more merchandise on credit, so she took her husband's advice and closed down her dry-goods shop. That's why she no longer comes to town. But today she had to go shopping for Passover, so her husband asked her to tell you to come to see him. Why are you afraid to show your face at the rabbi's house? Did they chase you away from the yeshiva?" Vella asked with dry anger.

"Who was chased away? Me? I'll go see him today!" Chaikl answered, even angrier.

Toward evening Chaikl went to visit the rabbi. He met Reb Avraham-Shaye on the street, wearing his coat, cane in one hand and an empty bucket in the other. The rabbi greeted him and spoke as if he'd seen him just yesterday.

"I'm going to collect fresh water to make the matzas. Would you like to help me?"

On the eve of every Passover Reb Avraham-Shaye baked his matzas in his own oven. He trusted no one with this mitzva—not even himself—and wasn't satisfied until the matzas were thoroughly baked, virtually burned. Now he was on his way to fill up a bucket of water which would, according to the law, remain standing overnight.

"Reb Tsemakh Atlas has already gone home," he whispered, as if to inform his pupil that he knew about his behavior at the Nareva yeshiva and wouldn't have to ask him about it. Chaikl took the bucket out of the rabbi's hand and followed without saying a word.

At sunset Poplaver Street looked as if it were paved with gold. The big square windows of the beth medresh gave off a homy glow that reminded him of the summers and winters he had spent there studying the Talmud. Here in the suburb, the mood of Passover was not apparent. The little street dozed, quiet and deserted, as if it were Sabbath afternoon.

The rabbi and his student came to the river, went down to the bank, and looked for a spot to draw the water. Reb Avraham-Shaye, eyes shut ecstatically in honor of the mitzva, filled the bucket, and Chaikl drew it out. He imagined that in the full bucket there lay a creature that trembled silently and pleaded with him not to cover the water with a piece of thick white linen because it was cold and dark under the cover, and the creature would die. Afraid of his crazy fantasy, Chaikl hurriedly covered the bucket, but when he lifted it, he felt that the water had become heavier, as if the invisible water creature had indeed died.

In the windows of the Poplaver beth medresh the gold of sunset had already faded, and the windowpanes sparkled mysteriously with violet, dark blue, and forest green—as if the beth medresh were bidding farewell forever to the student and the strange creature in the full bucket. "I'd help you carry it, but I have no strength," Reb Avraham-Shaye said, stopping on the sidewalk so that Chaikl would stop and rest too. "Do you know that I'm planning to go and settle in the Land of Israel?"

Reb Avraham-Shaye said it so softly and matter-of-factly that Chaikl thought he hadn't heard well or had misunderstood. He walked on, carrying the bucket and listening to what the rabbi was saying. "The Orthodox community of Jerusalem asked me to be their rabbi. I replied that I don't want to take upon myself the responsibility of being the head of a rabbinic court, but like any other Jew I do want to settle in the Land of Israel. Now I've received a letter telling me that even though the community very much regrets that I won't accept a rabbinic post, they're trying to get a visa for me from the British and that I will have it very soon.

"You've probably heard about the robbery at our house and that I persuaded Yudis to give up her business. So I think I'll be able to persuade her to go with me to the Land of Israel. But it's a secret meanwhile, and you mustn't discuss it with anyone. Come during the holiday and have some refreshments." Reb Avraham-Shaye stopped at the doorway of his house and called his rebbetsin out to take the bucket of water.

He invited me only for refreshments, as if I were some distant relative. He no longer considers me his pupil, so he has no regrets about departing and leaving me behind, Chaikl thought on his way down Zaretche Hill. He knew perfectly well that if it hadn't been for the rabbi, he would have left Torah studies sooner. Now that the rabbi had severed his links with him and would no longer be close by, the way to the world was open to him. And what would his mother say? She'll make me miserable with her weeping, he thought. She had supported him until now—and he was already past twenty—with her poor fruit baskets so that he would remain a ben Torah.

I won't visit him, Chaikl told himself. And indeed he didn't go during the first days of Passover. The festive mood of spring and the holiday was all around him; but he felt cold and gloomy and dark, like a mountain on which the shadow of another mountain falls and doesn't move as long as the sun shines.

During the middle days of Passover Yudis visited the fruit peddler again. Since Yudis had closed her dry-goods shop, she had begun wearing her Sabbath clothes during the week. Furthermore, she no longer cursed the wholesalers. But there was a dark emptiness in her eyes. Having been the breadwinner all these years, she could not make peace with the thought that her old man would now become the wage earner. And from what? Certainly not from his books. If a rabbi sent him one zloty more than the cost of the book, he always sent it back. Her husband had now entrusted her with the secret of their journey to the Land of Israel, and Yudis had become more dejected. She would have to leave behind so many kin in the villages and the cemeteries of Lithuania. "What's going to become of your pupil when you leave? He'll go completely astray. I feel sorry for his mother." The rebbetsin sighed.

"I know that," Reb Avraham-Shaye replied, and asked her to summon Chaikl's mother.

"May I tell my son that the rabbi has sent for me?" Vella asked Yudis.

"It would be better if he didn't know right now," Yudis replied. After she left, Vella remained sitting on her low stool, hands in her lap, puzzled and sad. The scale screwed into the wall above her head hung in perfect balance, a mute iron witness for this world and the next that the fruit peddler gave honest weight.

After three o'clock, when the peak hours of her business were over, Vella closed her shop, donned her black silk Sabbath shawl over her long coat with the big mother-of-pearl buttons, and went up Zaretche Hill.

Vella had never met Reb Avraham-Shaye Kosover. She had heard from Chaikl that his teacher wasn't tall or broad-shouldered, but still she hadn't expected him to look so ordinary. Her first thought was that her husband of blessed memory had a much nicer beard.

At the rebbetsin's request, Vella took off her coat and let herself be seated, but she didn't touch the proffered refreshments.

Reb Avraham-Shaye paced around the room and talked, trying to control his inner turmoil. "I know that you've toiled hard over the years to support your son, but you have to realize that you're losing him. He's leaving the path of Torah."

"Tell us once and for all what he's done!" the rebbetsin shouted to her husband. "His mother's sitting here scared to death."

"He had a fine father," Vella murmured.

"Your son could have grown up to be a rabbi. But by nature he's like the cow that lets herself be milked until she suddenly lets fly a kick at the pail and spills all the milk," Reb Avraham-Shaye answered. "If there's something that Chaikl wants, or if he gets angry, he forgets all the Torah he has studied."

"I'm not worthy before God to have my son grow up to be a rabbi. I'd be happy if he would just be a faithful Jew." Vella addressed the rebbetsin out of respect for the rabbi. "I'll tell you the truth, rebbetsin; if the rabbi couldn't succeed with my son, how can I? Nowadays the eggs think they're smarter than the hens."

In honor of the middle days of the festival, Reb Avraham-Shaye was wearing his soft, wide-brimmed Sabbath hat. He put on his coat and searched his pockets, not knowing himself what he was looking for. "I'm no longer worried about whether your son will grow up to be a Torah scholar. I have my doubts whether he'll even put on tefillin." Reb Avraham-Shaye tucked his earlocks behind his ears and pulled his beard out over the lapels of his coat. He wanted to console the poor fruit peddler and tell her how great her reward would be for the self-sacrifice that enabled her son to study Torah, but he was so grieved at the loss of his rebellious pupil, in spite of the time and energy he had expended, that he could no longer speak calmly. He strode hastily out to the street through the dim, empty shop.

Yudis purposely began to talk of other things. She complained about her apartment, where Egyptian darkness always reigned. Then she spoke of the robbery again, telling how the thieves had broken through the courtyard wall and carried off all her merchandise. Seeing that Vella sat with head bowed, not saying a word, Yudis defended her husband. "Don't be angry at my old man. Chaikl is as dear to him as if he were his own flesh and blood. That's why it torments him to see Chaikl leaving Torah studies. I just hope that his grief doesn't harm his health." The rebbetsin sighed and fell silent too. She thought about their journey to the Land of Israel, which still had to remain a secret to keep the Vilna rabbis and townsmen from pestering her husband with remarks like, "Indeed you're not a town rabbi, but everyone obeys your decisions, so you mustn't leave Vilna." That's what they'd say to him, and he'd have to argue with everyone and justify himself. But was she certain that in the Land of Israel itself they wouldn't plague him? After all, the Jews of Jerusalem wanted him to serve as rabbi. And how would the two of them earn their living there? The rebbetsin's sighs became louder, and Vella fell into a deeper and sadder silence. With the falling darkness the white tablecloth gleamed coldly, and from among the shadows the wrinkled, golden-yellow faces of the two women gave off a pale glow.

From his mother's tight lips and angry expression Chaikl knew that she had returned from somewhere in utter confusion. Vella told him where she had been, and although she was afraid to hear what her son had done, she implored him with a threat: "May I not live to bring you under the wedding canopy if you don't tell me what's come between you and your teacher."

"I'll tell you after I've had a chance to talk with him," Chaikl answered, sharpening his teeth in preparation for the argument he would have with his teacher: The author of *The Vision of Avraham* thinks that Reb Tsemakh's wife has come between me and the Torah. I'll show him that I'm not that frivolous or superficial. My outlook on life is a completely different one.

The Evening Service in the Poplaver shul had ended. The congregants had already dispersed, but in the big cool space of the room the echo of the minyan's prayers remained suspended. In honor of the middle days the beadle had left the chandeliers lighted, and their glow was reflected in the polished wine-colored benches and shone out of the sparkling wood as if from a hidden palace. The dark blue sky hovering over the windows made Chaikl uneasy; it reminded him that it was spring outside. Beside him, in a corner by the Holy Ark, Reb

Avraham-Shaye sat behind his broad oak prayer stand, burying his face deeper in the book as his pupil's impudence increased.

"The Talmud bids us drag the *yetzer ha-ra* into the beth medresh. If it's a stone, it will be worn away; if it's iron, it will crumble." Chaikl said, "But the whole street can't be dragged into the beth medresh. And what's more important, I like the plain people, and I don't want to run away from my street."

"A ben Torah cannot like the street which sinks into materiality and which doesn't observe Sabbath or keep kosher and has no respect for Torah scholars." Reb Avraham-Shaye did not take his nearsighted eyes from the book; he caressed the Rashi script with his beard as if consoling the Torah that it was not yet entirely abandoned. "And besides, I want to ask you—for a person doesn't simply roam the streets aimlessly—do you know where you're going or what you're looking for?"

"Of course I'm not roaming around aimlessly. I'm trying to get to know the people on my street. Torah scholars always talk about opposites, about good and evil, truth and falsehood, beautiful and disgusting. By so doing they think they're making good, true, and beautiful all one concept and bad, false, and disgusting the other concept, on the other side of the fence. Actually the world is full of things—like the stars and the grass—that are neither good nor bad, not true or false, not smart or foolish. They live their own lives and astonish us with their eternal laws, to which they are always subjected. Even the concepts of good and evil can be looked at from another point of view than that of the Torah scholars. Torah scholars control everyone to see if his deeds are in accord with the law and his feelings with the Musar books—but they are blind and callous toward people themselves. There is also the way of the poet and philosopher, which doesn't judge man, an approach that teaches until we understand that bad traits and habits can't be pulled out like rotten teeth or like thorns from a garden. Heredity affects man from within and environment from without. And by showing the entire chain of cause and effect that dominates man, the poets and philosophers redeem man from the darkness within him. They fulfill the mitzva of redemption of captives by helping man to better understand himself and, indeed, to become better . . ."

"Fine, Chaikl." Reb Avraham-Shaye closed the book and stood up. "If you show me one person whom the books of your poets and philosophers have made a better person, I'll carry his laundry to the bathhouse. I understand you want to tell me before I go to the Land of Israel that you have completely abandoned the path of Torah."

"I wanted you to know that I am not the cow who kicks the milk pail and spills the milk because a rage or a passion sweeps over me, as you told my mother. I'm not one of those rebellious slaves who doesn't want to bear the yoke of Torah and mitzvas because he is happy when his burden is light. I have a different outlook on life. Religious functionaries always complain because they have to deal with ordinary, everyday Jews, while I consider the plain Jew who struggles to make a living the most noble and admirable one of the thirty-six saints for whose sake God does not destroy the world."

Reb Avraham-Shaye did not reply. He didn't believe the debate would change anything. The two went outside, and the rabbi told Chaikl calmly, "A certificate that permits me to go to the Land of Israel will soon be ready. I'm making preparations to leave after Tisha B'Av. Until then I'll be in a vacation cottage in Nyementshin. Yudis will go with me this time, since she's closed the shop."

Chaikl kept his promise and told his mother why the rabbi had broken off with him. Vella gazed at her son with distrust and anger; she had demanded that he tell her the truth. Finally she realized from his appearance that he wasn't joking. She was speechless for a moment, then she looked toward the door, afraid someone outside the little shop might have overheard Chaikl's confession. Her amazement grew, and finally she broke the silence.

"You, a yeshiva student, were chasing romance in Nareva? And with none other than the wife of your former rosh yeshiva? Is she that beautiful? What a woman she must be! And your teacher heard about this and is still on speaking terms with you? The rabbi is indeed the world's greatest saint if he's still talking to a scamp like you! Blast you! May you go to the blazes!"

Vella tried to recover from her profound astonishment, and Chaikl was no less astonished. He felt that his mother was indignant without anger and chiding him without resentment.

The fruit peddler wiped her hands on her apron as if washing before reciting a blessing and made no effort to keep looking stern. But her eyes were shining with joy and her cheeks glowed. Against her will she broke into soft, happy laughter. "There's just one thing I want to know—when and where did you learn this? Not so long ago you were just a little boy!" Vella wiped her tear-filled eyes as if she'd received the glad tidings that soon she would be leading a son to the wedding canopy.

17

ON A HOT SUMMER DAY in the middle of the month of Av, Chaikl Vilner and Moshe Chayit Lohoysker sat on a hillside. Behind their backs the whitewashed walls of the Zaretche shul gleamed in the sun. The Vilenke River wound at the foot of the hill. A wooden bridge that spanned the river led to the Bernadine Garden. In the heights where the two youths sat, the ground was hard and whitish. The bushes and little trees around them stood numbly in the daytime heat, and the green fuzz of the leaves was covered with grayish dust. The water in the little river was low, and the current was yellowish and flat. The Vilenke streamed languidly among the shiny black stones in the river bed. Chaikl looked down into the Bernadine Garden, with its network of trails and broad, sandy footpaths, and its thick green treetops and rectangular flower beds which from afar twinkled white, yellow, red, and violet. The silver mist of a water fountain sparkled in the sun's rays. He couldn't see the faces of the people strolling in the garden, and he could tell the men and women apart only by their clothes. The benches along the river front were all taken. Couples ambled along the walkways. In a sunny little square were babies in their carriages, watched over by their young mothers. Chaikl saw a couple walking and imagined that the woman had a high, pale forehead. Her face was shadowed by her broad-brimmed hat, and her smile was amiable but cool. Of course she wasn't married yet, and her escort would not become her husband. He had a broad, crude face, greasy hair, and oxlike eyes; he was one of those rich idlers, a chatterbox, a fool. Chaikl couldn't understand what that bright, eager woman on the other side of the river could possibly talk about with such a vulgar and superficial creature.

Instead of looking at the depressed friend at his side, Chaikl preferred gazing down at the red brick Bernadine Church. Its gothic spires and towers seemed to be made of frozen sun rays and petrified flames. In the distance, beyond the checkerboard stone houses with their metal roofs and forests of chimneys, the three huge crosses at the Kreutzberg rose up to the sky. On the clear blue horizon, the castle hill with the ruins of the fortress of the ancient Lithuanian princes looked like a big ship at its mooring.

Chaikl could not see the broad Viliye River from the Zaretche Hill, so he closed his eyes and pictured what was happening on its banks this hot summer day. While he and Lohoysker were ashamed to look a woman in the face, at the beach men and women unashamedly paraded about half-naked and swam together. The white sailboats and the long narrow kayaks, filled with girls in colorful bathing suits, looked like basketsful of cherries and strawberries. At the Maccabee Stadium people were jumping from the high diving boards. They had water races, a radio blared, and the almost naked couples danced barefoot in the hot sand. Higher up the stream, beyond the section known as the Wild Beaches, began the pine forests of Antokol and Volokumpye. After sunning themselves all day and splashing in the Viliye, the couples went to "cool off" in the dark woods.

In the evening they strolled through the high corn. The young women wore short, flowered dresses and held sticks cut from thin twigs and adorned with little circles carved in the bark. After baking in the sun for so many hours, the girls felt a slight chill and at the same time a lusty fire in their bones. The boys had bronzed faces and disheveled tufts of hair. They wore sport socks, short, wide, knee-length pants held up by suspenders, and open-collared white shirts whose sleeves were rolled up over their muscular arms. While the youths sang and strummed on mandolins, the girls cast velvety, yearning glances at the horizon, where the sky touched the tall, golden, wind-blown cornstalks.

Behind Antokol and Volokumpye the fields and forests stretched to the village of Nyementshin. There in a forest cottage sat Reb Avraham-Shaye, studying his small Berlin edition of the Talmud. He gave no thought to what was happening in the surrounding summer cottages, and he no longer thought of his pupil in Vilna.

"My teacher should have come back from vacation. He said he was going to leave for the Land of Israel after Tisha B'Av, and now it's nearly a week later," Chaikl grumbled, his chin resting on his knees.

"From what you've told me about Reb Avraham-Shaye, I see that he's worlds removed from Tsemakh Atlas. If I'd had a teacher like that, perhaps I wouldn't have left the yeshiva," Moshe Chayit said, breaking twigs off a dry branch with his nervous fingers.

"You've said that before." Chaikl turned to him, looking as if he wanted to push him off the hill. "You must feel pretty awful if you left the yeshiva just to spite Tsemakh Atlas."

Lohoysker was silent. All his impudence had vanished. After much hardship, he had finally found a few students whom he taught Talmud in the Vilna Gaon's beth medresh—and, to appeal to his pupils' parents, he had to be pious. Hating himself for being such a shlimazel, he dressed sloppily and let his beard grow wild—the bench warmer was manifest in his every move. He had no friends among the nonreligious youths and didn't seek them out because he couldn't discuss his yeshiva years with them, and he wasn't interested in anything else. Chaikl too found it difficult to adapt to nonreligious companions.

"Are you thinking about Tsemakh Lomzher's wife again?" Moshe Chayit scraped his dirty nails in the dry, crumbly earth. "Before she left Vilna, she told me that when I stop hating her husband I'll stop loving her. I still hate her husband and I don't like her any more. Do you know why? Because she loves him."

"Then it's just the way she said it, only somewhat different." Chaikl shifted impatiently from side to side. "I don't think about her at all. Even though she pretended to be a wanton in Nareva, she's just an ordinary woman. She'll probably go as far as permitting herself to keep her own hair and not put on a marriage wig. Why should I think about her?"

"The Musarniks would enjoy their revenge if they could see how we suffer looking at the park from afar—at that Garden of Eden where the worldly enjoy life. When two boys sit together, it's as the Talmud says, 'eating bread with bread.' A sign of stupidity, monotony." Lohoysker yawned. He was stretched out on his back, hands behind his head, his eyes shut against the bright sun. "In Nareva I thought you were a typical Vilna Butchers Street boy. But I see now that compared to the gang on your street, you're a yeshiva student to the core."

"But I'll soon get that out of my system. Sooner or later I'll be rid of it, but you'll remain a bench warmer forever." Chaikl scratched his hands as if ants had run over them.

"We'll never be able to get the yeshiva out of our systems," Moshe Chayit answered, his pensive voice seeming to come from far away. Then he suddenly burst out laughing. "Remember how that wild Yankl Poltaver brought the trustee Sulkes a broom instead of a plate of sweets for his Purim feast?" Lohoysker sat up spiritedly, as he usually did when he spoke about the Nareva yeshiva. Chaikl hardly heard him; he bit his parched lips and wiped the perspiration that kept dripping down his forehead. He stood up, brushed the dust from himself, and pointed to the white stone building.

"Here in the Zaretche beth medresh Reb Israel Salanter, the founder of Musar and the teacher of all Musarniks from Kelm, Slobodke, and even our own Navaredok, had his first yeshiva. While we're sitting here, I can't escape the thought that Reb Israel Salanter's beth medresh is right behind us."

"You see?" Lohoysker crowed gaily. "I told you before that we'll never be able to get the yeshiva out of our systems. But you're drawn to this place because when you look down into that Garden of Eden of the worldly oriented people, you see Reb Israel Salanter's beth medresh mirrored in the back of your head."

The two young men climbed over a broken fence into the courtyard. The beth medresh door was open; the congregants were assembling for the Afternoon Service. In the small portal of the gate, the beadle stood looking for passers-by. Chaikl and Lohoysker were headed for the street, but the beadle grabbed their arms and cried, "The two of you will just make a minyan for us." Lohoysker was ready to go into the beth medresh, but Chaikl mumbled, "I don't have time," and walked on.

Lohoysker changed his mind and ran after Chaikl, who said angrily, "In Nareva you brought the yeshiva no end of troubles, and here you're dying for an Afternoon Service. I realize you have to be wary of the parents of the boys you tutor, but nobody knows you up here in Zaretche, so don't be a hypocrite. Don't try fooling anyone."

"First of all, I'm not fooling anyone. The beadle didn't ask me whether I could live without an Afternoon Service. He only wanted me to fill out a minyan. And second, you don't understand human nature. Sometimes a person wants to feel that he's not superfluous in this world—that someone still needs him, even if it's only for a little while, and even if it's only by being a tenth for a minyan."

Lohoysker's disheveled clothes and rickety gait made him look as if he were limping. His pathetic smile and odd manner of speaking upset Chaikl, who now regretted having refused the beadle at the Zaretche beth medresh. How would he have been compromising his views if he had gone in to pray, to enable the worshipers to have a minyan?

Chaikl noticed something and felt his heart stop: Reb Avraham-Shaye's apartment, bolted tight all summer long, was now open. The doors of the shop were open, and the shutter of the sole window of the living quarters was open.

"He's back! Reb Avraham-Shaye has come back from Nyementshin and is leaving for the Land of Israel!" Chaikl cried sadly, as if a mysterious clock had struck midnight. He knew that his nearsighted teacher could not see him through the window. Nevertheless, he quickly crossed the cobblestone street to the other side.

Moshe Chayit followed him, asking, "Aren't you going to say good-bye to your teacher?"

Chaikl was silent. If he had assented to the beadle's request, he thought, he would now have the courage to see the rabbi.

Vella was waiting impatiently for her son and his friend and told them immediately, "I had a surprise visitor today—the former Valkenik principal Reb Tsemakh Atlas. He asked me to tell you both to come to see him. He's at the same inn where you stayed when you came to Vilna, Moshe Chayit—at the corner of Vilna and Trock streets." Vella turned to her son. "Reb Tsemakh told me that he has come to see your teacher off. Don't you know that Reb Avraham-Shaye has come back from vacation and is leaving this week?"

"I know," Chaikl grunted, even more exasperated.

Lohoysker scratched his hairy chin, and his eyes glittered feverishly behind his glasses. "I'll go to see him; of course I'll go to see Reb

Tsemakh Atlas." Lohoysker left with his bedraggled walk, looking like a pauper who has slept curled up in rags on the steps of a house.

Vella watched him go, shaking her head. "May my enemies succeed the way you two have succeeded after leaving Torah studies. Reb Tsemakh told me that Reb Avraham-Shaye bade him good-bye in a letter. Still, he came to see him off. And when are you going to see your teacher?"

"I'll go, but I'm not going today," Chaikl shouted, and he ran out of the little shop.

As was her custom, Vella remained sitting on her stool, hands in her lap. She didn't know whether to be glad that her only son wasn't leaving her alone and going with his teacher, or whether this should be a cause for tears. His friend Lohoysker, the son of a rabbi, had left his parents in Russia and stolen across the border into Poland to learn in a yeshiva. But now he had left the yeshiva and was suffering in Vilna like a sinner in hell.

Vella had invited Lohoysker to join them for cholent every Sabbath. At the table the two friends argued, and Vella dreaded Chaikl's fury. He ought to give in to his friend, she thought, even if he thinks he's wrong. Lohoysker was, after all, a lonely youth and Chaikl's guest at the table. But, not wanting to interfere in their arguments, Vella instead tried to stop the squabbles by offering Lohoysker another piece of stuffed kishke, another couple of browned potatoes, or a spoonful of prune pudding. Even when Lohoysker came into the shop during the week to ask where Chaikl was, she would give him a bagful of fruit. First it was the season for cherries and plums. Now the new apples and pears had arrived. At first the youth would refuse the offer and Vella would have to assure him, "It won't make me any poorer." But she didn't offer food when Chaikl was there, because she saw that Lohoysker was more ashamed in Chaikl's presence than hers.

"Whoever studies Torah will succeed at everything," said Vella to herself. Of late this had become a maxim of hers. If someone jibed at her, saying that her son and his friend had left the proper path, she knew how to respond.

18

THE LOMZHE FLOUR MERCHANT Reb Tsemakh Atlas had become a sedate man. He was not brimming over with the joy of life, but he displayed no despair, not the slightest trace of anger, and no lust for admonition. On closer scrutiny, one could notice a weariness in the corners of his mouth and a certain apathy in his glance, like that of a person whose life is spent fulfilling only his duties. His pitch-black beard glistened here and there with snowy patches.

Moshe Chayit Lohoysker sat opposite him in his little room at the inn and said, "I support myself by teaching Talmud to a few middle-class youngsters, and because of that I have to lead the life of a pious ben Torah." He expected to hear the shout: Then what have you accomplished by leaving the yeshiva?

But Reb Tsemakh said nothing. After a period of silence, he merely asked, "And where do you sleep?"

"In a textile warehouse."

Astonished, Reb Tsemakh turned his head and half opened his mouth. But again he said nothing and listened silently to Lohoysker.

"The owners of textiles stores and warehouses are afraid of burglars. So shopkeepers on several streets got together to hire a night watchman who parades around all night in front of their warehouses. But he still can't prevent thefts. While he's at one street corner, the robbers are breaking into a warehouse on another. The merchants came up with the idea of admitting watchmen into the shops themselves. The owner locks the watchman in at night and lets him out the next morning. On Friday nights the watchmen have to come earlier because the merchant closes up earlier, and on Sabbath morning he's too lazy to get up. So the guard is locked up in his store like a mouse in a trap.

"At first the merchants used to pay these night watchmen, but then they discovered that such bargains could be had for nothing. There are enough people who have nowhere to sleep. That's the sort of free watchman I am," Lohoysker said. "When the merchant gave me the job, he listed two conditions. First, not to use up the electricity at night and early in the morning—because electricity costs money. And second, every morning before I leave the shop, I have to let myself be searched, in case I wrapped some cloth around my body. The owner told me about a previous night watchman who had impoverished him more than a burglar. I had no choice but to submit to these two conditions. As far as electricity is concerned, I tried to fool the owner, and I did turn on a light. You can go crazy lying awake all night in the dark without being able to read. But that textile merchant had the nasty habit of coming by late at night and looking in through the crevices to see if there was any light inside. So—no choice—I had to give up reading at night. But there's one thing I can't get used to. Every morning when I have to carry out my night pot and clean it, I don't know where to hide in my shame and fear that people will see me. I don't know myself why I'm so ashamed of this. Perhaps it's because I was—and still am—a yeshiva student, and as everyone knows, they're ashamed of their human needs."

Moshe Chayit spoke with apparent pleasure and arrogance, as if purposely wanting to further torment his listener's heart and conscience. But the more he talked to and looked at his old adversary, the more he felt that his deep-rooted hatred no longer made any sense. Opposite him sat a man who looked as if he had made peace with the notion that he was defeated forever.

"I was expecting a letter from you so that I could send you some money, as we agreed. But you didn't write, and I didn't know your address." Reb Tsemakh removed a bundle of folded bills from his jacket pocket. He gave the money to Lohoysker, and the latter, without counting it, put it into his pocket.

"I don't want your wife to know about my situation. That's why I didn't write. Does your wife know you brought me money?"

"She doesn't know, and even if she did, she wouldn't think the less of you." Reb Tsemakh rose so gently and quietly that his legs seemed to have no bones. "I came to Vilna to see Reb Avraham-Shaye off. He's going to the Land of Israel. I must go to him now. After he leaves, we'll meet again."

Lohoysker stood up too. "What do you think, Reb Tsemakh—if I returned to Nareva as a penitent, would they take me back into the yeshiva?"

"It seems to me that you neither want to nor should return to Nareva," Reb Tsemakh replied.

Lohoysker nodded. "True; I was joking. I don't want to return to the yeshiva, and they wouldn't take me back because they wouldn't believe I've repented." He stood still for a moment, face averted, thinking hard.

"You know, Reb Tsemakh, no matter what path in life you chose, it left you dissatisfied. That's the greatest injustice you committed against your pupils, and especially against me. You taught us a Torah for which you did indeed sacrifice yourself, but which you yourself weren't happy with. That's why your students grew up full of contradictions too, and became broken people. I don't hate you any more. I see what's become of you. But I have no respect for you. Don't give me any more money—in my heart I don't thank you for it. And when I know not to expect help from anyone, perhaps I'll succeed in something on my own."

Moshe Chayit Lohoysker left, and Reb Tsemakh understood that his former pupil would not see him again.

In the afternoon the Lomzhe flour merchant sat in Reb Avraham-Shaye's house silently articulating his sadness, which hung in the room like a cloud. As he liked to do, Reb Avraham-Shaye half sat, half lay on the sofa, his chin on the rim of the table beside it. His half-shut eyes twinkled as he thought: With that heavy silence, Reb Tsemakh can drive all his relatives away from his house. Reb Avraham-Shaye surprised himself by laughing joyously.

"If I'd known that you would get the idea of coming all the way from Lomzhe, I'd have told you about the trip after we reached the Land of Israel. How can you leave your business all of a sudden just to say good-bye to someone?"

"My wife also thought that I should come," Tsemakh said, smiling gloomily. He realized that Reb Avraham-Shaye wanted to know about his life at home. "My wife is compromising, as you correctly predicted, but I'm not what she expected me to be."

"Even if you're dissatisfied with your present way of life, you mustn't show it." Reb Avraham-Shaye raised his chin and crumpled beard from the edge of the table.

"But I can't hide it!" Reb Tsemakh's anguished smile faded like the cold light of a winter day. "On the one hand, it takes great effort for me to be a flour merchant. On the other, I have to take care not to become a flour merchant in my heart, and that is almost beyond my capacity. Thus I can't always pretend to be a man who is happy with his lot in life."

He came to share some of his sadness, Reb Avraham-Shaye thought. If Reb Tsemakh had devotedly studied Torah and fulfilled the mitzvas during his yeshiva years, he wouldn't be so afraid now of acquiring a merchant's soul just because he was standing in his shop. He would have enjoyed every Afternoon Service and been happy with every page of Talmud he managed to study. But he delved and speculated about the Creator of the Universe and the nature of man for so long that he has dug an abyss for himself that can't be filled. Reb Avraham-Shaye frowned. He was finding it extremely difficult to say what he considered it his duty to say.

"If it isn't impossible, then you must have a child. And then many of the problems you and your wife have will dissolve of their own accord. Please excuse me for saying this."

At this point Chaikl came into the room and stopped, bewildered, as if afraid he might have to offer a twofold account of himself to his former teacher and his former Valkenik rosh yeshiva. But the two men, glad that their talk had been interrupted, greeted him in friendly fashion and asked no questions at all. A silence that stretched from their beards and brows webbed the room. Chaikl didn't know what to say.

It was his good luck that the rebbetsin Yudis came in from the street, bustling with her travel preparations. "God Himself has sent you to help me pack, Chaikl. Do it for your teacher!" She spoke more crisply than usual.

Reb Avraham-Shaye smiled. "He'll help you for your sake, not for mine."

Dishes, bedding, and piles of books were scattered on the floor and benches of the empty shop. Everything had to be packed into bags, suitcases, wicker baskets. Chaikl stuffed the bags and bound them so tightly with rope that the sweat poured from him.

"What skill!" Yudis smacked her lips in admiration, then poured out a torrent of words. "I've known my old man, may he live and be well, for more than two dozen years. During the Great War we wandered through half a dozen towns and villages; nevertheless, I realize now that I still don't know him. How can a man be leaving to settle in the Land of Israel and act as if he were just moving into a summer cottage? I tell him that I would have wanted to go and weep at the graves of my grandparents in Chvaydan. But Chvaydan is in Lithuania and Vilna is in Poland and the two governments are at swords' points. How can I get there? I asked him if he would miss Vilna or his native village of Kosov. And he said, 'I don't know. Perhaps I won't miss them.' I asked him again where we'll live in the Land of Israel and what will support us. Again he said, 'I don't know.' Then I tried to find out if he's said good-bye to all his friends and who would come to the train station. So he shrugs and says, 'I don't want anyone to come to the train station.' He keeps studying the holy books, writing his commentaries in the note pads, and praying as if nothing was happening."

Chaikl calculated that by the time he finished packing, Reb Tsemakh would have gone, and he and Reb Avraham-Shaye would be alone. The rabbi had not seen him all summer long, and now he was leaving forever—a heart-to-heart talk was inevitable. But to his surprise he saw Reb Avraham-Shaye and Reb Tsemakh coming into the shop in their coats.

"I'm going with Reb Tsemakh to the Poplaver beth medresh for the Afternoon Service," Reb Avraham-Shaye told his wife, and gave Chaikl his hand.

"Since we're leaving tomorrow evening, I must say good-bye to you."

"I'll come to the station," Chaikl murmured. His throat was so dry that he thought he would choke. Reb Avraham-Shaye, silent, went out with Reb Tsemakh. Chaikl could pack no longer. His fingers were bleeding from pulling the string tight around the bundles, but the rabbi's conduct hurt him even more.

"Reb Avraham-Shaye does act as if going to the Land of Israel were like going off for a summer vacation," Chaikl grumbled.

"You see; I told you!" the rebbetsin cried. But noting the boy's dejection, she began to admonish him gently, "I'm not butting in. I'm just telling you that when I heard my old man sighing in the summer cottage, I knew he was sighing out of grief that his student was severing himself from Torah studies."

Chaikl returned home despondent and told his mother, "I won't go to the train station tomorrow because it almost seems as if the rabbi doesn't want to talk with me."

But his mother's reply was even more acerbic than the rebbetsin's. "You're a fool. He's probably annoyed at your behavior, so it's hard for him to talk with you." Then Vella the fruit peddler threatened again: "May I not live to bring you under the wedding canopy if you don't go to see the rabbi off."

Vella went to the station too. Rain during the day had cooled the sizzling air and washed away the dust. In the evening the damp cobblestones reflected the greenish light of the street gaslights. The glistening treetops were mirrored in the rain-washed windows. At the terminal, Chaikl and his mother found two minyans of Jews gathered around Reb Avraham-Shaye and his wife.

Reb Avraham-Shaye Kosover had managed to persuade members of his family and the Vilna Torah scholars not to come to see him off. Among the latter it was well-known that his desire to remain unnoticed was almost a sickness. When invited to a wedding, his condition was that he not be honored with any of the wedding blessings; and he warned that if called upon against his will, he would walk away from the canopy. So when he went to bid the older Vilna rabbis farewell, they responded to his request by quoting the famous passage: " 'A man's will must be respected.' If you don't want us to come to the station, we won't come." But he couldn't impose such conditions upon the simple Jews of his minyan at the Poplaver beth medresh. He had hoped, however, that if he said nothing, perhaps no one would think of coming to the train. As it turned out, not only did the regular contingent of the daily minyan show up, but those who prayed in the shul only on Sabbaths and holidays also came.

Leaning on his cane and immersed in an ecstatic stillness, the author of *The Vision of Avraham* stood amid the assembled Jews. They were silent too. Even his loquacious wife didn't say a word: she merely sighed occasionally as she had when standing in her empty shop, hands in her sleeves, waiting for a customer. Vella looked lovingly into Yudis' eyes and managed to hold back her tears. Chaikl, his lips numb with cold in midsummer, stood opposite Reb Avraham-Shaye, while the silent Reb Tsemakh Atlas towered over all the congregants' fedoras and the workingmen's caps.

A Pole in a blue-buttoned uniform sang out in the middle of the dim waiting room, "Train to Warsaw now leaving!" From all sides passengers rushed to the platform. Chaikl was dragged along with the crowd. His eyes suddenly grew misty; his ears rang. He saw shadows moving back and forth, up and down the steps of the cars—the men of the Poplaver shul carrying the rabbi's baggage into the train and returning to the platform. Reb Avraham-Shaye Kosover shook hands with everyone and thanked them with a nod. The crowd still wasn't noisy but whispered, as if in the Silent Devotion, "May you arrive in the Land of Israel in peace and good health."

Through his tears Chaikl saw the rabbi and Reb Tsemakh Atlas bidding each other farewell. They shook hands but did not kiss or say a word. Yudis was already in the train, and Reb Avraham-Shaye finally climbed up the steps.

"Go to your teacher," Chaikl's mother whispered, pushing him ahead of her.

The rebbetsin stood in the compartment putting the suitcases under the seats and on the luggage racks above. Seeing Chaikl's mother, she left her bundles; the two women embraced and burst into tears. The rebbetsin hugged Chaikl too; then she kissed him and shouted in her gruff, masculine voice, "If you stay with Torah studies, we'll bring you to the Land of Israel and marry you off."

"Thank you, rabbi." The fruit peddler wept before Reb Avraham-Shaye, who stood among the bundles in the dark, narrow corridor. "You've done more for my son than a flesh-and-blood father. Forgive him for having caused you anguish. I pray to the Eternal One that my son will never forget what you taught him."

A heavyhearted silence enfolded Reb Avraham-Shaye. He shook hands with Chaikl, hesitated for a moment over whether to say something, then sighed softly. "At a time like this, it's hard to talk."

Vella and her son came down the train steps and found the crowd still waiting on the platform. The well-wishers looked up to the window, but Reb Avraham-Shaye did not appear. The rebbetsin came to the window for a moment, waved, and moved her lips—but nothing could be heard through the thick glass.

The conductor shouted, "All aboard!" and at once closed doors and windows began whirling by. The wheels rumbled through Chaikl's temples. The metallic screech of the siren resounded in his ears with a weird, silent cry from the abyss: "Disperse, lest I destroy the world!" The bare, bright rails, quivering like a network of veins and nerves, blinded Chaikl momentarily. Gradually the clatter of the wheels abated, and the wind blew away the knots of smoke, the tousled mane of the locomotive.

The worshipers from the Poplaver beth medresh went back into the station. Vella too returned to the waiting room and stood by the glass door, watching her son and Reb Tsemakh Atlas, who had remained on the platform.

Reb Tsemakh looked at the departing train, his heart weeping within him: the author of *The Vision of Avraham* had told him that he should have a child. He wanted one and so did Slava, but she was waiting for him to be her husband again with all his heart—with joy—and not consider his life with her a torment. Then, she had said, she would have a child with him. Master of the Universe! There was a time when I doubted your existence because I didn't see you. My pride didn't let me believe in something I couldn't see and couldn't understand. Then you sent such suffering down upon me that I no longer doubted that you existed. Only a Creator can punish the way you have punished me. Now I believe in you, and yet I don't have enough faith, nor do I have a glad heart. Grant me a bit of Reb Avraham-Shaye's peace of soul and gladness of heart. We learn that heaven helps the one who wants to be better. Help me, Master of the Universe, help me! Reb Tsemakh shouted in his mind, his lips compressed and his eyes smarting with dryness. But Chaikl's eyes streamed hot tears; they burned his face and rolled down his neck.

The platform was now overrun with people waiting for another train. Reb Tsemakh Atlas and Chaikl Vilner still stood beside each other in the crowd; they were like an older brother with a younger one. They stood like two trees at the roadside on the edge of a town, while on the horizon a dense forest sways and rustles. But the two trees are always sad and pensive because the man who lived near them and watched over them has gone off into the wide world and will return no more, return no more. Reb Tsemakh Atlas and Chaikl Vilner realized that many other trials awaited them in life, but both had a feeling that all their struggles would be illuminated by the radiance of the man of God—Reb Avraham-Shaye Kosover, the author of *The Vision of Avraham*.

GLOSSARY

AGADA	The nonlegal, narrative, and anecdotal portion of the Talmud.
AGUDAH	The ultraorthodox religious party, opposed (in the time of the novel, but not nowadays) to Zionism.
AGUNAH	An abandoned wife.
ALENU	The concluding prayer of each of the three daily services.
AV	The eleventh month of the Jewish calendar (August).
BAAL TEFILLA	A congregant who leads a prayer service; not a trained cantor.
BEDIKAS CHOMETZ	The search for bread and other leaven products that takes place one night before the beginning of Passover.
BEN TORAH	A yeshiva student; a Torah scholar; literally, son of the Torah.
BETH MEDRESH	A house of study; also used as a place for prayer.
CHAFETZ CHAIM	The title of an ethical work written by Israel Meir Ha-Kohen (1838–1933), one of the most revered figures in modern Judaism. Beloved by the masses, he became known as the Chafetz Chaim, after his first book.
CHOLENT	A hot meal, usually consisting of beans and meat, cooked on Friday and kept warm to serve on the Sabbath.
CODE OF LAW	See *Shulchan Aruch.*
DAYS OF AWE	The ten-day period of High Holy Days between Rosh Hashana and Yom Kippur.
DYBBUK	The soul of one person which has entered another.
ELUL	The month (August and part of September) preceding Rosh Hashana.
ESROG	The citron used in services on Sukkos.

ETHICAL WILL	A last testament that guides the heirs along the proper path of conduct.
ETHICS OF THE FATHERS	A Talmudic tractate devoted to ethical teachings.
EYN YAAKOV	A collection of nonlegal narrative material mainly from the Babylonian Talmud, published in 1516, with commentary, by Rabbi Yaakov ibn Habib.
GAON	Great scholar.
GOLEM	Clod. Literally, a creature of clay.
KASHRUT	One who eats kosher foods and observes the Jewish dietary laws keeps kashrut.
KIDDUSH	Blessing chanted over wine at the beginning of the Sabbath or holiday evening meal.
KISLEV	The third month (November–December) of the Jewish calendar.
KOL NIDREI	The opening prayer, with its world-famous melody, of the night of Yom Kippur.
KOSHER	See *Kashrut*.
LAG B'OMER	A day of festivity, especially for children; they are released from their studies and taken into the fields and woods.
LAMED VOVNIK	One of the thirty-six hidden saints upon whose righteousness the world continues to exist.
LITVAK	A Jew who comes from Lithuania—traditionally thought of as being more reserved and scholarly than Jews from other regions.
LULAV	The palm branch adorned with myrtle and willow leaves that is used with the esrog during Sukkos.
MAIMONIDES	The great philosopher, physician, and sage (1135–1204), author of *The Guide to the Perplexed* and the *Mishneh Torah*, a codification of Jewish laws.
MASKIL	A follower of the Haskalah, the Jewish Enlightenment movement.
MAZEL TOV	Congratulations! Literally, "Good luck."
MENDELE MOCHER SEFORIM	Pen name of Shalom Jacob Abramowitz, a noted Hebrew and Yiddish writer (1836–1917).
MIDRASH	Rabbinic commentary and explanatory notes, homilies, and stories on Scriptural passages.
MIKVA	The ritual bath, used separately by both men and women.
MINYAN	The quorum of ten adult males needed for synagogue services.
MISHNA	The body of oral law redacted *c.* 200 C.E. by Rabbi Judah.

MISHNA BERURA	A six-volume (1894–1907) commentary on the laws of the *Shulchan Aruch* by Chafetz Chaim.
MITZVA	A Torah precept or commandment; a good deed.
MIZRACHI	The religious party that supported Zionism.
MOHEL	The man who performs circumcisions.
MUSAF	The additional prayer recited on Sabbaths and holidays and on the beginning of a new month.
MUSAR	A nineteenth-century movement in Judaism to educate the individual to strict ethical conduct; it also became a trend in certain yeshivas.
MUSARIST, MUSARNIK	A follower of Musar.
OVINU MALKENU	A prayer recited on fast days and during the Ten Days of Repentance.
PASSOVER	The eight-day festival during Nissan (March–April) that commemorates the Jew's freedom from Egyptian bondage.
THE PATH OF THE UPRIGHT	Written by Moses Chaim Luzzatto (1707–1747); one of the major texts on practical ethics.
PENITENTIAL PRAYERS	Prayers recited prior to Rosh Hashana.
PENTATEUCH	The Five Books of Moses.
PILPUL	The process of hair-splitting, especially in a discussion of a Talmudic text.
PURIM	The festival celebrating the Jews' deliverance from Haman's plan to exterminate them, as described in the Book of Esther. It is celebrated on the fourteenth day of Adar (March) and is noted for its gaiety. In the synagogues, where the Book of Esther is read from scrolls, children rattle noisemakers whenever Haman's name is mentioned.
RABBENU	Our Master; title given to the greatest Jewish scholars and sages.
RABBENU GERSHOM	A tenth-century sage and rabbi in Germany.
RAM'S HORN	Blown several times during Rosh Hashana and once after the Neilah service at the end of Yom Kippur.
RASHI	The great commentator of the Bible and the Talmud (1040–1105).
REB	Mister or sir; used in conjunction with a first name. A form of address for learned or pious Jews.
REBBE	Spiritual leader of a group of Hasidim.
REBBETSIN	The wife of a rabbi.
RITUAL FRINGES	Tsitses; a four-cornered, poncholike garment put on over the head and worn underneath the shirt by male Jews who observe the biblical commandment to wear a garment with fringes (Numbers 15:37–41).

ROSH HASHANA	The Jewish New Year, celebrated the first and second days of Tishrei. Rosh Hashana and Yom Kippur are the most solemn days of the year.
ROSH YESHIVA	The academic head of a yeshiva.
SABBATH OF CONSOLATION	The Sabbath that follows Tisha B'Av.
SANHEDRIN	The supreme court of ancient Israel.
SEDER	The festive ritual meal celebrated at home on the first and second nights of Passover.
SEVENTEENTH OF TAMMUZ	A fast day in the summer commemorating the day on which the city walls of Jerusalem were breached. This subsequently led to the razing of Jerusalem and the destruction of the Temple.
SHEVARIM	One of the sounds of the shofar.
SHEVAT	One of the winter months (January–February).
SHEVUOS	The Feast of Weeks, celebrated on the sixth and seventh of Sivan (May–June), seven weeks after Passover. It marks the day on which the Torah was given to Israel on Mount Sinai and also the day on which the firstfruits of the wheat harvest were offered to God.
SHLIMAZEL	A bungler.
SHMA YISROEL	The central affirmation of a Jew's faith: "Hear, O Israel, the Lord is our God, the Lord is One."
SHOFAR	See *Ram's horn*.
SHUL	Synagogue.
SHULCHAN ARUCH	The collection of laws by Joseph Caro, *The Code of Law*.
SIDDUR	The prayer book.
SILENT DEVOTION	One of the central prayers in the Jewish service, recited while standing.
SIMKHAS TORAH	The festival immediately following Sukkos on which the Torah is completed and begun anew. This joyous holiday is traditionally celebrated with singing and dancing with the Torah scrolls.
SUKKOS	The Feast of Booths celebrated in the middle of Tishrei, a few days after Yom Kippur. It commemorates the Jews' living in simple booths during their wanderings in the desert. It is also the harvest festival.
TALLIS	The prayer shawl worn by adult males during the Morning Service. Most men wear the prayer shawl only after their wedding; hence one can easily spot a bachelor.
TALMUD	The body of written Jewish law, comprising the Mishna (in Hebrew) and the Gemara (mostly in Aramaic).

TALMUD TORAH — The school in which children are taught Hebrew, the prayers, and the Pentateuch.

TEFILLIN — Phylacteries used in morning prayers. These are square boxes with leather thongs, containing scriptural passages worn on the arm and head during morning prayer every day, except Sabbaths and holidays, by male Jews over thirteen.

TEKIAH — One of the sounds of the shofar.

TEN DAYS OF REPENTANCE — The ten-day period beginning with Rosh Hashana and ending with Yom Kippur; a time when the Jew is supposed to examine his moral and religious state of being and change his ways.

TENTH OF TEVET — A fast day in the winter commemorating the beginning of the siege of Jerusalem by Nebuchadnezzar.

TERUAH — One of the sounds of the shofar.

THIRTEEN ARTICLES OF FAITH — A series of thirteen statements, each beginning with "I believe," originally formulated by Maimonides, and recited now by all Jews.

TISHA B'AV — The ninth day of the month of Av (July–August), marking the destruction of the Temple in 586 B.C.E. and 70 C.E.

TORAH — Not only the Five Books of Moses, and by extension the entire Bible, but the entire complex of Jewish learning, comprising the Talmud, the Commentaries, rabbinic writings, etc.

TRACTATE KIDDUSHIN — One of the tractates of the Talmud.

YARMULKE — A skullcap worn by Jewish boys and men.

YESHIVA — A Talmudic academy.

YETZER HA-RA — The evil inclination in man; his bad impulses. One interpretation given to *yetzer ha-ra* is "the evil tempter"; *yetzer ha-ra* can also be the tendency in man to do forbidden acts.

YEVSEKTSIYA — Jewish section of the Communist Party in the Soviet Union; active after the Revolution and liquidated in the 1930s.

YOM KIPPUR — The Day of Atonement, the holiest day in the Jewish year.

YORZEIT — The anniversary of a loved one's death.